# "I NEED TO GET OUT OF HERE. CAN YOU HELP ME?"

A smile tugged at the corner of John's mouth as he slid into the Corvette. He hadn't planned on having Miss January jump into his car. She looked like she'd been shrink-wrapped in satin from armpit to thigh. Her legs were long and tan, and she wore a pair of flimsy strapless high heels on her feet. He pulled out of the circular drive.

"Oh, no," she moaned. "I've really messed up this time."

"I could take you back," he offered.

"It's too late. I've done it now. And Sissy is going to kill me. I've left her there all by herself. She went to get a bouquet of lilac and pink roses, and I ran out! And Sissy doesn't like the groom. She thinks he's a lecherous old leprechaun."

A real bad feeling tweaked the back of John's neck. "But isn't Sissy the bride?"

"No." Miss January stared at him with her big green eyes and shook her head. "I am. And I can't believe I left Virgil at the altar!"

*Avon Books by*
**Rachel Gibson**

IT MUST BE LOVE
LOLA CARLYLE REVEALS ALL
SEE JANE SCORE
SIMPLY IRRESISTIBLE
TRUE CONFESSIONS
TRULY MADLY YOURS

*Coming Soon*

DAISY'S BACK IN TOWN

# Rachel Gibson

# Simply Irresistible

AVON BOOKS
*An Imprint of* HarperCollins*Publishers*

This is a work of fiction. Names, characters, places, and incidents are products of the author's imagination or are used fictitiously and are not to be construed as real. Any resemblance to actual events, locales, organizations, or persons, living or dead, is entirely coincidental.

AVON BOOKS
*An Imprint of* HarperCollins*Publishers*
10 East 53rd Street
New York, New York 10022-5299


Inside author photo by Sims Studios
Library of Congress Catalog Card Number: 97-93794
ISBN: 0-380-79007-6
**www.avonromance.com**



First Avon Books printing: January 1998



Printed in the U.S.A.

10 9 8

*For Jessica, Carrie, and Jamie,*
*who have eaten a lot of frozen pizza*
*so Mom could write*

# Prologue

*McKinney, Texas*
*1976*

Mathematics gave Georgeanne Howard a headache, and reading made her eyes hurt. At least when she was reading, she could move her finger along the tricky words and fake it sometimes. She couldn't fake math.

Georgeanne laid her forehead on the piece of paper sitting on her desk and listened to the sounds of her fourth grade classmates playing outside at recess beneath the warm Texas sun. She hated math, but she especially hated counting all those dumb bundles of sticks. Sometimes she stared at the little drawings of sticks so hard her head *and* eyes ached. But each time she counted, she came up with the same answers—the wrong answers.

To take her mind off the math, Georgeanne thought of the pink tea she and her grandmother planned to have after school. Grandmother would have already made the little pink petit fours, and the two of them would dress in pink chiffon and break out the pink tablecloth, napkins, and matching cups. Georgeanne loved pink teas and she was good at serving too.

"Georgeanne!"

She snapped to attention. "Yes, ma'am?"

"Did your grandmother take you to see the doctor like we talked about?" Mrs. Noble asked.

"Yes, ma'am."

"Did your grandmother take you to get tested?"

She nodded. For three days the week before, she read stories to a doctor with big ears. She answered his questions and wrote stories. She did math and drew pictures. She liked drawing pictures, but the rest had been real dumb.

"Are you finished?"

Georgeanne looked down at the scribbled-up page in front of her. She'd used her eraser so many times, the little answer boxes were a dull gray, and she'd ripped several three-corner tears next to the bundles of sticks. "No," she said, and covered the paper with her hand.

"Let me see what you've done."

Dread weighing her down, she rose from her chair, then made a great show of pushing it in at a precise angle. The soles of her patent leather shoes barely made a sound as she slowly walked to her teacher's desk. She felt sick to her stomach.

Mrs. Noble took the messy paper from Georgeanne's hand and studied the math problems. "You've done it again," she said, irritation punctuating her words. Displeasure narrowed her brown eyes and pinched her thin nose. "How many times are you going to write down the wrong answers?"

Georgeanne glanced over her teacher's shoulder to the social studies table where twenty small igloos had been constructed out of sugar cubes. There should have been twenty-one, but because of her poor penmanship, Georgeanne would have to wait to make her igloo. Maybe tomorrow. "I don't know," she whispered.

"I've told you at least four times that the answer to the first problem is not seventeen! So why do you keep writing it down?"

"I don't know." Over and over she'd counted each stick. There were seven in two bundles and three single twigs on the side. That made seventeen.

"I've explained this to you repeatedly. Look at the paper."

When Georgeanne did as she was told, Mrs. Noble pointed to the first bundle of sticks. "This bundle represents ten," she barked, and moved her finger over. "This bundle represents ten more, and we have three ones to the side. How many is ten plus ten?"

Georgeanne pictured the numbers in her head. "Twenty."

"Plus three?"

She paused to count it out silently. "Twenty three."

"Yes! The answer is twenty-three." The teacher shoved the paper at her. "Now, go sit down and finish the rest."

Once she was seated again, Georgeanne looked at the second problem on the page. She studied the three bundles, carefully counted each stick, then wrote down twenty-one.

As soon as the dismissal bell rang, Georgeanne grabbed the new purple poncho her grandmother had knitted for her and practically ran all the way home. When she entered the back door, she noticed the pink petit fours on the blue and white marbled counter. The kitchen was small, the yellow and red wallpaper peeling loose in places, but the room was Georgeanne's favorite. It smelled of nice comfortable things like cakes and bread, Pine-Sol and Ivory Liquid.

The silver service sat on the tea cart, and she was just about to call out to her grandmother when she heard a man's voice coming from the parlor. Since that particular room was off limits to anyone except really important company, Georgeanne walked quietly down the hall toward the front of the house.

"Your granddaughter doesn't seem to grasp abstract concepts at all. She reverses words or simply can't think of the word she wants to use. For example, when shown a picture of a doorknob, she called it 'that thing I turn to get into the house.' Yet at the same time, she accurately identified an escalator, pickax, and most of the fifty states," explained the man Georgeanne recognized as the doctor with the big ears who'd given her those dumb tests the week before. She stopped just short of the doorway and listened. "The good news is, she did score very high on comprehension," he continued. "Which means she understands what she reads."

"How can that be?" her grandmother asked. "She uses a doorknob every day, and as far as I know, has never even touched a pickax. How can she mix her words around, yet understand what she reads?"

"We don't know why some children suffer from brain dysfunction, Mrs. Howard. And we don't know what causes these disabilities, and we don't have a cure."

Georgeanne leaned against the wall out of sight. Her cheeks began to burn, and a lump settled in her stomach. Brain dysfunction? She wasn't so stupid that she didn't know what the man meant. He thought she was retarded.

"What can I do for my Georgie?"

"Perhaps with more testing we can pinpoint where she's having the most difficulties. Some children have been helped with medication."

"I won't put Georgeanne on drugs."

"Then enroll her in charm school," he advised. "She is a pretty little girl and will probably grow into a beautiful young woman. She won't have any trouble finding a husband to take care of her."

"A husband? My Georgie is only nine, Dr. Allan."

"No disrespect intended, Mrs. Howard, but you are the girl's grandmother. How many more years can you take care of her? It is my opinion that Georgeanne will never be real bright."

The lump in Georgeanne's stomach began to burn as she walked back down the hall and out the back door. She kicked a coffee can off the back steps and sent her grandmother's clothespins flying across the small, well-kept yard.

Parked in the dirt driveway sat an El Camino which Georgeanne had always thought was the exact color of root beer. The car rested on four flat tires and hadn't been driven since the death of her grandfather two years before. Her grandmother drove a Lincoln, so Georgeanne considered the El Camino hers and used it to transport herself to such exotic places as London, Paris, and Texarkana.

Today she didn't feel like going anywhere. Once she sat on the vinyl bench seat, she wrapped her hands around the cool steering wheel and stared at the Chevrolet insignia in the middle of the car's horn.

Her vision blurred and her grip tightened. Maybe her mother, Billy Jean, had known. Maybe she had known all along that Georgeanne would never be "real bright." Maybe that was why she'd dumped her at Grandmother's house and never come back. Grandmother always said that Billy Jean wasn't ready to be a mother yet, and Georgeanne had always wondered what she'd done to make her mother go away. Maybe now she knew.

As she stared into her future, her childhood dreams slipped away with the tears falling down her hot cheeks, and she realized several things. She'd never get to have recess again or build an igloo like the rest of the class. Her hopes of becoming a nurse or an astronaut were over, and her mother was never coming for her. The kids at school would probably find out and laugh at her.

Georgeanne hated to be laughed at.

Or they would make fun of her like they did Gilbert Whitley. Gilbert wet his pants in the second grade, and no one had ever let him forget it. Now they called him Gilbert Wetly. Georgeanne didn't even want to think about what they'd call her.

Even if it killed her, she was determined that no one ever find out she was different. She was determined no one ever discover that Georgeanne Howard had a brain dysfunction.

# One

*1989*

The night before Virgil Duffy's wedding, a summer storm pounded the Puget Sound. But by the next morning, the gray clouds were gone, leaving in their place a view of Elliot Bay and the spectacular skyline of downtown Seattle. Several of Virgil's wedding guests glanced up at the clear sky and wondered if he controlled Mother Nature the same way he controlled his shipping empire. They wondered if he could control his young bride as well or if she was just a toy like his hockey team.

While the guests waited for the ceremony to begin, they sipped from fluted champagne glasses and speculated as to how long the May-December marriage would last. Not long was the general consensus.

John Kowalsky ignored the buzz of gossip around him. He had more pressing concerns. Raising a crystal tumbler to his lips, he drained the hundred-year-old scotch as if it were water. An incessant thud pounded his head. His eye sockets throbbed and his teeth ached.

He must have had one hell of a good time last night. He just wished he could remember.

From his position on the terrace, he looked down on a cross-cut emerald lawn, immaculate flower beds, and sputtering fountains. Guests dressed in Armani and Donna Karan drifted toward rows of white chairs facing an arbor festooned with flowers and ribbon and some sort of pink gauzy stuff.

John's gaze moved to a cluster of his teammates looking out of place and uncomfortable in their matching navy blazers and scuffed loafers. They didn't look like they wanted to be stuck in the middle of Seattle society any more than he did.

To his left, a skinny woman in a flowing lavender dress with matching shoes sat down at her harp, leaned it back against her shoulder, and began to pluck the strings just slightly louder than the noises rolling off the Puget Sound. She looked up at him and gave him a warm smile he instantly recognized. He wasn't surprised by the woman's interest and purposely let his gaze travel down her body, then back up again. At the age of twenty-eight, John had been with women of all shapes and sizes, economic backgrounds, and differing levels of intelligence. He wasn't averse to taking a swim in the groupie pool, but he didn't particularly like bony women. Although some of his teammates dated models, John preferred soft curves. When he touched a woman, he liked to feel flesh, not bone.

The harpist's smile grew more flirtatious, and John looked away. Not only was the woman too skinny, but he hated harp music just about as much as he hated weddings. He'd been through two of his own, and neither had been real blissful. In fact, the last time he'd been this hungover had been in Vegas six months ago when he'd woken up in a red velvet honeymoon suite suddenly married to a stripper named DeeDee

Delight. The marriage hadn't lasted much longer than the wedding night. And the real bitch of it was, he couldn't remember if DeeDee had been all that delightful.

"Thanks for coming, son." The owner of the Seattle Chinooks approached John from behind and patted him on the shoulder.

"I didn't think any of us had a choice," he said, looking down into Virgil Duffy's lined face.

Virgil laughed and continued down the wide brick steps, the picture of wealth in his silver-gray tuxedo. Beneath the early afternoon sun, Virgil appeared to be exactly what he was: a member of the Fortune 500, owner of a professional hockey team, and a man who could buy himself a young trophy wife.

"Did you see him last night with the woman he's marrying?"

John glanced across his right shoulder at his newest teammate, Hugh Miner. Sportswriters had compared Hugh to James Dean in looks and reckless behavior on and off the ice. John liked that in a man. "No," he answered as he reached beneath his blazer and pulled a pair of Ray-Bans from the breast pocket of his oxford shirt. "I left fairly early."

"Well, she's pretty young. Twenty-two or so."

"That's what I hear." He shifted to one side and let a group of older ladies pass on their way down the stairs. Being a practicing womanizer himself, he'd never claimed to be a self-righteous moralist, but there was something pathetic and just a little sick about a man Virgil's age marrying a woman nearly forty years younger.

Hugh poked John in the side with his elbow. "And breasts that could make a man sit up and beg for buttermilk."

John slipped the sunglasses up the bridge of his nose and smiled at the ladies who glanced back at Hugh.

He hadn't been real quiet with his description of Virgil's fiancée. "You were raised on a dairy farm, right?"

"Yep, about fifty miles outside of Madison," the young goalie said with pride.

"Well, I wouldn't say that buttermilk thing too loud, if I were you. Women tend to get real pissed off when you compare them to cows."

"Yeah." Hugh laughed and shook his head. "What do you think she sees in a man old enough to be her grandfather? I mean, she isn't ugly or fat or anything. In fact, she's real good-lookin'."

At the age of twenty-four, Hugh was not only younger than John but obviously naive. He was on his way to being the best damn goalie in the NHL, but he had a real bad habit of stopping the puck with his head. In view of his last question, he obviously needed a thicker mask. "Take a look around," John answered. "The last I heard, Virgil's worth over six hundred millon."

"Yeah, well, money can't buy everything," the goalie grumbled as he started down the steps. "Are you coming, Wall?" He paused to ask over his shoulder.

"Nope," John answered. He sucked an ice cube into his mouth, then tossed the tumbler into a potted fern, showing the same disregard for the Baccarat as he had shown for the scotch. He'd put in an appearance at the party last night, and he'd shown his face today. He'd played his part, but he wasn't staying. "I've got one bitch of a hangover," he said as he descended the stairs.

"Where are you going?"

"My house in Copalis."

"Mr. Duffy isn't going to like it."

"Too bad," was his unconcerned comment as he walked around the side of the three-story brick mansion toward his 1966 Corvette parked in front. A year ago, the convertible had been a present to himself after he'd been traded to the Chinooks and had signed a multimillon-dollar contract with the Seattle hockey team. John loved the classic Corvette. He loved the big engine and all that power. He figured once he got on the freeway, he'd open the Corvette up.

As he shed his blue blazer, a flash of pink at the top of the wide brick steps caught his attention. He tossed his jacket in the shiny red car and paused to watch a woman in a light pink dress slip through the massive double doors. A beige overnight case banged against the hardwood, and a breeze tossed dozens of dark corkscrew curls about her bare shoulders. She looked like she'd been shrink-wrapped in satin from armpit to midthigh. The large white bow sewn to the top of the bodice did little to hide her centerfold bosom. Her legs were long and tan, and she wore a pair of flimsy strapless high heels on her feet.

"Hey, mister, wait a minute," she called to him in a slightly breathless, distinctly southern voice. The heels of her ridiculous shoes made tiny click-click sounds as she bounced down the stairs. Her dress was so tight, she had to descend sideways, and with each hurried step, her breasts strained and swelled against the top of the dress.

John thought about telling her to stop before she hurt herself. Instead he shifted his weight to one foot, folded his arms, and waited until she came to a halt on the opposite side of his car. "Maybe you shouldn't run like that," he advised.

From beneath perfectly arched brows, pale green eyes stared at him. "Are you one of Virgil's hockey players?" she asked, stepping out of her shoes and leaning down to pick them up. Several glossy dark curls slid over her tanned shoulder and brushed the tops of her breasts and the white bow.

"John Kowalsky," he introduced himself. With her full, kiss-me-daddy lips and tilty eyes, she reminded him of his grandfather's favorite sex goddess, Rita Hayworth.

"I need to get out of here. Can you help me?"

"Sure. Where are you headed?"

"Anywhere but here," she answered, and tossed her overnight case and shoes on the floor of his car.

A smile tugged at the corner of his mouth as he slid into the Corvette. He hadn't planned on having company, but having Miss January jump in his car wasn't such a bad fate. Once she sat in the passenger's seat, he pulled out of the circular drive. He wondered who she was and why she was in such a hurry.

"Oh God," she moaned, and turned to stare at Virgil's rapidly disappearing house. "I left Sissy there all by herself. She went to get her bouquet of lilac and pink roses and I ran out!"

"Who's Sissy?"

"My friend."

"Were you supposed to be in the wedding?" he asked. When she nodded he assumed she was a bridesmaid or some sort of attendant. As they sped past walls of fir trees, rolling farmland, and pink rhododendrons, he studied her out of the corner of his eye. A healthy tan tinted her smooth skin, and as John looked at her, he noticed that she was prettier then he'd first realized—younger, too.

She turned to face the front again, and the wind picked up her hair and sent it dancing about her face and straight shoulders. "Oh, God. I've really messed up this time," she groaned, drawing out the vowels.

"I could take you back," he offered, wondering what had happened to make this woman run out on her friend.

She shook her head and her pearl drop earrings brushed the smooth skin just below her jaw. "No, it's too late. I've done it now. I mean, I've done it in the past . . . but this . . . this beats all with a stick."

John turned his attention to the road. Female tears didn't really bother him much, but he hated hysterics, and he had a real bad feeling she was about to get hysterical on him. "Ahh . . . what's your name?" he asked, hoping to avoid a scene.

She took a deep breath, tried to let it out slowly, and grabbed at her stomach with one hand. "Georgeanne, but everyone calls me Georgie."

"Well, Georgie, what's your last name?

She placed one palm on her forehead. Her sculpted nails were painted light beige on the bottom and white at the ends. "Howard."

"Where do you live, Georgie Howard?"

"McKinney."

"Is that just south of Tacoma?"

"Cryin' all night in a bucket," she groaned, and her breathing quickened. "I can't believe it. I just can't believe it."

"Are you going to get sick?"

"I don't think so." She shook her head and gulped air into her lungs. "But I can't breathe."

"Are you hyperventilating?"

"Yes—no—I don't know!" She looked at him with nervous, wet eyes. Her fingers began to claw at the pink satin covering her ribs, and the hem of her dress slipped farther up her smooth thighs. "I can't believe it. I can't believe it," she wailed between big, hiccuping breaths.

"Put your head between your knees," he instructed, glancing briefly at the road.

She leaned slightly forward, then fell back against the seat. "I can't."

"Why the hell not?"

"My corset is too tight . . . Good Lord!" Her southern drawl rose. "I've done it up good this time. I can't believe it . . ." she continued with her now familiar litany.

John began thinking that helping Georgeanne was not the best idea. He pressed the gas pedal to the floor, propelling the Corvette across a bridge spanning a narrow strip of the Puget Sound, quickly leaving Bainbridge Island behind. Shades of green sped past as the Corvette chewed up highway 305.

"Sissy is never going to forgive me."

"I wouldn't worry about your friend," he said, somewhat disappointed to find that the woman in his car was as flaky as a croissant. "Virgil will buy her something nice, and she'll forget all about it."

A wrinkle appeared between her brows. "I don't think so," she said.

"Sure he will," John argued. "He'll probably take her someplace real expensive, too."

"But Sissy doesn't like Virgil. She thinks he's a lecherous old leprechaun."

A real bad feeling tweaked the back of John's neck. "Isn't Sissy the bride?"

She stared at him with her big green eyes and shook her head. "I am."

"That's not even funny, Georgeanne."

"I know," she wailed. "I can't believe I left Virgil at the altar!"

The tweak in John's neck shot to his head, reminding him of his hangover. He stomped on the brake as the Corvette swerved to the right and stopped on the side of the highway. Georgeanne fell against the door and grasped the handle with both hands.

"Jesus H. Christ!" John shoved the car into park and reached for the sunglasses on his face. "Tell me you're joking!" he demanded, tossing the Ray-Bans on the dash. He didn't even want to think about what would happen if he were caught with Virgil's runaway bride. But then, he really didn't have to think about it too hard, he knew what would happen. He knew he'd find himself traded to a losing team faster than he could clear out his locker. He liked playing for the Chinook organization. He liked living in Seattle. The last thing he wanted was a trade.

Georgeanne straightened and shook her head.

"But you're not wearing a wedding dress." He felt tricked and pointed an accusing finger at her. "What kind of bride doesn't wear a damn wedding dress?"

"This is a wedding dress." She grasped the hem and tried to yank it modestly down her thighs. But the dress hadn't been made for modesty. The more she tugged it toward her knees, the farther it slid down her breasts. "It's just not a traditional wedding dress," she explained as she grabbed the big white bow and pulled the bodice back up. "After all, Virgil has been married five times, and he thought a white gown would be tacky."

Taking a deep breath, John closed his eyes and ran a hand over his face. He had to get rid of her—fast. "You live south of Tacoma, right?"

"No. I'm from McKinney—McKinney, Texas. Until three days ago, I'd never been north of Oklahoma City."

"This just keeps getting better." He laughed without humor and turned to look at her sitting there as if she'd been gift wrapped just for him. "Your family is here for the wedding, right?"

Again she shook her head.

John frowned. "Naturally."

"I think I'm going to be sick."

Jumping out of the car, John ran to the other side. If she was going to vomit, he'd prefer she didn't do it in his new classic 'vette. He opened her door and grabbed her around the waist, and even though John was six foot five, weighed two twenty-five in his birthday suit, and could easily body-check any player against the boards, hauling Georgeanne Howard from his car was no easy task. She was heavier than she looked, and beneath his hands, she felt like she'd sealed herself up in a soup can. "Are you going to puke?" he asked the part in the top of her head.

"I don't think so," she answered, and looked up at him with pleading eyes. He'd been around enough women to spot a house cat when one landed in his lap. He recognized the "love me, feed me, take care of me" breed. They purred and rubbed, and other than making a man yowl, weren't good for anything else. He'd help her get where she needed to go, but the last thing he wanted was the care and feeding of the woman who'd jilted Virgil Duffy. "Where can I drop you off?"

Georgeanne felt like she'd swallowed dozens of butterflies and had difficulty catching her breath. She'd cinched herself into a dress two sizes too small and could only suck air into the top of her lungs. She looked way up into dark blue eyes surrounded by thick lashes and knew she'd rather slit her wrists with a butter knife than get sick in front of a man so outrageously good-looking. His thick lashes and full mouth should have made him look a little feminine, but didn't. The man exuded too much masculinity to be confused for anything but one hundred percent heterosexual male. Georgeanne, who stood five ten and weighed one hundred forty—on good days when she wasn't retaining water—felt almost small next to him.

"Where can I drop you off, Georgie?" he asked her again. A lock of rich brown hair curved over his forehead, drawing her attention to a thin white scar running through his left brow.

"I don't know," she whispered. For months now she'd lived with a horrible heaviness in her chest. A weight she'd been so sure a man like Virgil could make go away. With Virgil, she would have never had to dodge bill collectors or angry landlords again. She was twenty-two and had tried to take care of herself, but as with most things in her life, she'd failed—miserably. She'd always been a failure. She'd failed in school and at every job she'd ever had, and she'd failed to convince herself that she could love Virgil Duffy. That afternoon, as she'd stood before the cheval mirror studying her reflection, studying the wedding dress he'd chosen for her, the heaviness in her chest threatened to choke her and she'd known she couldn't marry Virgil. Not even for all that wonderful money could she go to bed with a man who reminded her of H. Ross Perot.

"Where's your family?"

She thought of her grandmother. "I have a great-aunt and uncle who live in Duncanville, but Lolly can't travel because of her lumbago, and Uncle Clyde had to stay home and take care of her."

The corners of his mouth turned downward. "Where are your parents?"

"I was brought up by my grandmother, but she took her final journey to heaven several years ago," Georgeanne answered, hoping he wouldn't ask about the father she'd never known or the mother she'd seen only once at her grandmother's funeral.

"Friends?"

"She's at Virgil's." Just the thought of Sissy made her heart palpitate. She'd been so careful to make sure everyone matched the lavender punch. Now coordinating dresses and dyed pumps seemed trivial and silly.

A frown bracketed his mouth. "Naturally." He removed his big hands from her waist and ran his fingers through the sides of his hair. "It doesn't sound to me like you have a real firm plan."

No, she didn't have a plan, firm or otherwise. She'd grabbed her vanity case and had run out of Virgil's house without a thought to where she was going or how she planned to get there.

"Well, hell." He dropped his hands to his sides and looked down the road. "You might want to think up something."

Georgeanne had a horrible feeling that if she didn't come up with an idea within the next two minutes, John would jump back in his car and leave her on the side of the road. She needed him, at least for a few days until she figured out what to do next, and so she did what had always worked for her. She placed one hand on his arm and leaned into him a little, just enough to make him think she was open to any suggestion he might make. "Maybe you could help me," she said in her smoothest bourbon-soaked voice, then topped it off with a you're-such-a-big-ol'-stud-and-I'm-so-helpless smile. Georgeanne might be a failure at everything else in her life, but she was an accomplished flirt and a bona fide success when it came to manipulating men. Lowering her lashes modestly, she gazed up into his beautiful eyes. One corner of her lips tilted in a seductive promise she had no intention of keeping. She slid her palms to his hard forearms, a gesture made to seem like a caress but that was purely a tactical maneuver to guard against quick hands. Georgeanne hated it when men pawed her breasts.

"You're real tempting," he said, placing a finger beneath her chin and lifting her face. "But you're not worth what it'd cost me."

"Cost you?" A cool breeze picked up several spiral curls and sent them dancing about her face. "What do you mean?"

"I mean," he began, then glanced pointedly at her breasts pressed against his chest, "that you want something from me and you're willing to use your body to get it. I like sex as much as any man, but, honey, you're not worth my career."

Georgeanne pushed away from him and batted her hair from her eyes. She'd been in several intimate relationships in her life, but as far as she was concerned, sex was highly overrated. Men seemed to really enjoy it, but for her, sex was just plain embarrassing. The only good thing she could say about it was that it only lasted about three minutes. She raised her chin and looked at him as if he'd just hurt and insulted her. "You're mistaken. I'm not that kind of girl."

"I see." He looked back at her as if he knew exactly what kind of girl she was. "You're a tease."

*Tease* was such an ugly word. She thought of herself more as an actress.

"Why don't you cut the bullshit and just tell me what you want."

"Okay," she said, changing tactics. "I need a little help, and I need a place to stay for a few days."

"Listen," he sighed, and shifted his weight to one foot. "I'm not the type of man you're looking for. I can't help you."

"Then why did you tell me you would?"

His eyes narrowed, but he didn't answer.

"Just for a few days," she pleaded, desperate. She needed time to think of what to do now—now that she'd royally messed up her life. "I won't be any trouble."

"I doubt that," he scoffed.

"I need to get in touch with my aunt."

"Where's your aunt?"

"Back in McKinney," she answered truthfully, although she didn't look forward to her conversation with Lolly. Her aunt had been extremely pleased with Georgeanne's choice in a husband. Even though Lolly had never been so tactless as to come right out and say so, Georgeanne suspected that her aunt envisioned a series of expensive gifts like a big-screen TV and a Craftmatic Adjustable Bed.

John's hard stare pinned her for several long moments. "Shit, get in," he said, and turned to walk around the front of the car. "But as soon as you get in touch with your aunt, I'm dropping you off at the airport or bus depot or wherever the hell else you're going."

Despite his less-than-enthusiastic offer, Georgeanne didn't waste any time. She jumped back in the car and slammed the door.

Once John was behind the wheel, he shoved the Corvette into gear, and the car shot back onto the highway. The sound of tires hitting the pavement filled an awkward silence between them—at least it felt awkward to Georgeanne. John didn't seem bothered by it at all.

For years she'd attended Miss Virdie Marshall's School of Ballet, Tap, and Charm. Although she'd never been the most coordinated girl, she'd outshined the others with her ability to charm anyone, anywhere, any time of the day. But this day she had a slight problem. John didn't seem to like her, which perplexed Georgeanne because men *always* liked her. From what she'd noticed of him so far, he wasn't a gentleman either. He used profanity with a frequency bordering on habitual, and he didn't apologize. The southern men she knew swore, of course, but they usually begged pardon afterward. John didn't strike her as the type of man to beg pardon for anything.

She turned to look at his profile and set about charming John Kowalsky. "Are you from Seattle originally?" she asked, determined that he would like her by the time they reached their destination. It would make things so much easier if he did. Because he might not realize it yet, but John was going to offer her a place to stay for a while.

"No."

"Where are you from?"

"Saskatoon."

"Where?"

"Canada."

Her hair blew about her face, and she gathered it all in one hand and held it by the side of her neck. "I've never been to Canada."

He didn't comment.

"How long have you played hockey?" she asked, hoping to drag a little pleasant conversation out of him.

"All of my life."

"How long have you played for the Chinooks?"

He reached for his sunglasses sitting on the dash and put them on. "A year."

"I've seen a Stars game," she said, referring to the Dallas hockey team.

"Bunch of candy-assed pussies," he muttered as he unbuttoned the white cuff above his driving hand and folded it up his forearm.

Not exactly *pleasant* conversation, she decided. "Did you go to college?"

"Not really."

Georgeanne had no idea what he meant by that. "I went to the University of Texas," she lied in a effort to impress him into liking her.

He yawned.

"I pledged a Kappa," she added to the lie.

"Yeah? So?"

Undaunted with his less-than-enthusiastic response, she continued, "Are you married?"

He stared at her through the lenses of his sunglasses, leaving little doubt she'd touched on a sore subject. "What are you, the friggin' *National Enquirer*?"

"No. I'm just curious. I mean, we will be spending a certain amount of time together, so I thought it would be nice to have a friendly chat and get to know each other."

John turned his attention back to the road and began to work on his other cuff. "I don't chat."

Georgeanne pulled at the hem of her dress. "May I ask where we're going?"

"I have a house on Copalis Beach. You can get in touch with your aunt from there."

"Is that near Seattle?" She shifted her weight to one side and continued to yank at the hem of her dress.

"Nope. In case you hadn't noticed, we're headed west."

Panic surged through her as they sped farther from anything remotely familiar. "How in the heck would I know that?"

"Maybe because the sun is at our backs."

Georgeanne hadn't noticed, and even if she had, she wouldn't have thought to judge direction by looking at the sun. She always messed up that whole north-south-east-west thing. "I assume you have a phone at your beach house?"

"Of course."

She'd have to make a few long-distance telephone calls to Dallas. She had to call Lolly, and she needed to phone Sissy's parents and tell them what had happened and how they could get in touch with their daughter. She also needed to call Seattle and find out where to send Virgil's engagement ring. She glanced at the five-carat diamond solitaire on her left hand and felt like crying. She loved that ring but knew she couldn't keep it. She was a flirt, and maybe even a tease, but she did have scruples. The diamond would have to go back, but not now. Now she needed to calm her nerves before she fell apart. "I've never been to the Pacific Ocean," she said, feeling her panic easing a bit.

He made no comment.

Georgeanne had always considered herself the perfect blind date because she could talk water uphill, especially when she felt nervous. "But I've been to the

Gulf many times," she began. "Once when I was twelve, my grandmother took me and Sissy in her big Lincoln. Boy, what a boat. That car must have weighed ten tons if it weighed an ounce. Sissy and I had just bought these really cool bikinis. Hers looked like an American flag while mine was made of a silky bandanna material. I'll never forget it. We drove all the way into Dallas just to buy that bikini at J.C. Penney's. I'd seen it in a catalog and I was just dying to have it. Anyway, Sissy is a Miller on her mother's side, and the Miller women are known throughout Collin County for their wide hips and piano ankles—not very attractive, but a lovely family just the same. One time—"

"Is there a point to all of this?" John interrupted.

"I was getting to it," she told him, trying to remain pleasant.

"Any time soon?"

"I just wanted to ask if the water off the coast of Washington is very cold."

John smiled and cast a glance at her then. For the first time, she noticed the dimple creasing his right cheek. "You'll freeze your southern butt off," he said before looking down at the console between them and picking up a cassette. He popped it in the tape player and a wailing harmonica put an end to any attempt at further conversation.

Georgeanne turned her attention to the hilly landscape dotted with fir and alder trees and painted with smears of blue, red, yellow, and of course, green. Up until now, she'd done fairly well at avoiding her thoughts, afraid they would overwhelm and paralyze her. But with no other distraction, they rolled over her like a Texas heat wave. She thought about her life and about what she'd done today. She'd left a man at the altar, and even though the marriage would have been a disaster, he hadn't deserved that.

All of her things were packed into four suitcases in Virgil's Rolls-Royce, except the carry-on sitting on the floor of John's car. She'd packed the little suitcase with essentials the night before in preparation for her and Virgil's honeymoon trip.

Now all she had with her was a wallet filled with seven dollars and three maxed-out credit cards, a liberal amount of cosmetics, a toothbrush and hairbrush, comb, a can of Aqua Net, six pairs of French-cut underwear with matching lace bras, her birth control pills, and a Snickers.

She had hit an all-time low, even for Georgeanne.

# Two

Flashes of blue and crystal sunlight, waving sea grass, and a salty breeze so thick she could taste it welcomed Georgeanne to the Pacific coast. Goose bumps broke out on her arms as she strained to catch glimpses of rolling blue ocean and foamy whitecaps.

The squall of seagulls pierced the air as John steered the Corvette up the driveway of a nondescript gray house with white shutters. An old man in a sleeveless T-shirt, gray polyester shorts, and a pair of cheap rubber thongs stood on the porch.

As soon as the car rolled to a stop, Georgeanne reached for the door handle and got out. She didn't wait for John to assist her—not that she believed he would have helped her anyway. After an hour and a half of sitting in the car, her merry widow had became so painful she thought she might get sick after all.

She tugged the hem of her pink dress down her thighs and reached for her overnight case and shoes. The metal stays in her corset dug into her ribs as she bent to shove her feet into her pink mules.

"Good God, son," the man on the porch growled in a gravelly voice. "Another dancer?"

A scowl creased John's forehead as he led Georgeanne to the front door. "Ernie, I'd like you to meet Miss Georgeanne Howard. Georgie, this is my grandfather, Ernest Maxwell."

"How do you do, sir." Georgeanne offered her hand and looked into the aged face, which bore a striking resemblance to Burgess Meredith.

"Southern . . . hmmm." He turned and walked back into the house.

John held the screen door open for Georgeanne, and she stepped inside a house furnished in plush blues, greens, and light browns, giving the impression that the view outside the large picture window had been brought into the living room. Everything appeared to have been chosen to blend with the ocean and sandy beach—everything but the black Naugahyde recliner patched with silver duct tape and the two broken hockey sticks placed like a sideways X above a packed trophy cabinet.

John reached for his sunglasses and tossed them on the wood and glass coffee table. "There's a guest room down the hall, last door on your left. Bathroom's on the right," he said as he crossed behind Georgeanne and walked into the kitchen. He grabbed a bottle of beer from the refrigerator and twisted off the top. Raising the bottle to his lips, he leaned his shoulders back against the closed refrigerator door. He'd messed up big this time. He never should have agreed to help Georgeanne, and he for damn sure never should have brought her with him. He hadn't wanted to, but then she'd stared up at him looking all vulnerable and scared, and he hadn't been able to leave her on the side of the road. He just hoped like hell Virgil never found out.

He pushed himself away from the refrigerator and returned to the living room. Ernie had plopped himself down in his favorite recliner, his attention riveted on Georgeanne. She stood next to the fireplace with her hair all windblown and her little pink dress wrinkled. She appeared exhausted, but by the look in Ernie's eyes, he found her more appealing than an all-you-can-eat buffet.

"Is there a problem, Georgie?" John asked, and raised the bottle to his lips. "Why aren't you changing?"

"I have a slight dilemma," she drawled, and looked at him. "I don't have any clothes."

He pointed with the bottle. "What's in that little suitcase?"

"Cosmetics."

"That's it?"

"No." She quickly glanced at Ernie. "I have underthings and my wallet."

"Where are your clothes?"

"In four suitcases in the back of Virgil's Rolls-Royce."

It figured he would have to feed, house, *and* clothe her. "Come on," he said, then he set his beer on the coffee table and led her down the hall into his bedroom. He walked to his dresser and pulled an old black T-shirt and a pair of green drawstring shorts from the drawers. "Here," he said, tossing them on the blue quilt covering his bed before turning toward the door.

"John?"

His name on her lips stopped him, but he didn't turn around. He didn't want to see that scared look in her green eyes. "What?"

"I can't get out of this dress by myself. I need your help."

He turned to see her standing within a golden slice of sunlight spilling in from the window.

"There are some little buttons at the top." She awkwardly pointed.

Not only did she want his clothes, she wanted him to undress her.

"They're really slippery," she explained.

"Turn around," he ordered, a harsh edge to his voice as he stepped toward her.

Without a word, she turned her profile to him and faced the mirror above the dresser. Between her smooth shoulder blades, four tiny buttons closed the very top of the dress. She pulled her hair to one side, exposing baby-fine curls just below her hairline. Her skin, her hair, her southern accent, everything about her was soft.

"How did you get into this thing?"

"I had help." She looked at him through the mirror. John couldn't remember a time that he'd helped a woman out of her clothes without taking her to bed afterward, but he didn't intend to touch Virgil's runaway bride any more than necessary. He raised his hands and tugged until one small button slipped from its slick loop.

"I can't imagine what they all must be thinking right now. Sissy tried to warn me against marrying Virgil. I thought I could go through with it, but I guess I couldn't."

"Don't you think you should have come to that conclusion before today?" he asked, then moved his fingers lower.

"I did. I tried to tell Virgil that I was having second thoughts. I tried to talk to him about it last night, but he wouldn't listen. Then I saw the silver." She shook her head and a soft spiral of hair fell down her back and brushed across her smooth skin. "I'd chosen Francis I for my pattern, and his friends had sent a good amount," she said, all dreamy as if he knew what the hell she was talking about. "Ohhh—just seeing all those pieces of fruit on the knife handles gave me the shivers. Sissy thinks I should have chosen repoussé, but I've always been a Francis I girl. Even when I was little . . ."

John had very little tolerance for girly chitchat. He wished he had a tape player and another Tom Petty cassette. Since he didn't, he tuned her out. More often than not, he was accused of being a real bastard, a reputation he considered an asset. That way he didn't have to worry about women getting ideas about a permanent connection.

"While you're there, could you unzip me? Anyway," she continued. "I almost wept with joy when I laid eyes on the pickle forks and grapefruit spoons and . . ."

John scowled at her through the mirror, but she wasn't paying any attention. Her gaze was directed downward toward the big white bow sewn on the front of her dress. John reached for the metal tab, and as he pulled, he discovered the reason Georgeanne had difficulty breathing. Between the gaping zipper of her wedding dress, silver hooks lashed together an undergarment John instantly recognized as a merry widow. Made out of pink satin, lace, and steel, the corset cut into her soft skin.

She raised a hand to the bow and clutched it to her large breasts to keep the dress from falling. "Seeing my favorite silver pattern went to my head, and I guess I let Virgil convince me that I just had prewedding jitters. I *really* wanted to believe him . . ."

When John finished with the zipper he announced, "I'm done."

"Oh." She looked up at him through the mirror, then quickly dropped her gaze. Her cheeks turned red as she asked, "Could you unfasten my ah . . . ah, thing partway?"

"Your corset?"

"Yes, please."

"I'm not a friggin' maid," he grumbled, and lifted his hands once more to tug at the hooks and eyes. While he worked at the tiny fasteners, his knuckles brushed the pink marks marring her skin. A shudder racked through her as a long, low sigh whispered deep within her throat.

John glanced up into the mirror and his hands stilled. The only time he ever saw such ecstasy on a woman's face was when he was buried deep inside her. A swift punch of lust hit him low in the belly. His body's reaction to the bliss-filled tilt to her eyes and lips irritated him.

"Oh, my." She breathed deep. "I can't tell you how wonderful that feels. I hadn't planned to wear this dress for more than an hour and it's been three."

His body might respond to a beautiful woman—in fact, he'd worry if it didn't—but he wasn't going to do anything about it. "Virgil is an old man," he said, not bothering to hide the irritation in his voice. "How in the hell did you expect him to pry you out of this?"

"That was unkind," she whispered.

"Don't expect kindness from me, Georgeanne," he warned her, and yanked at several more hooks. "Or I'm bound to disappoint you."

She looked at him and let her hair slide across her shoulders. "I think you could be nice if you wanted to."

"That's right," he told her, and raised his fingertips to brush the marks on her back, but before he could soothe her skin with his touch, he dropped his hand to his side. "If I wanted to," he said, and moved from the room, shutting the door behind him.

When he walked into the living room, he instantly felt Ernie's speculative gaze. John snagged his beer from the table, sat down on the couch across from his grandfather's old recliner, and waited for Ernie to start firing his questions. He didn't have to wait long.

"Where did you pick up that one?"

"It's a long story," he answered, then explained the situation, leaving nothing out.

"Good God, have you lost your mind?" Ernie leaned forward and about tipped himself out of the chair. "What do you think Virgil is going to do? From what you've told me, the man isn't exactly the forgiving kind, and you practically stole his bride."

"I did not steal her." John raised his feet to the coffee table and sank deeper into the cushions. "She'd already left him."

"Yeah." Ernie folded his arms across his thin chest and scowled at John. "At the altar. A man isn't likely to forgive and forget a thing like that."

John rested his elbows on his thighs and raised the bottle to his lips. "He won't find out," he said, and took a long swig.

"You better hope not. We've worked too damn hard to get this far," he reminded his grandson.

"I know," he said, although he didn't need reminding. He owed a lot of who he was to his grandfather. After John's father had died, he and his mother had moved right next door to Ernie. Every winter Ernie had filled his backyard with water so John would have a place to skate. It had been Ernie who'd practiced with John out on that cold ice until they were both frozen to the marrow of their bones. It had been Ernie who'd taught him how to play hockey, taken him to games, and stayed to cheer him on. It was Ernie who held things together when life got real bad.

"Are you going to *do* her?"

John looked over at his wrinkled grandfather. "What?"

"Isn't that what you young fellas say these days?"

"Jesus, Ernie," he said, though he really wasn't shocked. "No, I'm not going to *do* her."

"I sure as hell hope not." He crossed one callused and cracked foot over the other. "But if Virgil finds out she's here, he'll think you did anyway."

"She's not my type."

"She sure as hell is," Ernie argued. "She reminds me of that stripper you dated a while back, Cocoa LaDude."

John glanced at the hallway, grateful to find it empty. "Her name was Cocoa LaDuke, and I didn't *date* her." He looked back at his grandfather and frowned. Even though Ernie never said so, John had a feeling his grandfather didn't approve of his lifestyle. "I didn't expect to find you here," he said, purposely changing the subject.

"Where else would I be?"

"Home."

"Tomorrow is the sixth."

John turned his gaze to the huge window facing the ocean. He watched several white-tipped waves swell, then curl in on themselves. "I don't need you to hold my hand."

"I know, but I thought you might like a beer buddy."

John closed his eyes. "I don't want to talk about Linda."

"We don't have to. Your mama's worried about you. You should call her more often."

With his thumb, John picked at the label glued to the beer bottle. "Yeah, I should," he agreed, although he knew he wouldn't. His mother would bitch at him about his drinking and tell him that he was leading a self-destructive life. Since he knew she was pretty much right, he didn't need to hear it. "When I drove through town, I spotted Dickie Marks coming out of your favorite bar," he said, again changing the subject.

"I saw him earlier." Ernie pushed himself forward and rose slowly from the chair, reminding John that his grandfather was seventy-one. "We're going fishing in the morning. You should get up and come with us."

Several years ago, John would have been the first on the boat, but these days he usually woke up with a splitting headache. Getting up before dawn to freeze his butt off just didn't appeal to him anymore. "I'll think about it," he answered, knowing he wouldn't.

Georgeanne fastened her maroon bra, reached for the T-shirt, and pulled it over her head. A Seahawks baseball cap, a stopwatch, an Ace bandage, and a good amount of dust rested on the dresser in front of her. Her gaze rose to the big mirror above the dresser and she cringed. Soft black cotton fit tight across her breasts but loose everyplace else. She looked like a fashion nightmare, so she tucked the T-shirt into the baggy drawstring shorts, which only accentuated her large breasts and behind—the two places she'd rather not emphasize. She yanked the shirt out until it fell to her hips, then she threw her shoes into the overnight case and grabbed her Snickers. Sitting on the edge of the bed, she peeled back the dark brown wrapper and sank her teeth into the rich chocolate. A euphoric sigh escaped her lips as she chewed her candy bar. Lying back on the blue comforter, she stretched and stared up at the light fixture attached to the ceiling. Two dead moths lay in the bottom of the shallow white glass. As she devoured her candy, she listened to John and Ernie's muffled conversation through the wood door. Considering that John didn't seem to like her very much, she found it odd that the low timbre of his voice should soothe her. Perhaps it was because he was the only person she knew for miles, or maybe because she sensed he really wasn't a jerk as he pretended. Then again, the sheer size of the man would make just about any woman feel safe.

She scooted until her head rested on John's pillow

and her feet lay across her wedding dress, which she'd thrown on the end of the bed. Polishing off the Snickers, she thought about calling Lolly, but decided to wait. She wasn't in a big hurry to hear her aunt's reaction. She thought about getting up but closed her eyes instead. She thought of the first time she'd met Virgil in the fragrance department at the Neiman-Marcus in Dallas. It was still hard to believe that just a little over a month ago she'd been working as a perfume girl, handing out samples of Fendi and Liz Claiborne. She probably wouldn't have noticed him if he hadn't approached her. She probably wouldn't have agreed to have dinner with him that first time if he hadn't had roses and a limousine waiting by the curb for her after work. It had been so easy to crawl inside that air-conditioned limo, out of the heat, humidity, and bus fumes. If she hadn't felt so alone, and if her future weren't so uncertain, she probably wouldn't have agreed to marry a man she'd known for such a short time.

Last night she'd tried to tell Virgil she couldn't marry him. She'd tried to call it off, but he hadn't listened to her. She felt horrible for what she'd done, but she didn't know how to fix it.

Letting go of the tears she'd held back all day, she quietly sobbed into John's pillow. She cried for the mess she'd made of her life, and the emptiness she felt inside. Her future loomed before her, terrifying and uncertain. Her only relatives were an elderly aunt and uncle who lived off Social Security and whose lives revolved around *I Love Lucy* reruns.

She had nothing and knew no one besides a man who'd told her not to expect kindness from him. Suddenly she felt like Blanche Dubois in *A Streetcar Named Desire.* She'd seen every Vivien Leigh movie ever made, and she thought it a little eerie, and more than coincidental, that John's last name was Kowalsky.

She was scared and alone, but she also felt a sense of relief that she wouldn't have to pretend anymore. She wouldn't have to pretend to like Virgil's awful taste in clothes and the trashy things he liked for her to wear.

Exhausted, she cried herself to sleep. She hadn't realized she'd dozed off until she woke with a start, sitting straight up in bed.

"Georgie?"

One side of her hair fell over her left eye as she turned toward the sunlit doorway and looked into a face she was sure she'd dreamed off one of those studs calendars. His hands gripped the frame just above his head, and he wore a silver wristwatch turned so the face rested against his pulse. He stood with one hip higher than the other, and for several moments she stared at him, disoriented.

"Are you hungry?" he asked.

She blinked several times before it all came back to her. John had changed his clothes into a pair of worn Levi's with a shredded hole in one knee. A white Chinooks tank top stretched across his powerful chest, and fine hair shadowed his armpits. She couldn't help but wonder if he'd changed in the room while she slept.

"If you're hungry, Ernie's fixing chowder."

"I'm starving," she said, and swung her legs over the side of the bed. "What time is it?"

John lowered one hand and glanced at his wrist. "Almost six."

She'd slept for two and a half hours and felt more tired than before. She remembered passing the bathroom earlier and reached for her overnight case on the floor next to the bed. "I need a few minutes," she said, and avoided looking at herself in the mirror as she passed the dresser. "I shouldn't be too long," she added as she approached the doorway.

"Good. We're about to sit down," John informed her, although he didn't appear in a hurry to move. His shoulders practically filled the doorfame, forcing her to stop.

"Excuse me." If he thought she was going to squeeze past him, he'd better come up with a new plan. Georgeanne had figured out that game in the tenth grade. She felt a vague disappointment that John should belong to the caliber of sleazy men who thought they had the right to rub up against women and peer down their blouses, but when she looked up into his blue eyes, relief washed over her. A wrinkle appeared between his dark brows and he gazed at her mouth, not her breasts. He reached toward her and brushed his thumb across her bottom lip. He was so close, she could smell his Obsession, and after working with perfumes and colognes for a year, Georgeanne knew her fragrances.

"What's this?" he asked, and turned his hand to show her a smudge of chocolate on his thumb.

"My lunch," she answered, and felt a little flutter in her stomach. Looking up into his deep blue eyes, she realized that he wasn't frowning at her for a change. She ran the tip of her tongue along her lip and asked, "Better?"

Slowly he lowered his arms to his sides and raised his gaze to hers. "Better than what?" he asked, and just when Georgeanne thought he might smile and show her his dimple again, he turned and headed down the hall. "Ernie wants to know if you want beer or ice water with dinner," he said over his shoulder. The buns of his jeans were worn a lighter blue than the rest, and a wallet bulged one pocket. On his feet he wore a pair of cheap rubber thongs just like his grandfather.

"Water," she answered, but would have preferred iced tea. Georgeanne made her way to the bathroom and repaired the damage to her makeup. As she reapplied her burgundy lipstick, a smile curved her lips. She'd been right about John. He wasn't a jerk.

By the time she had arranged the curls about her shoulders and made her way to the small dining room, John and Ernie were already seated at the oak pedestal table. "Sorry I took so long," she said, noticing that they were so bad-mannered as to have begun without her. She sat across from John and reached for a paper napkin stuck in an olive green holder. She placed it on her lap, looked for her spoon, and found it on the wrong side of the bowl.

"Pepper's right there." Ernie motioned with his spoon to a red and white can in the middle of the table.

"Thank you." Georgeanne looked at the older man. She didn't really care for pepper, but after her first bite of creamy white chowder, it became obvious that Ernie did. The soup was thick and rich, and despite the pepper, it was delicious. A glass of ice water sat next to her bowl and she reached for it. As she took a sip, she glanced about the room and noticed the sparse decoration. In fact, the only other thing in the room besides the table was a large china hutch filled with trophies. "Do you live here year-round, Mr. Maxwell?" she asked, taking it upon herself to start the dinner conversation.

He shook his head, drawing her attention to his thinning white crew cut. "This is one of John's houses. I still live in Saskatoon."

"Is that close by?"

"Close enough to see my share of games."

Georgeanne set the glass on the table and began to eat. "Hockey games?"

"Of course. I see most of 'em." He turned his gaze to John. "But I could still kick myself in the ass for missing that hat trick last May."

"Quit worrying about it," John told him.

Georgeanne knew next to nothing about hockey. "What's a hat trick?"

"It's when a player scores three goals in one game," Ernie explained. "And I missed that damn Kings game, too." He paused to shake his head, his eyes filling with pride as he gazed at his grandson. "That candy-assed Gretzky rode the pines for a good fifteen minutes after you checked him into the boards," he said, genuinely delighted.

Georgeanne didn't have the faintest idea what Ernie was talking about, but getting "checked into the boards" sounded painful to her. She'd been born and raised in a state that lived for football, yet she hated it. She sometimes wondered if she was the only person in Texas who abhorred violent sports. "Isn't that bad?" she asked.

"Hell no!" the older man exploded. "He went up against The Wall and lived to regret it."

One corner of John's mouth lifted upward, and he smashed several crackers into his chowder. "I guess I won't be winning the Lady Bying any time soon."

Ernie turned to Georgeanne. "That's the trophy given for gentlemanly conduct, but screw that." He pounded the table with one fist and raised his spoon to his mouth with the other.

Personally, Georgeanne didn't think either of them was in danger of winning an award for gentlemanly conduct. "This is wonderful chowder," she said in an effort to change the subject to something a little less volatile. "Did you make it?"

Ernie reached for the beer next to his bowl. "Sure," he answered, and raised the bottle to his mouth.

"It's delicious." It had always been important to Georgeanne that people like her—never more than now. She figured her friendly overtures were wasted on John, so she turned her considerable charm on his grandfather. "Did you start with a white sauce?" she asked, looking into Ernie's blue eyes.

"Yeah, sure, but the trick to good chowder is in the clam juice," he informed her, then between bites, he shared his recipe with Georgeanne. She gave him the appearance of hanging on his every word, of concentrating on him fully, and within seconds, he dropped into the palm of her hand like a ripe plum. She asked questions and commented on his choice of spices, and all the while she was very aware of John's direct gaze. She knew when he took a bite, raised the beer bottle to his lips, or wiped his mouth with a napkin. She was aware when he shifted his gaze from her to Ernie and back again. Earlier, when he'd woken her from her nap, he'd been almost friendly. Now he seemed withdrawn.

"Did you teach John how to make chowder?" she asked, making an effort to pull him into the conversation.

John leaned back in his chair and crossed his arms over his chest. "No," was all he said.

"When I'm not here, John goes out to eat. But when I am here, I make sure his kitchen is good and stocked. I like to cook," Ernie provided. "He doesn't."

Georgeanne smiled at him. "I truly believe that people are born either hating it or loving it, and I can just tell that you"—she paused to touch his wrinkled forearm—"have a God-given talent. Not everyone can make a decent white sauce."

"I could teach you," he offered with a smile.

His skin felt like warm waxed paper beneath her touch, filling her heart with warm childhood memories. "Thank you, Mr. Maxwell, but I already know how. I'm from Texas and we cream everything, even tuna." She glanced at John, noticed his frown, and decided to ignore him. "I can make gravy out of just about anything. My grandmother was famous for her redeye, and I'm not talking about a late-night flight, if you know what I mean. When one of our friends or relatives took their final journey to heaven, it was understood that my grandmother would bring the ham and redeye gravy. After all, Grandmother was raised on a hog farm near Mobile, and she was famous on the funeral circuit for her honeyed hams." Georgeanne had spent her life around elderly people, and talking to Ernie felt so comfortable she leaned closer to him and her smile brightened naturally. "Now, my aunt Lolly is famous as well, but unfortunately not in a flattering way. She's known for her lime Jell-O because she'll throw anything into the mold. She got really bad when Mr. Fisher took his final journey. They're still talking about it at First Missionary Baptist, which in no way should be confused with the First Free Will Baptists, who used to foot-wash, but I don't believe they practice—"

"Jeez-us," John interrupted. "Is there a point to any of this?"

Georgeanne's smile fell, but she was determined to remain pleasant. "I was getting to it."

"Well, you might want to do that real soon because Ernie isn't getting any younger."

"Stop right there," his grandfather warned.

Georgeanne patted Ernie's arm and looked into John's narrowed eyes. "That was incredibly rude."

"I get a lot worse." John pushed his empty bowl aside and leaned forward. "The guys on the team and I want to know, can Virgil still get it up, or was it strictly his money?"

Georgeanne could feel her eyes widen and her cheeks burn. The idea that her relationship with Virgil had been fodder for locker-room jock talk was beyond humiliating.

"That's enough, John," Ernie ordered. "Georgie is a nice girl."

"Yeah? Well, *nice* girls don't sleep with men for their money."

Georgeanne opened her mouth, but words failed her. She tried to think of something equally hurtful, but she couldn't. She was sure a perfectly witty and sarcastic response would come to her later, long after she needed it. She took a deep breath and tried to stay calm. It was a sad fact of her life that when she became flustered, words flew from her head—simple words like *door, stove,* or—as was the case earlier when she'd had to ask John for help—*corset.* "I don't know what I've done to make you say such cruel things," she said, placing her napkin on the table. "I don't know if it's me, if you hate women in general, or if you're just terminally bad-tempered, but my relationship with Virgil is none of your business."

"I don't hate women," John assured her, then deliberately lowered his gaze to the front of her T-shirt.

"That's right," Ernie broke in. "Your relationship with Mr. Duffy isn't our business." Ernie reached for her hand. "The tide is almost out. Why don't you go on down and look for some tide pools near those big rocks down there. Maybe you can find something from the Washington coast to take back to Texas with you."

Georgeanne had been raised to respect her elders too much to argue or question Ernie's suggestion. She glanced at both men, then stood. "I'm truly sorry, Mr. Maxwell. I didn't mean to cause trouble between y'all."

Without taking his eyes from his grandson, Ernie answered, "It's not your fault. This has nothing to do with you."

It certainly felt like her fault, she thought as she stepped behind her chair and slid it forward. As Georgeanne walked through the narrow, foam green kitchen toward the multipaned back door, she realized that she'd let John's good looks impair her judgment. He wasn't pretending to be a jerk. He was one!

Ernie waited until he heard the back door close before he said, "It's not right for you to take out your bad temper on that little girl." He watched one brow rise up his grandson's forehead.

"Little?" John planted his elbows on the table. "By no stretch of the imagination could you ever mistake Georgeanne for a 'little girl.' "

"Well, she can't be very old," Ernie continued. "And you were disrespectful and rude. If your mother were here, she'd give your ear a good hard twist."

A smile curved one corner of John's mouth. "Probably," he said.

Ernie stared into his grandson's face and pain wrenched his heart. The smile on John's lips didn't reach his eyes—it never did these days. "It's no good, John-John." He placed his hand on John's shoulder and felt the hard muscles of a man. Before him, he recognized nothing of the happy boy he'd taken hunting and fishing, the boy he'd taught to play hockey and drive a car, the boy he'd taught everything he'd known about being a man. The man before him wasn't the boy he'd raised. "You have to let it out. You can't hold it all in, walking around blaming yourself."

"I don't have to let anything out," he said, his smile disappearing altogether. "I told you that I don't want to talk about it."

Ernie looked into John's closed expression, into the blue eyes so much like his own had been before they'd clouded with age. He'd never pressed John about his first wife. He'd figured John would come to terms with what Linda had done on his own. Even though John had been a dumb-ass and married that stripper six months ago, Ernie had hopes that he'd begun to work things out in his own mind. But tomorrow marked the first anniversary of her death, and John seemed just as angry as the day he'd buried her. "Well, I think you need to talk to someone," Ernie said, deciding that maybe he should force the issue for John's own good. "You can't keep it up, John. You can't pretend nothing happened, yet at the same time drink to forget what did." He paused to remember what he'd heard on the television the other day. "You can't use booze to self-medicate. Alcohol is just a symptom of a greater disease," he said, pleased that he remembered.

"Have you been watching *Oprah* again?"

Ernie frowned. "That isn't the point. What happened is eating a hole in you, and you're taking it out on an innocent girl."

John leaned back in his chair and folded his arms over his chest. "I'm not taking anything out on Georgeanne."

"Then why were you so rude?"

"She gets on my nerves." John shrugged. "She rambles on and on about absolutely nothing."

"That's because she's a southerner," Ernie explained, letting the subject of Linda drop. "You just have to sit back and enjoy a southern gal."

"Like you were? She had you eating out of the palm of her hand with all that white sauce and funeral bullshit."

"You're jealous," Ernie laughed. "You're jealous of an old guy like me." He slapped his hands on the table and slowly stood. "I'll be damned."

"You're crazy," John scoffed, snagging his beer as he stood also.

"I think you like her," he said, and turned toward the living room. "I saw the way you were looking at her when she didn't know you were looking. You may not want to like her, but you're attracted to her, and it's pissing you off." He walked into his bedroom and stuffed a few things in a duffel bag.

"Where are you going?" John asked from the doorway.

"I'm gonna stay with Dickie for a few days. I'm just in the way here."

"No you're not."

Ernie glanced back at his grandson. "I told you, I saw the way you were eyeing her."

John shoved one hand in the front pocket of his Levi's and leaned a shoulder against the doorframe. With his other hand, he impatiently tapped the beer bottle against his thigh. "And I told you, I'm not going to have sex with Virgil's fiancée."

"I hope you're right and I'm wrong." Ernie zipped the duffel bag closed and reached for the straps with his left hand. He didn't know if he was doing the right thing by leaving. His first instinct was to stay and make sure his grandson didn't do anything he might regret in the morning. But Ernie had done his job. He'd helped raise John already. There was nothing he could do now. There was nothing he could do to save John from himself. "Because you'll end up hurting that girl and damaging your career."

"I don't plan to do either."

Ernie looked up and smiled sadly. "I hope not," he said, unconvinced, and strode toward the front door. "I sure as hell hope not."

John watched his grandfather leave, then he walked back into the living room. His bare feet sank into the thick beige carpet as he moved toward the picture window. He owned three houses; two were on the West Coast. He loved the ocean, the sounds and smells of it. He could lose himself in the monotony of the waves. This house was a haven from life. Here, he didn't have to worry about contracts or endorsements or anything attached to being one of the most talked about centers in the NHL. He found a peace here that he couldn't find anywhere else.

Until today.

He stared out the big window at the woman who stood at the edge of the surf, the breeze whipping her dark hair about her head. Georgeanne definitely disturbed his peace. He brought the bottle of beer to his lips and took a long pull.

An unwitting smile tugged one corner of his mouth as he watched her tiptoe cautiously into the cold waves. Without a doubt, Georgeanne Howard was a walking fantasy. If it weren't for her irritating habit of rambling, and if she weren't Virgil's fiancée, John didn't think he'd be in such a hurry to get rid of her.

But Georgeanne was entangled with the owner of the Chinooks, and John had to get her out of town as soon as possible. He figured he'd take her to the airport or bus depot in the morning, which still left the long night ahead.

He hooked one thumb in the waistband of his faded jeans and turned his gaze to a pair of kids flying a kite down the beach. He wasn't worried that he'd end up in bed with Georgeanne. Because contrary to what Ernie believed, John thought with his head, not his dick. As he raised the beer to his mouth again, his conscience took the opportunity to remind him of his asinine marriage to DeeDee.

Slowly he lowered the bottle and looked back at Georgeanne. He never would have done anything so stupid as marry a woman he hadn't known more than a few hours if he hadn't been drunk, no matter how great her body. And DeeDee's body had been great.

A dark scowl turned John's mouth downward. His eyes followed Georgeanne as she played in the surf, then with a foul curse on his lips, he stormed into the kitchen and poured out his beer.

The last thing he needed was to wake up in the morning with a pounding headache and married to Virgil's fiancée.

# Three

Georgeanne flinched each time a frigid wave rose up her thighs. A shudder shook her shoulders, but despite the cold, she dug her feet into the sand and grabbed ahold of the large rock shaped like a loaf of bread. Bending forward slightly, she planted her hand on the jagged stone. For several moments she stared, fascinated, at the numerous purple and orange starfish fastened to the rock. Then like a woman reading braille, she lightly ran her fingers across the lines of a hard, rough back. The five-carat diamond solitaire on her left hand caught the evening sun and shot blue and red fire across her knuckles.

The surf pounding in her ears, and the view before her eyes, kept her head clear—clear of everything—everything but the simple pleasure of experiencing the Pacific Ocean for the first time.

When she'd first walked down to the beach, her dark thoughts had threatened to overwhelm her. Her destitution, the day's unfortunate wedding catastrophe, and her dependency on a man like John, who didn't seem to possess two ounces of compassion, weighed heavy on her shoulders. But worse than her money problems, John, or Virgil was the feeling that she was so incredibly alone in a vast world where nothing felt familiar. She was surrounded by trees and mountains, and everything was so green. The textures were different here, the sand coarser, the water colder, and the wind harsher.

As she'd stood staring out at the ocean, feeling like the only person alive, she'd fought the panic swelling within her, but she'd lost the battle. Like a high-rise building experiencing blackout, Georgeanne had felt and heard the familiar click-click-hum of her brain shutting down. From as far back as she could remember, her mind had always gone blank when she felt overwhelmed. She hated when it happened, but was powerless to prevent it. The events of the day had finally caught up with her, and she was so overloaded, it had taken longer than usual for the lights to come back on. When they had, she'd closed her eyes, taken deep, cleansing breaths, then pushed the day's troubling thoughts from her head.

Georgeanne was good at clearing her mind and refocusing on one certain thing. She'd had years of practice. She'd had years to learn to cope with a world that danced to a different beat—a beat she didn't always know or understand. But a beat she'd learned to fake. Since the age of nine, she'd worked hard to make it appear as if she were in perfect step with everyone else.

Since that afternoon twelve years ago when her grandmother had told her she had a brain dysfunction, they'd tried to hide her disability from the world. She'd been enrolled in charm and cooking schools, yet she'd never been taken to a scholastic tutor. She understood design compositions and could make beautiful flower arrangements with her eyes closed, yet she could not read past the fourth-grade level. She hid her problems behind charm and flirtations, behind her beautiful face and body. Even though she now knew she was dyslexic rather than retarded, she still hid it. And even though she felt tremendous relief with the discovery, she was still too embarrassed to seek help.

A large wave hit the front of her thighs and soaked the bottom of her shorts. She braced her feet wider apart and dug her toes even deeper into the sand. Close to the top of Georgeanne's list of life's rules, right under making sure people liked her, and directly above being a good hostess, was her determination to appear just like everyone else. As a result, she tried to learn *and* remember two new words a week. She rented movie adaptations of classic literature, and she owned the video of what she considered the best movie ever put on celluloid, *Gone with the Wind*. She owned the book, too, but had never read it. All those pages and all those words were just too overwhelming.

Moving her hand to a lime green sea anemone, she lightly brushed the edge. The sticky tentacles closed around her fingers. Startled, she jumped back. Another large wave hit her thighs, her knees buckled, and she splashed backward into the surf. A breaker pushed her away from the rock, flipped her several times, and propelled her toward the shore. Icy cold ocean slapped her chest and sucked her breath away. Salt water and sand filled her mouth as she kicked and clawed to keep her head above the surface. A piece of slimy seaweed wrapped around her neck and an even larger wave caught her from behind and shot her up the beach like a torpedo. By the time she finally came to a stop, the surf was already rushing back out to meet the next wave. With one hand she pushed herself to her feet and scrambled up the beach. When she reached the safety of the shore, she dropped to her hands and knees and took several deep breaths. She spit sand from her mouth, grabbed the seaweed from around her neck, and tossed it aside. Her teeth began to chatter, and when she thought of all the plankton she'd just swallowed, her stomach pitched like the Pacific behind her. She could feel grit in very uncomfortable places and looked toward John's house, hoping her misadventure had gone unobserved.

It hadn't. Sunglasses shading his eyes and his rubber thongs kicking up sand, John strolled toward her looking good enough to lick up one side and down the other. Georgeanne wanted to crawl back into the ocean and die.

Above the sound of the surf and seagulls, his rich, deep laughter reached her ears. In a flash she forgot about the cold, the sand, and the seaweed. She forgot about her appearance and wanting to die. Red-hot rage shot through her veins and ignited her temper like a blowtorch. She'd worked all of her life to avoid ridicule, and there was nothing she *hated* more than being *laughed* at.

"That was the funniest thing I've seen in a long time," he said with a flash of his straight white teeth.

Georgeanne's anger rumbled in her ears, blocking even the sound of the ocean. Her fists closed around two clumps of wet sand.

"Damn, you should have seen yourself," he told her with a shake of his head. The breeze ruffled the dark hair about his ears and forehead as he roared with laughter.

Rising to her knees, Georgeanne threw a handful of sandy mud, hitting him in the chest with a satisfying splat. She'd never been particularly coordinated or light on her feet, but she'd always been a good shot.

His laughter died instantly. "What the hell?" he swore, and looked down at the front of his tank top. When he raised his stunned gaze, Georgeanne nailed him on the forehead. The sand glob knocked his Ray-Bans askew before the sand fell to his feet. Over the top of the black frames his blue eyes stared back at her, promising retribution.

Georgeanne smiled and reached for another handful. She was beyond fearing anything John might do. "Why aren't you laughing now, you stupid jock?"

He slid the sunglasses from his face and pointed them at her. "I wouldn't throw that."

She stood and, with a brisk toss of her head, flipped a hunk of soggy hair out of her face. "Afraid of a little dirt?"

One dark brow rose up his forehead, but otherwise, he didn't move.

"What are you going to do?" she taunted the man who suddenly represented every injustice and insult ever inflicted on her. "Something really macho?"

John smiled, then before Georgeanne could utter a scream, he moved like the athlete he was and body-checked her to the ground. The sand flew from her hand. Stunned, she blinked and looked into his face only a few inches from hers.

"What in the hell is the matter with you?" he asked, sounding more incredulous than angry. A dark lock of hair fell over his forehead and touched the white scar running through his brow.

"Get off of me," Georgeanne demanded, and socked him on the upper arm. His warm skin and hard muscle felt good beneath her clenched fist, and she punched him again, venting her rage. She hit him for laughing at her, for insinuating she'd planned to marry Virgil for money, and for being right. She struck out against her grandmother, who'd died and left her alone—alone to make bad choices.

"Jesus, Georgie," John cursed, grabbed her wrists, and pinned them to the ground next to her head. "Stop it."

She looked up into his handsome face, and she hated him. She hated herself, and she hated the moisture blurring her vision. She took a deep breath to keep herself from crying, but a sob caught in her throat. "I hate you," she whispered, and ran her tongue over her salty lips. Her breasts heaved with the effort to keep her tears inside.

"At the moment," John said, his face so close she could feel his warm breath on her cheek, "I can't say that I'm real fond of you either."

The heat from John's body penetrated her anger, and Georgeanne became acutely aware of several things at once. She became aware of his right leg crammed snugly between both of hers and his groin shoved intimately into her inner thigh. His wide chest covered her, but his weight wasn't at all unpleasant. He was solid and incredibly warm.

"But damn if you don't give me ideas," he said, a smile twisting one corner of his mouth. "Bad ideas." He shook his head as if he were trying to convince himself of something. "Real bad." His thumb stroked the inside of her wrist as his gaze drifted across her face. "You shouldn't look this good. You've got dirt on your forehead, your hair is a damn mess, and you're as wet as a drowned cat."

For the first time in days, Georgeanne felt as if she'd been plopped down on familiar ground. A satisfied little smile curved her lips. No matter how he behaved to the contrary, John liked her after all. And with a little tactical maneuvering, he might be willing to let her stay at his house until she figured out what to do with her life. "Please let go of my wrists."

"Are you going to punch me again?"

Georgeanne shook her head, mentally calculating exactly how much of her considerable charm to use on him.

One of his brows lifted. "Throw sand?"

"No."

He released his hold but didn't move to get off her. "Did I hurt you?"

"No." She placed her palms on his shoulders, and beneath her hands his hard muscles bunched, reminding her of his strength. John didn't strike her as the type of man to force himself on a woman, but she *was* staying in his house. That fact alone could give a man the wrong idea. Before, when he hadn't seemed to even like her, it hadn't occurred to her that John might expect more than gratitude. It occurred to her now.

Then she remembered Ernie and a breathy laugh escaped her throat. "I've never been tackled before. Does this usually work for you?" Surely John wouldn't expect her to sleep with him while his grandfather was in the next room. Relief washed through her.

"What's the matter? Didn't you like it?"

Georgeanne smiled up into his eyes. "Well, I could make a suggestion."

Rising to his knees, he looked down at her. "I'll just bet you could," he said as he stood.

Instantly she felt the loss of body heat and struggled to a sitting position. "Flowers. They're more subtle, but get your message across just the same."

John held out a hand to Georgeanne and helped her to her feet. He never sent flowers to women anymore, not since the day he'd ordered dozens of pink roses placed on the lid of his wife's white coffin.

He dropped Georgeanne's hand and pushed the memory aside before it got too painful. Focusing his attention on Georgeanne, he watched her turn at the waist to wipe sand from her behind. He deliberately let his gaze slide down her body. She had tangles in her hair, sand on her knees, and her red toenails were a strange contrast to her dirty feet. The green shorts clung to her thighs, and his old black T-shirt looked as if it had been laminated to her breasts. Her nipples were hard from the cold and stuck out like little berries. Beneath him she'd felt good—too good. And he'd stayed much too long pressed into her soft body and staring down into her pretty green eyes.

"Did you get ahold of your aunt?" he asked as he bent down to pick up his sunglasses from the ground.

"Ahh . . . not yet."

"Well, you can call again once we get back." John straightened, then turned to walk across the beach toward his house.

"I'll try," she said, catching up with him and matching his long strides. "But it's Aunt Lolly's bingo night, so I don't think she'll be home for a few more hours."

John glanced at her, then slipped on his Ray-Bans. "How long do her bingo games last?"

"Well, that depends on how many of those little cards she buys. Now, if she decides to play at the old grange hall, she doesn't play as long because they allow smoking, and Aunt Lolly absolutely hates cigarette smoke, and of course, Doralee Hofferman plays at the grange. And there's been real bad blood between Lolly and Doralee since 1979 when Doralee stole Lolly's peanut patty recipe and called it her own. The two had been the best of friends, you understand, up until—"

"Here we go again," John sighed, interrupting her. "Listen, Georgie," he said, and stopped to look at her. "We're never going to get through tonight if you don't stop this."

"Stop what?"

"Rambling."

Her pouty mouth fell open and she placed an innocent palm on the top of her left breast. "I ramble?"

"Yes, and it gets on my nerves. I don't give a goddamn about your aunt's Jell-O, foot-washing Baptists, or peanut patties. Can't you just talk like a normal person?"

She dropped her gaze, but not before he saw the

wounded look in her eyes. "You don't think I talk like a normal person?"

A twinge of guilt pricked his conscience. He didn't want to hurt her, but at the same time, he didn't want to listen to hours of her meandering chitchat either. "Not really, no. But when I ask you a question that should require a three-second answer, I get three minutes of bullshit that has nothing to do with anything."

She bit her bottom lip, then said, "I'm not stupid, John."

"I never meant that you were," he contended, even though he didn't figure she'd been valedictorian at that university she said she'd attended. "Look, Georgie," he added because she looked so hurt, "I'll tell you what, if you don't ramble, I'll try not to be an ass."

The corners of her mouth formed a doubtful frown.

"Don't you believe me?"

Shaking her head, she scoffed, "I told you that I wasn't stupid."

John laughed. Damn, he was beginning to like her. "Come on." He motioned with his head toward the house. "You look like you're freezing."

"I am," she confessed, then fell into step beside him.

They walked across the cool sand without speaking while the sounds of crashing waves and crying seabirds filled the breeze. When they reached the weathered stairs leading to the back door of John's house, Georgeanne took the first step, then turned to face him. "I don't ramble," she said, her eyes squinted against the glare of the setting sun.

John stopped and looked into her face on about the same level as his. Several corkscrew curls were beginning to dry and dance about her head. "Georgie, you ramble." He reached for his sunglasses and slipped them down the bridge of his nose. "But if you can manage to control yourself, we'll get along fine. I think for one night we can be"—he paused and placed the Ray-Bans on her face—"friends," he finished for lack of a better word, although he knew it was impossible.

"I'd like that, John," she said, and pulled her lips into a seductive smile. "But I thought you told me you weren't a nice guy."

"I'm not." She was so close, her breasts almost touched his chest—almost, and he wondered if she was playing the tease again.

"How can we possibly be friends if you're not nice to me?"

John slid his gaze to her lips. He was tempted to show her just how *nice* he could be. He was tempted to lean forward just a little and brush his mouth across hers, to taste her sweet lips and explore the promise of her seductive smile. He was tempted to raise his hands a few inches to her hips and pull her tight against him, tempted to learn just how far she'd let his hands roam before she stopped him.

He was tempted, but not insane. "Easy." He placed his palms on her shoulders and moved her to the side. "I'm going out," he announced, and walked past her up the stairs.

"Take me with you," she said as she followed closely behind.

"No." He shook his head. There wasn't a chance that he was going to be seen with Georgeanne Howard. Not a chance in hell.

Warm water ran over Georgeanne's chilled flesh as she slowly worked shampoo into her hair. Before she'd entered the shower fifteen minutes ago, John had asked her to keep it short because he wanted to shower before he went out for the evening. Georgeanne had other plans.

Closing her eyes, she leaned her head back to rinse the suds away and cringed to think of what the cheap shampoo was doing to the ends of her spiral perm. She thought of the Paul Mitchell packed in her suitcase in the back of Virgil's Rolls-Royce, and she felt like crying as she ripped open a sample packet of conditioner she'd found beneath the bathroom sink. A pleasant floral scent filled the steam of the shower as her thoughts turned from shampoo and conditioner to the bigger problem at hand.

Ernie had left for the evening, and John planned to follow him. Georgeanne couldn't very well persuade John to let her stay for a few days if he wasn't even in the house. When he'd announced that they could be friends, she'd felt a moment of relief, only to have it dashed by his second announcement that he was going out.

Georgeanne took great care to work the conditioner into her hair before she stepped back into the stream of warm water. For a brief moment she thought about using sex to entice John into remaining home for the night, but she quickly dismissed the idea. Not so much because she found the idea morally distasteful, but because she didn't *like* sex. The few times she'd allowed men to become that intimate with her, she'd felt acutely self-conscious. So self-conscious that she couldn't enjoy herself.

By the time she emerged from the shower, the water had turned cold and she greatly feared that she smelled like manly soap. She quickly dried herself, then dressed in a pair of emerald lace underwear and a matching bra. She'd bought the fancy underwear in anticipation of her honeymoon, but she couldn't say she was real sorry that Virgil would never see her in it.

The ceiling fan pulled the steam from the room, but the silk robe she'd borrowed from John clung to her moist skin as she tied the belt around her waist. Despite the soft texture of the material, the robe was very masculine and smelled of cologne. The pitch black silk hit her just below the knees, while a big red and white Japanese symbol had been embroidered on the back.

She ran the big teeth of her comb through her hair and pushed away the memory of her Estée Lauder lotion and powder locked in Virgil's car. Pulling open cabinet drawers, she looked for anything she might use in her beauty regime. She found a few toothbrushes, a tube of Crest, a bottle of foot powder, a can of shave cream, and two razors.

"That's it?" With a frown marring her forehead, she turned and rummaged through her overnight case. She pushed aside the plastic container of prescription birth control pills she'd started to take three days prior and pulled out her cosmetics. She found it extremely unjust that John could look so handsome with such a paltry effort while she had to spend hundreds of dollars and a good amount of time on her appearance.

Lifting a towel, she dried a spot on the mirror and peered at herself. Through the circle she'd wiped on the glass, she brushed her teeth, then applied mascara to her lashes and blusher to her cheeks.

A knock on the bathroom door startled her so bad she almost streaked her face with a tube of Luscious Peach lipstick.

"Georgie?"

"Yes, John?"

"I need in there, remember?"

She remembered, all right. "Oh, I forgot." She fluffed the hair around her face with her fingers and critically viewed her appearance. She smelled like a man and looked less than her best.

"Are you coming out anytime tonight?"

"Give me a second," she said, and tossed her cosmetics into the overnight case sitting on the closed toilet seat lid. "Should I put the wet clothes over the towel rack?" she asked as she gathered them from the white and black linoleum floor.

"Yeah. Sure," he answered through the door. "Are you going to be much longer?"

Georgeanne carefully laid her wet bra and underwear over the aluminum rod, then covered them with the green shorts and T-shirt. "All done," she said as she opened the door.

"What happened to keeping it short?" He held up his hands as if he were catching rain in his palms.

"Wasn't that short? I thought that was short."

His hands fell to his sides. "You were in there so long, I'm surprised your skin isn't wrinkled like a California raisin." Then he did what she'd expected the moment she'd opened the door. He let his gaze wander down her body, then climb back up again. A spark of interest flashed behind his eyes, and she relaxed. He liked her. "Did you use all the hot water?" he asked as a deep scowl darkened his features.

Georgeanne's eyes widened. "I guess I did."

"It doesn't matter now anyway, damn it," he cursed as he turned his wrist over and looked at his watch. "Even if I left now, the bar will run out of oysters before I can get there." He turned and walked down the hall toward the living room. "I guess I'll eat beer nuts and stale popcorn."

"If you're hungry, I could cook something for you." Georgeanne followed close behind him.

He glanced over his shoulder at her. "I don't think so."

She wasn't about to let this opportunity to impress him pass her by. "I'm a wonderful cook. I could make you a beautiful dinner before you go out."

John stopped in the middle of the living room and turned to face her. "No."

"But I'm hungry also," she said, which wasn't precisely the truth.

"You didn't get enough to eat earlier?" He buried his hands up to his knuckles in the front pocket of his jeans and shifted his weight to one foot. "Ernie sometimes forgets that not everyone eats as little as he does. You should have said something."

"Well, I didn't want to impose any more than I already have," she said, and smiled sweetly at him. She could see his hesitation and pressed a little further. "And I didn't want to hurt your grandfather's feelings, but I hadn't eaten all day and was starving. But I know how older people are. They eat soup or salad and call it a meal while the rest of us call it first course."

His lips curved slightly.

Georgeanne took the slight smile as a sign of acquiescence and walked past him into the kitchen. For a jock who admitted he didn't like to cook, the room was surprisingly modern. She opened the almond-colored refrigerator and mentally inventoried its contents. Ernie had mentioned that the kitchen was well stocked, and he hadn't been kidding.

"Can you really make gravy with tuna fish?" he asked from the doorway.

Recipes flipped through her head like a Rolodex as she opened a cupboard filled with a variety of pasta and spices. She glanced at John, who stood with one shoulder propped against the frame. "Don't tell me you want creamed tuna? Some people like it, but if I never have to see or smell it again, I could live quite happy."

"Can you make a big breakfast?"

Georgeanne shut the cupboard and turned to face him. The silky black belt at her waist came loose. "Of course," she said as she tightly retied it into a bow. "But why would you want breakfast when you have all that wonderful seafood in your refrigerator?"

"I can have seafood anytime," he answered with a shrug.

She'd accumulated a variety of culinary skills from years of cooking classes and was eager to impress him. "Are you sure you want breakfast? I make a killer pesto and my linguine with clam sauce is to die for."

"How about biscuits and gravy?"

Disappointed she asked, "You're kidding, right?" Georgeanne couldn't remember being taught how to make biscuits and gravy, it was just something she'd always known how to do. She supposed it had been bred into her. "I thought you wanted oysters."

He shrugged again. "I'd rather have a big, greasy breakfast. A real southern artery clogger."

Georgeanne shook her head and opened the refrigerator again. "We'll fry up all the pork we can find."

"We?"

"Yep." She placed a summer ham on the counter, then opened the freezer. "I need you to slice the ham while I make biscuits."

His dimple creased his tan cheek as he smiled, and he pushed himself away from the doorframe. "I can do that."

The pleasure of his smile sent a flutter to the pit of Georgeanne's stomach. As she placed a package of sausage links in the sink and ran hot water over them, she imagined that with a smile like his, he'd have no problem getting women to do anything he wanted anytime he wanted it. "Do you have a girlfriend?" she asked, as she turned off the water and began pulling flour and other ingredients out of cupboards.

"How much of this do I slice?" he asked instead of answering her question.

Georgeanne glanced across her shoulder at him. He held the ham in one hand and a wicked-looking knife in the other. "As much as you think you'll eat," she responded. "Are you going to answer my question?"

"Nope."

"Why?" She dumped flour, salt, and baking powder into a bowl without measuring.

"Because," he began, and hacked off a hunk of ham, "it's none of your business."

"We're friends, remember," she reminded him, dying to know details of his personal life. She spooned Crisco into the flour and added, "Friends tell each other things."

The hacking stopped and he looked up at her with his blue eyes. "I'll answer your question if you answer one of mine."

"Okay," she said, figuring she could always tell a little white lie if she had to.

"No. I don't have a girlfriend."

For some reason his confession made her stomach flutter a little more.

"Now it's your turn." He tossed a piece of ham in his mouth, then asked, "How long have you known Virgil?"

Georgeanne pondered the question as she moved past John and took milk from the refrigerator. Should she lie, tell the truth, or perhaps reveal a bit of both? "A little over a month," she answered truthfully, and added several splashes of milk to the bowl.

"Ahh," he said through a flat smile. "Love at first sight."

Hearing his bland, patronizing voice, she wanted to clobber him with her wooden spoon. "Don't you believe in love at first sight?" She settled the bowl on her left hip and stirred as she'd seen her grandmother do a thousand times, as she herself had done too many times to count.

"No." He shook his head and began to slice the ham once more. "Especially not between a woman like you and a man as old as Virgil."

"A woman like me? What is that supposed to mean?"

"You know what I mean."

"No," she said, even though she had a pretty good idea. "I don't know what you're talking about."

"Come on." He frowned and looked at her. "You're young and attractive and built like a bri—like aaa . . ." He paused and pointed the knife at her. "There's only one reason a girl like you marries a man who parts his hair by his left ear and combs it over the top of his head."

"I was fond of Virgil," she defended herself, and stirred the dough into a dense ball.

He lifted a skeptical brow. "Fond of his money, you mean."

"That's not true. He can be real charming."

"He can also be a *real* son of a bitch, but being that you've only known him a month, you might not know that."

Careful not to lose her temper and throw something at him again, and in turn damage her chances of receiving an invitation to stay for a few more days, Georgeanne prudently placed the bowl on the counter.

"What made you run out on your wedding?"

She certainly wasn't about to confess her reasons to him. "I just changed my mind is all."

"Or did it finally dawn on you that you were going to have to have sex with a man old enough to be your grandfather for the rest of his life?"

Georgeanne folded her arms beneath her breasts and scowled at him. "This is the second time you've brought up the subject. Why are you so fascinated by my relationship with Virgil?"

"Not fascinated. Just curious," he corrected, and continued to cut a few more slices of ham, before setting down the knife.

"Has it occurred to you that I might not have had sex with Virgil?"

"No."

"Well, I haven't."

"Bullshit."

Her hands fell to her sides and curled into fists. "You have a dirty mind and a filthy mouth."

Nonchalant, John shrugged and leaned one hip into the edge of the counter. "Virgil Duffy didn't make his millions by leaving anything to chance. He wouldn't have paid for a sweet young bed partner without testing the springs."

Georgeanne wanted to yell in his face that Virgil hadn't paid for her, but he had. He just hadn't received a return on his investment. If she'd gone through with the wedding, he would have. "I didn't sleep with him," she insisted while her emotions pitched from anger to hurt. Anger that he should judge her at all and hurt that he should judge her so trashy.

The corners of his mouth lifted slightly and a lock of his thick hair brushed his brow as he shook his head. "Listen, sweetheart, I don't care if you slept with Virgil."

"Then why do you keep talking about it?" she asked, and reminded herself that no matter how aggravating he was, she couldn't lose her temper again.

"Because I don't think you realize what you've done. Virgil is a very rich and powerful man. And you humiliated him today."

"I know." She lowered her gaze to the front of his white tank top. "I thought I might call him tomorrow and apologize."

"Bad idea."

She looked back up into his eyes. "Too soon?"

"Oh, yeah. Next year might be too soon. If I were you, I'd get the hell out of this state altogether. And as soon as possible."

Georgeanne took a step forward, stopping several inches from John's chest, and looked up at him as if she were on the edge of scared when, in truth, Virgil

Duffy didn't frighten her one bit. She felt bad for what she'd done to him today, but she knew he'd get over it. He didn't love her. He only wanted her, and she didn't intend to dwell on him tonight. Especially not when she had a more pressing concern, like finagling an until-you-can-get-your-life-together invitation out of John. "What's he gonna do?" she drawled. "Hire someone to kill me?"

"I doubt he'll go that far." His gaze lowered to her mouth. "But he could make you one miserable little girl."

"I'm not a little girl," she whispered, and inched closer. "Or maybe you haven't noticed."

John pushed away from the counter and looked down into her face. "I'm neither blind nor retarded. I noticed," he said, and slid his hand around her waist to the small of her back. "I've noticed a lot about you, and if you drop that robe, I'm sure you could keep me happy and smiling for hours." His fingers drifted up her spine and brushed between her shoulders.

Even though John stood close, Georgeanne didn't feel threatened. His broad chest and big arms reminded her of his strength, but without a doubt, she instinctively knew she could walk away at any time. "Sugar buns, if I dropped this robe, your smile would have to be surgically removed from your face," she teased, her voice oozing southern seduction.

He lowered his hand to her bottom and cupped her right cheek in his palm. His eyes dared her to stop him. He was testing her, seeing just how far she'd let him go. "Hell, you might be worth a little surgery," he said, and eased her close.

Georgeanne froze for an instant, testing the sensation of his touch. Even though his hand caressed her behind, and the tips of her breasts touched his chest, she didn't feel pawed and pulled like a piece of taffy. She relaxed a little and slipped her palms up his chest.

Beneath her hands she felt the definition of muscle.

"But you're not worth my career," he said as his fingers smoothed the silk material back and forth across her behind.

"Your career?" Georgeanne rose onto the balls of her feet and placed soft kisses at the corner of his mouth. "What are you talking about?" she asked, prepared to carefully free herself from his grasp if he did something she didn't care for.

"You," he answered against her lips. "You're a real good-time baby, but you're bad for a man like me."

"Like you?"

"I have a hard time saying no to anything excessive, shiny, or sinful."

Georgeanne smiled. "Which am I?"

John laughed silently against her mouth. "Georgie girl, I do believe you are all three, and I'd love to find out just how bad you get, but it isn't going to happen."

"What isn't?" she asked cautiously.

He pulled back far enough to look into her face. "The wild thing."

"What?

"Sex."

Enormous relief washed through her. "I guess this just isn't my lucky day," she drawled through a big smile she tried but failed to suppress.

# Four

John glanced at the folded napkin by his fork and shook his head. He couldn't tell if it was supposed to be a hat, a boat, or some sort of lid. But since Georgeanne had informed him that she'd set the table with a North-meets-South theme, he guessed it was supposed to be a hat. Two empty beer bottles sprouted yellow and white wildflowers out the long necks. Down the middle of the table, a thin line of sand and broken shells had been woven through the four lucky horseshoes that used to hang on the stone fireplace. John didn't think Ernie would mind the use of the horseshoes, but why Georgeanne would drag all that crap to the table was beyond him.

"Would you like some butter?"

He looked across the table into her seductive green eyes and shoved a bite of warm biscuit and sausage gravy in his mouth. Georgeanne Howard was a tease, but she was also one hell of a good cook. "No."

"How was your shower?" she asked, and gave him a smile as soft as her biscuits.

Since he'd sat down at the table ten minutes ago, she'd tried her hardest to engage him in conversation, but he wasn't in an obliging mood. "Fine," he answered.

"Do your parents live in Seattle?"

"No."

"Canada?"

"Just my mother."

"Are your parents divorced?"

"Nope." Her deep cleavage drew his gaze to the front of the black robe.

"Where's your father?" she asked as she reached for her orange juice. The front of the robe gaped, exposing the scalloped edge of green lace and the swell of smooth white skin.

"Died when I was five."

"I'm sorry. I know how it feels to lose a parent. I lost both of mine when I was quite young myself."

John glanced back up into her face, unmoved. She was gorgeous. Curvy and soft in an overblown, breathy sort of way. Her long legs were beautifully shaped, and she was exactly the type of woman he preferred naked and in bed. Earlier today he'd accepted the fact that he couldn't have Georgeanne. That didn't bother him all that much, but it bugged the hell out of him that she only *pretended* she couldn't wait to get her hot little hands all over his body. When he'd told her they couldn't make love, her pouty little mouth had ooohed and cooed her disappointment, but her eyes had sparked with utter relief. In fact, he'd never seen such relief on a woman's face.

"It was a boating accident," she informed him as if he'd asked. She took a sip of orange juice, then added, "Off the coast of Florida."

John stabbed a bite of ham, then reached for his coffee. Women liked him. Women shoved their phone numbers and underwear in his pockets. Women didn't look at John as if sex with him were tantamount to root canal.

"It was a miracle that I wasn't with them. My parents hated to leave me, of course, but I'd contracted the chicken pox. So reluctantly they'd left me with my grandmother, Clarissa June. I remember . . ."

Tuning out her words, John lowered his gaze to the soft hollow of her throat. He wasn't a conceited man, or at least he didn't think he was. But the fact that Georgeanne found him so totally *resistible* irritated him more than he liked to admit. He set his coffee mug on the table and folded his arms across his chest. After his shower, he'd changed into a clean pair of jeans and a plain white T-shirt. He still planned to go out. All he had to do was grab his shoes and go.

"But Mrs. Lovett was as cold as a Frigidaire," Georgeanne continued, leaving John to wonder how the subject had shifted from her parents to refrigerators. "And tacky . . . cryin' all night, she was tacky. When LouAnn White got married, she gave her"—Georgeanne paused, her green eyes sparkling with animation—"a Hot Dogger. Can you believe it? Not only did she give an appliance, she gave a little machine that electrocutes weenies!"

John tilted his chair back on two legs. He distinctly remembered a conversation he'd had with her about rambling. He guessed she just couldn't help herself. She was a tease and a chatter hound.

Georgeanne pushed her plate to the side and leaned forward. The robe parted as she confided, "My grandmother used to say that Margaret Lovett was just too tacky for Technicolor."

"Are you doing that on purpose?" he asked.

Her eyes rounded. "What?"

"Flashing me your breasts."

She looked down, eased away from the table, and clutched the robe to her throat. "No."

The front legs of the chair hit the floor as John rose to his feet. He looked into her wide eyes and gave in to insanity. Holding out his hand, he ordered, "Come here." When she stood before him, he wrapped his arms around her waist and pulled her tight against his chest. "I'm leaving now," he said, sinking into her soft curves. "Kiss me good-bye."

"How long will you be gone?"

"Awhile," he answered, feeling his body grow heavy.

Like a cat stretching on a warm windowsill, Georgeanne arched against him and wound her arms around his neck. "I could go with you," she purred.

John shook his head. "Kiss me and mean it."

She rose onto the balls of her feet and did what he asked. She kissed like a woman who knew what she was doing. Her parted lips pressed softly into his. She tasted of orange juice and the promise of something sweeter. Her tongue touched, swirled, caressed, and teased. She ran her fingers through his hair as the arch of her foot slipped up his calf. Pure lust shot up the backs of his legs, took hold of his insides, and gave a good hard tug.

She was a pro, and he eased back far enough to look into her face. Her lips were shiny, her breath slightly uneven, and if her eyes had shown the slightest hint of the same hunger he felt, he would have turned and walked out the door. Satisfied.

John's gaze shifted to the soft mahogany curls surrounding her face. The light shimmered in each silky corkscrew, and he wanted to bury his hands in them. He knew he should leave. Just turn and walk out. Instead, he looked back into her eyes.

He wasn't satisfied. Not yet. He planted one hand on the back of her head, tilted her face to the side, and soul-kissed her to the bottoms of her feet. While his mouth feasted at hers, he walked her backward until her behind hit the edge of the china hutch doubling as a trophy cabinet. His kiss continued, across her cheek and along her jaw. His lips slipped to the side of her neck, and he pushed her hair down her back. She smelled of flowers and warm feminine skin, and he slid the silk robe from her shoulder. He felt her stiffen in his arms and told himself that he should stop. "You smell good," he said into the side of her throat.

"I smell like a man," she laughed nervously.

John smiled. "I've been around men all of my life. Believe me, honey, you don't smell like a man." He slipped his fingertips beneath one emerald strap of her bra and kissed the soft skin of her throat.

Instantly she covered his hand with hers. "I thought we weren't going to make love."

"We're not."

"Then what are we doing, John?"

"Foolin' around."

"Doesn't that lead to making love?" She grabbed her other shoulder and crossed her arms over her breasts.

"Not this time. So relax." John moved his hands to the backs of her smooth thighs, grabbed ahold, and lifted. Before she could utter an objection, he plopped her down on top of the hutch, then stepped between her thighs.

"John?"

"Hmmm?"

"Promise you won't hurt me."

He raised his head and looked into her face. She was serious. "I won't hurt you, Georgie."

"Or do anything that I don't like."

"Of course not."

She smiled and moved her palms to his shoulders.

"Do you like this?" he asked, slipping his hands up the outsides of her thighs, pushing up the silk robe at the same time.

"Mmm-hmm," she answered, then softly licked his earlobe and slid the very tip of her tongue down the side of his neck. "Do *you* like this?" she asked against the side of his throat. Then she lightly sucked his sensitive skin into her mouth.

"Nice," he chuckled quietly. He smoothed his hands to her knees, then back up until his fingers came into contact with the elastic and lace of her underwear. "Everything about you is real nice." John tilted his head to the side and closed his eyes. He couldn't remember ever touching a woman as soft as Georgeanne. His fingers sank into her warm thighs and he pushed them farther apart. While her mouth did incredible things to his throat, he slid his hands beneath the robe and cupped her behind. "You have soft skin, great legs, and a nice butt," he said as he pulled her against his pelvis. Heat flooded his groin, and he knew that if he wasn't careful, he could sink into Georgeanne and stay there awhile.

Georgeanne lifted her face. "Are you making fun of me?"

John looked down into her clear eyes. "No," he answered, looking for a reflection of the desire he felt and not really finding it. "I would never make fun of a half-naked woman."

"You don't think I'm fat?"

"I don't like skinny women," he answered flatly, and moved his hands down her hips to her knees, then back up again. A flash of interest flicked in her eyes, and finally, a spark of desire.

Georgeanne looked into his sleepy gaze for a sign that he was lying to her. Since the onset of puberty, she'd done constant battle with her weight and had tried more diets than she could count. She planted her hands on the side of his face and kissed him then. Not the practiced and perfect kiss she'd given him earlier, a kiss meant to tease and tantalize. This time she wanted to swallow him whole. She meant to show him how much his words meant to a girl who'd always considered herself overweight. She let herself go, let herself melt into the hot, dizzying desire. The kiss turned ravenous as his hands touched, caressed, molded, and sent shivers clear to her toes. She felt the silk belt slacken and the robe part. He slid his hands across her stomach and up her waist. His warm palms slipped up her ribs, and his thumbs fanned the undersides of her heavy breasts. An unexpected and intense tremor shook her. For the first time in her life, a man's touch on her breasts didn't feel like an attack. She sighed her surprise into his mouth.

John raised his head and looked into her eyes. He smiled as if what he saw there pleased him, and he pushed the robe from her shoulders.

Georgeanne lowered her arms and let the black silk pool about her thighs. Before she knew his intention, John moved his hands to her back and unhooked her bra. Startled by his quick work, she raised her own hands and kept the lacy green cups in place. "I'm big," she stated in a rush, then wanted to die for saying something so obvious and stupid.

"So am I," he teased through a provocative grin.

Nervous laughter escaped her throat as one bra strap drifted down her arm.

"Are you going to sit like that all night?" he asked, and slid his knuckles along the lace edge of her bra.

His light touch sent tingles along her skin. She liked the things he said and the way he made her feel, and she didn't want him to stop yet. She liked John and wanted him to like her. She looked into his sexy eyes and lowered her hands. Her bra slowly fell to her lap and she held her breath, waiting for him to make some lewd comment about her breasts—hoping he wouldn't.

"Jesus, Georgie," he said. "You told me you're big. You should have warned that you're perfect." He cupped her heavy breast and kissed her lips, long and hard. His thumb slowly brushed her nipple, back and forth, around and over. No one had ever caressed her as John was doing at the moment. His feathery touch made her feel as if she were made of something delicate and breakable. He didn't pull and twist or pinch. He didn't grab her with rough hands and expect her to enjoy the attention.

Desire, appreciation, and love shot through her veins to her heart and beat between her legs. As she kissed him, her thighs closed around his hips, pulling him closer until she felt his hard bulge against her crotch. Her hands tugged at his T-shirt, and she pulled away from his mouth to yank his shirt over his head. Swirls of dark hair covered his big chest, shot down his flat abdomen, circled his navel, and disappeared in the waistband of his jeans. She tossed the T-shirt aside and ran her hands up and down his chest and stomach. Her fingers furrowed through the short, fine hair covering hard muscles and hot skin. She felt the pounding of his heart and heard his rapid breath.

He moaned her name just before his mouth captured hers in another hot kiss. The tips of her breasts grazed his chest and spread an ache throughout her. Each place he touched pulsed with a hot passion she'd never experienced before. It was as if her body had known, waiting her whole life for John to love her. She ran her hands across the hard planes of his smooth back, down his spine and around to his stomach. He sucked in air as her fingers curled into the waistband of his jeans. When she pulled the metal button from its hole, his hands curled around her wrists. He tore his mouth from hers, took a step back, and looked at her with heavy eyes. A wrinkle creased his forehead and his tan cheeks were flushed. He looked like a hungry man who'd just been given his favorite dish, but he didn't look very happy about it. He looked as if he were about to refuse.

"Ahh, the hell with it," he swore at last, and reached for the top of her underwear. "I'm a dead man either way."

Georgeanne planted her hands behind her on the cabinet and raised her bottom as he pulled her underwear down her legs. When he stepped between her thighs once more, he was naked. And he *was* big. He hadn't been teasing about that. She reached for him and closed her fist around the thick shaft of his penis. His hand fastened around hers, and he moved her palm up to the plump head, then back down. He was incredibly hard and very hot within her grasp.

He looked at their hands and at her open thighs. "Are you taking birth control?" he asked, and moved his free hand to the top of her pelvis bone.

"Yes," she sighed as his fingers slipped through her pubic hair and stroked her slick flesh, arousing her until she thought she might shatter.

"Put your legs around my waist," he ordered, and when she did, he plunged inside of her. His head snapped up and his gaze shot to hers. "Oh God, Georgie," he uttered from the back of his throat. He withdrew slightly, then pushed until he was seated fully inside of her. He grabbed her hips and moved within her, slowly at first, then faster. The trophies in the hutch rattled, and with each thrust, Georgeanne felt as if he were pushing her toward a dark ledge. With each thrust her skin grew hotter and her craving for him more ravenous. Each drive of his body was torture and sweet bliss all at the same time.

She said his name over and over as her head fell back against the hutch and her eyes closed. "Don't stop," she cried out as she felt herself pitched over the edge. Fire spread across her flesh and her muscles involuntarily clenched as she fell into a long, hot orgasm. She uttered things that normally would have shocked her. She didn't care. John made her feel things, incredible things, that she'd never known before, and her every thought and feeling centered around the man she held close.

"Jesus H. Christ," John hissed as his face descended to the crook of her neck. His grasp tightened on her hips and, with a deep, guttural groan, he thrust into her one last time.

Darkness enclosed John's naked form, matching his grim mood. The house was quiet. Too quiet. If he listened closely, he could almost hear Georgeanne's steady breathing. But she lay asleep in his bedroom, and he knew hearing her was impossible.

It was the night. The darkness. The silence. It conspired against him, breathed down his neck and plagued him with memories.

Raising a bottle of Bud to his mouth, he drained the first quarter. He moved to the large picture window and gazed out at a big yellow moon and silver-tipped black waves. Of his own reflection in the glass, all he could see was a hazy silhouette. A blurry outline of a man who'd lost his soul and wasn't real interested in finding it again.

Unbidden, the image of his wife, Linda, rose before him in the darkness. The vision of how she'd looked the last time he'd seen her—sitting in a tub of bloody water, her appearance so different from the fresh-faced girl he'd known in high school.

His mind did a quick spin, back to that short time in school when he'd dated her. But after graduation, he'd moved hundreds of miles away to play hockey in the junior leagues. His life had revolved around his sport. He played hard and, at the age of twenty, was the first player taken by the Toronto Maple Leafs in the 1982 drafts. His size made him a dominating force and quickly earned him the nickname "The Wall." His on-ice skill made him a star on the rise. His off-ice skill made him a star with the rink bunnies, who considered him the Mark Spitz of the groupie pool. John played for the Maple Leafs for four seasons before the New York Rangers offered him a big-money contract, and he became one of the highest-paid players in the NHL. He forgot all about Linda.

When he did see her again, six years had passed. They were the same age but vastly different in experience. John had seen a lot of the world. He was young, rich, and had done things other men could only dream about doing. Over the years, he'd changed a great deal while Linda had changed very little. She was pretty much the same girl he'd driven around in Ernie's Chevy. The same girl who'd used the rearview mirror to smear on red lipstick so he could smear it back off.

He ran into Linda again during a break in the hockey season. He took her out on the town. He took her to a hotel, and three months later when she told him she was pregnant, he took her as his wife. His son, Toby, was born five months into the pregnancy. For the next four weeks, as he watched his son struggle for breath, he dreamed of teaching Toby all the things he'd been taught about life and hockey. But his dreams of a rowdy little boy died painfully with his son.

While John grieved in silence, Linda's sorrow was plain to everyone around her. She cried all the time, and within a short period became obsessed with having another child. John knew he was the reason behind her obsession. He'd married her because she was pregnant, not because he loved her.

He should have left then. He should have gotten out, but he hadn't been able to leave her. Not while she was in pain, and not while he felt responsible for her grief. For the next year he stayed. He stayed while she sought doctor after doctor. He stayed while she suffered a series of miscarriages. He stayed because for a while there had been a part of him that wanted another baby, too. He stayed while she sank deeper into despair.

He stayed, but he wasn't a good husband. Her preoccupation with having a baby became manic. The last few months of her life, he couldn't stand to touch her. The more she grasped, the harder he pushed. His affairs with other women became flagrant. On a subconscious level, he wanted her to leave him.

She chose to kill herself instead.

John raised the bottle of beer to his lips and took a long pull. She'd wanted him to find her, and he had. A year later, he could still remember the exact color her blood had turned the bath water. He could see her chalky white face and damp blond hair. He could smell the shampoo she'd used and see the cuts she'd made up her wrists almost to her elbows. He could still feel that awful kick in the gut.

Every day he lived with the awful guilt. Every day he sought diversion from his memories and the part he'd played in them.

John walked into his bedroom and looked down at the sultry girl wrapped up in his sheet. The light from the hall shined on the bed and the dark curls fanning her head. One arm rested across her stomach while the other lay out to one side.

He figured he should feel bad for usurping Virgil's wedding night. But he didn't. He didn't regret what he'd done. He'd had too good a time, and if anyone found out she'd spent the night in his house, they would assume he'd had sex with her anyway. So what the hell?

She had a body made for sex, but as he'd found out, she wasn't as experienced as her teasing had suggested. He'd had to show her how to give and receive pleasure. He'd kissed and caressed her body with his tongue, and in turn he'd taught her what to do with that pouty mouth of hers. She was sensual and naive, and he found her incredibly erotic.

John moved to the side of the bed and slid the white sheet to her waist. She looked like she'd been dropped naked into a huge dollop of whipped cream. He felt himself grow hard again and covered her with his body. Moving his hands to the sides of her breasts, he lowered his face to her cleavage and tenderly kissed her there. Here, with soft, warm flesh beneath him, he didn't have to think of anything. All he had to do was feel pleasure. Hearing Georgeanne's deep moan, he looked up into her face. Her slumberous green eyes stared back at him.

"Did I wake you up?" he asked.

Georgeanne watched his dimple crease his right cheek and felt her heart swell. "Wasn't that your intention?" she asked, caring about him so much she felt it deeply in her soul, and while he hadn't said he cared for her, she knew he must feel something. He'd risked Virgil's anger by being with her. He'd jeopardized his career, and Georgeanne found the gamble he'd taken for her exciting and terribly romantic.

"I could control my hands and let you go back to sleep. But it won't be easy," he said as he moved his palm to the outside of her bare thigh.

"Do I have another option?" she asked, and ran her fingers through the short hair at his temples.

He slid upward until his face was above hers. "I could make you scream again with pleasure."

"Hmm." She pretended to consider her choices. "How long do I have to make up my mind?"

"Time just ran out."

John was young and handsome, and in his arms, she felt secure and protected. He was a wonderful lover and could take care of her. And most important, she was falling madly in love with him.

He placed his lips on hers and kissed her with sweet passion, and she felt like singing that old country and western song. She was "the happiest girl in the whole U.S.A."

She wanted to make John happy, too. Ever since her first relationship at the age of fifteen, Georgeanne had always changed like a chameleon to become whatever her current boyfriend wanted. In the past, she'd done everything from dying her hair an ungodly shade of red to bruising her body on a mechanical bull. Georgeanne had always gone out of her way to please the men in her life, and in return, they loved her for it.

John might not love her now, but he would.

# Five

Georgeanne raised a hand to the ache in her chest. Her fingers grasped the white satin bow sown to her bodice, while within her breast, love and hatred collided like a wrecking ball and shattered her heart. Bound in her pink wedding dress and flimsy high-heeled mules, she fought against the stinging in the backs of eyes. But as she watched John's red Corvette pull back out into traffic, she felt herself losing the fight. Her vision blurred, but the release of her tears brought no comfort.

Even as she watched John disappear, she couldn't believe that he had actually dumped her on the side-walk in front of the Seattle-Tacoma International Airport. Not only had he abandoned her, but he'd left without looking back.

All around her people dressed for business, or in light summer clothes, hurried by. Taxi drivers unloaded luggage while the exhaust from the cabs choked the hot air. Skycaps joked with customers while an expressionless male voice warned that the marked area in front of the airport was for loading and unloading only. The jumbled sounds around Georgeanne matched the confused hum in her head. Last night John had behaved so unlike the indifferent man who'd awakened her this morning with a Bloody Mary in his hand. Last night he'd made love to her repeatedly, and she'd never felt closer to a man. She'd been so sure John had felt close to her, too. Surely he wouldn't have taken such a risk unless he cared. If he'd felt nothing for her, he wouldn't have jeopardized his career with the Chinooks. But this morning he'd behaved as if they'd spent the night watching reruns on television instead of making love. When he'd announced that he'd booked her a flight to Dallas, he'd sounded as if he were doing her a big favor. When he'd helped her into the corset and pink wedding dress, his touch had been impersonal. So unlike the hot caresses of her lover the night before. While he'd helped her dress, Georgeanne had struggled with her confused feelings. She'd struggled to find the right words to convince him to let her stay with him. She'd hinted at her willingness to do and be anything he wanted, but he'd ignored her subtle suggestions.

On the way to the airport, he'd played his music so loud that conversation had been impossible. During the hour she'd spent in his car, she'd tortured herself with questions. She'd wondered what she'd done and what had happened to change everything. Only her pride kept her from switching off the cassette player and demanding an answer. Only pride had held back her tears when he'd helped her out of his car.

"Your plane leaves in just under an hour. You have plenty of time to pick up your ticket at the counter and still make the flight," John had informed her as he'd handed her overnight case to her.

A tight fist of panic seized her stomach. Fright pushed her beyond pride, and she opened her mouth to plead with him to take her back to the beach house, where she felt safe. His next words stopped her. "In that dress, you're sure to get at least two marriage proposals before you reach Dallas. I don't want to tell you how to live your life, God knows I've messed up mine, but maybe you should put a little more thought into your next fiancé."

She loved him so much she ached, and he didn't care if she married another man. The night they'd shared hadn't meant *anything* to him.

"It's been great knowing you, Georgie," he'd said, then turned away.

"John!" His name burst from her lips, past her pride.

He'd turned, and the look on her face must have revealed everything she felt inside. He'd sighed with resignation. "I never wanted to hurt you, but I told you from the beginning, I wouldn't risk my position with the Chinooks for you." He'd paused, then added, "It's nothing personal." Then he'd walked away, down the sidewalk, and out of her life.

Georgeanne's hand began to ache, and she looked down at the overnight case she held in her tight grasp. Her knuckles were white and she loosened her grip.

The thick exhaust fumes made her nauseous, and she finally turned and walked into the airport. She had to get out of here. She had to go away, but she didn't know where to go. She felt all of her circuits overloading and tried to push everything from her mind. She found the Delta ticket counter, and no, she told the agent, she didn't have any luggage to check. With her ticket in one hand and her overnight case in the other, she turned away.

She walked past gift shops, restaurants, and flight-information boards. Misery surrounded her, pressing down like a thick black fog. She kept her gaze lowered, positive her heartache showed on her face, certain if people looked at her too closely, they would see the truth.

They would see that there wasn't one person alive

who gave a damn about Georgeanne Howard. Not in this state or any other. She'd deserted her only friend, Sissy, and if Georgeanne died, there wasn't one person who would care, not truly. Oh, her aunt Lolly would act as if she cared. She'd make her green funeral Jell-O and cry as if she weren't secretly relieved that she wouldn't have to feel responsible for Georgeanne anymore. Briefly Georgeanne wondered if her mother would grieve, but she knew the answer before she finished the thought. No. Billy Jean would never grieve for the child she'd never wanted.

She entered the Delta boarding room just as her fragile control slipped. Taking a seat facing a bank of windows, she moved aside a copy of the *Seattle Times* and set her overnight case on the vinyl seat beside her. She looked out onto the runway and an image of her mother's face rose before her, reminding her of the one and only time she'd met Billy Jean.

It had been the day of her grandmother's burial, and she'd looked up from the casket into the face of an elegant-looking woman with stylish brown hair and green eyes. She wouldn't have known who the woman was if Lolly hadn't told her. In an instant the grief of her grandmother's death mixed with apprehension, joy, hope, and a myriad of conflicting emotions. For all of Georgeanne's life she'd anticipated the moment she would finally meet her mother.

Growing up, she'd been told that Billy Jean was young and that she just didn't want children yet. As a result, Georgeanne had dreamed of the day her mother would change her mind.

But by the time Georgeanne had reached adolescence, she'd given up on dreams of reunions. She'd discovered that Billy Jean Howard was now Jean Obershaw, wife of Alabama representative Leon Obershaw, and the mother of their two small children. The day she'd learned of her mother's other family was the day she'd had to face a cruel reality. Grandmother had lied to her. Billy Jean did want children. She just didn't want *her*.

At her grandmother's funeral, when Georgeanne had finally laid eyes on Billy Jean, she'd expected to feel nothing. She was surprised to find that buried deep in her heart, she still harbored the fantasy of a loving mother. She'd held on to the dream that her mother could fill the empty place inside her. Georgeanne's hands had shaken and her knees quaked as she'd introduced herself to the woman who'd abandoned her shortly after giving birth. She'd held her breath . . . waiting . . . wanting. But Billy Jean had hardly looked at her when she'd said, "I know who you are." Then she'd turned and walked to the back of the church. After the service she'd disappeared, presumably back to her husband and children. Back to her life.

The announcement of an arriving Delta flight drew Georgeanne's attention from the past. Other passengers were beginning to fill up the boarding room, and she grabbed her overnight case and set it on her lap. An older woman with tight white curls and a polyester smock made her way toward the now empty chair. Out of habit, Georgeanne automatically reached for the *Seattle Times* newspaper and moved it out of the woman's way. She set it on top of her suitcase and looked back out the windows at a passing tow tractor and baggage trailer. Normally she would have smiled at the woman and perhaps engaged her in pleasant chitchat. But she didn't feel like being pleasant. She thought of her life and her attraction to people who couldn't return her love.

She'd fallen in love with John Kowalsky in less than a day. Her feelings for him had happened so fast she could hardly believe it herself. Yet she knew it was true. She thought of his blue eyes and the dimple dent-ing his right cheek whenever he smiled. She thought of his strong arms around her, making her feel safe. If she closed her eyes, she could feel his hands on her behind, lifting her onto the china hutch as if she weighed nothing. No other man she'd ever known, not even old boyfriends she'd thought she loved, had ever made her feel the way John had.

*You should have warned me that you're perfect,* he'd said, making her feel like the reigning Queen of the San Antonio Fiesta. No man had ever made her feel so desirable. No man had left her feeling so wretched inside.

Her eyes began to sting again and her vision blurred. Lately she'd made some pretty poor choices in her life. At the top of the list was her decision to marry a man old enough to be her grandfather. A close second was running from her wedding like a coward. But falling in love with John hadn't been a choice. It had just happened.

A single tear slipped down her cheek and she wiped at it. She had to get over John now. She had to get on with her life.

*What life?* She had no home and no job waiting for her. She had no real family to speak of, and her only friend probably hated her now. All of her clothes were at Virgil's, and there was no doubt in her mind that he despised her. The man she loved didn't love her in return. He'd dumped her on the curb without looking back.

She had nothing and no one but herself.

"Attention," a female voice announced, "passengers holding tickets for Delta flight 624, Dallas–Fort Worth International Airport, will begin boarding in fifteen minutes."

Georgeanne looked at the ticket in her hand. Fifteen minutes, she thought. Fifteen minutes before she boarded an airplane that would take her back to nothing. No one would be there to greet her. She had no one. No one to take care of her. No one to tell her what to do.

No one but herself. Only Georgeanne.

Panic grabbed ahold of her stomach, and she lowered her gaze to the *Seattle Times* on the overnight case in her lap. She could feel an emotional overload just below the surface. In order to avoid a complete shutdown, she concentrated on the newsprint. Her lips moved as she slowly read the want ads.

The sign above Heron Catering hung awkwardly to the right. Thursday night's storm had knocked it around until one of the chains had snapped. Now the great majestic bird painted on the sign looked as if it were about to take a nosedive onto the sidewalk. The rhododendrons planted on each side of the door had survived the heavy winds, but the hanging red geraniums were pretty much history.

Inside the small building, everything was in perfect order. The office in the front of the converted store had a desk and a round table. A large picture of two people with matching clothing and identical faces hung on the wall. Each held an opposite end of a dollar bill. In the kitchen an industrial slicer, grinder, and stainless steel pots and pans shined. A selection of menu samples sat on a tray in one of the refrigerators, while the owner's doubler-decker air-flow oven dominated the opposite corner.

The owner herself stood in the bathroom with a blue rubber band clamped between her lips. A fluorescent light flickered and buzzed and cast a grayish tint over Mae Heron's face. Her brown eyes studied her reflection in the mirror above the sink as she brushed her blond hair into a ponytail high on the back of her head.

Mae was the epitome of an Ivory Soap girl. She

didn't have any use for fruity skin cleansers or toners or fancy creams. She hated the feel of makeup on her face. Sometimes she wore a little mascara, but because she had little practice, she wasn't any good at applying it, not like Ray had been. Ray had always been so good at dress-up.

Mae turned to look at herself from the side and raised a hand to smooth a lump of hair at her crown. She might have taken the ponytail out and started over if the bell above the front door hadn't signaled the arrival of the customer Mae had been expecting. Mrs. Candace Sullivan was a frequent client of Heron's, and she'd called Mae to cater her parents' fiftieth wedding anniversary. Candace was the wife of a respected cardiologist. She was wealthy and Mae's last hope to keep her and Ray's dream alive.

She looked down to make sure her blue polo shirt was tucked neatly into her khaki shorts and took a deep breath. She wasn't very good at this part of the business. Kissing ass and schmoozing customers had been Ray's forte. She was the accountant. The bookkeeper. She wasn't good with people. She'd spent the previous night and much of today crunching numbers until her eyes felt gritty, but no matter how many creative ways she'd figured it, if the catering business she and Ray had opened three years ago didn't receive a generous cash flow soon, then she'd have to close the doors. She needed Mrs. Sullivan; she needed her money.

Mae reached for the manila job envelope on the sink and headed out of the bathroom. She walked through the kitchen, but stopped short in the doorway to the front office. The young woman standing in the room bore not the slightest resemblance to Mrs. Sullivan. In fact, she looked like an escapee from the Playboy Mansion. She was everything Mae was not: tall, busty, with thick dark hair and nice tanned skin. All Mae had to do was think of the sun and she burned a nice shade of lobster red. "Ahh . . . can I help you?"

"I'm here to apply for the job," she answered with an obvious southern drawl. "The chef's assistant job."

Mae glanced at the newspaper the woman held in one hand, then let her gaze travel up the pink satin dress with the big white bow. Her brother Ray would have loved that dress. He would have wanted to wear it. "Have you ever worked for a caterer before?"

"No. But I'm a good cook."

From the looks of her, Mae sincerely doubted the woman could boil water. But she knew better than anyone not to judge a person by the color of his or her party dress. She'd spent most of her life defending her twin brother against cruel people who judged him harshly, including members of her own family.

"I'm Mae Heron," she said.

"It's a pleasure, Ms. Heron." The other woman set the newspaper on a table by the door, then walked toward Mae and shook her hand. "My name is Georgeanne Howard."

"Well, Georgeanne, I'll get you an application," she said as she moved behind her desk. If she got the Sullivan job, she would need a chef's assistant, but she really doubted she would hire this woman. Not only did she prefer to hire experienced cooks, but she questioned the judgment of someone who would wear a provocative dress to apply for a job in a kitchen.

Even though she didn't plan to hire Georgeanne, she figured that she'd let her fill out an application and send her on her way. She reached inside a bottom drawer as the bell above the door rang once again. She looked up and recognized her wealthy client. Like most cocktail-drinking, tennis-playing, country-club women, Mrs. Candace Sullivan's hair resembled a platinum helmet. Her jewelry was real, her nails fake, and she was typical of every other rich woman with whom Mae had ever worked. She drove an eighty-thousand-dollar car yet quibbled over the price of raspberries. "Hello, Candace. I have everything ready for you." Mae pointed to the round table where three photo albums lay. "Why don't you take a seat and I'll be with you in a moment."

Mrs. Sullivan turned her curious gaze from the girl in pink and smiled at Mae. "Thursday's storm seems to have played havoc on the exterior of your building," she said as she took a seat.

"It sure did." Mae knew she'd have to repair the sign and buy new plants, but she didn't have the money right now. "You can sit here," she told Georgeanne, and laid an application on the desk. Then, with the job envelope still in her hand, she moved across the room and took a seat at the round table. "I've created several menus for you to choose from. When we talked on the phone, we discussed duck as your entrée." She removed the menus from the envelope, laid them on the table, and pointed to the first choice. "With roasted duck, I would recommend hunter wild rice and either mixed vegetables or green beans. A small dinner roll will—"

"Oh, I don't know," Mrs. Sullivan sighed.

Mae was prepared for that response. "I have samples in the refrigerator for you to try."

"No, thank you. I just had lunch."

Tamping down her irritation, she moved her finger to the next choice of side dishes. "Perhaps you would prefer asparagus spears. Or artichoke—"

"No," Candace interrupted. "I don't think so. I don't think I like the idea of duck anymore."

Mae moved to the next menu. "Okay. How about prime rib of beef au jus, browned potato, green beans, sliced—"

"I've been to three parties this year where prime rib was served. I want something different. Something special. Ray used to come up with the most wonderful ideas."

Mae shuffled the pages before her and set a third menu on top. She had a notoriously short amount of patience and wasn't any good at this. She didn't deal well with picky customers who didn't know what they wanted, except that they didn't want any of the suggestions she'd worked hard to put together. "Yes, Ray was wonderful," she said, missing her brother so much it felt like a part of her heart and soul had died six months ago.

"Ray was the best," Mrs. Sullivan continued. "Even though he was a . . . well . . . you know."

Yes, Mae knew, and if Candace wasn't careful, she'd find herself escorted out the door. Even though Ray could no longer be hurt by bigotry, Mae wouldn't tolerate it. "Have you given any thought to Chateaubriand?" she asked as she pointed out her third suggestion.

"No," Candace answered. Then in less than ten minutes she rejected all of Mae's other ideas. Mae wanted to kill her and had to remind herself that she needed the money.

"For my parents' fiftieth wedding anniversary, I was hoping for something a little more unique. You haven't shown me anything special. I wish Ray was here. He'd come up with something really nice."

All the menus Mae had showed her were nice. In fact, they were from Ray's menu file. Mae felt her temper rise and forced herself to ask as pleasantly as possible, "What did you have in mind?"

"Well, I don't know. You're the caterer. You're supposed to be creative."

But Mae had never been the creative one.

"I haven't seen anything special. Do you have anything else?"

Mae reached for a photo album and flipped it open.

She doubted Candace would find anything to suit her. She was convinced that Mrs. Sullivan's sole reason for coming was to drive Mae to drink. "These are pictures of jobs we've catered. Perhaps you'll see something you like."

"I hope so."

"Excuse me," the girl in pink at the desk cut in. "I couldn't help but overhear y'all. Maybe I could help."

Mae had forgot Georgeanne was even in the room, and turned to look at her.

"Where did your parents honeymoon?" Georgeanne asked from her seat behind the desk.

"Italy," Candace replied

"Hmm." Georgeanne placed the tip of the pen on her full bottom lip. "You could start with Pappa col Pomodoro," she advised, her Italian sounding peculiar with that southern accent of hers drawing out all those vowels. "Then Florentine roast pork served with potatoes, carrots, and a thick slice of bruschetta. Or if you prefer duck, it could be served Arezzo style with pasta and a fresh salad."

Candace looked at Mae, then back at the other woman. "Mother loves lasagna with basil sauce."

"Lasagna with a nice radicchio salad would be perfect. Then you could top off the meal with a delicious apricot anniversary cake."

"Apricot cake?" Candace asked, sounding less than enthusiastic. "I've never heard of it."

"It's wonderful," Georgeanne gushed.

"Are you sure?"

"Absolutely." She leaned forward and placed her elbows on the desk. "Vivian Hammond, of the San Antonio Hammonds, is positively mad for apricot cake. She loves it so much, she broke a hundred-and-thirty-year tradition and served it to the ladies at the annual Yellow Rose Club meeting." Her eyes narrowed and she lowered her voice as if she were sharing a tasty piece of gossip. "You see, until Vivian, the club had always served lemon pound cake at their meetings, lemon being the same color as yellow roses and all." She paused, leaned back in her chair, and tilted her head to one side. "Naturally, her mama was mortified."

Mae lowered her brows and stared at Georgeanne. There was something a little familiar about her. She couldn't quite put her finger on it and wondered if they'd met before.

"Really?" Candace asked. "Why didn't she serve both?"

Georgeanne shrugged her bare shoulders. "Who knows. Vivian is a peculiar woman."

The more Georgeanne talked, the stronger Mae's feeling of familiarity grew.

Candace looked at her watch, then at Mae. "I like the idea of Italian, and I'll need a big enough apricot anniversary cake to feed about one hundred people." By the time Mrs. Sullivan left the building, Mae had a menu plan, a contract written, and a check for the deposit. She leaned her behind against the table and folded her arms beneath her breasts.

"I have a few questions for you," she said. When Georgeanne looked up from the application she pretended to study, Mae looked at the menu she held in her own hand. "What is Pappa col Pomodoro?"

"Tomato soup."

"Can you make it?"

"Sure. It's real easy."

Mae set the menu on the table by her right hip. "Did you make up that apricot cake story?"

Georgeanne tried to look contrite, but a little smile tilted the corners of her lips. "Well . . . I did embellish somewhat."

Now Mae knew why she recognized the other woman. Georgeanne was an unrepentant bullshit artist just as Ray had been. For a brief moment she felt the emptiness of his death recede just a fraction. She pushed herself away from the table and walked over to her desk. "Have you ever worked as a cook's assistant or done any waitressing?" she asked, and glanced down at the employment application.

Georgeanne quickly covered the paper with her hands, but not before Mae noticed the poor penmanship and that on the job-you're-applying-for line she'd written *chief's* assistant instead of chef's.

"I was a waitress at Luby's before I worked at Dillard's, and I've taken just about every cooking class imaginable."

"Have you ever worked for a caterer?"

"No, but I can cook anything from Greek to Szechwan, baklava to sushi, and I'm real good with people."

Mae looked Georgeanne over and hoped she wasn't making a mistake. "I have one more question. Would you like a job?"

# Six

*Seattle*
*June 1996*

Escaping the chaos in the kitchen, Georgeanne walked the banquet room one last time. With a critical eye, she scrutinized the thirty-seven linen-draped tables carefully placed about the room. In the center of each table, pressed-glass bowls had been artfully piled with a variety of wax-dipped roses, baby's breath, and fern fronds.

Mae had accused her of being obsessed, possessed, or both. Georgeanne's fingers still ached from all that hot paraffin, but as she gazed at each centerpiece, she knew the aggravation, pain, and mess had been worth it. She'd created something unique and beautiful. She, Georgeanne Howard, the girl who'd been raised to depend on others to take care of her, had created a wonderful life. She'd done it by herself. She'd learned methods to help her deal with her dyslexia. She no longer hid her problems, yet she didn't talk about them openly either. She'd concealed her dyslexia too many years to announce it to the world now.

She'd overcome many of her old obstacles, and at the age of twenty-nine, she was a partner in a successful catering business and owned a modest little house in Bellevue. She took tremendous satisfaction from everything the backward little girl from Texas accomplished. She'd walked through fire, been burned to her soul, but she'd survived. She was a stronger person now, perhaps less trusting, and extremely reluctant to ever give her heart to a man again, but she didn't view those two qualities as impedances to her happiness. She'd learned her lessons the hard way, and although she'd much rather give a vital organ than relive her life before she'd walked into Heron Catering seven years ago, she was the woman she was today because of what had happened to her then. She didn't like to think of the past. Her life was full now and filled with things she loved.

She'd been born and raised in Texas, but she'd quickly come to love Seattle. She loved the hilly city surrounded by mountains and water. It had taken her a few years to get used to the rain, but like most natives, it didn't bother her much now. She loved the tactile feel of Pike Place Market and the vibrant colors of the Pacific Northwest.

Georgeanne raised her forearm, pushed back the wrist of her black tuxedo jacket, and peered at her watch. Elsewhere in the old hotel, her waiting staff served sliced cucumber topped with salmon, stuffed mushrooms, and glasses of champagne to three hundred guests. But in a half hour, they would make their way to the banquet room and dine on veal scallopini, new potatoes with lemon butter, and endive and watercress salad.

She reached for a wineglass and plucked the napkin stuffed inside. Her hands trembled as she refolded the white linen to resemble a rose. She was nervous. More so than usual. She and Mae had catered parties of three hundred before. Nothing new. No sweat. But they'd never catered for the Harrison Foundation. They'd never catered a fund-raiser that charged its guests five hundred dollars a plate. Oh, realistically she knew the guests weren't paying that amount of money for the food. The money raised tonight would go to The Children's Hospital and Medical Center. Still, just the thought all those people, paying all that money for a piece of veal, gave her palpitations.

A door at the side of the room opened and Mae slipped through. "I thought I'd find you in here," she said as she walked toward Georgeanne. In her hand she held the green folder that contained work and purchase orders, a running inventory of all supplies, and a cluster of receipts.

Georgeanne smiled at her close friend and business partner and placed the folded napkin back in the glass. "How are things in the kitchen?"

"Oh, the new cook's assistant drank all that special white wine you bought for the veal."

Georgeanne felt her stomach drop. "Tell me you're kidding."

"I'm kidding."

"Really?"

"Really."

"That's not funny," Georgeanne sighed as Mae came to stand next to her.

"Probably not. But you need to lighten up."

"I won't be able to lighten up until I'm on my way home," Georgeanne said as she turned to adjust the pink rose pinned to the lapel of Mae's cutaway tuxedo jacket. Although the two of them were dressed in identical suits, they were complete physical opposites. Mae had the smooth porcelain skin of a natural blonde, and at five feet one inch, was as slim as a ballerina. Georgeanne had always envied Mae's metabolism, which allowed her to eat almost anything and never gain a pound.

"Everything is progressing right on schedule. Don't get excited and zone out like you did at Angela Everett's wedding."

Georgeanne frowned and walked toward the side door. "I'd still like to get my hands on Grandma Everett's little blue poodle."

Mae laughed as she strolled beside Georgeanne. "I'll never forget that night. I was serving the buffet and I could hear you screeching from the kitchen." She lowered her voice a fraction, then proceeded to mimic Georgeanne's accent. "Cryin' all night. A dawg ate my balls!"

"I said *meatballs*."

"No. You didn't. Then you just sat down and stared at the empty tray for a good ten minutes."

Georgeanne didn't quite remember it that way. But even she had to admit that she still wasn't all that good at handling sudden stress. Although she was better at it than she used to be. "You're a horrid liar, Mae Heron," she said, reaching up to give her friend's ponytail a little tug, then turned to cast one more glance at the room. The china shined, the silver flatware gleamed, and the folded napkins looked as if hundreds of white roses hovered just above the tabletops. Georgeanne was extremely pleased with herself.

A frown furrowed John Kowalsky's brow as he leaned slightly forward in his chair and took a closer look at the napkin stuffed in his wineglass. It appeared to be a bird or a pineapple. He wasn't sure which.

"Oh, this is nice," his date for the evening, Jenny Lange, sighed. He glanced at her shiny blond hair and had to admit that he'd liked Jenny a lot better the day he'd asked her out. She was a photographer, and he'd met her two weeks ago when she'd come to take pictures of his houseboat for a local magazine. He didn't know her very well. She seemed like a perfectly nice lady, but even before they'd arrived at the benefit, he'd discovered he wasn't attracted to her. Not even a little bit. It wasn't her fault. It was him.

He turned his attention back to the napkin, plucked it from the glass, and laid it across his knee. Lately he'd been thinking about getting married again. He'd been talking to Ernie about it, too. Maybe tonight's benefit had triggered something dormant in him. Maybe it was because he'd just had his thirty-fifth birthday; but he'd been thinking about finding a wife and having a few kids. He'd been thinking about Toby, thinking about him more than usual.

John leaned back in his chair, brushed aside the front of his charcoal Hugo Boss suit jacket, and shoved his hand in the pocket of his gray trousers. He wanted to be a father again. He wanted the word "Daddy" added to his list of names. He wanted to teach his son to skate, just as he'd been taught by Ernie. Like every other father in the world, he wanted to stay up late on Christmas Eve and put together tricycles, bicycles, and race-car sets. He wanted to dress up his son as a vampire, or a pirate, and take him trick-or-treating. But when he looked at Jenny, he knew she wasn't going to be the mother of his children. She reminded him of Jodie Foster, and he'd always thought Jodie Foster looked a little like a lizard. He didn't want his children to look like lizards.

A waiter interrupted his thoughts and asked if he wanted wine. John told him no, then leaned forward and turned his glass upside down on the table.

"Don't you drink?" Jenny asked him.

"Sure," he answered, and taking his hand from his pocket, he reached for the glass he'd carried in with him from the cocktail hour. "I drink soda water and lime."

"You don't drink alcohol?"

"No. Not anymore." He set down his glass as another waiter placed a plate of salad before him. He'd been dry for four years this time, and he knew he'd never drink again. Alcohol turned him into a dumb shit, and he'd finally grown tired of it.

The night he'd hit Philadelphia forward Danny Shanahan was the night he'd hit rock bottom. There were those who thought "Dirty Danny" had deserved what he'd been given. But not John. As he'd stared down at the man lying prone on the ice, he'd known he was out of control. He'd been cracked in the shins and elbowed in the ribs more times than not. It was part of the game. But that night something in him had snapped. Before he'd even realized what he was doing, he'd thrown his gloves and had bare-knuckle sucker-punched Shanahan. Danny had received a concussion and a trip to the infirmary. John had been ejected from play and suspended for six games. The next morning he'd awakened in a hotel with an empty bottle of Jack Daniel's and a bed filled with two naked women. As he'd stared up at the textured ceiling, thoroughly disgusted with himself and trying to recall the night before, he'd known he had to stop.

He hadn't had a drink since. He hadn't even wanted one. And now when he went to bed with a woman, he woke up the next morning knowing her name. In fact, he had to know a lot about her first. He was careful now. He was lucky to be alive and he knew it.

"Isn't the room beautifully decorated?" Jenny asked.

John glanced at the table, then at the podium in the front of the room. All the flowers and candles were a little too fruity for his tastes. "Sure. It's great," he said, and ate his salad. When he finished, the plate was taken and another set before him. He'd attended a lot of banquets and benefits in his life. He'd eaten a lot of bad food at them, too. But tonight the food was pretty good; skimpy, but good. Better than last year. Last year he'd been served a rubbery game hen with really shitty pine nuts stuffed inside. But then, he wasn't here for the food. He was here to give money. A lot of money. Very few people knew of John's philanthropy, and he wanted it to stay that way. He did it for his son and it was private.

"What do you think of the Avalanche winning the Stanley Cup?" Jenny asked as the dessert was set before them.

John figured she was asking just to make conversation. She didn't want to know what he really thought, so he toned down his opinion and kept it nice and clean. "They've got one hell of a goaltender. You can always count on Roy to pull through in the playoffs and save your ass." He shrugged. "They've got some good muckers, but Claude Lemieux is a gutless sissy boy." He reached for his dessert spoon, then looked at her. "They'll probably make it into the finals again next season." And he'd be waiting for them, because John expected to be there, too, battling for the Cup.

He turned to let his gaze sweep the room in search of the president of the Harrison Foundation. Ruth Harrison usually took the podium first and got things rolling. He spotted her two tables away looking up at a woman who stood beside her. The woman's back was to John, but she stuck out in the crowd of silk dresses around her. She wore a tuxedo with long tails and appeared overdressed, even for a fancy fund-raiser. Her hair was pulled back and secured at the nape of her neck with a big black bow. From the bow, soft curls fell to the middle of her shoulders. She was tall, and when she turned her profile toward him, John choked on his sorbet. "Jesus," he wheezed.

"Are you okay?" Jenny asked, and placed a concerned hand on the shoulder of his jacket.

He couldn't answer. He could only stare, feeling as if he'd been high-sticked in the forehead. When he'd delivered her to Sea-Tac Airport seven years ago, he'd never thought they'd meet again. He remembered the last time he'd seen her, a voluptuous baby doll in a little pink dress. He remembered a lot more about her, too, and what he remembered usually brought a smile to his lips. For reasons he couldn't recall at the moment, he hadn't been drunk the night he'd spent with her. But he didn't think it would have mattered if he'd been drinking or not, because drunk or sober, Georgeanne Howard wasn't the type of woman a man forgot.

"What's the matter, John?"

"Ahh . . . nothing." He glanced at Jenny, then turned his gaze back to the woman who'd caused such a stir when she'd run out on her wedding. After that fateful day, Virgil Duffy had left the country for eight months. The Chinooks' summer training camp that year had been thick with speculation. A few players thought she'd been kidnaped while others theorized on the mode of her escape. Then there was Hugh Miner, who figured that rather than marry Virgil, she'd killed herself in his bathroom and Virgil had covered it up. Only John knew the truth, but he had been the only Chinook not talking.

"John?"

Now here she was, standing in the middle of a banquet room, looking as beautiful as he remembered. Maybe more so. Maybe it was the tuxedo, which seemed to emphasize the shape of her body rather than disguise it. Maybe it was the light shining on her dark hair, or the way her profile defined her full lips. He didn't know if it was one or all of those things, but he found the more he looked at her, the deeper his curiosity grew. He wondered what she was doing in

Seattle. What she'd done with her life, and if she'd found a rich man to marry.

"John?"

He turned his attention to his date.

"Is something wrong?" she asked.

"No. Nothing." He turned to look at Georgeanne again and watched her place a black purse on the table. She reached out and shook Ruth Harrison's hand. Then she smiled, grabbed the purse, and walked away.

"Excuse me, Jenny," he said as he rose to his feet. "I'll be right back."

He followed Georgeanne as she wove her way through tables, keeping his eyes on the straight set of her shoulders. "Pardon me," he said as he shoved his way past two older gentlemen. He caught up with her just as she was about to open a side door.

"Georgie," he said as her hand reached for the brass knob.

She stopped, glanced over her shoulder at him, and stared for a good five seconds before her mouth slowly fell open.

"I thought I recognized you," he said.

She closed her mouth. Her green eyes were huge as if she'd been caught in the act of a felony.

"Don't you remember me?"

She didn't answer. She just continued to stare at him.

"I'm John Kowalsky. We met when you ran away from your wedding," he explained, although he wondered how she could possibly forget that particular debacle. "I picked you up and we—"

"Yes," she interrupted him. "I remember you." Then she said nothing more, and John wondered if there was something wrong with his memory because he remembered her as a real chatter hound.

"Oh, good," he said to cover the awkward silence

that stretched between them. "What are you doing in Seattle?"

"Working." She took a deep breath, which raised her breasts, then said on a rush of expelled air, "Well, I have to go now." She turned so fast that she ran into the closed door. The wood rattled noisily and her purse fell from her hand, spilling some of the contents on the floor. "Cryin' all night," she gasped with her breathy southern drawl, and stooped to retrieve her things.

John lowered to one knee and picked up a tube of lipstick and a ballpoint pin. He held them out to her in his open hand. "Here you go."

Georgeanne looked up and her eyes locked with his. She stared at him for several heartbeats, then reached for her lipstick and pen. Her fingers brushed his palm. "Thank you," she whispered, and pulled away her hand as if she'd been burned. Then she stood and opened the door.

"Wait a minute," he said, and reached for a floral-printed checkbook. In the short amount of time it took him to grab it and rise to his feet, she was gone. The door shut in his face with a loud bang, leaving John to feel like an idiot. She'd acted as if she were afraid. While it was true that he didn't remember every detail of the night they'd spent together, he would have remembered if he'd hurt her. Before he could contemplate the possibility, he dismissed it as absurd. Even at his drunkest, he'd never hurt a woman.

Baffled, he turned and walked slowly back toward his table. He couldn't figure out why she'd practically run from him. His memories of Georgeanne weren't at all unpleasant. They'd shared a night of great raw sex, then he'd bought her a plane ticket home. Oh, he'd known he'd hurt her feelings, but at that time in his life, it was the best he could offer.

John looked down at the checkbook in his hand and

flipped it open. He was surprised to see her checks had crayon pictures on them like a kid would draw. He glanced at the left-hand corner and was further surprised to see that her last name hadn't changed. She was still Georgeanne Howard and she lived in Bellevue.

More questions were added to the list of others in his head, but they would all go unanswered. For whatever reason, she obviously didn't want to see him. He slipped the checkbook into the pocket of his jacket. He'd mail it back to her Monday.

Georgeanne hurried up the sidewalk edged on each side by colorful primroses and purple pansies. Her hand shook as she fit her key into the brass knob on the door. A chaotic mix of lush hydrangea and cosmos planted in front of the house spilled out onto the lawn. Panic held her in its tight grasp, and she knew she wouldn't feel relieved of her fear until she was safely inside her house.

"Lexie," she called out as she opened the door. She glanced to the left and a bit of calm eased the racing of her heart. Her six-year-old daughter sat on the couch surrounded by four stuffed dalmatians. On the television, Cruella De Vil laughed wickedly, and her eyes glowed red as she drove her car off a snowy embankment. Sitting next to the dalmatians, Rhonda, the teenage girl from next door, looked up at Georgeanne. Her nose ring caught a glint of light and her burgundy hair shined like rich wine. Rhonda looked odd, but she was a nice girl and a wonderful baby-sitter.

"How did everything go tonight?" Rhonda asked as she stood.

"Great," Georgeanne lied, opened her purse, and pulled out her wallet. "How was Lexie?"

"She was fine. We played Barbies for a while and then she ate the macaroni and cheese with the little hot dogs cut up in it that you left for her."

Georgeanne handed Rhonda fifteen dollars. "Thank you for sitting for me tonight."

"Any time. Lexie is a pretty cool kid." She raised a hand. "See ya."

"'Bye, Rhonda." Georgeanne smiled as she let the baby sitter out. She moved to sit down on the peach and green floral-print couch next to her daughter. She took a deep breath and let it out slowly. *He doesn't know,* she told herself. *And even if he did, he probably wouldn't care anyway.*

"Hey, precious darlin'," she said, and patted Lexie on the thigh. "I'm home."

"I know. I like this part," Lexie informed her without taking her eyes from the television. "It's my favorite. I like Rolly the best. He's fat."

Georgeanne brushed several locks of Lexie's hair behind her shoulder. She wanted to grab her daughter and hold her tight; instead she said, "If you give me some sugar, I'll leave you alone."

Lexie automatically turned, lifted her face, and puckered her dark red lips.

Georgeanne kissed her, then held Lexie's chin in her palm. "Have you been into my lipstick again?"

"No, Mommy, it's mine."

"You don't have that shade of red."

"Uh-huh. I do, too."

"Where did you get it then?" Georgeanne lifted her gaze to the dark purple shadow Lexie had liberally applied from eyelids to brows. Bright pink streaks colored her cheeks, and she'd doused herself in Tinkerbell perfume.

"I found it."

"Don't lie to me. You know I don't like it when you lie to me."

Lexie's heavily coated bottom lip trembled. "I forget

sometimes," she cried dramatically. "I think I need a doctor to help me remember!"

Georgeanne bit the inside of her cheek to keep from laughing. As Mae was fond of saying, Lexie was a drama queen. And according to Mae, she knew queens very well. Her brother, Ray, had been one. "A doctor will give you a shot," Georgeanne warned.

Lexie's lip stopped trembling and her eyes rounded.

"So maybe you can remember to stay out of my things without going to the doctor."

"Okay," she agreed a little too easily.

"Because if you don't, the deal is off," Georgeanne warned, referring to the bargain they'd agreed to several months ago. On the weekends, Lexie could dress in whatever she wanted and wear as much makeup as her little heart desired. But during the week, she had to have a clean face and dress in the clothes her mother picked out for her to wear. For now, the deal seemed to be working.

Lexie was mad for cosmetics. She loved them and thought the more the better. The neighbors stared when she rode her bicycle down the sidewalk, especially if she wore the lime green boa Mae had given her. Taking her to a grocery store or to the mall was embarrassing, but it was only on the weekends. And it was easier to live with the deal they'd made than the daily battles that used to ensue every morning when it was time for Lexie to get dressed.

The threat of no more makeup got Lexie's attention. "I promise, Mommy."

"Okay, but only because I'm a sucker for your face," Georgeanne said, then she kissed her on the forehead.

"I'm a sucker for your face, too," Lexie repeated back.

Georgeanne rose from the couch. "I'll be in my bedroom if you need me." Lexie nodded and turned her attention to the barking dalmatians on the television screen.

Georgeanne walked down the hallway, past a small bathroom, then into her bedroom. She shrugged out of her tuxedo jacket and tossed it on a pink and white striped chaise.

John didn't know about Lexie. He couldn't. Georgeanne had overreacted, and he'd probably thought she was a lunatic, but seeing him again had been such a shock. She'd always been careful to avoid John. She didn't move in the same social circle, and she never attended a Chinooks game, which was no hardship because she found hockey appallingly violent. For fear of running into him, Heron's never catered athletic functions, which didn't bother Mae since she hated jocks. Never in a million years had she thought she might run into him at a hospital charity.

Georgeanne sank down on the floral chintz comforter covering her bed. She didn't like to think about John, but forgetting about him completely was impossible. Occasionally she would walk through a grocery store and see his handsome face staring at her from the cover of a sports magazine. Seattle was crazy about the Chinooks and John "The Wall" Kowalsky. During the hockey season he could be seen on the nightly news slamming other men against the boards. She saw him on local television commercials, and she'd seen his face on a billboard advertising milk, of all things. Sometimes the smell of a certain cologne, or the sound of crashing waves, would remind her of lying on a sandy beach and staring up into deep blue eyes. The memory no longer hurt as it had once. It wasn't a sharp ache to the heart. Still, she always pushed away the images of that time and of that man. She didn't like to dwell on them.

She'd always thought Seattle was big enough for the both of them. She'd thought that if she made every effort to avoid him, she'd never have to actually see him in person. But even though she didn't think it would ever happen, there was a part of her that had always wondered what he would say if he saw her again. Of course, she'd known what she would say. She'd always pictured herself acting indifferent. Then she'd say, as cool as a December morning, "John? John who? I'm sorry, I don't remember you. *It's nothing personal.*"

That hadn't happened. She'd heard someone call out the name she hadn't used in seven years, the name she no longer associated with the woman she was now, and she'd turned to look at the man who'd used it. For several heartbeats her brain hadn't registered what her eyes had seen. Then complete shock had taken over. The fight-or-flight instinct had kicked in and she'd run.

But not before she'd looked into his blue eyes and accidentally touched his hand. She'd felt the warm texture of his palm beneath her fingers, seen the curious smile on his lips, and recalled the touch of his mouth pressed to hers. He looked so much like she remembered, and yet he seemed bigger and age had etched fine lines at the corners of his eyes. He was still extremely nice to look at, and for a few brief seconds, she'd forgotten that she hated him.

Georgeanne rose and moved to stand in front of the cheval mirror across the room. Her hand lifted to the front of her tuxedo shirt and she unbuttoned it. Because of Lexie's dark hair and coloring, people often commented that she resembled Georgeanne, but Lexie looked just like her father. She had the same blue eyes and long, thick lashes. Her nose was the same shape as his, and when she smiled, a dimple creased her cheek. Just like John.

Pulling her shirt from the waistband of her pants, she unbuttoned her cuffs. Lexie was the most important thing in Georgeanne's life. She was her heart, and the thought of losing her was unbearable. Georgeanne was scared. More afraid than she'd been in a long time. Now that John knew she lived in Seattle, he could find Lexie. All he had to do was ask someone at the Harrison Foundation, and he could find Georgeanne.

*But why would John want to seek me out?* she asked herself. He'd dumped her at the airport seven years ago, making his feelings painfully obvious. And even if he did find out about his daughter, he probably wouldn't want anything to do with her. He was a big hockey player. What would he want with one little girl?

She was just being paranoid.

The next morning Lexie finished her cereal and put the bowl in the sink. From the back of the house she could hear her mom turn on the faucet, and she knew she had a long wait before they left for the mall. Her mom loved to take long showers.

The doorbell rang and she walked into the living room, dragging her boa behind her. She moved to the big front window and pushed the lace curtain aside. A man in jeans and a striped shirt stood on the porch. Lexie stared at him a moment, then let the curtain fall back in place. She wrapped her boa around her neck and walked across the room to the front entrance. She wasn't supposed to open the door for strangers, but even though the man standing on the porch had on black sunglasses, he wasn't a stranger. She knew who he was. She'd seen him on the TV, and last year Mr. Wall and his friends had come to her school to sign their names on some of the kids' shirts and notebooks and stuff. Lexie had been way at the back of the gym and hadn't gotten anybody's name on anything.

He'd probably come to sign some of her stuff now,

she thought as she opened the door. Then she looked up—way up.

John removed his sunglasses and stuffed them in the pocket of his polo shirt. The door opened and he looked down—way down. Almost as shocking as finding a child in Georgeanne's house was the little girl staring up at him wearing pink snakeskin cowboy boots, a little pink skirt, a purple polka-dot T-shirt, and a wild green boa around her neck. But her electric clothing was nothing compared to her face. "Ahh . . . hi," he said, taken back by the powder blue eye shadow, bright pink cheeks, and shiny red lips. "I'm looking for Georgeanne Howard."

"My mom's in the shower, but you can come in." She turned and walked into the living room. A scraggly ponytail high on the back of her head swayed with each step of her boots.

"Are you sure?" John didn't know very much about children, and absolutely nothing about little girls, but he did know that they weren't supposed to invite strangers into the house. "Georgeanne might not like it when she finds out you let me in," he said, but then, he figured she probably wouldn't like finding him in her house whether she was in the shower or not.

The little girl glanced over her shoulder. "She won't mind. I'll go get my stuff," she said, and disappeared around a corner, presumably to get her *stuff*. Whatever that meant.

John slipped Georgeanne's checkbook into his back pocket and stepped inside the house. The checkbook was an excuse. His curiosity had brought him here. After Georgeanne had left the banquet last night, he hadn't been able to stop thinking about her. He closed the door behind him and walked into the living room, immediately feeling out of his element, like the time he'd bought underwear for an old girlfriend at Victoria's Secret.

The house was filled with the pastel colors and fussy decorations feared by even the most confident heterosexual man. Her flowery couch had lace pillows that matched the curtains. There were vases of daisies and roses and baskets of dried flowers. Some of the photographs sitting around had angels on the silver frames. He kind of liked that and wondered if he should worry about himself.

"I've got some good stuff," the little girl said as she pushed a miniature shopping cart made of orange plastic into the living room. She sat on the couch, then patted the cushion next to her.

Feeling even more out of place, he sat next to Georgeanne's little girl. He looked into her face and tried to determine how old she was, but he wasn't any good at guessing a kid's age. Her makeup job didn't help any.

"Here," she said, plucking a T-shirt with a dalmatian on the front from her basket and handing it to him.

"What's this for?"

"You have to sign it."

"I do?" he asked, feeling huge next to the little girl.

She nodded and gave him a green marker.

John really didn't want to sign the kid's shirt. "Your mom might get mad."

"Nuh-uh. That's my Saturday shirt."

"Are you sure?"

"Yep."

"Okay." He shrugged and took the cap from the marker. "What's your name?"

Her brows lowered over her dark blue eyes, and she looked at him as if he were a few sandwiches short of a picnic. "Lexie." Then she pronounced it again just in case he didn't get it the first time. "Leexxiiiie. Lexie Mae Howard."

*Howard?* Georgeanne hadn't married the child's father. He wondered what kind of man she'd been involved with. What kind of man abandoned his daughter? He flipped the shirt over as if he were planning to write on the back. "Why do you want me to ruin your perfectly good shirt, Lexie Mae Howard?"

"'Cause the other kids got stuff that you wrote on and I don't."

He wasn't sure what she meant, but he thought he'd better ask Georgeanne before he marked up her daughter's shirt.

"Brett Thomas has lots of stuff. He showed me in school last year." She sighed heavily and her shoulders drooped. "He gots a cat too. Do you have a cat?"

"Ahh . . . no. No cat."

"Mae gots a cat," she confided as if he knew Mae. "His name is Bootsie 'cause he gots white boots on his feet. He hides from me when I go to Mae's. I used to think he didn't like me, but Mae says he runs away 'cause he's shy." She grasped the end of her boa, held it up for him to see, then shook it. "This is how I get him, though. He chases it and I grab him real tight."

If John hadn't known before that this little girl was Georgeanne's daughter, the more he listened to her talk, the more obvious it became. She talked quickly about wanting a cat. Then the subject moved to dogs and somehow progressed to mosquito bites. While she talked, John studied her. He thought she must resemble her father because he didn't think she looked all that much like Georgeanne. Maybe their mouths were similar, but not much else.

"Lexie," he interrupted her as it occurred to him that he might be talking to Virgil Duffy's daughter. He never figured Virgil for the type of man to abandon his child. Then again, Virgil could be a real jerk. "How old are you?"

"Six. I had my birthday a few months ago. My friends came over and we had cake. I got the movie

*Babe* from Amy and so we watched it. I cried when Babe was taken from his mommy. That was really really sad, and I got sick. But my mommy said he got to go visit on weekends, so I felt better. I want a pig, but my mommy says I can't have one. I like that part when Babe bites the sheep," she said, and then began to laugh.

Six, but he'd last seen Georgeanne seven years ago. Lexie couldn't be Virgil's child. Then he realized that he'd forgotten the nine months she would have been pregnant, plus if Lexie had just had her birthday a few months ago, she might very well be Virgil's child. But she didn't look anything like Virgil. He looked at her more closely. Her laughter turned to a big smile, and a dimple dented her right cheek. "I'm a sucker for that little pig's face." She shook her head and began to giggle again.

In another part of the house, the water shut off, and John's heart stopped beating in his chest. He swallowed hard. "Holy shit," he whispered.

Lexie's laughter stopped on a scandalized breath. "That's a bad word."

"Sorry," he muttered, and looked beneath the makeup. Her long lashes curled up at the very end. As a boy, John had been relentlessly teased about lashes like that. Then he stared into her dark blue eyes. Eyes like his. An unexplainable current ran though him and he felt as if he'd stuck his finger in an electrical outlet. Now he knew why Georgeanne had behaved so strangely last night. She'd had his child. A little girl.

*His daughter.*

"Holy shit."

# Seven

Georgeanne unwound the towel from around her head and tossed it on the end of her bed. She reached for her hairbrush sitting on the dresser, but her hand stilled before she grasped the round handle. From the living room, Lexie's childish giggles mixed with the unmistakable low pitch of a man's voice. Concern overrode modesty. She grabbed her green summer robe and shoved her arms through the sleeves. Lexie knew better than to let a stranger in the house. They'd had a nice long talk about it the last time Georgeanne had walked into the living room and found three Jehovah's Witnesses sitting on her couch.

She tied the belt around her waist and hurried down the narrow hall. The scolding she planned to unleash died on her tongue, and she stopped in her tracks. The man sitting on the couch next to her daughter hadn't come to offer heavenly salvation.

He raised his gaze to hers, and she looked into the dreamy blue eyes of her worst nightmare from hell.

She opened her mouth, but she couldn't talk past the shock clogging her throat. Within a split second, her world stopped, shifted beneath her feet, then went spinning out of control.

"Mr. Wall came to sign my stuff," Lexie said.

Time stood still as Georgeanne stared into blue eyes staring back at her. She felt disoriented and unable to fully comprehend that John Kowalsky was actually sitting in her living room looking as big and handsome as he had seven years ago, as he had in all the magazine pictures she'd ever seen of him, as he had last night. He sat in her house, on her couch, next to her daughter. She placed a hand on her bare throat and took a deep breath. Beneath her fingers she felt the rapid beating of her pulse. He looked out of place in her home, like he didn't belong. Which, of course, he didn't. "Alexandra Mae," she finally managed on a rush of air, and shifted her gaze to her daughter. "You know better than to let a stranger in the house."

Lexie's eyes widened. Georgeanne's use of her proper name let her know she was in very deep trouble. "But—but," she stuttered as she hopped to her feet. "But, Mommy, I know Mr. Wall. He came to my school, but I didn't get nothin'."

Georgeanne didn't have a clue what her daughter meant. She looked back at John and asked, "What are you doing here?"

He slowly rose, then reached into the back pocket of his faded Levi's. "You dropped this last night," he answered as he tossed her checkbook to her.

Before she could catch it, it bounced off her chest and hit the floor. Rather than bend down and pick it up, she left it lying there. "You didn't have to bring it by." A small measure of relief soothed her nerves. He'd come to bring her checkbook, not because he'd found out about Lexie.

"You're right," was all he said. His masculine presence filled the feminine room, and she suddenly became very aware of her nakedness beneath the cotton robe. She glanced down and was relieved to discover that she was fully covered.

"Well, thank you," she said as she walked toward the entryway. "Lexie and I were just getting ready to leave, and I'm sure you have important places to go yourself." She reached for the brass knob and opened the door. "Good-bye, John."

"Not yet." His eyes narrowed, accentuating the small scar running through his left brow. "Not until we talk."

"About what?"

"Oh, I don't know." He shifted his weight to one foot and tilted his head to one side. "Maybe we can have that conversation we should have had seven years ago."

She eyed him warily. "I don't know what you're talking about."

He looked at Lexie, who stood in the middle of the room switching her interest from one adult to the other. "You know exactly *who* I'm talking about," he countered.

For several long seconds they stared at each other. Two combatants bracing for confrontation. Georgeanne didn't relish the thought of being alone with John, but whatever was said between them, she was sure it was best if Lexie didn't hear. When she spoke, she turned her attention to her daughter. "Run across the street and see if Amy can play."

"But, Mommy. I can't play with Amy for a week 'cause we cut the hair off my Birthday Surprise Barbie, remember?"

"I've changed my mind."

The bottoms of Lexie's pink cowboy boots dragged across the peach carpet as she moved toward the door. "I think Amy gots a cold," she said.

Georgeanne, who normally kept her daughter as far away from germs as possible, recognized Lexie's ploy for what it was: a blatant attempt to stay and eavesdrop on adult conversation. "It's okay this one time."

When Lexie reached the entryway she looked over her shoulder at John. "'Bye, Mr. Wall."

John stared at her for several drawn-out moments before a slight smile curved his mouth. "See ya, kid."

Lexie turned her attention to her mother and, out of habit, puckered her lips.

Georgeanne kissed her and came away with the taste of Cherry Lip Smackers. "Come home in about an hour, okay?"

Lexie nodded, then walked through the door and down the two front steps. One end of her green boa dragged behind her as she strolled down the sidewalk. At the curb, she stopped, looked both ways, then dashed across the street. Georgeanne stood in the doorway and watched until Lexie entered the neighbor's house. For a few precious seconds she avoided the confrontation ahead of her, then she took a deep breath, stepped back, and closed the door.

"Why didn't you ever tell me about her?"

He couldn't know. Not for certain. "Tell you what?"

"Don't jerk me around, Georgeanne," he warned, his scowl as stormy as a funnel cloud. "Why didn't you tell me about Lexie a long time ago?"

She could deny it, of course. She could lie and tell him that Lexie wasn't his child. He might believe her and leave them alone. But the stubborn set of his jaw, and the fire in his eyes, told her he wouldn't believe her. Leaning back against the wall behind her, she folded her arms beneath her breasts. "Why would I?" she asked, unwilling to just come right out and admit everything up front.

He pointed a finger at the house across the street. "That little girl is mine," he said. "Don't deny it. Don't force me to prove paternity because I will."

A paternity test would only confirm his claim.

Georgeanne didn't see any point in denying anything. The best she could hope for was to answer his questions and get him out of her house and, hopefully, her life. "What do you want?"

"Tell me the truth. I want to hear you say it."

"Fine." She shrugged, trying to appear composed, as if her admission cost her nothing. "Lexie is your biological child."

He closed his eyes and took a deep breath. "Jesus," he whispered. "How?"

"The usual way," she answered dryly. "I would have thought that a man of your experience would know how babies are made."

His gaze snapped to hers. "You told me you were on birth control."

"I was." *Only apparently not long enough.* "Nothing is one hundred percent."

"Why, Georgeanne?"

"Why what?"

"Why didn't you tell me seven years ago?"

She shrugged again. "It was none of your business."

"What?" he asked, incredulous, staring at her as if he couldn't quite believe what she'd just said to him. "None of my business?"

"No."

His hands fisted at his sides and he took several steps toward her. "You have *my* child, and yet you don't think it's *my* business?" He stopped less than a foot in front of her and frowned down into her face.

Even though he was a lot bigger than she was, she looked up at him unafraid. "Seven years ago I made a decision I thought was best. I still think so. And anyway, there is nothing that can be done about it now."

One dark brow lifted up his forehead. "Really?"

"Yes. It's too late. Lexie doesn't know you. It's best if you just leave and never see her again."

He planted both of his palms on the wall beside her

head. "If you believe that's going to happen, then you're not a very bright girl."

She might not be afraid of John, but being so close to him was very intimidating. His wide chest and thick arms made her feel as if she were completely surrounded by testosterone and hard muscles. The smell of soap on his skin and the hint of aftershave clogged her senses. "I'm not a girl," she said, lowering her arms to her sides. "Seven years ago I may have been very immature, but that isn't the case any longer. I've changed."

His eyes lowered deliberately, and his grin wasn't very nice when he said, "From what I can see, you haven't changed all that much. You still look like a real good time."

Georgeanne fought the urge to deck him. She glanced down at herself and felt heat rush up her throat to her cheeks. The edges of her big green robe lay open to the belted waist, exposing an embarrassing amount of cleavage and the entire top of her right breast. Horrified, she quickly grabbed the edges and closed the robe.

"Leave it," John advised. "Seeing you like that just might put me in a more forgiving mood."

"I don't want your forgiveness," she said as she ducked beneath his arm. "I'm getting dressed. I think you should leave."

"I'll be right here," John promised as he turned and watched her hurry down the hall. His gaze narrowed as he noticed the sway of her hips and the bottom of her robe flutter around her bare ankles. He wanted to kill her.

Moving across the living room, he pushed aside a prissy lace curtain and stared out the front window. He had a child. A daughter he didn't know and who didn't know him. Until the moment Georgeanne had confirmed his suspicions, he hadn't been completely certain Lexie was his. Now he knew, and the thought of it burned a hole in his chest.

*His daughter.* He fought a strong urge to march across the street and bring Lexie back. He wanted to just sit and look at her. He wanted to watch her and listen to her little voice. He wanted to touch her, but he knew he wouldn't. Earlier, he'd felt big and awkward sitting next to her, a big man who sent vulcanized rubber pucks hurling across the ice at ninety-six miles an hour and who used his body as a human steamroller.

*His daughter.* He had a child. His child. He felt his anger swell, and he pushed it back behind the rigid control he kept on his temper.

John turned and walked to the brick fireplace. Spread across the mantel was a series of photographs in a variety of frames. In the first, a baby girl sat on a stool with the bottom edge of her T-shirt tucked beneath her chin while she found her belly button with her chubby index finger. He studied the picture, then turned his attention to the other photos illustrating various stages of Lexie's life.

Fascinated by the likeness of his little girl, he reached for a small picture of a toddler with big blue eyes and pink chubby cheeks. Her dark hair stood straight up on the top of her head like a feather duster, and her little lips were pursed as if she were about to give the photographer a kiss.

A door down the hall opened and closed. He slipped the thin-framed photograph into his pocket, then turned and waited for Georgeanne to appear. When she entered the room, he noticed that she'd pulled her hair back into a slick ponytail and had dressed in a white summer sweater. A gauzy skirt hung down to her ankles and clung to her long legs. She wore little white sandals with straps that crisscrossed up her calves. Her toenails were painted a dark purple.

"Would you care for some iced tea?" she asked as she came to stand in the middle of the room.

Under the circumstances, her hospitality surprised him. "No. No iced tea," he said, lifting his gaze to her face. He had a lot of questions he needed answered.

"Why don't you have a seat," she offered, and swept her hand toward a white wicker chair covered in fluffy, frilly cushions.

"I'd rather stand."

"Well, I'd rather not have to look up at you. Either we sit down and discuss this, or we don't discuss it at all."

She was ballsy. John didn't remember that about her. The Georgeanne he remembered was a chatty tease. "Fine," he said, and sat on the couch rather than the chair he didn't trust to hold him. "What have you told Lexie about me?"

She took the wicker chair. "Why, nothing," she drawled with her Texas accent not quite as heavy as he remembered.

"She has never asked about her father?"

"Oh, that." Georgeanne sat back on the floral cushions and crossed one leg over the other. "She thinks you died when she was a baby."

John was irritated by her answer, but he wasn't surprised. "Really? How did I die?"

"Your F-16 was shot down over Iraq."

"During the Gulf War?"

"Yes." She smiled. "You were a very brave soldier. When Uncle Sam called for the finest fighter pilots, he phoned you first."

"I'm Canadian."

She shrugged. "Anthony was a Texan."

"Anthony? Who the hell is Anthony?"

"You are. I made you up. I've always liked the name Tony for a man."

Not only had she lied about his auspicious demise and his occupation, but she'd changed his name as well. John felt this temper flare, and he leaned forward and placed his forearms on his knees. "What about pictures of this nonexistent man? Has Lexie asked to see pictures?"

"Of course. But all the pictures of you were burned up in a house fire."

"How unfortunate." He frowned.

Her smile brightened. "Isn't it, though?"

Seeing her smile tugged at his anger. "What happens when she finds out that your maiden name is Howard? She'll know you lied."

"By then she'll probably be in her teens. I'll confess that Tony and I were never actually married, although we were very much in love."

"You have it all worked out then."

"Yes."

"Why all the lies? Did you think I wouldn't help you?"

Georgeanne looked in his eyes for a few moments before she said, "Frankly, John, I didn't think you would want to know or that you would care. I didn't know you and you didn't know me. But you did make your feelings for me abundantly clear the morning you dumped me at the airport without a backward glance."

John didn't quite remember things that way. "I bought you a ticket home."

"You didn't bother to ask me if I wanted to go home."

"I did you a favor."

"You did yourself a favor." Georgeanne looked down at her lap and gathered the gauzy material between her fingers. So much time had passed that remembering that day shouldn't have had the power to hurt, but it did. "You couldn't get rid of me fast enough. We had sex that one night and then—"

"We had a lot of sex that one night," he interrupted. "A lot of down-and-dirty, no-holds-barred, hot, sweaty sex."

Georgeanne's fingers stilled and she glanced up him. For the first time she noticed the fire in his eyes. He was angry and trying his best to antagonize her. Georgeanne couldn't allow herself to be baited, not when she needed to remain calm and keep her head clear. "If you say so."

"I know so, and so do you." He leaned forward a little and said slowly, "Then because I didn't declare undying love the next morning, you kept my child from me. You got back at me real good, didn't you?"

"My decision had nothing to do with retaliation." Georgeanne thought back on the day she'd realized that she was pregnant. After she'd recovered from the shock and fear, she'd felt blessed. She'd felt as if she'd been given a gift. Lexie was the only family that Georgeanne had, and she wasn't willing to share her daughter. Not even with John. Especially not John. "Lexie is mine."

"You weren't alone in my bed that night, Georgeanne," John said as he stood. "If you think I'm going to walk away now that I've found out about her, then you're crazy."

Georgeanne rose also. "I expect you to leave and forget about us."

"You're dreaming. Either we come to an agreement we both can live with, or I'll have my lawyer contact you."

He was bluffing. He had to be. John Kowalsky was a sports figure. A hockey star. "I don't believe you. I don't think you really want people to know about

Lexie. That kind of publicity could potentially harm your image."

"You're wrong. I don't give a good goddamn about publicity," he said as he came to stand very close to her. "I'm not exactly a poster boy for the Moral Majority, so I doubt one little girl could do any damage to my less-than-clean image." He pulled his wallet out of his back pocket. "I'm leaving town tomorrow afternoon, but I'll be back by Wednesday." He pulled out a business card. "Call the bottom number on the card. I never answer the phone, even if I'm at home. My answering machine will pick up, so leave a message, and I'll get right back to you. I'm also giving you my address," he said as he wrote on the back, then he took her hand in his and placed the pen and business card in her palm. "If you don't want to call me, write. Either way, if I don't hear from you by Thursday, one of my lawyers will contact you Friday."

Georgeanne stared down at the card in her hand. His name had been printed in bold black letters. Beneath his name three different telephone numbers were listed. On the back of the card, he'd written his address. "Forget about Lexie. I won't share her with you."

"Call by Thursday," he warned, and then he was gone.

John shifted his forest green Range Rover into high gear and merged onto the 405. Wind from the open window ruffled the sides of his hair but did little to cool his chaotic mind. He flexed the cramps from his fingers, then eased his grip on the steering wheel.

Lexie. His daughter. A little six-year-old who wore more makeup than Tammy Faye Bakker and who wanted a cat, a dog, and pig. He lifted his right hip and reached into his back pocket. Retrieving the picture of Lexie he'd stolen, he propped it on the dashboard. Her big blue eyes stared back at him above her puckered pink lips. He thought of the kiss she'd given her mother, then he returned his gaze to the road.

Whenever he'd thought of having a child, he'd thought of a boy. He didn't know why. Maybe because of Toby, the son he'd lost, but he'd always pictured himself the father of a rowdy boy. He'd imagined junior league hockey games, cap pistols, and Tonka trucks. He'd always envisioned dirty fingernails, holey jeans, and scabby knees.

What did he know of little girls? What did little girls do?

He stole another glance at the photograph as he drove the Range Rover across the 520. Little girls wore green boas and pink cowboy boots and cut the hair off their Barbies. A little girl chattered and giggled and kissed her mother good-bye with sweetly pursed lips.

*Her mother.* At the thought of Georgeanne, John's hands tightened on the steering wheel once more. She'd kept his child a secret from him. All of those years of wanting, of watching other men with their children, and the whole time he had a daughter.

He'd missed so much. He'd missed her birth, her first steps, and her first words. She was a part of him. The same genes and chromosomes that made him were a part of her. She was a part of his family, and he'd had a right to know about her. Yet Georgeanne had decided that he hadn't needed to know, and he could not separate the bitterness of that deed from the person responsible. Georgeanne had made the decision to keep his child's existence from him, and he knew that he could never forgive her. For the first time in several years, he craved a bottle of Crown Royal, one shot glass, no ice to pollute the smooth whiskey. He blamed Georgeanne for the craving, because almost as much as he hated what she'd done, he hated what she made him feel.

How could he want to place his hands around her throat and squeeze, yet at the same time want to slip his hands lower and fill his palms with her breasts? Harsh laughter rumbled within his chest. When he'd had her against the wall, he was surprised that she hadn't noticed his physical reaction. A reaction he'd been unable to control.

Where Georgeanne was concerned, he obviously had no control over his body. Seven years ago he hadn't *wanted* to want her. She'd spelled trouble for him the minute she'd jumped into his car, but what he'd wanted hadn't seemed to matter all that much, because right or wrong, good or bad, he'd been overwhelmingly attracted to her. From the tilt of her seductive green eyes and cover-girl lips, to the lure of her centerfold body, he had responded to her regardless of the situation.

Apparently that old saying about some things never changing was true, because he wanted her again, and it didn't seem to make a whole hell of a lot of difference that she'd kept his daughter from him. He didn't even like Georgeanne, but he wanted her. He wanted to touch her all over. Which he figured made him one sick bastard.

As he drove around the south end of Lake Union toward the western shore, he endeavored to push the memory of Georgeanne in her light green robe from his mind. He stole glances at the picture of Lexie propped up on the dashboard, and once he'd pulled the Range Rover into his parking spot, he grabbed the photograph and headed to the end of the dock where his nineteen-hundred-square-foot, two-story houseboat was moored.

Two years ago he'd bought the fifty-year-old houseboat and had hired a Seattle architect and an interior designer to redesign it from the floats up. When the job was finished, he owned a three-bedroom floating home with a gabled roof, several balconies, and wrap-around windows. Until two hours ago, the houseboat had fit him perfectly. Now, as he shoved his key in the heavy wood door and pushed it open, he wasn't so sure that it was the right place for a child.

*Lexie is mine. I expect you to leave and forget about us.* Georgeanne's words echoed in his head, prodding his resentment and stirring the anger he held deep in his gut.

The soles of John's loafers squeaked on the newly polished hardwood floor of the entry, then fell silent as he walked across plush rugs. He set the photograph of Lexie on an oak coffee table, which, like the floors, had been polished the day before by the cleaning service he employed. One of the three telephones sitting on a desk in the dining room rang and, after three rings, was picked up by one of three answering machines. John stilled, but when he heard his agent's voice reminding him of his flight schedule for the following day, he turned his attention once again to the events of the past two hours. He moved toward a set of French doors and gazed out at the deck beyond.

*Forget about Lexie.* Now that he knew about his daughter, there wasn't a chance that he'd forget. *I won't share her with you.* John's eyes narrowed on a pair of kayakers paddling across the lake's smooth surface, then suddenly he turned and moved into the dining room. He reached for one of the telephones sitting on the mahogany desk and dialed the home telephone number of his lawyer, Richard Goldman. Once he had Richard on the phone, he explained the situation.

"Are you sure the child is yours?" his attorney asked.

"Yeah." He glanced into the living room at the photograph of Lexie sitting on the coffee table. He'd told Georgeanne that he'd wait until Friday to contact an attorney, but he didn't see any point in waiting. "Yeah, I'm sure."

"This is a pretty big shock."

He had to know where he stood legally. "Tell me about it."

"And you don't think she's willing to let you see the girl again?"

"Nope. She was real clear about that." John picked up a rock paperweight, tossed it in the air, then caught it in his palm. "I don't want to take my daughter away from her mother. I don't want to hurt Lexie, but I want to see her. I want to get to know her, and I want her to know me."

There was a long pause before Richard said, "I specialize in business law, John. The only thing I can do is give you the name of a good family attorney."

"That's why I called you. I want someone good."

"Then you want Kirk Schwartz. He specializes in child custody, and he's good. Real good."

"Mommy, Amy gots a Pizza Hut Skipper just like mine, and we played like both our Skippers work at the Pizza Hut, and we fight over Todd."

"Hmm." Georgeanne turned the handle of her Francis I fork, wrapping spaghetti around the tines. She twirled the pasta around and around as she stared at the narrow basket of French bread in the center of the table. Like a survivor of a bloody battle, she was exhausted, yet restless at the same time.

"And we made clothes for our Skippers out of Kleenex, and mine was a princess, so I drove in the empty box like it was a car. But I wouldn't let Todd drive 'cause he gots a ticket and likes Amy's Skipper more than mine."

"Hmm." Again and again Georgeanne replayed what had happened that morning. She tried to remember what John had said and the way he'd said it. She tried to recall her response, but she couldn't remember everything. She was tired, and confused, and afraid.

"Barbie was our mom and Ken was our dad and we went to Fun Forest and had a picnic by where the big fountain is. And I had magic shoes and could fly up higher than that one big building. I flew to the roof—"

Seven years ago she'd made the right decision. She was sure she had.

"—but Ken got drunk and Barbie had to drive him home."

Georgeanne looked up at her daughter as Lexie sucked a saucy noodle between her lips. Her face was clean of cosmetics and her dark blue eyes shined with the excitement of her story. "What? What are you talking about?" Georgeanne asked.

Lexie licked the corners of her mouth, then swallowed. "Amy says her daddy drinks beer at the Seahawks and that her mommy gots to drive him home. He needs a ticket," Lexie announced before she twirled more spaghetti with her fork. "Amy says that he walks around in his underwear and scratches his bum."

Georgeanne frowned. "So do you," she reminded her daughter.

"Yeah, but he's big and I'm just a little kid." Lexie shrugged and took a bite of pasta. One noodle slipped down her chin, and she pulled in her cheeks and sucked it between her lips.

"Have you been asking Amy about her daddy lately?" Georgeanne inquired cautiously. From time to time Lexie asked questions about daddies and daughters, and Georgeanne would try to answer. But since Georgeanne had been raised almost solely by her grandmother, she didn't really have the answers.

"No," Lexie replied around a mouthful of food. "She just tells me stuff."

"Please don't talk with your mouth full."

Lexie's eyes narrowed; she reached for her milk and raised it to her lips. After she'd set her glass back on the table she said, "Well, don't ask me questions when I'm chewin'."

"Oh, sorry." Georgeanne laid her fork on the plate and placed her hands on the beige linen tablecloth. Her thoughts returned to John. She hadn't lied to him about the reason she'd kept Lexie's birth from him. She really hadn't thought he'd want to know or that he would have cared. But whether he would have cared or not hadn't been her main motivation. Her primary reason had been much more selfish. Seven years ago she'd been alone and lonely. Then she'd had Lexie and suddenly she wasn't alone any longer. Lexie filled the hollow places in Georgeanne's heart. She had a daughter who loved her unconditionally. Georgeanne wanted to keep that love all for herself. She was selfish and greedy, but she didn't care. She was both mommy and daddy. She was enough. "We haven't had a pink tea for a while. I'm working at home tomorrow. Do you want to have a tea?"

Lexie's smile lifted the milk mustache at the corners of her mouth, and she nodded vigorously, flipping her ponytail up and down.

Georgeanne returned her daughter's smile as she brushed at crumbs with her little finger. Seven years ago she'd pointed her flimsy mule shoes toward the future, and she rarely looked back. She'd done pretty well for herself and Lexie. She co-owned a successful business, paid mortgage on her own home, and just last month she'd bought a new car. Lexie was healthy and happy. She didn't need a daddy. She didn't need John.

"When you're finished, go see if your pink chiffon dress still fits you," Georgeanne said as she picked up her plate and carried it to the sink. She'd never known her daddy and she'd survived. She'd never known what it was like to curl up on her father's lap and hear his heart beating beneath her ear. She'd never known the security of her daddy's arms or the reassuring timbre of his voice. She'd never known and she'd done just fine.

Georgeanne looked out the window above the sink and stared into the backyard. She'd never known, but many times she'd tried to imagine.

She remembered peeking through fences to watch the neighbors barbecue chicken on burn barrels cut lengthwise. She remembered riding her blue Schwinn with the silver banana seat down to Jack Leonard's gas station to watch him change tires, fascinated by the big, filthy hands he always wiped on a greasy towel hanging from the back pocket of his dirty gray coveralls. She remembered the nights she'd sit on the hard, age-pocked porch at her grandmother's house, a confused and curious little girl with a dark ponytail and red cowboy boots, watching the men in her neighborhood return from work and wishing she had a daddy, too. She had watched and waited and the whole time wondered. She had wondered what daddies did when they came home. She had wondered because she hadn't known.

The sound of Lexie's bootheels on the kitchen linoleum pulled Georgeanne from her memories. "All finished?" she asked as she turned to take the dirty plate and empty glass from Lexie's hands.

"Yep. Tomorrow can I serve the petit fours?"

"Yes, you may," Georgeanne answered as she placed the plate and glass in the sink. "And I think you're old enough to pour the tea now."

"All right!" Lexie clapped her hands with excitement, then wrapped her thin arms around Georgeanne's thighs. "I love you," she gushed.

"I love you, too." Georgeanne looked down at the top of her daughter's head and placed her palm on

Lexie's back. Her grandmother had loved her, but her love hadn't been enough to fill the empty places inside. No one had been able to fill the holes in her soul until Lexie.

Georgeanne rubbed her hand up and down Lexie's spine. She was very proud of all she'd accomplished. She'd learned to live with the disability of dyslexia rather than hide from it. She'd worked hard to improve herself, and everything she had, everything she'd become, she'd done on her own. She was happy.

Still, she wanted more for her daughter. She wanted better.

# Eight

Muscle and bone and gritty determination collided, hockey sticks slapped the ice, and the roar of thousands of frenzied fans filled John's living room. On the big-screen television, the "Russian Rocket," Pavel Bure, high-sticked Ranger defenseman Jay Wells in the face, dropping the bigger New York player to the ice.

"Damn, you've got to admire a guy Bure's size mixing it up with Wells." A smile of admiration tilted John's lips as he cast a glance at his three guests: Hugh "The Caveman" Miner, Dmitri "Tree" Ulanov, and Claude "The Undertaker" Dupre.

His three teammates had originally dropped by John's houseboat to watch the Dodgers play the Atlanta Braves on his huge television. The game had lasted two innings before they'd shaken their collective heads as if to say, "And they make more money than I do for that!" and had slipped a tape of the 1994 Stanley Cup Championships into the VCR.

"Have you seen Bure's ears?" Hugh asked. "He's got great big goddamn ears."

As blood ran from Jay Wells's broken nose, Pavel,

with his shoulders slumped, skated from the rink, ejected on a game misconduct.

"And girly curls," added Claude in his soft French-Canadian accent. "But not as bad as Jagr. He's a sissy."

Dmitri tore his eyes from the television screen as his fellow countryman, Pavel Bure, was escorted to the locker room. "Jaromir Jagr iz sissy?" he asked, referring to the Pittsburgh Penguin's star winger.

Hugh shook his head with a grin, then paused and looked at John. "What do you think, Wall?"

"Nah, Jagr hits too hard to be a sissy," he answered with a shrug. "He's no pansy-ass."

"Yeah, but he does wear all those gold chains around his neck," argued Hugh, who was famous for talking trash just to get a reaction. "Either Jagr is a sissy-man or a fan of Mr. T."

Dmitri bristled and pointed to the three gold necklaces around his neck. "Chains does not mean sissy."

"Who's Mr. T?" Claude wanted to know.

"Didn't you ever watch *The A-Team* on television? Mr. T is the big black dude with the Mohawk and all the gold jewelry," Hugh explained. "He and George Peppard worked for the government and blew up stuff."

"Chains does not mean sissy," Dmitri insisted.

"Maybe not," Hugh conceded. "But I know for a fact that wearing a lot of chains has something to do with the size of a guy's dick."

"Bullsheet," Dmitri scoffed.

John chuckled and stretched his arm along the back of the beige leather couch. "How do you know, Hugh? Have you been peeking?"

Hugh rose to his feet and pointed an empty Coke can at John. His eyes narrowed and a smile curved his mouth. John knew that look. He'd seen it hundreds of times just before "The Caveman" went for the kill and verbally kicked the guts out of any opposing player who dared to skate too close to the goalie crease. "I've showered with guys all my life, and I don't have to peek to know that the guys who are weighed down with gold are compensating for lack of dick."

Claude laughed and Dmitri shook his head. "Not true," he said.

"Yes it is, Tree," Hugh assured him as he walked toward the kitchen. "In Russia lots of gold chains might mean you're a real stud, but you're in America now and you can't just walk around advertising something like a small dick. You have to learn our ways if you're not going to embarrass yourself."

"Or if you want to date American women," John added.

The doorbell rang as Hugh passed the entry. "Do you want me to get that?" he asked.

"Sure. It's probably Heisler," John answered, referring to the Chinooks' newest forward. "He said he might drop by."

"John." Dmitri got John's attention and scooted to the edge of the leather chair in which he sat. "Iz true? American woman think chains mean no deek?"

John fought to hold back his laughter. "Yes, Tree. It's true. Have you been having trouble finding dates?"

Dmitri looked perplexed and scooted back into his chair again.

Losing the fight, John burst into laughter. He glanced at Claude, who found Dmitri's confusion hilarious.

"Ahh, Wall. It's not Heisler."

John glanced over his shoulder, and his laughter died instantly when he saw Georgeanne standing in the entry to his living room.

"If I'm interrupting y'all, I could come back another time." Her gaze darted from one male face to the next, and she took several steps backward toward the door.

"No." John quickly jumped to his feet, shocked by her sudden appearance. He reached for the remote control on the coffee table, then cut the power to the television. "No. Don't go," he said as he tossed the remote on the couch.

"I can see that you're busy and I should have called." She glanced at Hugh, who stood beside her, then she looked back at John. "I did call actually, but you didn't pick up. Then I remembered that you said you never answer your phone, so I took the chance and drove here, and . . . well, what I wanted to say was . . ." Her hand fluttered at her side and she took a deep breath. "I know that arriving uninvited is incredibly rude, but may I have a few moments of your time?"

She was obviously rattled at finding herself the object of four big hockey players' interest. John almost felt sorry for Georgeanne. Almost. But he couldn't forget what she'd done. "No problem," he said as he rounded the couch and walked toward her. "We can go upstairs to the loft or outside on the deck."

Once again Georgeanne looked at the other men in the room. "I think the deck would be best."

"Fine." John motioned to a pair of French doors across the room. "After you," he said, and as she walked past, he let his gaze take a slow journey down her body. Her sleeveless red dress buttoned around her throat, exposed her smooth shoulders, and hugged her breasts. The dress brushed her knees, and wasn't especially tight, or revealing. But she still managed to look like his favorite selection of sins all wrapped up in one convenient snack pack. Annoyed that he should notice her appearance at all, he shifted his gaze from the big, soft curls touching her shoulders to Hugh. The goalie stared at Georgeanne as if he knew her but just couldn't recall when they'd met. Even though Hugh sometimes played as if he were dense, he wasn't, and it wouldn't take long before he remembered her as Virgil Duffy's runaway bride. Claude and Dmitri hadn't played for the Chinooks seven years ago and hadn't been at the wedding, but they'd probably heard the story.

John moved to the doors and opened one side for Georgeanne. When she walked outside, he turned back to the room. "Make yourselves at home," he told his teammates.

Claude stared after Georgeanne with a smile twisting one corner of his mouth. "Take your time," he said.

Dmitri didn't say anything; he didn't have to. The conspicuous absence of his gold chains spoke louder than the dopey look on his young Russian face.

"I shouldn't be long," John said through a frown, then stepped outside and shut the door behind him. A slight breeze ruffled the blue and green whale banner hanging from the rear balcony while waves softly slapped the side of John's twenty-three-foot runabout tied to the deck. The bright evening sun shimmered on the ripples cut from a sailboat slicing peacefully through the water. The people on the boat called to John, and he waved automatically, but his attention was focused on the woman who stood near the water's edge with one hand raised to her brow, gazing out onto the lake.

"Is that Gas Works Park?" she asked, and pointed across to the other shore.

Georgeanne was beautiful and seductive and so malicious that he had visions of tossing her into the water. "Did you come to see my view of the lake?"

She dropped her hand and looked over her shoulder. "No," she answered, then turned to face him. "I wanted to talk to you about Lexie."

"Sit down." He pointed to a pair of Adirondack chairs, and when she sat, he took the chair facing her.

With his feet spread wide, his hands on the armrests, he waited for her to begin.

"I really did try to call you." She glanced at him briefly, then slid her gaze to his chest. "But your answering machine picked up and I didn't want to leave a message. What I want to say is too important to leave on an answering machine, and I didn't want to wait until you returned from your trip to talk to you. So I took a chance that you might be home and I drove here." Again she glanced at him, then looked over his left shoulder. "I really am sorry if I'm interrupting something important."

At the moment John couldn't think of anything more important than what Georgeanne had to say to him. Because whether or not he would like what she had to say, it would have a big effect on his life. "You aren't interrupting anything."

"Good." She finally looked at him as a tiny smile flitted across her lips. "I don't suppose you would reconsider leaving Lexie and me alone?"

"No," he answered flatly.

"I didn't think so."

"Then why are you here?"

"Because I want what is best for my daughter."

"Then we want the same thing. Only I don't think we will agree on exactly what is best for Lexie."

Georgeanne looked down at her lap and took a deep breath. She felt jumpy and as nervous as a cat looking at a big Doberman pinscher. She hoped John hadn't noticed her anxiety. She needed to take command, not only of her emotions but of the situation as well. She couldn't allow John and his lawyers to control her life or dictate what was best for Lexie. She couldn't let things get that far. Georgeanne, not John, wanted to dictate terms. "You mentioned this morning that you planned to contact an attorney," she began, and moved her gaze up his gray Nike T-shirt, over his strong chin darkened by a five-o'clock shadow, and into his deep blue eyes. "I think we can come to a reasonable compromise without involving lawyers. A court battle would hurt Lexie, and I don't want that. I don't want lawyers involved."

"Then give me an alternative."

"Okay," Georgeanne said slowly. "I think Lexie should get to know you as a family friend."

One dark brow lifted up his forehead. "And?"

"And you can get to know her, too."

John looked at her for several long seconds before he asked, "That's it? That's your 'reasonable compromise'?"

Georgeanne didn't want to do this. She didn't want to say it, and she hated John for forcing her. "When Lexie knows you well, and is comfortable with you, and when I think the time is right, I'll tell her you are her father." *And my child will probably hate me for the lie,* she thought.

John tilted his head slightly to one side. He didn't look real happy with her proposition. "So," he said. "I'm supposed to wait until *you* think it's the right time to tell Lexie about me?"

"Yes."

"Tell me why I should wait, Georgie."

"No one calls me Georgie anymore." She didn't tease and flirt to get what she wanted these days. She wasn't Georgie Howard now. "I would prefer that you call me Georgeanne."

"I don't care what you prefer." He folded his arms across his wide chest. "Now, why don't you tell my why I should wait, *Georgeanne.*"

"This is bound to be a great shock to her, and I think it should be done as gently as possible. My daughter is only six, and I'm sure a custody battle would hurt and confuse her. I don't want my daughter hurt by a court—"

"First of all," John interrupted, "the little girl you keep referring to as *your* daughter is in fact just as much mine as she is yours. Second, don't make me out to be the bad guy here. I wouldn't have mentioned lawyers if you hadn't made it very clear to me that you weren't going to let me see Lexie again."

Georgeanne felt her resentment stir and took a deep breath. "Well, I've changed my mind." She couldn't afford a fight with him, not yet anyway. Not until she got a few concessions.

John sank farther down in his chair and hooked his thumbs in the front pockets of his jeans. His gaze narrowed and distrust pulled at the corners of his mouth.

"Don't you believe me?"

"Frankly, no."

On the drive over this evening, she'd run through several if-he-says-this-then-I'll-say-that scenarios in her mind, but she'd never thought he wouldn't believe her. "You don't trust me?"

He looked at her as if she were crazy. "Not for a second."

Georgeanne figured they were even then, because she didn't trust him either. "Fine. We don't have to trust each other as long as we both want what is best for Lexie."

"I don't want to hurt her, but as I said before, I don't think we will agree on what is best. I'm sure it would please you clear down to your southern toes if I died tomorrow. However, that wouldn't please me. I want to get to know Lexie, and I want her to know me. If you think I should wait to tell her that I'm her father, then okay, I'll wait. You know her better than I do."

"I have to be the one to tell her, John." She expected an argument and was surprised when she didn't get one.

"Fine."

"I have to insist that you give me your word on

this," she persisted, because she wasn't convinced that a few months down the road, John wouldn't change his mind and decide that being a daddy cramped his style. If he abandoned Lexie, after she knew he was her father, it would break her heart. And Georgeanne knew from experience that the pain of abandonment from a parent was worse than not knowing at all. "The truth has to come from me."

"I thought we didn't trust each other. What good is my word?"

He had a point. Georgeanne thought about it, and having no other alternative, she said, "I'll trust you if you give me your word."

"You have it, but just don't expect me to wait a long time. Don't jerk me around," he warned. "I want to see her when I get back into town."

"That's another reason I came here tonight," Georgeanne said as she rose from the chair. "Next Sunday Lexie and I are planning a picnic at Marymoor Park. You are welcome to join us if you don't have plans."

"What time?"

"Noon."

"What should I bring?"

"Lexie and I are providing everything except alcoholic beverages. If you want beer, you'll have to bring it yourself, although I'd prefer you didn't."

"That's not a problem," he said as he stood also.

Georgeanne looked up at him, always a little surprised by his height and the width of his shoulders. "I'm bringing a friend along, so you're welcome to include one of your friends also." Then she smiled sweetly and added, "Although I would prefer that your friend wasn't a hockey groupie."

John shifted his weight to one foot and scowled at her. "That's not a problem either."

"Great." She turned to go, but stopped and looked

back at him. "Oh, and we have to pretend to like each other."

He stared at her, his eyes narrowed, his mouth in a straight line. "Now, that," he said dryly, "might be a problem."

Georgeanne tucked the floral-print comforter around Lexie's shoulders and looked into her sleepy eyes. Lexie's dark hair fanned over her pillow, and her cheeks were pale from exhaustion. As a baby, she'd always reminded Georgeanne of a wind-up toy. One moment she'd be crawling across the floor, and in the next she'd lie down and fall asleep in the middle of the kitchen. Even now, when Lexie was tired, she went out fairly fast, which Georgeanne considered a blessing. "Tomorrow we'll have our tea after we watch *General Hospital*," she said. It had been over a week since they'd found the time to catch an episode of their favorite soap opera together.

"Okay," Lexie yawned.

"Give me some sugar," Georgeanne ordered, and when Lexie puckered her lips, she bent to kiss her daughter good night. "I'm a sucker for your pretty face," she said, then stood.

"Me, too. Is Mae coming to tea tomorrow?" Lexie wiggled onto her side and rubbed her face against the Muppet blanket she'd had since she'd been a baby.

"I'll ask her." Georgeanne walked across the floor, stepped over a Barbie camper and a pile of naked dolls. "Cryin' all night, this room's a pigsty," she declared as she tripped over a baton with purple streamers hanging from the ends. She glanced over her shoulder and saw Lexie's eyes were closed. She reached for the switch by the door, turned out the light, and headed down the hall.

Before Georgeanne entered the living room, she could feel Mae impatiently waiting for her. Earlier when Mae had come to sit with Lexie, Georgeanne had briefly explained the situation with John to her friend and business partner. And while they'd sat around waiting for Lexie's bedtime, Mae had seemed ready to burst with questions.

"Is she asleep?" Mae asked barely above a whisper as Georgeanne entered the room.

Georgeanne nodded and sat on the opposite end of the couch from Mae. She reached for a pillow embroidered with flowers and her monogram, then she dropped it on her lap.

"I've been thinking about it," Mae began as she turned to face Georgeanne. "And a lot of things make sense now."

"What things?" she asked, thinking that with Mae's new shorter haircut, she looked a little like Meg Ryan.

"Like how we both hate men who are athletes. You know that I hate jocks because they used to beat up my brother. And I always assumed you didn't like them because of your boobs," she said as she cupped her palms in front of her chest as if she were holding a pair of cantaloupes. "I always figured you must have been groped by the football team, or something equally hellish, and just never wanted to talk about it." She dropped her hands to her thighs, bare below her jean shorts. "I never imagined Lexie's father was a jock. But now that makes sense, too, because she's a lot more athletic than you."

"Yes, she is," Georgeanne agreed. "But that's not saying much."

"Remember when she was four and we took the training wheels off of her bike?"

"I didn't take them off, you did." Georgeanne looked into Mae's brown eyes and reminded her friend, "I wanted them left on in case she fell."

"I know, but they were all bent upward and didn't even touch the ground anyway. They wouldn't have helped her." Mae dismissed Georgeanne's concern with a wave of her hand. "I remember thinking then that Lexie must have inherited coordination from her daddy's gene pool, because she didn't get it from you."

"Hey, that's not nice," Georgeanne complained, but she really didn't take offense; it was the truth.

"But never in a million years would I have guessed John Kowalsky. My God, Georgeanne, the man is a hockey player!" She pronounced the last two word with the same horrified disdain usually reserved for serial killers or used-car salesmen.

"I know that."

"Have you ever seen him play?"

"No." She looked down at the pillow in her lap and frowned at a brown smudge on one corner. "Although occasionally I have seen sports clips on the evening news."

"Well, I've seen him play! Do you remember Don Rogers?"

"Of course," she said as she picked at the spot on the linen pillow. "You dated him for a few months last year, but you dumped him because you thought the amount of affection he afforded his Labrador was very peculiar." She paused and looked back up at Mae. "Did you let Lexie eat in the living room tonight? I believe there is chocolate on this pillow."

"Forget about the pillow," Mae sighed, and ran her fingers through the sides of her short blond hair. "Don was this incredible Chinooks fanatic, so I went to a game with him. I couldn't believe how hard those guys hit each other, and no one hit harder than John Kowalsky. He sent one guy somersaulting through the air. Then he just kind of shrugged and skated off."

Georgeanne wondered where this was going. "What does that have to do with me?"

"You slept with him! I can't believe it. Not only is he a jock, but he's a jerk!"

Secretly Georgeanne agreed, but she was becoming slightly ticked off. "It was a long time ago. And besides, being that you reside in a glass house, let's not throw stones at each other, shall we?"

"What's that supposed to mean?"

"It means that any woman who slept with Bruce Nelson has no right to judge anyone else."

Mae crossed her arms over her chest and sank back farther into the couch. "He wasn't that bad," she grumbled.

"Really? He was a wormy little mama's boy, and you only dated him because you could push him around—like all the guys you go out with."

"At least I have a normal sex life."

They'd had this same conversation many times. Mae considered Georgeanne's lack of sex unhealthy, while Georgeanne felt that Mae should practice saying the word "no" a bit more often.

"You know, Georgeanne, abstinence isn't normal, and one of these days you're just going to explode," she predicted. "And Bruce wasn't wormy, he was cute."

"Cute? He was thirty-eight years old and still lived at home with his mother. He reminded me of my third cousin Billy Earl down in San Antonio. Billy Earl lived with his mama until she took her final journey, and believe you me, he was as twisted as a piece of taffy. He used to steal reading glasses just in case he developed astigmatism. Which, of course, he never did, because all my people have perfect twenty-twenty vision. My grandmother used to say we should pray for him. We should pray he never developed a fear of cavities in his teeth or people with dentures wouldn't be safe around Billy Earl."

Mae Laughed. "You're full of it."

Georgeanne raised her right hand. "My lips to God's ear. Billy Earl was a nut ball." She looked back down at the pillow in her lap and ran her fingers over the white embroidered flowers. "Anyway, you obviously cared for Bruce or you wouldn't have slept with him. Sometimes our hearts do the choosing."

"Hey." Mae patted the back of the couch with her hand to get Georgeanne's attention. When she looked up, Mae said, "I didn't care for Bruce. I felt *sorry* for him, and I hadn't had sex in a while, which is a really bad reason to go to bed with a man. I wouldn't recommend it. If I sounded like I was judging you, I'm sorry. I didn't mean to, I swear."

"I know," Georgeanne said easily.

"Good. Now, tell me. How did you first meet John Kowalsky?"

"Do you want the whole story?"

"Yep."

"Okay. Do you remember when I first met you, I was wearing a little pink dress?"

"Yes. You were supposed to marry Virgil Duffy in that dress."

"That's right." Years ago Georgeanne had told Mae of her botched wedding plans to Virgil, but she'd left out the part about John. She told Mae now. She told her all of it. All except the private details. She'd never been a person to talk openly and freely about sex. Her grandmother had certainly never discussed it, and everything she'd learned, she'd learned from a health class at school, or from inept boyfriends who either hadn't known or hadn't cared about giving pleasure.

Then she'd met John, and he'd taught her things she hadn't thought were physically possible until that night. He'd set her ablaze with his hot hands and hungry mouth, and she'd touched him in ways she'd only heard whispered about. He'd made her want him so much, she'd done everything he'd suggested and then some.

Now she didn't even like to think of that night. She no longer recognized the young woman who'd given her body and her love so easily. That woman didn't exist anymore, and she didn't feel there was any reason to discuss her.

She skipped over the lurid details, then told Mae of the conversation she'd had with John that morning and of the agreement they'd reached at his houseboat. "I don't know how things are going to work out, I just pray Lexie doesn't get hurt," she concluded, suddenly feeling exhausted.

"Are you going to tell Charles?" Mae asked.

"I don't know," she answered as she hugged the pillow to her chest, leaned her head against the back of the couch, and stared up at the ceiling. "I've only been out with him twice."

"Are you going to see him again?"

Georgeanne thought of the man she'd dated for the past month. She'd met him when he'd hired Heron's to cater his daughter's tenth birthday. He'd called the next day and they'd met for dinner at The Four Seasons. Georgeanne smiled. "I hope so."

"Then you better tell him."

Charles Monroe was divorced and one of the nicest men Georgeanne had ever known. He owned a local cable station, was wealthy, and had a wonderful smile that lit up his gray eyes. He didn't dress flashy. He wasn't *GQ* gorgeous, and his kisses didn't set her eyebrows on fire. They were more like a warm breeze. Nice. Relaxing.

Charles never pushed or grabbed, and given more time, Georgeanne could see herself becoming involved in an intimate relationship with him. She liked him a lot, and just as important, Lexie had met him once, and she liked him, too. "I guess I'll tell him."

"I don't think he's going to like this news one bit," Mae predicted.

Georgeanne rolled her head to the left and looked at her friend. "Why?"

"Because even though I abhor violent men, John Kowalsky is a stud boy, and Charles is bound to be jealous. He might worry that there is still something between you and the hockey jock."

She figured that Charles might get upset with her because she'd told him her standard lie about Lexie's father, but she wasn't worried he'd be jealous. "Charles has nothing to worry about," she said with the certainty of a woman who knew for a fact that there wasn't even a remote possibility she would ever become romantically involved with John again. "And besides, even if I were so delusional as to fall for John, he hates me. He doesn't even like to look at me." The idea of a reunion between herself and John was so absurd that she didn't waste any brain power giving it a second thought. "I'll tell Charles when I have lunch with him on Thursday."

But four days later, when she met Charles at a bistro on Madison Street, she didn't get a chance to tell him anything. Before she could explain what had happened with John, Charles hit her with a proposal that left her speechless.

"What do you think about hosting your own live television show?" he asked over pastrami sandwiches and coleslaw. "A kind of Martha Stewart of the Northwest. We'd slip you into the Saturday twelve-thirty-to-one time slot. That's just after *Margie's Garage* and right before our afternoon sports programming. You'd have the freedom to do what you wanted. You could cook one show, and the next you could arrange dried flowers or retile a kitchen."

"I can't retile a kitchen," she whispered, shocked clear down to her beige pumps.

"I just threw that out as an idea. I trust you. You've got natural talent, and you'd look great on television."

Georgeanne placed a hand on her chest, and her voice squeaked when she said, "Me?"

"Yes, you. When I talked it over with my station manager, she thought it was a great idea." Charles gave her an encouraging smile, and she almost believed she could go in front of a television camera and host her own show. Charles's offer did appeal to the creative side of her, but reality interceded. Georgeanne was dyslexic. She'd learned to compensate, but if she wasn't careful, she still read the words wrong. If she was flustered, she still had to stop and think about which way was left and which was right. And then there was her weight. A camera was supposed to add five pounds to a person. Well, Georgeanne was already several pounds overweight, add five pounds to that, and not only would she appear on TV reading words that didn't exist, but she'd look fat. Plus there was Lexie to consider. Georgeanne already felt horrible for the amount of time her daughter spent in day care or with sitters.

She looked into Charles's gray eyes and said, "No, thank you."

"Aren't you going to think it over?"

"I have," she said as she picked up her fork and speared her coleslaw. She didn't want to think about it any longer. She didn't want to think of the possibilities or the opportunity she'd just turned down.

"Don't you want to know how much it pays?"

"Nope." The government would take half, and she'd be left looking like a fat idiot for half of what she was worth.

"Will you think about it a little longer?"

He seemed so disappointed that she said, "I'll think about it." But she knew she wouldn't change her mind.

After lunch he walked her to her car, and once they stood beside her maroon Hyundai, he took the key from her hand and fit it into the lock.

"When can I see you again?"

"This weekend is impossible," she said, feeling a little guilty that she'd never gotten around to mentioning John. "Why don't you and Amber come over next Tuesday night and have dinner with me and Lexie?"

Charles reached for her wrist and placed her keys in her palm. "That sounds nice," he said as he moved his hand up her arm to the back of her neck. "But I want to see you alone more often." Then he touched his lips to hers, and his kiss was like a nice pause in a busy day. A relaxing ahh, or a dip in a warm pool. So what if his kisses didn't make her crazy? She didn't want a man who made her lose control. She didn't want any man's touch to turn her into a raving nymphomaniac ever again. She'd been there, done that, and she'd been burned big time.

She touched her tongue to his and felt his quick intake of breath. His free hand found her waist, and he pulled her closer into his chest. His grip tightened. He wanted more. If they hadn't been standing in a parking lot in downtown Seattle, she might have given him what he wanted.

She cared for Charles, and in time, she could see herself maybe falling in love with him. It had been years since she'd made love. Years since she'd given herself to a man. When she stepped back and looked into Charles's heavy eyes, she thought it might be time to change that. It might be time to try again.

# Nine

"Hey, look at me!"

Mae glanced up from the carefully folded napkins in her hands as Lexie ran by dragging a pink Barbie kite behind her. Her denim hat with the big sunflower in front flew off her head and landed on the grass.

"You're doing great," Mae hollered. She set down the napkins and stood back to view the picnic table with a critical eye. The ends of the blue and white striped cloth fluttered in the slight breeze while Lexie's Chia Pet sat on an overturned bowl in the center of the table. The grassy pig wore little sunglasses cut out of poster board, and a bright pink scarf had been tied around its neck. "What are you trying to prove?" she asked.

"I'm not trying to prove anything," Georgeanne answered, wedging a tray of salmon-asparagus bundles, smoked-bluefish pâté, and rounds of toast on one end of the table. For some reason, a small porcelain cat sat in the middle of the tray licking its paws. On the cat's head was a pointed hat made out of yellow felt. Mae knew Georgeanne well enough to know that there was a theme to this picnic somewhere. She just hadn't figured it out yet, but she would.

She moved her gaze from the cat to the variety of food she recognized from jobs they'd catered the week before. She recognized the cheese blintzes and the loaf of traditional challah bread from little Mitchell Wiseman's bar mitzvah. The crab cakes and checkerboard canapés looked like they'd come from Mrs. Brody's annual garden party. And the roasted chicken and baby back ribs with plum sauce had been served at the barbecue they'd catered the night before. "Well, it looks like you're trying to prove to someone that you can cook."

"I just cleaned out the freezer at work, that's all," Georgeanne answered.

No, that wasn't all. The artfully arranged and carefully polished tower of fruit hadn't come from work. The apples, pears, and bananas were perfect. The peaches and cherries had been meticulously positioned, and a blue-feather bird wearing a paisley cape looked down from a perch high atop a mound of shiny green and purple grapes. "Georgeanne, you don't have to prove to anyone that you're a successful woman or a good mother. I know you are and you know it, too. And since you and I are the only grownups around here that count, why kill yourself to impress a bonehead hockey player?"

Georgeanne looked up from the crystal duck in a muumuu that she'd placed beside the canapés. "I told John to bring a friend, so I don't think he'll be alone. And I'm not trying to impress him. I certainly don't care what he thinks."

Mae didn't argue. Instead, she grabbed a stack of clear plastic glasses and set them on the table next to the iced tea. Whether intentional or not, Georgeanne had set out to impress the man who'd dumped her at Sea-Tac seven years ago. Mae understood Georgeanne's need to prove she'd made a success of her life. Although she did think the designer brownies Georgeanne had molded into the shapes of dogs was going a bit too far.

And Georgeanne's appearance was a little too perfect for a day at the park, too. Mae wondered if she was trying to convince John Kowalsky that she was as perfect as June Cleaver. Her dark hair was pulled up on each side of her head and held in place with gold combs. The gold hoops in her ears shined, and her makep was flawless. Her emerald green halter dress matched her eyes, and her pink fingernail polish matched her toenails. She'd kicked off her sandals, and the thin gold ring on her third toe gleamed in the sun.

Just a little too perfectly put together for a woman who didn't care if she impressed the father of her child.

When Mae had first hired Georgeanne, she'd felt a little drab standing beside her, like a pound mutt next to a highbred poodle. But her self-conscious feelings hadn't lasted long. Georgeanne couldn't help being a glamour queen any more than Mae could help feeling most comfortable in T-shirts and jeans. Or wearing a pair of cutoffs and a tank top like today.

"What time is it?" Georgeanne asked as she poured herself a glass of tea.

Mae looked at the big Mickey Mouse watch strapped to her wrist. "Eleven-forty."

"We've got twenty minutes then. Maybe we'll get lucky and he won't show."

"What did you tell Lexie?" Mae asked as she dropped ice cubes into a glass.

"Just that John might come to our picnic." Georgeanne raised a hand to her brow and watched Lexie run with her kite.

Mae reached for the tea pitcher and poured. "*Might* come to your picnic?"

Georgeanne shrugged. "A girl can hope. And besides, I'm not convinced John will really want to be a part of Lexie's life forever. I can't help but think that sooner or later he'll get tired of being a daddy. I just hope it happens sooner than later, because if he abandons her after she's come to care for him, it will break her heart. You know how protective I am, and of course, something like that would bring out my bad temper. I'd naturally feel compelled to retaliate."

Mae considered Georgeanne one of the genuinely nicest women she knew, except when she lost her temper. "What would you do?"

"Well, the thought of putting termites in his houseboat does hold a certain appeal."

Mae shook her head. She was fiercely loyal to both mother and daughter, and she considered them her family. "Too slow."

"Running him down with my car?"

"You're getting warmer."

"Drive-by shooting?"

Mae smiled, but dropped the subject as Lexie walked toward them, dragging her kite behind her. The little girl collapsed on the ground at her mother's feet, the hem of her denim sundress riding up to her Pocahontas underwear. Clumps of grass were stuck to her clear jelly sandals.

"I can't run no more," she gasped. For a change, her face was clean of cosmetics.

"You did a real good job, precious darlin'," Georgeanne praised. "Would you like a juice box?"

"No. Will you run with me and help get my kite in the air?"

"We've talked about this. You know I can't run."

"I know," Lexie sighed, and sat up. "It hurts your boobs and it's tacky." She shoved her hat back on her head and looked up at Mae. "Can you help me?"

"I would, but I don't wear a bra."

"Why not?" Lexie wanted to know. "Mommy does."

"Well, Mommy needs to, but Aunt Mae doesn't." She studied the little girl for a brief moment, then asked, "Where's all the goop you usually wear on your face?"

Lexie rolled her eyes. "It's not goop. It's my makeup, and Mommy told me that I could have a Kitten Surprise if I didn't wear it today."

"I told you I'd buy you a real kitten if you didn't wear it at all. You're too young to be a slave to Max Factor."

"Mommy says I can't have a kitty or a dog or nothin'."

"That's right," Georgeanne said, and looked at Mae. "Lexie isn't old enough for the responsibility of a pet, and I don't want the burden. Let's drop this subject before Lexie gets started on it." Georgeanne paused, then lowered her voice. "I think she might finally be over her fixation with my having a . . . well, you know."

Yes, Mae knew, and she thought Georgeanne was wise not to say it out loud and remind Lexie. For about the last six months, Lexie had been preoccupied with the notion that Georgeanne should provide her with a little brother or sister. She'd driven everyone nuts, and Mae was relieved she wouldn't have to hear about babies anymore. The kid already had a long-standing obsession with owning a pet and had been a certified hypochondriac since birth, which was one hundred percent Georgeanne's fault since she'd always made a big deal out of every little scratch and scrape.

Mae reached for her tea, raised it halfway to her lips, then set it back down. Walking toward her were two very big, very athletic men. She recognized the man wearing a white collarless shirt tucked inside faded jeans as John Kowalsky. The other man, who was slightly shorter with less bulk, she'd never seen before.

Big, strong men had always intimidated Mae, and not just because she was five one and weighed one hundred five pounds either. Her stomach took a tumble, and she figured that if she was this nervous, then Georgeanne was close to a complete wig-out. She glanced at her friend and saw the anxiety in her eyes.

"Lexie, get up and wipe the grass from your dress," Georgeanne said slowly. Her hand shook as she reached down and helped her daughter to her feet.

Mae had seen Georgeanne nervous many times, but she hadn't seen her this bad for several years. "Are you going to be okay?" she whispered.

Georgeanne nodded, and Mae watched as she pasted a smile on her face and flipped on her hostess switch. "Hello, John," Georgeanne said as the two men approached. "I hope you didn't have trouble finding us."

"No," he answered, stopping directly in front of them. "No trouble." His eyes were covered by a pair of expensive dark sunglasses. His lips were set in a straight line, and for several awkward seconds, the two just stared at each other. Then Georgeanne abruptly turned her attention to the other man, whom Mae estimated to be around six feet tall. "You must be a friend of John's."

"Hugh Miner." He smiled and stuck out his hand.

While Georgeanne took his hand in both of hers, Mae studied Hugh. With one cursory glance, she determined that his smile was too pleasant for a man with such intense hazel eyes. He was too big, too handsome, and his neck was too thick. She didn't like him.

"I'm so glad you were able to join us today," Georgeanne said as she let go of Hugh's hand, then she introduced the two men to Mae.

John and Hugh said hello at the same time. Mae,

who wasn't as good at hiding her feelings as Georgeanne, managed a smile, sort of. It was really more of a lip twitch.

"This is Mr. Miner, and you remember Mr. Kowalsky, don't you, Lexie?" Georgeanne inquired, continuing with the introductions.

"Yes. Hello."

"Hi, Lexie. How have you been?" John asked.

"Well," Lexie began on a dramatic sigh, "yesterday I stubbed my toe on the front porch at our house, and I hit my elbow really hard on the table, but I'm better now."

John shoved his hands up to his knuckles into the front pockets of his jeans. He looked down at Lexie and wondered what fathers said to little girls who stubbed their toes and hit their elbows. "I'm glad to hear you're better," was all he could come up with. He couldn't think of anything else, and so he just stared. He indulged himself and watched her as he'd wanted to since he'd first realized she was his child. He looked into her face, without layers of lipstick and eye shadow, really seeing her for the first time. He saw tiny brown freckles dusting her small, straight nose. Her skin looked as smooth as cream, and her plump cheeks were pink as if she'd been running. Her lips were pouty like Georgeanne's, but her eyes were his, from the color to the lashes he'd inherited from his mother.

"I have a kite," she told him.

Her dark brown hair fell in curls from beneath a denim hat with a big sunflower sewn on it. "Oh? That's good," he uttered, wondering what in the hell was the matter with him. He signed trading cards for kids all the time. Some of his team members brought their children to practices, and he'd never had any trouble talking to them. But for some reason, he couldn't think of anything to say to his own child.

"Well, it's a lovely day for a picnic," Georgeanne said, and Lexie turned away. "We've put together a little lunch. I hope you gentlemen are hungry."

"I'm starved," Hugh confessed.

"What about you, John?"

As Lexie walked toward her mother, John noticed grass stains on the back of her denim dress. "What about me?" he asked, and looked up.

Georgeanne walk around to the opposite side of the table and looked over at him. "Are you hungry?"

"No."

"Would you like a glass of iced tea?"

"No. No tea."

"Fine," Georgeanne said, her smile faltering. "Lexie, will you hand Mae and Hugh a plate while I pour the tea?"

His answer obviously irritated Georgeanne, but he didn't particularly care. He felt the same as when he had pregame jitters. Lexie scared the holy shit right out of him and he didn't know why.

In his life, he'd faced some of the toughest enforcers the NHL had thrown at him. He'd had his wrist and ankle broken, his clavicle snapped like a twig twice, and he'd had five stitches in his left eyebrow, six on the right side of his head, and fourteen to the inside of his mouth. And those were just the injuries he could recall at the moment. After recovering from each incident, he'd grabbed his stick and had skated back out onto the ice, unafraid.

"Mr. Wall, would you like a juice box?" Lexie asked as she climbed onto the bench.

He looked at the backs of her skinny legs and knees, and he felt as if someone had elbowed him in the gut. "What kind of juice?"

"Blueberry or strawberry."

"Blueberry," he answered. Lexie jumped down and ran around the table to a cooler.

"Hey, Wall, you should try these salmon asparagus things," Hugh advised, stuffing his face as he moved to stand across from John and next to Georgeanne.

"I'm so glad you like them." Georgeanne turned toward Hugh and smiled, and not the phony smile she'd given John either. "I wasn't sure I'd sliced the salmon thin enough. Oh, and be sure that you try the baby back ribs. The plum barbecue sauce is just to die for." She glanced at her friend who stood by her other side. "Don't you think so, Mae?"

The short blonde with the bad attitude shrugged. "Yeah, sure."

Georgeanne's eyes widened as she stared at her friend. Then she turned back to Hugh. "Why don't you try the pâté while I carve you some chicken?" She didn't wait for an answer before she grabbed a large knife. "While I do this, why don't y'all look around the table. If you look real close, you will see a variety of little animals in their picnic attire."

John folded his arms across his chest and stared at a Chia Pig wearing sunglasses and a scarf. A funny tingle started at the base of his skull.

"Lexie and I thought today would be a perfect opportunity for her to unveil her summer collection of animal couture."

"Oh, I get it now," Mae said as she reached for a crab cake.

"Animal couture?" Hugh sounded as incredulous as John felt.

"Yes. Lexie likes to make clothes for all the little glass and porcelain animals in our house. I know it may sound strange," Georgeanne continued as she sliced, "but she comes by it honestly. Her great-grandmother Chandler, that's on my grandfather's side of the family, used to design clothes for pullets. Being northerners, you may not know this, but a pullet is a young hen. Young because they don't get to be very old before . . ." She paused and raised the knife about five inches from her throat and made choking sounds. "Well, you know." She shrugged and lowered the knife once more. "And hens because it goes without saying that it would be a colossal waste of time and talent to make clothing for roosters, being that they are predisposed to nasty temperaments. Anyway, Great-grandmother used to make little capes with matching hoods for the family's pullets. Lexie has inherited her great-grandmother's eye for fashion and is carrying on a time-honored family tradition."

"Are you serious?" Hugh asked as Georgeanne slid slices of chicken onto his plate.

She raised her right hand. "My lips to God's ears."

The tingle in John's skull shot to his brain as déjà vu enveloped him. "Oh, God."

Georgeanne glanced across the table at him, and he saw her as she'd been seven years ago, a beautiful young woman who had rambled on about Jell-O and foot-washing Baptists. He saw her killer green eyes and sexy mouth. He saw her come-to-papa body all wrapped up in his black silk robe. She'd driven him crazy with her teasing glances and honey-coated voice. And as much as he hated to admit it, he wasn't immune to her.

"Mr. Wall."

John felt a tug on the belt loop of his pants, and he looked down at Lexie.

"Here's your juice box, Mr. Wall."

"Thank you," he said, and took the little blue carton from her.

"I put the straw in it already."

"Yes, I see." He raised the box to his mouth and sucked the blue juice through the straw.

"Good, huh?"

"Mmm," he said, trying not to grimace.

"I brung you this, too."

She shoved a paper napkin at him, and he grabbed it with his free hand. It was folded into a shape he didn't readily recognize.

"It's a rabbit."

"Yes. I see that," he lied.

"I have a kite."

"Oh?"

"Yeah, but it won't fly. My mommy wears a real big bra, but she still can't run." She shook her head sadly. "And Mae can't run either 'cause she doesn't wear a bra at all."

Silence fell on the picnic like a curtain of doom. John raised his gaze to the two women on the other side of the table. They stood as if freeze-dried. Mae gripped a black olive positioned before her mouth, while Georgeanne held the big knife in midair with a piece of chicken stuck on the end. Their eyes were huge, and bright red stained their cheeks.

John coughed into his rabbit napkin to hide his laughter, but no one said a word.

Except Hugh. He leaned forward, looked past Georgeanne to her shorter friend. "Is that right, sweetheart?" he asked with a big grin.

Both women lowered their hands at the same time. Georgeanne got real busy cutting and straightening while Mae turned to frown at Hugh.

Hugh either didn't notice Mae's scowl or he didn't care. Knowing his friend, John would bet the latter was the case. "I've always been partial to a liberated woman," he continued. "In fact, I've been thinking of becoming a member of NOW."

"Men can't belong to NOW," Mae informed him tersely.

"That's where you're wrong. I believe Phil Donahue is a member."

"That's not true," Mae argued.

"Well, if he's not, he should be. He's more feminist than any woman I've ever met."

"I doubt you would know a feminist if she bit you on the butt."

The Caveman smiled. "I've never been bitten on the butt by any woman, feminist or not. But I'm willing if you are."

Folding her arms beneath her breasts, Mae said, "By your lack of manners, the size of your neck, and the slope to your forehead, I assume you play hockey."

Hugh glanced at John and laughed. Giving shit and taking it when it was thrown right back at him was one of the things John like about Hugh. "'Slope to your forehead,' " Hugh chuckled as his gaze returned to Mae. "That was a good one."

"Do you play hockey?"

"Yep. I'm goalie for the Chinooks. What is it you do, wrestle pit bulls?"

"Pickle?" Georgeanne reached for the relish plate and shoved it at Hugh. "I made them myself!"

Once more John felt a tug on his belt loop. "Do you know how to fly a kite, Mr. Wall?"

He looked down into Lexie's upturned face; her eyes were squinted against the sun. "I could try."

Lexie smiled and a dimple indented her right cheek. "Mommy," she hollered as she spun around and raced toward the other side of the table. "Mr. Wall is gonna fly my kite with me!"

Georgeanne's gaze swung to him. "You don't have to do that, John."

"I want to." He placed his juice box on the table.

Setting down the relish plate, Georgeanne said, "I'll come with the two of you."

"No." He needed and wanted time alone with his daughter. "Lexie and I can manage."

"But I don't think that's a good idea."

"Well, I do."

She quickly glanced over her shoulder at Lexie, who knelt on the ground untangling string. She grabbed his arm and pulled him several feet away. "Okay, but not too far," she said, stopping in front of him. She rose onto the balls of her feet and looked over his shoulder toward the others.

She whispered something about Lexie, but he wasn't really listening. She was so close he could smell her perfume. He lowered his gaze to her slim fingers resting on his biceps. The only thing keeping her double Ds from brushing against his chest was a tiny slice of empty space. "What do you want?" he asked, raising his eyes up her smooth arm to the hollow of her soft throat. She was still a tease.

"I just told you." She lowered her hand and dropped to her heels.

"Why don't you tell me again, but this time keep your breasts out of the conversation."

A wrinkle appeared between her brows. "My what? What are you talking about?"

She looked so genuinely perplexed, John almost believed her innocent expression. Almost. "If you want to talk to me, don't use your body to do it. Unless, of course, you want me to take you up on your offer."

She shook her head, disgusted. "You're a sick man, John Kowalsky. If you can manage to keep your eyeballs off the front of my dress, and your mind out of the gutter, we have something more important to discuss than your absurd fantasies."

John rocked back on his heels and looked down into her face. He wasn't sick. At least he didn't think so. He wasn't as sick as some of the guys he knew.

Georgeanne tilted her head to the side. "I want you to remember your promise."

"What promise?"

"Not to tell Lexie you're her father. She should hear it from me."

"Fine," he said, and reached for his sunglasses on the bridge of his nose. He shoved a side piece down the front pocket of his jeans, leaving the glasses to hang by his hip. "And I want you to remember that Lexie and I are going to get to know each other. Alone. I'm taking her to fly her kite, and don't you follow us in ten minutes."

She thought for a moment, then said, "Lexie's too shy. She'll need me."

John seriously doubted there was a shy bone in Lexie's body. "Don't bullshit me, Georgie."

Her green eyes narrowed. "Just don't go where I can't see you."

"What do you think I'm going to do, kidnap her?"

"No," she said, but John knew she didn't trust him any more than he trusted her. He had a feeling that was exactly what she thought.

"We won't go too far." He turned back toward the others. He'd told Hugh about Georgeanne and Lexie, and he knew he could count on his friend's discretion. "Are you ready, Lexie?" he asked.

"Yep." She stood with her pink kite in hand, and together the two of them headed away from people throwing Frisbees, toward a nice grassy expanse. After Lexie got her feet tangled in the kite's tail the second time, John took it from her. The top of her head barely reached his waist, and he felt huge walking next to her. Again he didn't know what to say and did very little talking. But then, he didn't need to.

"Last year, when I was a little kid, I was in kindergarten," his daughter began, then she proceeded to name each child in her class, relate whether they owned a pet, and describe the breed.

"And he gots three dogs." She held up three fingers. "That's just not fair."

John looked over his shoulder, determined that

they'd walked a couple of hundred feet, and stopped. "I think this is a good spot."

"Do you gots any dogs?"

"No. No dogs." He handed her back the spool of string with the stick through the center.

She shook her head sadly. "Me neither, but I want a dalmatian," she said as she grasped each side of the stick. "A great big one with lots of spots."

"Keep the string tight." He held the pink kite above his head and felt the gentle pull of the breeze.

"Don't I have to run?"

"Not today." He moved the kite to the left and the wind tugged harder. "Now walk backward, but don't let out any string until I tell you." She nodded and looked so serious he almost laughed.

After ten tries, the kite rose about twenty feet in the air. "Help me." She panicked, her face turned skyward. "It's gonna fall again."

"Not this time," he assured her as he came to stand next to her. "And if it does, we'll put it back up."

She shook her head and her denim hat fell on the ground. "It's gonna fall, I just know it. You take it!" She shoved the spool toward him.

John lowered himself to one knee beside her. "You can do it," he said, and when she leaned her back against his chest, he felt his heart stop for a few beats. "Just let the string out slowly." John stared into her face as she watched her kite soar higher. Her expression turned quickly from trepidation to delight.

"I did it," she whispered, and turned to look over her shoulder at him.

Her soft breath brushed his cheek and swept deep down to his soul. A moment before, his heart had felt as if it had stopped; now it swelled. It felt as if a balloon were being inflated beneath his sternum. It grew big and fast and intense, and he had to look away. He looked at the people flying kites around him. He looked at fathers and mothers and children. Families. He was a daddy again. *But for how long this time?* his cynical subconscious asked.

"I did it, Mr. Wall." She spoke quietly, as if a raised voice would bring her kite crashing to the ground.

He looked back at his child. "My name is John."

"I did it, John."

"Yes, you did."

She smiled. "I like you."

"I like you, Lexie."

She looked up at her kite. "Do you gots kids?"

Her question took him by surprise, and he waited a moment before answering, "Yes." He wasn't going to lie to her, but she wasn't ready for the truth, and of course, he'd promised Georgeanne. "I had a little boy, but he died when he was a baby."

"How?"

John glanced up at the kite. "Let out a little more string." When Lexie did as he advised he said, "He was born too early."

"Oh, what time?"

"What?" He looked into the small face so close to his.

"What time was he born?"

"About four o'clock in the morning."

She nodded as if that answered everything. "Yep, too early. All the doctors are still asleep. I was born late."

John smiled, impressed with her logic. She was obviously quite bright.

"What was his name?"

"Toby." *And he was your big brother.*

"That's a weird name."

"I like it," he said, feeling himself relax a bit for the first time since he'd driven into the park.

Lexie shrugged. "I want to have a baby, but my mommy says no."

John carefully settled her more comfortably against his chest, and everything seemed to slip into place, like a smooth one-timer: slide, hit, score. He placed his hands on each side of the stick next to hers and relaxed a bit more. His chin touched her soft temple when he said, "Good, you're too young to have a baby."

Lexie giggled and shook her head. "Not me! My mom. I want my *mom* to have a baby."

"And she said no, huh?"

"Yep, 'cause she don't got no husband, but she could get one if she just tried harder."

"A husband?"

"Yep, and then she could have a baby, too. My mom said she went to the garden and pulled me up like a carrot, but that's not true. Babies don't come from a garden."

"Where do they come from?"

She bumped his chin as she looked up at him. "Don't you know?"

He'd known for a *very* long time. "Why don't you tell me."

She shrugged and returned her gaze to the kite. "Well, a man and a woman gets married, and then they go home and lie on the bed. They close their eyes really, really tight and think really, really hard. Then a baby goes into the mommy's tummy."

John laughed, he couldn't help it. "Does your mom know that you think babies are conceived through telepathy?"

"Huh?"

"Never mind." He'd heard or read somewhere that parents should talk to their children about sex at an early age. "Maybe you better tell your mom that you know babies aren't grown in a garden."

She thought for a few moments before she said, "No. My mommy likes to tell that story at night sometimes. But I did tell her that I'm too big to believe in the Easter Bunny."

He tried to sound shocked. "You don't believe in the Easter Bunny?"

"Nope."

"Why not?"

She looked back at him as if he were stupid. "'Cause rabbits gots little paws and can't dye eggs."

"Ah . . . that's true." Again he was impressed with her six-year-old logic. "Then I bet you're too old to believe in Santa."

She gasped, scandalized. "Santa is for real!"

He guessed the same reasoning that told her rabbits couldn't dye eggs didn't apply to flying reindeer, a fat man sliding down her chimney, or jolly little elves who lived to make toys three hundred-sixty-four days a year. "Let out some more of your kite string," he said, then he just relaxed. He listened to her perpetual chatter and noticed little details about her. He watched the breeze toss her soft hair about her head, and he noticed the way she hunched her shoulders and raised her fingers to her lips whenever she giggled. And she giggled a lot. Her favorite subjects were obviously animals and babies. She had a flair for the dramatic, and was undoubtedly a hypochondriac.

"I skinned my knee," she told him after reciting a long list of the injuries she'd suffered in the past few days. She pulled her dress up her skinny thighs, raised one leg out in front of her, and touched a finger to a neon green Band-Aid. "And see my toe," she added, pointing to a pink Band-Aid visible beneath her plastic sandal. "Stubbed it at Amy's. Do you have any ouchies?"

"Ouchies? Hmm . . ." He thought a moment, then came up with, "I cut my chin shaving this morning."

Her eyes almost crossed as she looked at his chin.

"My mom gots a Band-Aid. She gots lots of Band-Aids in her purse. I could get one for you."

He pictured himself with a neon pink bandage. "No. No, thanks," he declined, and began to take note of Lexie's other peculiarities, like the way she often said the word "gots" instead of "has" or "have." He focused all of his attention on her and pretended that they were the only two people in the park. But of course, they weren't, and it didn't take long before two boys walked up to them. They looked about thirteen, and both wore baggy black shorts, big T-shirts, and baseball caps with the bills turned backward.

"Aren't you John Kowalsky?"

"Sure am," he said as he rose to his feet. Usually he didn't mind the intrusion, especially by kids who liked to talk hockey. But today he would have preferred that no one approach him. He should have known better. After their last season, the Chinooks were bigger and more popular in the state than ever before. Next to Ken Griffey and Bill Gates, his was the most recognized face in the state of Washington, especially after those billboards he'd done for the Dairy Association.

His teammates had given him a whole shit load of razzing for the white milk mustache, and although he'd pretended otherwise, he had felt like a weenie whenever he'd driven by one of those billboards. But John had learned a long time ago not to take the whole celebrity-athlete thing too seriously.

"We saw you play against the Black Hawks," said one of the boys, with a picture of a snowboarder on his T-shirt. "I loved the way you hip-checked Chelios at center ice. Man, he flew."

John remembered that game, too. He'd received a minor penalty and a bruise the size of a cantaloupe. It had hurt like hell, but that was part of the game. Part of his job.

"I'm glad to hear you enjoyed it," he said, and

looked into their young eyes. The hero worship he saw there made him uncomfortable; it always did. "Do you play hockey?"

"Just street," the other boy answered.

"Where?" He turned to Lexie and reached for her hand so that she wouldn't feel left out.

"Over at the elementary school by my house. We get a whole bunch of guys together and play."

As the two boys filled him in on their street hockey, he noticed a young woman walking straight toward them. Her jeans were so tight they looked painful, and her tank top didn't reach her navel. John could detect a sexually aggressive rink bunny at fifty paces. They were always around. Waiting in a hotel lobby, outside the locker room, and positioned next to the team bus. Women eager to get it on with celebrities were easy to spot in a crowd. It was all in the way they walked and flipped their hair. It was the determined look in their eyes.

He hoped this woman would walk right on past.

She didn't.

"David, your mom wants you," she said as she stopped next to the two boys.

"Tell her in just a second."

"She said now."

"Dang!"

"It was good to meet you guys." John reached out to shake their hands. "The next time you're at a game, wait for me outside the locker room and I'll introduce you to some of the guys."

"Really?"

"All right!"

When the two walked away, the woman stayed behind. John let go of Lexie's hand and glanced down at the top of her head. "It's time to reel in your kite," he said. "Your mom will wonder what happened to us."

"You John Kowalsky?"

He looked up. "That's right," he answered, his tone clearly letting her know that he wasn't interested in her company. She was pretty enough, but she was skinny and had that fake blond look to her, like she'd been left out in the sun too long. Determination hardened her light blue eyes, and he wondered how rude she was going to force him to get with her.

"Well, John," she said, and slowly pushed the corners of her lips upward into a seductive smile. "I'm Connie." Her eyes raked him from head to toe. "And you look pretty good in those jeans."

He was fairly certain he'd heard that line before, but it had been a while and he couldn't remember it exactly. Not only was she encroaching on his private time with Lexie, she wasn't very original either.

"But I think I'd look better. Why don't you take them off and we'll see?"

Now John remembered. The first time he'd heard it, he'd been twenty and had just signed with Toronto. He'd probably been stupid enough to bite. "I think both of us should keep our pants on," he said, and wondered why men were the only gender accused of using cheap old pickup lines. Women's come-ons were equally bad, and most often downright raunchy.

"Okay. I could just crawl right on inside." She ran the tip of one long red fingernail along his waistband, then down.

John reached out to remove her finger from his fly, but Lexie took care of the problem. She batted the woman's hand away, then stepped between them.

"That's a bad touch," Lexie said as she glared up at Connie. "You could get into really big trouble."

The woman's smile faltered as she glanced down. "Is she yours?"

John chuckled softly, amused by Lexie's fierce expression. He'd certainly needed his share of security before, especially in the City of Brotherly Love, where the fans could get real nasty if someone put the big hurt on their team. But he'd never been guarded by a girl, much less a girl under four feet. "Her mother is a friend of mine," he said through his smile.

She looked back up at John and flipped her hair. "Why don't you send her to Mama, and you and I can go for a drive in my car. I have a big backseat."

A quickie in the back of a Buick didn't even arouse his curiosity. "I'm not interested."

"I'll do things to you that no other woman has done."

John seriously doubted her claim. He figured he'd pretty much done everything at least once; more often than not, he'd done it twice just to make sure. He placed his hand on Lexie's shoulder and considered several different ways to tell Connie to get lost. With his daughter so close, he had to be careful how he phrased his rejection.

Georgeanne's approach saved him the trouble. "I hope I'm not interrupting anything," she said with that honeyed voice of hers.

He turned to Georgeanne and wrapped an arm around her waist. With his hand on her hip, he looked into her stunned face and smiled. "I knew you couldn't stay away."

"John?" she gasped.

Rather than answer the question in her voice, he raised his hand from Lexie's shoulder and pointed to the blond woman. "Georgie, honey, this is Connie."

Georgeanne forced one of her phony smiles and said, "Hello, Connie."

Connie gave Georgeanne a thorough once-over, then shrugged. "It could have been a kick," she told John, and turned to leave.

As soon as Connie walked away, John watched the corners of Georgeanne's full lips fall into a straight line. She looked as if she wanted to hit him with a sharp elbow.

"Are you high?"

John smiled and whispered in her ear. "We're supposed to be friends, remember? I'm just doing my part."

"Do you grope all your friends?"

John laughed. He laughed at her, at the whole situation, but mostly he laughed at himself. "Only the pretty ones with green eyes and sassy mouths. You might want to remember that."

# Ten

That evening, after the picnic, Georgeanne still felt raw. Dealing with John had snapped her last nerve, and Mae certainly hadn't helped one bit. Instead of offering support, Mae had spent her time insulting Hugh Miner, who seemed to have enjoyed the abuse. He'd eaten with relish, laughed tolerantly, and had teased Mae until Georgeanne worried for the man's safety.

Now all Georgeanne wanted was a hot bath, a cucumber facial, and a loofah. But her bath would have to wait until she came clean to Charles. If she wanted any kind of a future with him, she would have to tell him about John. She would have to tell him she lied about Lexie's father. She would have to tell him tonight. She wasn't looking forward to the conversation, but she wanted to get it over with.

The doorbell rang and she ushered Charles into the house. "Where's Lexie?" he asked, glancing about the living room. He looked comfortable and relaxed in a pair of chinos and a white polo shirt. The light brush of gray at his temples lent dignity to his handsome face.

"I put her to bed."

Charles smiled and placed his hands on the sides of Georgeanne's face. He gave her a long, gentle kiss. A kiss that offered more than hot passion. More than a one-night stand.

The kiss ended and Charles looked into her eyes. "You sounded worried on the phone."

"I am, a little," she confessed. She took his hand and sat next to him on the couch. "Do you remember when I told you Lexie's daddy was dead?"

"Sure, his F-16 was shot down during the Gulf War."

"Well, I may have embellished a bit—actually, a lot." She took a deep breath and told him about John. She told him about their meeting seven years ago, and she told him about the picnic that afternoon. When she was finished, Charles didn't look pleased, and she was afraid she'd damaged their relationship.

"You could have told me the truth the first time," he said.

"Maybe, but I've just gotten so used to lying about it that I never really stopped to think about the truth after a while. Then when John walked back into my life, I thought he'd hurry and grow tired of playing daddy, and I wouldn't have to tell her or anyone."

"You don't think he'll grow tired of Lexie now?"

"No. Today in the park he was very attentive to her, and he made a date to take her to the exhibit at the Pacific Science Center next week." She shook her head. "I don't think he's going away."

"How will seeing him affect you?"

"Me?" she asked as she looked into his gray eyes.

"He's in your life. You'll see him from time to time."

"That's right. And your ex-wife is in your life."

He looked down. "It's not the same."

"Why not?"

He smiled slightly. "Because I find Margaret extremely unappealing."

He wasn't angry. He was jealous, just as Mae had predicted.

"And John Kowalsky," he continued, "is a good-looking guy."

"So are you."

He reached for her hand. "You have to tell me if I'm competing with a hockey player."

"Don't be ridiculous." Georgeanne laughed at such absurdity. "John and I hate each other. On a scale from one to ten, he's a negative thirty. I find him as appealing as gum disease."

He smiled and pulled her close to his side. "You have a unique way of expressing yourself. It's one of the many things I like about you."

Georgeanne laid her head on his shoulder and sighed with relief. "I was afraid I'd lose your friendship."

"Is that all I am to you? A friend?"

She looked up at him. "No."

"Good. I want more than friendship." His lips brushed her forehead. "I could fall in love with you."

Georgeanne smiled and ran her palm up his chest to his neck. "I could maybe fall in love with you, too," she said, then she kissed him. Charles was exactly the kind of man she needed. Reliable and sane. Because of their hectic careers and busy lives, they didn't get to spend a lot of time together completely alone. Georgeanne worked weekends, and if she had a free night, she spent it with Lexie. Charles usually didn't work evenings or weekends, and as a result of their conflicting schedules, they met most often for lunch. Maybe it was time to change that. Maybe it was time to meet for breakfast. Alone. At the Hilton. Suite 231.

* * *

Georgeanne closed the door to her office, shutting out the hum of mixers and the chatter of her employees. Like her home, the office she shared with Mae was filled with flowers and lace. And pictures. Dozens of them sat round the room. Most were of Lexie, several were of Mae and Georgeanne taken together at different jobs they'd catered. Three were of Ray Heron. Mae's deceased twin brother had been captured in resplendent drag in two of the framed photographs, while in the third he looked fairly normal in jeans and a fuchsia sweater. Georgeanne knew Mae missed her twin and thought of him daily, but she also knew that Mae's pain wasn't as great as it had been. She and Lexie had filled the empty place left by Ray's death, while Mae had become both sister to her and aunt to Lexie. The three of them were a family.

Moving to the window and lifting the shade, Georgeanne let in the early afternoon sunlight. She placed a three-page contract on the antique desk and sat. Mae wasn't expected until later that afternoon, and Georgeanne had an hour before her lunch date with Charles. She pored over the itemized lists, rereading to make sure she didn't miss anything important. When she lowered her gaze to the bottom line, her eyes widened, and she cut her finger on the edge of the paper. If Mrs. Fuller wanted her September birthday party to have a medieval theme, then she was going to have to pay *big* money for it. Absently she sucked her finger between her lips and reread the cost of the rare food. Hiring the Medieval Society to perform, and transforming the backyard of Mrs. Fuller's home into a medieval fair, would take a lot of work and a lot of cash.

Georgeanne lowered her hand and sighed heavily as she eyed the special menu. Usually she thrived on challenge. She had fun creating wonderful events and planning unusual menus. She loved the feeling of accomplishment she got at the end when everything was packed back up and loaded into her vans. But not this time. She was tired and didn't feel up to the task of catering a sit-down dinner for one hundred people. She hoped she would by September. Maybe her life would be more settled then, but for two weeks now, beginning with the day John had walked back into her life, she'd felt as if she were riding a roller coaster. Since the picnic in the park, he'd met her and Lexie at the Seattle Aquarium, and he'd taken them to Lexie's favorite restaurant, the Iron Horse. Both events had been tense, but at least in the darkened warrens of the aquarium, Georgeanne hadn't had to think of anything more mentally taxing than sharks and sea otters. The Iron Horse had been different. As they'd waited for their burgers brought to the table by a small train, attempting polite conversation had been excruciating. The whole time she'd felt as if she were holding her breath, waiting for the other shoe to drop. The only time she'd felt she could breathe was when hockey fans approached their table and asked for John's autograph.

If things were strained between Georgeanne and John, Lexie hadn't seemed to notice at all. Lexie had immediately warmed to her father, which didn't surprise Georgeanne. Lexie was friendly, outgoing, and genuinely liked people. She smiled, laughed easily, and assumed that everyone just naturally thought she was the most wonderful little invention since Velcro. John obviously agreed with her. He listened attentively to her repeated dog and cat stories and laughed at all of her elephant jokes, which were pretty bad and not in the least bit funny.

Georgeanne set the contract aside and reached for a bill from the electrician who'd spent two days fixing the ventilation in the kitchen. She tried not to let the situation with John bother her. Lexie behaved no differently with John than she did with Charles. Still, there was a risk with John that wasn't there with any other man. John was Lexie's daddy, and there was a part of Georgeanne that feared their relationship. It was a relationship she couldn't share. A relationship she'd never known, would never understand, and could only watch from a distance. John was the only man who could threaten Georgeanne's closeness with her daughter.

A knock rapped her door as it swung open at the same time. Georgeanne looked up as her first cook stuck her head in the room. Sarah was a bright university student and a gifted pastry chef. "There's a man here to see you."

Georgeanne recognized the excited spark in Sarah's eyes. Over the past two weeks, she'd seen it on a myriad of female faces. It was usually followed by giggles, ridiculous fawning, and requests for autographs. The door opened wide, and she glanced past Sarah to the man who reduced women to such embarrassing behavior. The man who looked oddly at ease in a formal tuxedo.

"Hello, John," she greeted, and rose to her feet. He walked into the office, filling the small, feminine room with his size and masculine presence. A black silk tie hung loose down the front of a white pleated shirt. The top gold stud was left unfastened. "What can I do for you?"

"I was in the neighborhood and I thought I'd drop by," he answered, and shrugged out of the jacket.

"Do you need anything?" Sarah inquired.

Georgeanne moved toward the doorway. "Please have a seat, John," she said over her shoulder. She looked out into the kitchen at her employees, who weren't even bothering to hide their interest. "No, thank you," she said, and closed the door on their curious faces. She turned around and assessed John's appearance in one glance. His jacket lay over his shoulder, held in place by the hook of two fingers. Against the stark white shirt, black suspenders ran up his wide chest and made a Y down his back. He looked good enough to eat with a spoon.

"Who's this?" he asked, holding a photograph in a porcelain frame. Staring back at him, Ray Heron looked especially fetching in a pageboy wig and a red kimono. Although Georgeanne had never met Ray, she admired his skill with eyeliner and his flair for dramatic color. Not every woman, or man, could wear that particular shade of red and look so good in it.

"That's Mae's twin brother," she answered, and walked behind her desk once more. She waited for him to say something derogatory and cruel. He didn't. He just lifted one eyebrow and set the photograph back on her desk.

Once again Georgeanne was reminded of how out of place he looked in her environment. He didn't fit. He was too big, too masculine, and too incredibly handsome. "Are you getting married?" she joked as she sat.

He glanced around, then tossed the jacket on the back of an armchair. "Hell no! This isn't mine." He pulled the chair forward and took a seat. "I was in Pioneer Square doing an interview," he explained casually, and shoved his hands into the front pockets of the wool trousers.

Pioneer Square was about five miles from Georgeanne's business. Not exactly in the neighborhood. "Nice tux. Whose is it?"

"I don't know. The magazine probably borrowed it from somewhere."

"What magazine?"

"*GQ*. They wanted a couple of pictures by the waterfall," he answered so nonchalantly, Georgeanne wondered if he was being purposely blasé.

"I needed a little break, so I took off. Do you have a few minutes?"

"A few," she answered, and glanced at the clock on the corner of her desk. "I'm catering a party at three."

He cocked his head to the side. "How many parties do you cater a week?"

Why was he fishing? "Depends on the week," she answered evasively. "Why?"

John glanced about the office. "You seem to be doing real well."

She didn't trust him for a second. He wanted something. "Are you surprised?"

He looked back at her. "I don't know. I guess I just never figured you for a businesswoman. I always thought you'd gone back to Texas and snagged yourself a rich husband."

His unflattering speculation irritated her, but she supposed he wasn't completely without justification. "As you know, that didn't happen. I stayed here and helped build this business." Then, because she couldn't help bragging just a bit, she added, "We do very well."

"I can see that."

Georgeanne stared at the man in front of her. He looked like John. He had the same smile, same scar running through his eyebrow, but he wasn't acting like him. He was acting . . . well, almost nice. Where was the guy who scowled and loved to provoke her? "Is that why you're here? To talk about my business?"

"No. I have something I want to ask you."

"What?"

"Do you ever take a vacation?"

"Sure," she answered, suspicious about where his questions were leading. Did he think that she never took Lexie on a vacation? Last summer they'd flown to Texas to visit Aunt Lolly. "July is typically slow in the catering business. So Mae and I close for a few weeks."

"Which weeks?"

"The middle two."

He tilted his head again and stared into her eyes. "I want Lexie to come with me to Cannon Beach for a few days."

"Cannon Beach, Oregon?"

"Yes. I have a house there."

"No," she answered easily. "She can't go."

"Why not?"

"Because she doesn't know you well enough to take a trip with you."

He frowned. "Obviously you'd come with her."

Georgeanne was incredulous. She placed her hands on the top of her desk and leaned forward. "You want me to stay in your house? With you?"

"Of course."

It was an impossible idea. "Are you completely nuts?"

He shrugged. "Probably."

"I have to work."

"You just said you close for two weeks next month."

"That's true."

"Then say yes."

"No way."

"Why?"

"Why?" she repeated, amazed that he should even ask her to consider staying at another beach house with him. "John, you don't like me."

"I've never said I didn't like you."

"You don't have to say it. You just look at me and I *know* it's true."

His brows drew together. "How do I look at you?"

She sat back. "You scowl and frown at me as if I'd done something tacky, like scratch myself in public."

He smiled. "That bad, huh?"

"Yes."

"What if I promise not to scowl at you?"

"I don't think that's a promise you can keep. You are a very moody person."

He removed one hand from his pocket and placed it over the even pleats of his shirt. "I'm very easygoing."

Georgeanne rolled her eyes. "And Elvis is alive and raising minks somewhere in Nebraska."

John chuckled. "Okay, I'm usually easygoing, but you've got to admit, this situation between us is unusual."

"That's true," she conceded, although she doubted he would ever be mistaken for a nice sensitive guy.

John placed his elbows on his knees and leaned forward. The ends of his tie dangled above his thighs while his suspenders stayed flat against his chest. "This is important to me, Georgie. I don't have a lot of time before I have to leave for training camp. I need to be with Lexie someplace where people don't recognize me."

"People won't recognize you in Oregon?"

"Probably not, and if they do, no one in Oregon gives a damn about a Washington hockey player. I want to give Lexie my full attention, without interruption. I can't do that here. You've been out with me. You've seen what it's like."

He wasn't bragging, just stating a fact. "I imagine getting asked for your autograph all the time must get fairly annoying."

He shrugged one shoulder. "I usually don't mind. Except when I'm standing in front of a urinal and my hands are full."

*Hands.* What an ego! She tried not to laugh. "Your fans must really like you to follow you into the bathroom."

"They don't know me. They like who they think I

am. I'm just a regular guy who plays hockey for a living instead of driving a backhoe." A self-deprecating smile twisted one corner of his mouth. "If they really knew me, they probably wouldn't like me any more than you do."

*I never said that I didn't like you.* The sentence hung between them, unspoken and waiting for Georgeanne to employ some tact and repeat it. She could tell him she liked him—easily. She'd been raised on polite lies. But when she looked into his cobalt blue eyes, she wasn't sure how much would be a lie. As he sat there looking like every woman's fantasy, charming her with his smiles, she wasn't sure how much she really disliked him anymore. Somehow, he'd moved up from a negative thirty to about a minus ten. An improvement over an hour ago. "I like you more than this paper cut," she admitted as she held up her index finger. "But less than a bad hair day."

He looked at her for several prolonged moments. "So . . . I'm somewhere between a paper cut and a bad hair day?"

"That's correct."

"I can live with that."

Georgeanne didn't know what to say to him when he was being so agreeable. She was saved the trouble by the ringing of the telephone. "Excuse me for a moment," she said, and picked up the receiver. "Heron Catering, this is Georgeanne." The male voice on the other end didn't waste any time telling her exactly what he wanted.

"No," she said in answer to his inquiry. "We don't do naked-torso cakes."

John chuckled beneath his breath as he stood. He glanced about the room, then moved toward a bookcase beneath the window. The sun glinted off a gold cuff link at his wrist as he reached behind a thriving fern and picked up one of Georgeanne's least favorite pictures. Mae had snapped the photo during Georgeanne's eighth month of pregnancy, which was why it was hidden behind the plant.

"I'm sure," she said into the receiver, "you have us confused with someone else." The gentleman adamantly argued that he was positive Heron's had catered his friend's bachelor party. He went into detail, and Georgeanne was forced to lower her voice and say, "I know for a fact that we have never provided topless pool waitresses for any occasion. And I don't even know what a bootie girl is." She looked at John's profile, but his expression gave no indication that he'd heard her. His brows were lowered as he stared at the picture of Georgeanne looking as big as a circus tent in a pink and white polka-dot maternity dress.

When she hung up the telephone, she stood and walked around the side of her desk. "That's an awful picture," she said as she came to stand beside him.

"You were huge."

"Thanks." She made a grab for the photograph, but he held it out of her reach.

"I didn't mean fat," he said as he stared at the picture. "I meant very pregnant."

"I was *very* pregnant." She reached for it again and missed. "Now give it to me."

"What did you crave?"

"What are you talking about?"

"Pregnant women are supposed to crave pickles and ice cream."

"Sushi."

He grimaced and looked at her out of the corners of his eyes. "You like sushi?"

"Not anymore. I ate so much of it that I couldn't hardly stand the smell of fish for a long time. And kisses. I craved kisses every night at about nine-thirty."

His gaze lowered to her mouth. "From who?"

She felt her stomach go a little squishy. A very dangerous feeling. "Chocolate kisses."

"Raw fish and chocolate, hmm." He stared at her mouth for a few more seconds, then looked back at the picture. "How much did Lexie weigh when she was born?"

"Nine pounds three ounces."

His eyes widened, and he smiled as if he were very proud of himself. "Holy shit!"

"That's what Mae said when they weighed Lexie." She grabbed for the picture again and this time snatched it from his grasp.

He turned to her and held out his hand. "I wasn't finished looking at that."

Georgeanne hid it behind her back. "Yes, you were."

He dropped his hand to his side. "Don't make me body-check you."

"You wouldn't."

"Oh, yes I would," he said, his voice low, silky. "It's my job and I'm a professional."

It had been a long time since Georgeanne had flirted and teased. She didn't do that sort of thing anymore. She retreated a few steps backward. "I don't know what body-check means. Is it like being frisked?"

"No." He tilted his head back and looked at her from beneath lowered lids. "But I might be willing to change the rules for you."

The edge of the desk stopped Georgeanne. The room felt as if it had suddenly gotten a whole lot smaller, and the look in his eyes made her heart flutter like a debutante's fake lashes.

"Come on now, give it up."

Before she knew exactly how it happened, seven years of self-improvement flew out the window. She opened her mouth and words poured out like warm butter. "I haven't heard such sweet talk since high school," she drawled.

John grinned. "Did it work?"

She smiled and shook her head.

"Are you going to make me get rough with you?"

"That didn't work, either."

His deep, rich laugher filled her office and lit his eyes. The man standing before her was intriguing and magnetic. This was the John who'd charmed her out of her clothes seven years, ago then dumped her faster than toxic waste. "Aren't the people from *GQ* waiting for you?"

Without taking his eyes from her, he raised his arm and pushed back his cuff. He turned his wrist pulse side up and quickly glanced at his gold watch. "Are you kicking me out?"

"Absolutely."

He tugged his cuff down and reached for his tuxedo jacket. "Think about Oregon."

"I don't need to think about it." She wasn't going. Period.

The door swung opened and Charles entered, putting an end to any further discussion and bringing with him a change in the air. With his brows raised, Charles looked from Georgeanne to John, then back again. "Hello," he said.

Georgeanne straightened. "I thought we weren't meeting until noon." She set the picture on the desk.

"I finished with my meeting early, and I thought I'd come by and pick you up." He looked back at John and something passed between the two men. Some primal and intrinsic male *thing*. A nonverbal encoded language that she didn't understand. Georgeanne broke the silence and introduce the two of them.

"Georgeanne tells me you're Lexie's father," Charles said after several strained moments.

"That's right." John was ten years younger than Charles. He was tall and athletic. A beautiful man with a beautiful body. His mind was as twisted as a curly fry.

Charles stood an inch taller than Georgeanne and was thin rather than beefy. His looks were more distinguished, like a senator or congressman. He was sane. "Lexie's a wonderful little girl."

"Yes. She is."

Charles slid a possessive arm around Georgeanne's waist and pulled her against his side. "Georgeanne is a fantastic mother, and an incredible woman." He gave her a little squeeze. "She's a talented cook, too."

"Yes. I remember."

Charles's brows lowered. "She doesn't need anything."

"From who?" John asked.

"From you."

John looked from Charles to Georgeanne. A knowing smile showed his straight white teeth. "You still crave kisses at night, baby doll?"

She felt like socking him a good one. He was purposely trying to provoke Charles. And Charles . . . She didn't know what was the matter with him. "Not anymore," she said.

"Maybe you're not kissing the right person." He shrugged into his jacket and tugged at his cuffs.

"Or maybe I'm satisfied."

He cast a skeptical glance at Charles before turning his gaze back to Georgeanne. "See ya later," he said, and left the room.

She watched him leave, then turned to Charles. "What was that all about? What was going on between you two?"

Charles was silent a moment, his brows still lowered over his gray eyes. "An old-fashion pissing contest."

Georgeanne had never heard Charles use a swear word before. She was shocked and alarmed. She didn't want him to feel he had to compete with John. The two men were in different leagues. John was crude and lewd and used profanity as if it were a second language. Charles had polish and was a gentleman. John was a down-and-dirty, win-at-all-costs fighter. Charles didn't stand a chance against a man who used both hands at the urinal.

Charles shook her head. "I'm sorry for using vulgar language."

"It's okay. John seems to bring out the worst in people."

"What did he want?"

"To talk about Lexie."

"What else?"

"That's all."

"Then why did he ask you about craving kisses?"

"He was provoking me. Something he does quite well. Don't let him bug you." She wrapped her arms around his neck, reassuring him and herself. "I don't want to talk about John. I want to talk about us. I thought maybe this Sunday we could load the girls up and spend the day looking for whales near the San Juans. I know it's a real touristy thing to do, but I've never done it, and I've always wanted to. What do you think?"

He kissed her lips and smiled. "I think you're gorgeous, and I'll do anything you want."

"Anything?"

"Yes."

"Then take me to lunch. I'm starving." She took Charles's hand, and as they walked from the room, she noticed the picture of her looking like a circus tent was gone.

# Eleven

For the first time in seven years, Mae was almost glad her twin brother was dead. Ray's friends were moving out of state or checking out altogether, and he'd never been able to handle desertion. No matter that the person deserting hadn't been given a choice.

Mae shoved her sunglasses on the bridge of her nose and walked across the hospital lobby. If Ray were alive, he wouldn't have been able to endure watching his good friend and lover, Stan, waste away from AIDS-related cancer. He would have become too emotional, unable to hide his grief. But not Mae. Mae had always been stronger than her twin.

She ducked her head and pushed open one of the heavy glass doors. She was a control nut. So what. If she weren't, she might not have been able to come to the hospital to say her final good-bye to Stan. If it weren't for her self-control, she just might lose it before she got home. She might break down right there and weep for the man who'd helped her through the death of her brother. The man who loved a good joke, an early tee-off, and Liberace memorabilia. Stan was so much more than a skeleton waiting for his family to take him home to die. He was so much more than the latest AIDS casualty. He was her friend and she loved him.

Mae took a deep breath of the cool morning breeze and cleared her lungs of antiseptic hospital air. She started up Fifteenth Avenue toward the house she shared with her cat, Bootsie.

"Hey there, Mae."

She paused midstride, and glancing over her shoulder, she looked right into the grinning face of Hugh Miner. A blue baseball cap shaded his eyes, and his light brown hair curled up like little fishhooks along the edges. He grasped three big hockey sticks in one hand, hooking the blades over a broad shoulder. Seeing him in her neighborhood was a surprise. Mae lived on Capital Hill, an area just east of downtown Seattle well known for its substantial gay and lesbian population. Mae had been around gay men all of her life and could tell sexual preference within minutes of meeting a person. The first and only time she'd met Hugh, she'd known within *seconds* that he was one hundred percent heterosexual. "What are you doing here?" she asked.

"I'm dropping these sticks off at the hospital."

"Why?"

"For an auction."

She turned to face him. "People actually pay for your old hockey sticks?"

"You bet." His smile grew and he rocked back on his heels. "I'm a great goalie."

She shook her head. "You're an egomaniac."

"You say that as if it's a bad thing. Some women actually like that about me."

Mae didn't care for his type of man, handsome and cocky. "Some women are desperate."

He chuckled. "What are you doing today, beside spreading sunshine?"

"Walking home."

His smile fell. "Do you live around here?"

"Yep."

"Are you a lesbian, sweetheart?"

She thought of how Georgeanne would have howled with laughter over that question. "Does it matter?"

He shrugged. "It'd be a damn shame, but it would explain why you're so ornery."

Mae wasn't usually ornery to men. She loved men. Just not the athletic type. "Just because I'm rude to you doesn't mean I'm a lesbian."

"Well, are you?"

She hesitated. "No."

"That's good." He smiled again and shifted his weight to one foot. "Do you want to go get a cup of coffee or a beer somewhere?"

Mae laughed without humor. "Get real," she scoffed, and moved to the curb. She glanced up and down Fifteenth and waited for the traffic to slow.

"Sorry about that, sunshine," Hugh called after her as if she'd asked him a question. "But I don't go in for that kinky stuff."

Mae looked at him as she stepped between two parked cars. He was walking backward toward the hospital entrance and pointing the hockey sticks at her. "But if you're real good and wear something slutty, maybe I'll take you to that triple-X theater down on First. The *French Orgy* is playin', and I know how you love those foreign films."

"You're sick," she muttered, and crossed Fifteenth. She easily dismissed Hugh from her mind. She had more important things to think about than a jock with a thick neck. Her circle of friends was getting smaller all the time. Just last week she'd had to say good-bye to her longtime pal and neighbor, Armando "Mandy" Ruiz. She hadn't even known he was thinking of leaving until the day she'd watched him pack up his Chevy. He'd left Seattle for L.A. Left to answer the call of bright lights and to chase his dream of becoming the next RuPaul. Mae would miss Stan, and she'd miss Mandy, too.

But she still had her family. She still had Georgeanne and Lexie. They were enough for now. For now she was satisfied with her life.

John opened his front door and sized up Georgeanne in one quick glance. At ten in the morning, she looked fresh and perfectly flawless. She'd brushed her dark hair into a twisted bun on the back of her head, and diamond studs adorned each earlobe. She wore one of those awful female power suits that hid her deep cleavage and covered her to her knees. "Did you bring them?" he asked, and stepped aside to let her into his houseboat. When she walked past, he raised his arm a little and took a quick sniff. He didn't smell too bad, but maybe he should have taken a shower after his run. Maybe he should have changed out of his jogging shorts and ratty gray T-shirt.

"Yes, I brought several." Georgeanne walked into the living room, and he shut the door behind her. "Just make sure you keep your part of the bargain."

"Let me see the goods first." As she dug into her beige briefcase, his eyes slid down her body. The severity of her hair and the blue and white pinstripes made her appear almost sexless—almost. But her eyes were a little too green, her mouth a bit too full and a shade too red. And her body . . . well, hell, there wasn't a damn thing she could wear to conceal her breasts. Just looking at her made a man think evil thoughts.

"Here." She shoved a framed picture at him.

He took the photograph of Lexie and moved to the leather sofa. It was a school picture, with Lexie giving the camera a real cheesy smile. "What kind of grades did she get in school?" he asked.

"They don't give grades in kindergarten."

He sat with his knees wide. "Then how do you know if she's learning what she needs?"

"She's had two years of preschool. She reads and writes simple words really well, thank God. I was so afraid she might struggle."

When she sat next to him, he looked at her. "Why?"

Georgeanne pushed up the corners of her mouth. "No reason."

She was lying, but he didn't want to argue with her—not yet. "I hate when you do that."

"What?"

"Smile when you don't mean it."

"Too bad. There are a lot of things I don't like about you."

"Like what?"

"Like you stealing that awful picture from my office yesterday and holding it for ransom. I don't appreciate blackmail."

He hadn't intended to blackmail her. He'd taken the photograph because he liked it. No other reason. He liked to look at her beautiful face and her pregnant belly, huge with his baby. When he looked at it, his chest swelled with pride, nearly choking him with good old-fashioned testicular machismo. "Georgie, Georgie," he sighed. "I thought we'd cleared up these ugly accusations last night on the phone. I told you, I simply *borrowed* that picture," he lied. He'd never had any intention of giving it back, but then she'd called and yelled at him about it, and he'd decided to use her emotions to his advantage.

"Now give me the photograph you stole."

John shook his head. "Not until you replace it with

something of equal or greater value. This one is kind of cheesy," he said, and set the school picture on the coffee table. "What else ya got?"

She handed him a portrait taken in one of those glamour studios in the mall. He stared at his little girl, looking like a tart in heavy makeup, long rhinestone earrings, and a fluffy purple boa. He frowned and tossed it on the table. "I don't think so."

"It's her favorite."

"Then I'll think about it. What else?"

She scowled and bent forward to dig deeper into her briefcase. A slit in the side of her skirt parted and slid up her thigh, gracing him with a glimpse of bare flesh above tan hose and powder blue garter. Holy Mother of God. "Where are you going dressed like that?"

She straightened. The skirt closed, and the show was over.

"I'm meeting a client in her home on Mercer." She handed him another photograph, but he didn't look at it.

"Are you sure you're not meeting your boyfriend?"

"Charles?"

"Do you have more than one?"

"No, I don't have more than one, and I'm sure I'm not meeting him."

John didn't believe her. Women didn't wear underwear like that unless they were planning on showing it to someone. "Do you want some coffee?" He stood before his imagination sucked him into a fantasy of soft thighs and blue lace.

"Sure." Georgeanne followed him into the kitchen, filling the room with the sound of her heels tapping the hardwood floors.

"Charles doesn't like me, you know," John informed her as he poured coffee into two navy mugs.

"I know, but I wasn't under the impression that you liked him either."

"No. I don't," he said, but his dislike of the man wasn't personal. The guy was a real dickweed, true enough, but that wasn't his primary objection. John hated the thought of any man in Lexie's life—period. "How serious is your relationship?"

"That's none of your business."

Maybe, but he was going to press the issue anyway. He handed her the mug. "Cream or sugar?"

"Do you have Equal?"

"Yep." He dug in a cupboard for the little blue packet and gave her a spoon. "Your boyfriend is my business if he spends time with my daughter."

Georgeanne's long fingers emptied the sweetener into her coffee and she slowly stirred. Her nails were mauve, long, and perfect. Sunlight poured in through the window above the sink, catching in her hair and earrings. "Lexie has met Charles twice and she seems to like him. He has a daughter who is ten, and she and Lexie play well together." She set the spoon in the sink and looked up at him. "I think that's all you need to know."

"If Lexie has only met him twice, then you haven't known him very long."

"No, not long." She pursed her lips a little and blew into her coffee. John rested one hip against the white tile counter and watched her take a sip. He'd bet she hadn't slept with him yet. It would explain why the man had been so hostile toward John. "What is he going to say when he finds out that you and Lexie are coming to Cannon Beach with me?"

"Easy. We're not going."

He'd spent the previous night figuring out a way to coerce her into agreeing with his vacation plans. He would appeal to her emotions; God knew she had those in spades. Everything she felt was right there in her green eyes. Even though she tried to hide her feelings behind bland smiles, John had spent his life reading the faces of tough, coolheaded men. Men who reined in emotion while uncorking haymakers with detached precision. Georgeanne didn't stand a chance. He would appeal to her maternal side. If that didn't work, he'd improvise. "Lexie needs to spend time with me, and I need to build a relationship with her. I don't know a lot about little girls," he confessed with a shrug, "but I bought a book written on the subject by a woman doctor. She writes that the relationship a girl has with her father could determine how she relates to the men in her life. Say, if a girl's father isn't around, or if he's a jerk, she could really be fuc—ahh... messed up."

Georgeanne looked at John for several long moments, then carefully set her mug on the counter. She knew from personal experience that he was right. She'd been messed up for a lot of years. But his being right didn't persuade her to spend a vacation with him. "Lexie can get to know you here. The three of us alone would be a disaster."

"It's not the three of us you're worried about. It's the *two* of us." He pointed at her and then himself. "You and me."

"You and I don't get along."

He folded his arms across his wide chest, and the worn collar of his gray T-shirt dipped, exposing his clavicle and the base of his throat. "I think you're afraid we'll get along too well. You're afraid you'll end up in my bed."

"Don't be absurd." She rolled her eyes. "I don't even like you very much, and I'm not the least little bit attracted to you."

"I don't believe you."

"I don't care what you believe."

"You're afraid that once we're alone, you won't be able to resist jumping in bed with me."

Georgeanne laughed. John was rich and handsome.

He was a well-known athlete and had the powerful body of a warrior. She wasn't concerned she'd jump in bed with him. Not even if he were that last man on earth and held a gun to her head. "You need to get over yourself."

"I think I'm right."

"No." She shook her head and walked out of the kitchen. "You're delusional."

"But you don't need to worry," he continued, and followed close behind. "I'm immune to you."

Georgeanne reached for her briefcase and set it on the couch.

"You're beautiful and Christ knows you've got a body to make a priest weep, but I'm just not tempted."

His announcement stung a little more than she liked to admit. Secretly she wanted him to eat his heart out every time he laid eyes on her. She wanted him to kick himself for dumping her the way he had. She raised an eyebrow as if she didn't believe him and pointed to the coffee table. "Which pictures do you want?"

"Leave all of them."

"Fine." She had copies at home. "Give me the photo you stole from my office."

"In a minute." He grabbed her arm and stared into her eyes. "I'm trying to tell you that you'd be completely safe in my house. You could rip your clothes off and walk around bare-assed, and I wouldn't even look."

She felt her old self emerge to salvage her pride, the old Georgeanne who had been sure of nothing but her effect on men. "Honey, if I stripped my clothes off, you'd pop blood vessels in your eyeballs and your heart would palpitate. I'd have to give you mouth-to-mouth resuscitation."

"You're wrong about that, Georgie. Sorry to hurt your feelings, but I find you completely resistible," he said, dropping his hand and stinging her pride a bit more. "You could put me in a headlock and stick your tongue in my mouth, and I wouldn't respond."

"Are you trying to convince me or yourself?"

He looked her up and down. "Just stating facts."

"Uh-huh. Well, here's a fact for you." She treated him to the same up-and-down body browse. Her gaze started at his taut calves and moved up his muscular thighs, waist, broad chest, and wide shoulders to his handsome face. He looked macho and kind of sweaty. "I'd rather kiss a dead fish."

"Georgie, I've seen your boyfriend. You do kiss dead fish."

"Better than a dumb jock like you."

His eyes narrowed. "You sure about that?"

She smiled, satisfied that she'd provoked him. "Absolutely."

Before she knew what happened, John wrapped an arm around her waist and jerked her forward. He shoved his fingers into the twisted bun on the back of her head. "Open up and say ahh," he said as his mouth came down hard on hers. She gasped her surprise, and shock kept her arms limp at her sides. His blue eyes stared into hers, then he softened the kiss, and she felt the tip of his tongue lightly touch her top lip. He licked the corner of her mouth and applied a little suction. His eyes drifted closed and he pulled her tighter against his chest. A warm shiver ran up her spine and her scalp tingled. His mouth was hot and wet, and before she had a chance to think about it, she kissed him back. She touched her tongue to his and turned up the heat a little more. Then just as suddenly as it began, he pushed her away.

"See?" he said, taking a deep breath and letting it out slowly. "Nothing."

Georgeanne blinked and looked up at him standing there as cool as a day in December. She could still feel the pressure of his mouth against hers. He'd kissed her and she'd let him.

"There isn't any reason why the two of us can't share a house for a week." He wiped his thumb across his bottom lip, removing a red smear. "Unless, of course, you felt something from that kiss."

"No. Not a thing," she tried to assure him, and pushed the corners of her mouth upward, but she had felt something. She still did. Something warm and weightless in the pit of her stomach. She'd let him kiss her and she didn't know why. She grabbed her briefcase and headed for the door before she screamed or cried and made a fool of herself. Perhaps it was too late. Responding to John's kiss had certainly been foolish.

As she walked toward her car, she realized she'd hurried out of his house so fast, she'd forgot the picture he'd stolen from her. Well, she wasn't going back to get it. Not now. And she wasn't going to Oregon with him either. No way. *Nada.* Not going to happen.

John stood on the deck attached to the back of his house and looked out at Lake Union. He'd kissed her. Touched her. And now he regretted it. He'd told her he hadn't felt anything. If she'd bothered to check, she would have known he lied.

He didn't know why he'd kissed her, except that maybe he'd wanted to assure her she'd be safe at his house in Oregon. Or maybe because she'd told him she'd rather kiss a dead fish. But mostly likely because she was gorgeous and sexy and wore blue lace garters, and he'd wanted a quick taste of her lips. Just one quick kiss. Just for science. That's all he'd wanted. He got more. He got a swift kick of lust and a throb in his groin. He got a hell of an ache and no real pleasurable way to take care of it.

John kicked off his shoes and dove into the cold water, letting it cool his body. He wouldn't make the same mistake again. No kissing. No touching. No thinking about Georgeanne naked.

# Twelve

Georgeanne hadn't meant to agree to John's vacation plans. She'd meant to remain firm in her opposition to Cannon beach. She would have, too, if it weren't for Lexie and her interest in her fictional daddy, Anthony.

The day after they'd gone sailing near the San Juan Islands, Lexie's questions started. Perhaps watching Charles with Amber had triggered her curiosity. Perhaps it was her age. Periodically Lexie had always asked about Anthony, but for the first time, Georgeanne tried to answer without prevarication. Then she'd called John and told him they'd meet him in Oregon. If Lexie was going to have a relationship with John, then she needed to spend time with him before she was told that he was her daddy. Now as Georgeanne drove toward the city of Cannon Beach, she hoped she wasn't making a colossal mistake. John had promised her that he wouldn't try to provoke her, but she didn't really believe him.

"I'll be on my best behavior," he'd promised.

Yeah. Right. And elephants roosted in trees.

She looked over at her daughter belted in the seat

next to her. While Lexie meticulously colored a picture of a Muppet Baby, her black smiley-face ball cap shaded her forehead and her kiddie blue sunglasses covered her eyes. It was Saturday, so her lips were painted a vivid red. And at last, those little red lips were stilled, and quiet filled the inside of the Hyundai.

The trip had started out pleasant enough, but then somewhere around Tacoma, Lexie had started to sing . . . and sing . . . and sing. She'd sung the only verse she knew of "Puff the Magic Dragon" and all verses of "Where Is Thumbkin?" She'd belted out the words to "Deep in the Heart of Texas" and had clapped as enthusiastically as any proud Texan. Unfortunately she sang it clear to Astoria.

Just when Georgeanne had finished calculating the number of years before she could ship Lexie safely off to college, the singing had stopped and Georgeanne had felt like a horrible mother for visually kicking Lexie from the nest.

But then the questions began. "Are we there yet?" "How much longer?" "Where are we?" "Did you remember to pack blankie?" From Astoria to Seaside, she'd become worried about where she was going to sleep and the number of bathrooms in John's house. She couldn't remember if she'd packed her press-on fingernails, and she fretted over whether she'd brought enough Barbies to play with for five whole days. She did remember her beach toys, but what if it rained the whole time? And she wondered if there were kids in his neighborhood, how many and how old?

Now as Georgeanne drove through Cannon Beach, she was reminded of dozens of other artsy communities that dotted the coastal Northwest. Studios and cafés and gift shops lined the main street. The storefronts wore subdued shades of blues and grays and foamy greens, and whales and starfish were painted everywhere. The sidewalks were filled with tourists, and colorful flags fluttered in the always present breeze.

She glanced at the digital clock above the radio in the dash of her car. She had been raised on punctuality and usually arrived on schedule, but today she was early by about a half hour. Somewhere between Tacoma and Gearhart, her foot got real heavy on the accelerator. Somewhere between the first round of "Where Is Thumbkin?" and "Are we there yet?" she'd gassed the Hyundai up past eighty-five. The possibility of getting stopped by a cop and given a ticket hadn't concerned her. In fact, she would have welcomed the adult conversation.

She looked at the map John had drawn for her and drove past weathered homes sandwiched between beachside resorts. She slowed to read his bold, scrawling handwriting, then she turned onto a heavily shaded street and drove straight ahead as instructed and easily found the house. She pulled her Hyundai next to John's dark green Range Rover parked in the driveway of a white single-story house with a steep roof of wooden shingles. Gnarled pine and acacia shaded the wood porch, stained a light gray. She left the luggage in the car and, with Lexie's hand in hers, walked to the front door. With each step Georgeanne's heart picked up its pace. With each step her concern that she was making a big mistake grew.

She rang the bell and knocked several times. No one answered. Looking at the map, she read it carefully again. If she'd drawn it herself, she would have felt the familiar uncertainty that usually sat on her chest when she feared she'd transposed numbers again.

"Maybe he's takin' a nap," Lexie suggested. "Maybe we should go in and wake him up."

"Yeah, maybe." Georgeanne looked at the numbers on the house once more, then she moved to the mailbox nailed to the house and opened the top. She peered inside and hoped neither a neighbor nor a gun-toting postal employee was watching. She pulled out a business reply card addressed to John.

"Do you think he forgot?" Lexie asked.

"I hope not," Georgeanne answered as she turned the handle and opened the door. What if he had forgotten? she asked herself. What if he was somewhere in the house asleep? Or taking a shower—with a woman? She knew she was a little early; what if he was in bed, his body entwined with some gullible woman?

"John?" she called out, and stepped into the entryway. Her feet sank into plush carpeting the color of champagne, and with Lexie following close behind, Georgeanne walked into the living room. She immediately realized that the house was not a single story as it appeared from the front. To her left, steps led downward, while to her right a second set went up to an open loft above the dining room. The house was built into the hillside overlooking the beach and ocean, and the entire back wall was made of massive windows framed with bleached oak. Three matching skylights dominated the ceiling above the living room.

"Wow," Lexie gasped as she spun around in a circle. "Is John rich?"

"It looks that way, doesn't it?" The furnishings were modern and made primarily of bleached wood and iron. An overstuffed sectional, upholstered in deep blue, was angled to take in the view of the ocean or the fireplace on the left wall. Above the mantel hung a large picture of John's grandfather standing next to one of those big blue fish tourists catch off the coast of Florida. It had been a long time since Georgeanne had seen Ernie, but she easily recognized him.

"I wonder if John fell down somewhere." Lexie moved toward one of three sliding glass doors off the living and dining rooms. "Maybe he broke his leg or got a cut."

Together the two of them moved to the doors and looked out on a wraparound deck which went down to the beach. Beyond the deck, Haystack Rock jutted toward the clear blue sky. Seabirds circled and hovered above the green vegetation clinging to the top half of the enormous rock while their continuous squawks mingled with the crash of waves.

"John!" Lexie called out in a raised voice. "Where are you?"

Georgeanne opened the sliding door and let in a breeze heavy with the scents of salt water and seaweed and the sounds of the sea. She stepped out onto the deck, took a deep breath, and let it out slowly. Maybe spending the week in such a beautiful house on such a wonderful piece of real estate wasn't going to be such a hardship after all. If she didn't let John charm her into moving him up further on her likable scale, and if he kept his lips to himself, then perhaps this trip wouldn't turn into a big mistake.

Beneath her feet, Georgeanne felt a heavy thud, thud, thud through the soles of her espadrilles. She heard the steady thumping of footsteps pounding up the stairs, and her insides got a little mushy. Then John emerged one slice at a time. A pair of yellow headphones was strapped across his sweat-dampened hair, and the lower half of his face was covered with a dark shadow of a beard. Next came his wide shoulders and powerful chest. He wore a loose-fitting mesh tank top that looked like he'd hacked off the bottom with a pair of hedge trimmers. Georgeanne wondered why he'd even bothered to wear it. His stomach was flat and bare except for short, dark hair swirling around his navel, then disappearing like the shaft of an arrow into his navy running shorts. He had thighs thick with muscle, and his legs were long and tanned.

"You're early," she heard him say as he tried to catch his breath. She looked up as he pushed his headphones to circle his neck. He glanced at his sports watch turned backward on his wrist. "If I'd known, I would have been here."

"Sorry," she said, refusing to blush at the sight of him. She was an adult. She could handle a hot, sweaty, half-naked man. She could certainly handle John Kowalsky—no problem. She just had to think of him as one big bad hair day. Uncooperative, annoying, and real messy. "My foot got a little heavy on the gas petal," she explained.

"How long have you been here?" He reached for a white towel hanging on the rail. He dried his face and hair as if he'd just gotten out of the shower, then his whole head disappeared beneath the thick cotton.

"Just a few minutes."

"Umm, we thought you fell down and hurt yourself," Lexie informed him, distracted by the sight of his stomach. Up to this point in her life, she'd never been close to a half-dressed man. She stared at all that skin and hair and took a step forward to get a better look. "I thought maybe you broke your leg or got a cut," she said.

His head poked out from beneath the towel. He looked a Lexie and smiled. "Did you get a Band-Aid ready just in case?" he asked as he slid the towel around his neck, holding on to the ends with both hands.

She shook her head. "You gots a hairy tummy, John. Really hairy!" she said, then turned to the railing, her short attention drawn to the activity on the beach below.

He looked down and placed a big hand on his hard abdomen. "I don't think I'm that bad," he said as he rubbed his palm across his stomach. "I know guys who are a lot worse. At least I don't have hair on my back."

Georgeanne watched his hand slide lower on his abdomen, his long fingers slipping through short hair, and memories shimmering in her head like a mirage. She remembered a night a long time ago when she'd touched him, when she'd felt him warm and virile beneath her hands.

"What are you looking at, Georgeanne?"

She raised her gaze up his chest to his eyes. She'd been caught. She could act mortified and guilty or lie. "I was checking out your shoes."

He chuckled silently. "You were checking out my package."

Or she could admit it. "It was a long drive." She shrugged. "I'll go get our things out of the car."

John stepped in front of her. "I'll get your stuff."

"Thank you."

He slid the door open. "You're welcome," he said though an arrogant smile, and walked across the living room.

"Hey, John!" Lexie hollered, and ran past her mother, leaving Georgeanne to follow behind them both. "I brung my roller skates. And guess what."

"What?"

"My mom bought me new Barbie knee pads."

"Barbie?"

"Yeah."

He opened the front door. "Cool."

"And guess what else."

"What?"

"I gots new sunglasses." She took the blue frames from the bridge of her nose and held them up in the air. "See?"

John turned toward her. "Hey, those are real nice." He stopped and stared into her face. "Are you going to wear all that purple stuff while you're here?" he asked, referring to her liberal application of eye shadow.

She nodded. "I get to wear it on Saturdays and Sundays."

He walked to the back of the Hyundai and said, "Maybe, since you're on vacation, you could take a break from wearing all that makeup."

"No way. I like it. It's my most favorite thing."

"I thought dogs and cats were your most favorite."

"Well, makeup is my most favorite thing that I can *have*."

His sigh was heavy with resignation as he took two suitcases and a duffel bag of toys from the backseat of the car. "Is this all?" he asked.

Georgeanne smiled and unlocked the trunk.

"Jesus," John swore as he stared at three more suitcases, two yellow rain slickers, one big umbrella, and a Barbie Beauty Parlor. "Did you pack your whole house?"

"This has been condensed several times since the original load," she told him, and reached for the jackets and umbrella. "Please don't swear in front of Lexie."

"Did I swear?" John asked, looking innocent.

Georgeanne nodded.

Lexie giggled and grabbed her Barbie Beauty Parlor.

Georgeanne and Lexie followed him back into the house and downstairs. He showed them to a guest room decorated in shades of beige and green, then he left to retrieve their luggage. When he'd carried in all their things, he gave a quick tour of the lower floor. A room filled with free weights and exercise equipment separated the guest room from the master bedroom.

"I need to take a shower," John told them as they headed into the hall after Lexie's inspection of all three bathrooms. "When I get out, we can go look in tide pools if you want."

"Why don't you meet us down there," Georgeanne suggested, wanting to take advantage of the sunbreak while it lasted, before the skies clouded and became overcast.

"Sounds good. Do you need beach towels?"

Georgeanne had never been a Girl Scout but was usually prepared for anything and everything. She'd brought her own. After John left them, Lexie and Georgeanne changed. Lexie slipped into her pink and purple plaid two-piece swimsuit, then pulled her DON'T MESS WITH TEXAS T-shirt over her head. Georgeanne changed into a pair of orange and yellow tie-dyed drawstring shorts, a matching halter that left her abdomen bare, and because she felt a bit too exposed, she slipped her arms into a light cotton blouse. The yellow fabric fell past her behind and she left it unbuttoned. Both she and Lexie shoved their feet into Teva sandals, grabbed beach towels and sunscreen, then headed outside.

By the time John joined them on the beach, Lexie had found a broken sand dollar, half a shell, and a little crab claw. She put them in her pink pail and crouched down beside Georgeanne to inspect a sea anemone stuck to one of many small rocks exposed by the low tide.

"Touch it," Georgeanne told her. "It's sticky."

Lexie shook her head. "I know it's sticky, but I don't like to touch 'em."

"It won't bite you," John told her, casting a shadow over the two of them.

Georgeanne glanced up and slowly stood. John had shaved and changed into beige cargo shorts and an olive T-shirt. He looked clean and casual, but too rough and too sensuous to ever look completely respectable. "I think she's afraid it will grab her finger and won't let go." Georgeanne said.

"No, I'm not," Lexie objected, and shook her head again. She scrambled to her feet and pointed to Haystack Rock about a hundred feet away. "I want to go there."

Together the three of them picked their way toward the huge formation. John helped Lexie jump from rock to rock, and when the terrain got a little rough for her short legs, he picked Lexie up and swung her up on his shoulders as effortlessly as if she weighed nothing.

Lexie grabbed the sides of John's head, and her pail swung and hit him on his right cheek. "Mommy, I'm high!" she shrieked.

John and Georgeanne looked at each other and laughed. "Just what every mother longs to hear," she said.

When their laughter died and was drowned out by the sound of waves, John's smile remained. "I was beginning to think that you only wore dresses or skirts," he said as he reached up to wrap his hands around Lexie's ankles.

She wasn't surprised he'd noticed. He was that kind of guy. "I don't usually wear shorts or pants."

"Why?"

Georgeanne didn't really want to answer that question. Lexie, however, had no problem providing personal information. "Because she has a big bum."

John looked up at Lexie, his eye squinted against the sun. "Really?"

Lexie nodded. "Yep. That's what she says all the time."

Georgeanne felt her face flush. "Let's not discuss it."

Reaching for the hem of her yellow shirt, John raised the back and tilted his head to the side for a better look. "It doesn't look big," he said as casually as if they were discussing the weather. "Looks pretty good to me."

Georgeanne felt a little foolish for the ember of pleasure in the pit of her stomach. She batted his hand away and pulled the bottom of her shirt down. "Well, it is," she said, then she stepped around John and walked ahead of him and Lexie. She remembered what had happened seven years ago when he'd turned her head with his smooth compliments. Every southern girl dreamed of being a beauty queen, and with very little effort, he'd made her feel like Miss Texas. She'd eagerly jumped in his bed. Now, as she walked around a medium-sized boulder, she reminded herself that while he could be charming, he could also get real nasty.

Once they reached the base of the rock, the three of them explored. John set Lexie back on her feet, and together they examined the usual variety of ocean life. The sky remained cloudless and the day beautiful.

Georgeanne watched John and Lexie together. She watched them discover orange and purple starfish, mussels, and more sticky anemone. She watched their dark heads bent over a tide pool and tried to bury her insecurities.

"It's lost," Lexie said as Georgeanne crouched down next to her beside the tide pool.

"What is?" she asked.

Lexie pointed to a little brown and black fish swimming beneath the surface of the clear, cold water. "It's a baby and its mommy is gone."

"I don't think it's a baby," John told her. "I think it's just a small fish."

She shook her head. "No, John. It's a baby, all right."

"Well, once the tide comes back in, its mommy can come and get it," Georgeanne assured her daughter, attempting to stop Lexie before she got too agitated. When it came to orphans, Lexie was known to get very emotional.

"No." She shook her head again and her chin quivered as she said, "Its mommy is lost, too."

Because Lexie had only known the security of one

parent, and she had no other family besides Mae, Georgeanne had to carefully screen Lexie's movies and videos to make sure that every child and animal had a mother or a father. On her last birthday Georgeanne had let Lexie convince her that she was old enough to watch the movie *Babe.* Major mistake. Lexie had cried for a week afterward. "Its mommy isn't lost. When the tide comes back in, it can go home."

"No, mommies don't leave their babies unless they're lost. The little fish can't ever go home now." She rested her forehead on her knee. "It's gonna die without its mommy." She squeezed her eyes shut and a tear ran down her nose.

Georgeanne gazed across Lexie's bent head toward John. He stared back with a desperate look in his deep blue eyes. He clearly expected her to do something. "I'm sure its daddy is out there swimming around looking for it."

Lexie wasn't buying. "Daddies don't take care of babies."

"Sure they do," John said. "If I were a daddy fish, I'd be out there looking for my baby."

Turning her head, Lexie looked at John for a few moments, weighing his words in her mind. "Would you look until you found it?"

"Absolutely." He glanced at Georgeanne, then back at Lexie. "If I knew I had a baby, I'd look forever."

Lexie sniffed and stared back into the clear water. "What if it dies before the tide comes back?"

"Hmm." John reached for Lexie's bucket, dumped out her shells, and scooped the tiny fish inside.

"What are you doing?" Lexie asked as the three of them stood.

"Taking your little fish to its daddy," he said, and turned toward the tide. "Stay here with your mother."

Georgeanne and Lexie stood on a flat rock and watched John wade out into the surf. Gentle waves swept up his thighs, and she heard his gasp as the cold water soaked the bottom of his shorts. He looked about him, and after a few moments, he carefully lowered the pail into the ocean.

"Do you think it found the daddy fish?" Lexie asked anxiously.

Georgeanne stared at the big man with the little pink pail and said, "Oh, I'm certain he did."

He walked back toward them. A smile on his face. John "The Wall" Kowalsky, big bad hockey player, hero of small girls and guardian of tiny fish, had just sneaked past Bad Hair Day on her likable scale.

"Did you find him?" Lexie jumped off the rock and waded in up to her knees.

"Yep, and boy, was he happy to see his baby."

"How did you know it was the daddy?"

John gave Lexie her pail, then took her little hand in his. "Because they look alike."

"Oh, yeah." She nodded. "What did he do when he saw his baby?"

He stopped in front of the rock where Georgeanne stood and looked up at her. "Well, he jumped up in the air, and then he swam around and around his little fish just to make sure it was all right."

"I saw him do that."

John laughed and little lines appeared at the corners of his eyes. "Really? From clear over here?"

"Yep. I'm gettin' my towel 'cause I'm freezin'," she announced, then took off up the beach.

Georgeanne looked into his face and matched his smile with her own. "How does it feel to be a hero?" she asked.

John grabbed Georgeanne's waist and easily lifted her from the rock. Her hands grasped his shoulders as he lowered her feet into the frigid surf. Waves swirled about her calves and the breeze tousled her hair. "Am

I your hero?" he asked, his voice gone all low and silky. Dangerous.

"No." She dropped her hands from his hard shoulders and took a step backward. He was a big, powerful man, and yet he was very gentle and caring with Lexie. He was slicker than an oil spill, and if she wasn't careful, he could make her forget the painful past. "I don't like you, remember?"

"Uh-huh." His smile told her he didn't believe her for a minute. "Do you remember the time we were together on the beach in Copalis?"

She turned toward shore and spotted Lexie bundled up on the beach. "What about it?"

"You told me you hated me, and look what happened." As they walked through the surf, he looked at her out of the corners of his eyes.

"Then it's a good thing you find me completely resistible."

He glanced at her chest, then turned his gaze toward the shore. "Yeah, good thing."

When the three of them got back to the house, John insisted on making lunch. They sat at the dining room table and ate shrimp cocktail, slices of fresh fruit, and pita bread filled with crab salad. While Georgeanne and Lexie helped John put things away, she spied a deli sack stuck back in the corner by his answering machine.

By four o'clock the morning spent in the car with Lexie and the anxiety of the trip left Georgeanne exhausted. She found a soft chaise lounge on the deck and curled up with Lexie in her lap. John took the chair next to her, and the three of them stared out at the ocean, content with the world. She didn't have anywhere to go or anything to do. She savored the calmness of it all. Although she couldn't say that the man sitting next to her was relaxing company—John was too big a presence and there was too much painful history between them for that—this house on the coast went a long way toward making up for the strained moments when he did his best to provoke her.

The peaceful sounds and the soft breeze lulled Georgeanne to sleep, and when she awoke, she was alone. A handcrafted blanket with shells on it covered her legs. She pushed it aside, stood, and stretched the kinks from her bones. Voices from the beach rose on the breeze, and she moved to the rail and leaned over the edge. John and Lexie weren't on the beach. She pulled her hand back and a sharp sliver stabbed the soft pad of her middle finger. Her finger throbbed, but she had a more pressing concern.

Georgeanne really didn't think John would take Lexie anywhere without talking to her about it first. But he wasn't the sort of man who would think he needed her permission. If he'd left with her daughter, then Georgeanne figured she had a right to kill him and consider it justifiable homicide. But in the end, she didn't have to kill him. She found both Lexie and John downstairs in the weight room.

John sat on a fancy exercise bike in the corner, pedaling at a steady pace. His gaze was lowered to Lexie, who lay on the floor, her hands behind her head and one dirty little foot resting on her bent knee.

"How come you gotta ride that so fast?" Lexie asked him.

"It helps my stamina," he answered above the soft whirring of the front wheel. He still wore the olive T-shirt he'd worn earlier, and for one short second, Georgeanne let her gaze travel to his strong thighs and calves, and she took in the pleasure of watching him.

"What's stam-na?"

"It's endurance. The stuff a guy needs so that he doesn't run out of steam and let the young guys kick his ass all over the ice."

Lexie gasped. "You did it again."

"What?"

"You swore."

"I did?"

"Yep."

"Sorry. I'll work on it."

"That's what you said last time," Lexie complained from her position on the floor.

He smiled. "I'll do better, Coach."

Lexie was quiet for a moment before she said, "Guess what."

"What?"

"My mom gots a bike like that." She pointed in John's direction. " 'Cept I don't think she rides it."

Georgeanne's exercise bicycle wasn't like John's. It wasn't as expensive, and Lexie was right, she didn't ride it anymore. In fact, she never really had ridden it. "Hey," she said as she stepped into the room, "I use that bike all the time. It has a very important job as a shirt hanger."

Lexie turned her head and smiled. "We're working out. I rode first and now it's John's turn."

John looked over at her. The bicycle pedals stopped, but the wheel kept spinning. "Yes. I can see that," she said, wishing she'd brushed her hair before she'd found them. She was sure she looked scary.

John didn't agree. She looked tousled and flushed from sleep. Her voice a bit lower than normal. "How was your nap?"

"I hadn't even known I was that tired." She combed her fingers through her hair and shook her head.

"Well, keeping up with the twists and turns of a certain little mind is exhausting," he said, and wondered if she was doing that hair-shaking stuff on purpose.

"Very." Georgeanne walked over to Lexie and held out a hand to help her to her feet. "Let's go find something to do and let John finish."

"I am finished," he said as he stood, keeping his eyes above chest level and trying not to stare like a schoolboy at her cleavage. He really didn't want her to catch him ogling her body and think he was some kind of perverted bastard. She was the mother of his child, and although she never really said anything specific, he knew she didn't have a very high opinion of him as it was. Maybe he deserved her low opinion. Maybe not. "Actually, I wasn't going to do this today, but Lexie and I got a little bored waiting for you. It was either ride the exercise bike or play Barbie Beauty Parlor."

"I can't see you playing Barbies."

"That makes two of us." But there was just one problem with his good intentions; the halter top she wore was sapping his willpower. Kind of like Superman and kryptonite. "Lexie and I have been talking about finding some oysters for dinner."

"Oysters?" Georgeanne turned her attention to Lexie. "You won't like oysters."

"Yeah-huh. John said I would."

Georgeanne didn't argue, but an hour later as they sat in a seafood restaurant, Lexie took one look at the picture of oysters on the menu and wrinkled her nose. "That's yucky," she said. When their waitress approached the table, Lexie ordered a toasted cheese sandwich on "fresh" bread, fries on a separate plate, and Heinz ketchup.

The waitress turned her attention to Georgeanne, and John sat back and observed the power of her southern charm and megawatt smile.

"I know you're very busy, and I know from experience that your job is thankless and extremely hectic, but you look like a sweetheart, and I was so hoping I might make just a few little changes," she began, her voice oozing compassion for the woman and her "thankless" job. By the time she was finished, she'd ordered salmon with a "lemon-chive brown-butter sauce" that wasn't even on the menu. She substituted new potatoes for the rice, with "no butter, just a dash of salt, and a pinch of chives." She ordered her cantaloupe served on a separate plate because "cantaloupe should never be served warm." John half expected the woman to tell Georgeanne to go to hell, but she didn't. The waitress seemed only too happy to change the menu for Georgeanne.

Compared to his two female companions, John's order was extremely easy. Oysters on the half shell. Nothing extra. Nothing on the side. As soon as the waitress left, he looked across the table at the two females with him. Both wore light summer dresses. Georgeanne's matched the green of her eyes. Lexie's matched the blue of her eye *shadow*. He tried not to frown, but he hated to see all that makeup on his little girl. It was embarrassing and made him grateful for the darkness of the booth.

"Are you gonna eat those?" Lexie asked once their food arrived. She leaned forward, fascinated yet repulsed by his dinner.

"Yep." He reached for a half shell and raised it to his lips. "Mmm," he said, then sucked the oyster into his mouth and down his throat.

Lexie squealed, and Georgeanne looked a little squeamish and turned her attention to her salmon with lemon-chive brown-butter sauce.

The rest of the meal progressed fairly well. They chatted with a bit less tension than usual, but the ease of the evening ended when the waitress set the check next to him. Georgeanne reached for it, but he stopped her with his hand. Her eyes met his across the table, and she looked like a woman who wanted to drop the gloves and fight for the check.

"I'll get it," she said.

"Don't make me get rough with you," he warned,

and squeezed her hand. He wasn't opposed to the match, just the arena.

Rather than argue, she let him win, but the look she gave him said she clearly meant to discuss it again later when they were alone.

On the way home from the restaurant, Lexie fell asleep in the backseat of John's Range Rover. He carried her into the house, feeling her warm breath on the side of his neck. He would have liked to hold her longer, but he didn't. He would have liked to stay while Georgeanne got her ready for bed, but he felt a little funny about it and left.

Georgeanne watched John leave and reached for Lexie's shoes. She dressed Lexie in her pajamas and put her to bed. Then she went in search of John. She wanted to ask him about tweezers for the sliver in her finger, and she needed to talk to him about the money he was spending on her and Lexie. She wanted him to stop. She could pay for herself. And she could pay for Lexie, too.

She found John standing at the bank of windows, staring out at the ocean. His hands were shoved in the front pockets of his jeans. The sleeves of his denim shirt were rolled up his forearms, and the setting sun cast him in a fiery glow, making him appear bigger than life. When she entered the room, he turned to face her.

"I need to talk to you about something," she said as she walked toward him, bracing herself for an argument.

"I know what you're going to say, and if it will keep that scowl off your pretty forehead, then you can pick up the check next time."

"Oh." She stopped in front of him. She'd won before she'd begun, and felt somewhat deflated. "How did you know that's what I wanted to talk about?"

"You've been frowning at me since the waitress

placed the check by my plate. For a few seconds I thought you really were going to leap across the table and wrestle me for it."

For a few seconds she had thought of it, too. "I would never wrestle in public."

"I'm glad to hear it." In the gray wash of approaching night, she saw a corner of his mouth lift slightly. "'Cause I could take you."

"Maybe," she said, unwilling to concede. "Do you have a pair of tweezers?"

"What are you going to do, pluck my eyebrows?"

"No. I have a sliver."

John walked into the dining room and flipped on the light above the pedestal table. "Let me see it."

Georgeanne didn't follow. "It's no big deal."

"Let me see it," he repeated.

With a sigh, she gave up and walked into the dining room. She held out her hand and showed him her middle finger.

"That's not too bad," he announced.

She leaned closer for a better look, and their foreheads almost touched. "It's huge."

A frown lowered his brows. "I'll be right back," he said, and left the room, only to return with a pair of tweezers. "Have a seat."

"I can do it myself."

"I know you can." He turned a chair backward and straddled it. "But I can get it out easier because I can use both hands." He placed his forearms on the top rung and motioned to another chair. "I promise I won't hurt you."

Warily she took a seat and shoved her hand toward him, purposely keeping an arm's length between them. John closed the short distance by scooting his chair until her knees touched the back of the wooden seat, so close that she had to press her legs together so they wouldn't brush the insides of his thighs. She leaned back as far as she could. He took her hand in his palm and squeezed the pad of her middle finger.

"Ouch." She tried to pull free, but he tightened his grasp.

He glanced up at her. "That didn't hurt, Georgie."

"Yes, it did!"

He didn't argue, but he didn't let go either. He lowered his gaze and poked at her skin with the tweezers.

"Ouch."

Once again he lifted his gaze and looked at her over their joined hands. "Baby."

"Jerk."

He laughed and shook his head. "If you weren't such a girly girl, this wouldn't be so bad."

"Girly girl? What's a girly girl?"

"Look in the mirror."

That didn't tell her much. She tried to pull her hand back again.

"Just relax," he said as he continued to work at the sliver. "You look like you're about to jump out of your chair. What do you think I'm going to do, stab you with a pair of tweezers?"

"No."

"Than relax, it's almost out."

*Relax?* He was so close he took up all the space. There was only John with his callused palm cupping her hand and his dark head bent over the tips of her fingers. He was so close she could feel the warmth of his thighs through his jeans and the thin cotton of her kiwi-colored dress. John had such a strong presence that relaxing with him so close was impossible. She raised her gaze from the side part in his hair and looked across the living room. Ernie and his big blue fish stared back at her. Her memories of John's grandfather were of a nice older gentleman. She wondered about him now, and she wondered what he thought of Lexie. She decided to ask.

He didn't look up, just shrugged and said, "I haven't told my grandfather or my mother yet."

Georgeanne was surprised. Seven years ago she'd thought John and Ernie were close. "Why?"

"Because both of them have been bothering me to get married again and start a family. When they find out about Lexie, they'll shoot to Seattle faster than a smoker from the sweet spot. I want time to get to know Lexie first, before I'm blitzed by my family. Besides, we agreed to wait to tell her, remember? And with my mother and Ernie hanging around, staring, it might make Lexie uncomfortable."

*Married again?* Georgeanne hadn't heard anything he'd said after he'd uttered those two words. "You were married?"

"Yeah."

"When?"

He let go of her hand and placed the tweezers on the table. "Before I met you."

Georgeanne looked at her finger, and the sliver was gone. She wondered which meeting he was referring to. "The first time?"

"Both times." He grasped the top rung of the chair, leaned back, and frowned a little.

Georgeanne was confused. "Both times?"

"Yep. But I don't think the second marriage really counts."

She couldn't help it. She felt her brows raise and her jaw drop. "You were married twice?" She held up two fingers. "Two times?"

His brows lowered and he drew his mouth into a straight line. "Two isn't that many."

To Georgeanne, who'd never been married, two sounded like a lot.

"Like I said, the second time didn't count anyway. I was only married as long as it took to get a divorce."

"Wow, I didn't know you were ever married at all."

She began to wonder about these two women who'd married John, the father of her child. The man who'd broken her heart. And because she couldn't stand not knowing, she asked, "Where are these women now?"

"My first wife, Linda, died."

"I'm sorry," Georgeanne uttered lamely. "How did she die?"

He stared at her for several prolonged moments. "She just did," he said, subject closed. "And I don't know where DeeDee Delight is. I was real drunk when I married her. When I divorced her, too, for that matter."

*DeeDee Delight?* She stared at him, at a compete loss. *DeeDee Delight? Cryin' all night in a bucket!* She had to ask. She simply couldn't help it. "Was DeeDee a . . . a . . . an entertainer?"

"She was a stripper," he said blandly.

Even though Georgeanne had guessed as much, it was a shock to hear John actually confess to marrying a stripper. It was so shocking. "Really! What did she look like?"

"I don't remember."

"Oh," she said, her curiosity unsatisfied. "I've never been married, but I think I'd remember. You must have been *real* drunk."

"I said I was." He made an exasperated sound. "But you don't have to worry about Lexie around me. I don't drink anymore."

"Are you an alcoholic?" she asked, the question slipping out before she thought better of it. "I'm sorry. You don't have to answer such a personal question."

"It's okay. I probably am," he answered more candid than she would have suspected. "I never checked into Betty Ford, but I was drinking pretty heavily and turning my brain to shit. I was pretty much out of control."

"Was it hard to quit?"

He shrugged. "It wasn't easy, but for my physical and mental well-being, I've had to give up a few things."

"Like what?"

He grinned. "Alcohol, loose women, and the Macarena." He moved forward and hung his wrists over the top rung of the chair. "Now that you know the skeletons in my closet, answer something for me."

"What?"

"Seven years ago, when I bought you a ticket home, I was under the impression you were broke. How did you live, let alone start a business?"

"I was very lucky." She paused a moment before adding, "I answered a help wanted ad for Heron's." Then because he'd been so truthful with her—and because nothing she'd ever done could equal marrying a stripper—she added a little fact about her life that no one knew but Mae. "And I was wearing a diamond that I sold for ten thousand dollars."

He didn't bat an eye. "Virgil's?"

"Virgil gave it to me. It was mine."

A slow smile, which could have meant anything, worked the corners of his mouth. "He didn't want it back?"

Georgeanne folded her arms beneath her breasts and tilted her head to one side. "Sure he did, and I'd planned to give the ring back, too, but he'd taken my clothes and donated them to the Salvation Army."

"That's right. He had your clothes, didn't he?"

"Yep. When I left the wedding, I left everything but my makeup. All I had was that stupid pink dress."

"Yes. I remember that little dress."

"When I called him to ask about my things, he wouldn't even talk to me. He had his housekeeper tell me to drop the ring off at his offices and leave it with his secretary. The housekeeper wasn't very nice about it either, but she did tell me what he'd done with my stuff." Georgeanne wasn't especially proud of selling the ring, but Virgil was partly to blame. "I had to buy all my clothes back at four and five dollars a pop, and I didn't have any money."

"So you sold the ring."

"To a jeweler who was happy to get it for half of what it was worth. When I first met Mae, her catering business wasn't doing real well. I gave her a lot of that ring money to pay off some of her creditors. That money might have given me a little help, but I've worked my tail off to get where I am today."

"I'm not judging you, Georgie."

She hadn't realized that she sounded so defensive. "Some people might, if they knew the truth."

Amusement appeared in the corners of his eyes. "Who am I to judge you? Jesus, I married DeeDee Delight."

"True," Georgeanne laughed, feeling a little like Scarlett O'Hara unburdening her dishonorable deeds to Rhett Butler. "Does Virgil know about Lexie yet?"

"No. Not yet."

"What do you think he'll do when he finds out?"

"Virgil is a smart businessman, and I'm his franchise player. I don't think he'll do anything. It's been seven years, and it's water under the bridge, anyway. Now, I'm not saying he'll be real happy when I tell him about Lexie, but he and I work together fairly well. Besides, he's married now and seems happy."

Of course, she'd known he'd married. Local papers had reported on his marriage to Caroline Foster-Duffy, director of the Seattle Art Museum. Georgeanne hoped John was right and that Virgil was happy. She harbored him no ill will.

"Answer me something else?"

"No. I answered your question, it's my turn to ask you."

John shook his head. "I told you about DeeDee and

my drinking. That's two skeletons. So you owe me one more."

"Fine. What?"

"The day you brought the pictures of Lexie to my houseboat, you mentioned being relieved that she didn't struggle in school. What did you mean?"

She didn't really want to talk about her dyslexia with John Kowalsky.

"Is it because you think I'm a dumb jock?" He gripped the top rung of the chair and leaned back.

His question surprised her. He looked calm and cool as if her answer didn't matter one way or the other. She had a feeling it mattered more than he wanted her to know. "I'm sorry I called you dumb. I know what it's like to be judged for what you do or how you look." A lot of people suffered from dyslexia, she reminded herself, but knowing that famous people like Cher, Tom Cruise, and Einstein endured it also didn't make it any easier to reveal herself to a man like John. "My concern for Lexie had nothing to do with you. When I was a child, I struggled in school. The three Rs gave me bit of trouble."

Except for a slight crease between his brows, he remained expressionless. He said nothing.

"But you should have seen me in ballet and charm school," she continued, forcing levity into her voice and attempting to coax a smile from him. "While I may have been the worst ballerina to have ever leaped across a stage, I do believe I excelled at charm. In fact, I graduated at the head of my class."

He shook his head and the crease disappeared from his forehead. "I don't doubt it for a second."

Georgeanne laughed and let down her guard a bit. "While other children memorized their multiplication tables, I studied table settings. I know the correct positions for everything, from shrimp forks to finger bowls. I read silver patterns while some girls read

Nancy Drew. I had no problem distinguishing between luncheon silver and dinner silver, but words like *how* and *who,* and *was* and *saw,* gave me fits."

His eyes narrowed a little. "You're dyslexic?"

Georgeanne sat up straighter. "Yes." She knew she shouldn't feel ashamed. Still, she added, "but I've learned to cope. People assume that someone who suffers from dyslexia can't read. That's not true. We just learn a little differently. I read and write like most people, but math will never be my forte. Being dyslexic doesn't really bother me now."

He stared at her for a moment, then said, "But it did as a child."

"Sure."

"Were you tested?"

"Yes. In the fourth grade I was tested by some sort of doctor. I don't really remember." She scooted back her chair and stood, feeling resentment build inside of her. Resentment toward John for forcing her problem into the open as if it were his business. And she felt the old bitterness toward the doctor who'd turned her young life upside down. "He told my grandmother I had a brain dysfunction, which isn't altogether a misstatement, but it is a rather harsh term and a blanket diagnosis. In the seventies, everything from dyslexia to mental retardation was considered a brain dysfunction." She shrugged her shoulders as if none of it really mattered and forced a little laugh. "The doctor said I'd never be real bright. So I grew up feeling a little retarded and a bit lost."

Slowly John stood and moved his chair out of the way. His eyes got real narrow. "No one ever told that doctor to go fuck himself?"

"Well, I—I—" Georgeanne stuttered, taken back by his anger. "I can't imagine my grandmother ever using the F word. She was Baptist."

"Didn't she take you to another doctor? Have you

tested somewhere else? Find a tutor? Any damn thing?"

"No." *She enrolled me in charm school,* she thought.

"Why not?"

"She didn't think there was anything else that could be done. It was the mid-seventies and there wasn't as much information as there is today. But even today, in the nineties, children are still misdiagnosed sometimes."

"Well, it shouldn't happen." His gaze roamed her face, then returned to her eyes.

He still looked angry, but she couldn't think of one reason why he should care. This was a side of John she'd never seen. A side filled with what felt like compassion. This man standing in front of her, the man who looked like John, confused her. "I should go to bed now," she uttered.

He opened his mouth to say something, then closed it again. "Sweet dreams," he said, and took a step back.

But Georgeanne didn't have sweet dreams. She didn't dream at all for a very long time. She lay in bed, staring up at the ceiling and listening to Lexie's even breathing beside her. She lay awake, thinking of John's angry reaction, and her confusion grew.

She thought of his wives, but mostly she thought of Linda. After so many years, he still couldn't bring himself to talk about her death. Georgeanne wondered what sort of woman inspired such love in a man like John. And she wondered if there was a woman somewhere who could fill Linda's place in John's heart.

The more she thought about it, the more she came to realize that she hoped not. Her feelings weren't very nice, but they were real. She didn't want John to find happiness with some skinny woman. She wanted him to regret the day he'd dumped her at Sea-Tac. She wanted him to walk around kicking his own behind for the rest of his life. Not that she'd ever get together with him again, because, of course, she wouldn't even consider it. She just wanted him to suffer. Then maybe when he'd suffered a long time, she'd forgive him for being an insensitive jerk and breaking her heart.

Maybe.

# Thirteen

Georgeanne had a choice between riding a sand bike, driving bumper cars, or in-line skating along the Promenade in Seaside. None of the choices thrilled her—in fact, they all sounded like her idea of hell—but since she had to choose or go along with Lexie's choice of bumper cars, she picked Rollerblading. She hadn't chosen it because of her ability. The last time she'd tried it, she'd fallen so hard she'd had to blink back the tears stinging her eyes. She'd sat there while little kids zipped past, lights flashing, and her tailbone throbbing so bad it had taken all her strength not to grab her behind with both hands.

Her experience with Rollerblades was so vivid, she'd almost chosen bumper cars and taken her chances with whiplash, but then she'd seen the Promenade. The Prom was a nice expanse of sidewalk stretching along the beach and was bordered on the ocean side with a stone wall about two to three feet high. The benches built into the stone caught her eye immediately, and she'd made her choice.

Now as the ocean breeze picked up the ends of her ponytail, Georgeanne sighed happily. She stretched one arm along the top of the stone bench and crossed one knee over the other; the Rollerblade on her left foot swayed to and fro like the tide of the ocean several hundred feet in the distance. She thought she probably looked a little strange sitting there in her sleeveless white silk blouse that laced up the front, her white and purple gauzy skirt, and her rented Ultra Wheels. But she figured it was better to look weird than get up and fall on her behind.

She was more than content just to sit right where she was and watch John teach Lexie to Rollerblade. At home, Lexie buzzed the neighborhood on her Barbie roller skates, but learning to balance on a row of rubber wheels took practice, and Georgeanne was relieved that there was someone more athletic than herself to help Lexie. She was also a little surprised to discover that instead of feeling deserted, she felt as if she'd been released from hazardous duty.

At first, Lexie's ankles had wobbled a little, but John positioned her in front of him, took her arms in his hands, and placed both of his Rollerblades on the outsides of hers. Then he pushed off and the two of them began to move. Georgeanne couldn't hear what he said to Lexie, but she watched her daughter nod and move her feet at the same time as John.

With the added height of the wheels, John looked huge. The back of Lexie's head barely reached the waistband of his jean shorts where he'd tucked in his "Bad Dog" T-shirt. Lexie, with her neon pink bicycle shorts and pink kitty shirt, looked very small and very dainty skating between her father's large feet.

Georgeanne watched them skate away, then she turned her gaze to the tourists who walked the Promenade. A young couple strode past, pushing a two-seated stroller, and Georgeanne wondered, as she often did, what it would be like to have a husband, to have a typical family, and even though she did well on her own, to have a man to share half the worry.

She thought of Charles and felt guilty. She'd told him of her and Lexie's plans to vacation at Cannon Beach, but she'd left out one important detail. She'd left out John. Charles had even called the night before she'd left to wish her a safe trip. She could have told him then, but she hadn't. She'd have to tell him sometime. He wouldn't like it, and she couldn't blame him.

A flock of seagulls squawked above her, drawing her attention from her problems with Charles to several children tossing bread crusts over the Promenade wall toward the beach. Georgeanne watched the birds and the people for a while before she spotted John and Lexie. John skated backward toward her, and she let her gaze slowly slip up his muscular calves, over the backs of his knees and hard thighs, to the wallet making a bulge in his back pocket. Then he crossed one foot behind the other and was suddenly skating forward, beside Lexie. Georgeanne looked at her daughter and laughed. Lexie's brows were lowered and her face pinched as she concentrated on what John was telling her. The two of them slowly wheeled past and John glanced at Georgeanne. His brows lowered when he saw her, and Georgeanne was struck by how much he and Lexie resembled each other. She'd always thought Lexie looked more like John than herself, but with both of them scowling, the similarities were striking.

"I thought you were going to practice around here," he reminded her.

That's what she'd told him, and he'd believed her. "Oh, I did," she lied.

"Then come on." He motioned with his head.

"I need to practice a little more. Y'all go on without me."

Lexie raised her gaze from her feet. "Look, Mommy, I'm good now."

"Yes, I see that." As soon as they wheeled past, Georgeanne resumed her people watching once more. She hoped when John and Lexie returned next time, they would have grown tired of skating and the three of them could retire their Rollerblades and get serious in the gift shops lining Broadway.

But her hopes were dashed when Lexie boldly rolled past as if she'd been born with wheels on her feet.

"Don't go too far now," John called after Lexie, and took a seat by Georgeanne on the stone bench. "She's pretty good for a kid her age," he said, then he smiled, obviously pleased with himself.

"She has always picked things up quickly. She walked a week before she turned nine months old."

He looked down at his feet. "I think I did, too."

"Really? I worried that she'd become bowlegged from walking so early, but there was no way, short of hog-tying, that I could stop her. Besides, Mae said all that bowlegged stuff is an old wives' tale anyway."

They were silent for a moment while both of them watched their daughter. She fell onto her behind, picked herself up, and was off again.

"Wow, that's a first," she said, surprised that Lexie didn't skate toward her with big fat tears in her eyes.

"What?"

"She isn't howling and demanding Band-Aids."

"She told me she was going to be a big girl today."

"Hmm." Georgeanne's eyes narrowed on her daughter. Perhaps Mae was right. Perhaps Lexie was more drama queen than Georgeanne realized.

John nudged her bare arm with his elbow. "You ready?"

"For what?" she asked, although she had a real bad feeling she knew the answer.

"To skate."

She uncrossed her legs and turned toward him on the bench. Through the thin fabric of her skirt, her knee brushed his. "John, I'll be real honest with you. I hate skating."

"Then why did you pick it?"

"Because of this bench. I thought I could just sit here and watch."

He stood and held out his hand. "Come on."

Her gaze traveled from his open palm and up his arm. She looked into his face and shook her head.

He responded by making chicken sounds.

"That's so juvenile." Georgeanne rolled her eyes. "You can coat me with secret herbs and spices and serve me in a bucket, but I'm not skating."

John laughed and creases appeared in the corners of his blue eyes. "Since I promised to be on my best behavior, I won't comment on how I'd like to see you served."

"Thank you."

"Come on, Georgie, I'll help you."

"I need more help than you can provide."

"Five minutes. In five minutes you'll be skating like a pro."

"No, thanks."

"You can't just sit here, Georgie."

"Why not?"

"Because you'll get bored." Then he shrugged and said, "And because Lexie will worry about you."

"Lexie won't worry about me."

"Sure she will. She told me she didn't want you to sit here all by yourself."

He was lying. Like any six-year-old, Lexie was basically self-centered and took her mother for granted. "After five minutes you'll leave and let me hold down the bench?" she asked, compromising so he'd leave her alone.

"I promise, and I promise that I won't let you fall either."

Georgeanne sighed with resignation, placing one

hand in his palm and the other on the stone wall. "I'm not very athletic," she warned him as she carefully stood.

"Well, your other talents make up for it."

She was about to ask him what he meant, but he moved behind her and placed his strong hands on her hips.

"Outside of a good pair of skates," he said close to her left ear, "the most important thing is balance."

Georgeanne felt his breath on the side of her neck and became so flustered her skin tingled. "Where do I put my hands?" she asked.

He took so long to answer she didn't think he was going to. Then just when she opened her mouth to repeat her question, he said, "Wherever you want."

She balled her fingers into fists and held them down at her sides.

"You need to relax," he said as they slowly rolled down the Prom. "You're like a totem pole on wheels."

"I can't help it." Her back collided with his chest, and his hands tightened on her hips.

"Sure you can. First off, you need to bend your knees a little bit and balance your weight over your feet. Then push out with your right foot."

"Isn't the five minutes up yet?"

"No."

"I'll fall."

"I won't let you fall."

Georgeanne took one quick glance down the Promenade, spotted Lexie a short distance away, then looked down at her skates. "Are you sure?" she asked one last time.

"Of course. I do this for a living. Remember?"

"Okay." Carefully she bent her knees slightly.

"Good. Now give a little push," he instructed, but when she did, her feet began to slide out from under her. John wrapped one forearm around her middle and his other hand grabbed her and kept her from falling. She found herself pressed tightly against his chest, her breath frozen in her lungs. She wondered if he knew what he'd grabbed.

There wasn't a doubt that John knew. If he'd been blind, he would have known he'd grabbed one of Georgeanne's big, soft breasts. In a split second his battered control shattered completely. Up until now, he'd done reasonably well at governing his body's reaction to her. Now, for the first time since he'd seen her standing on his deck yesterday morning, his control completely deserted him.

"Are you all right?" he managed, and carefully slid his hand from her breast.

"Yes."

He'd told himself that being around Georgeanne would not pose a problem. That he could handle having her stay with him for five days. He'd been wrong. He should have left her sitting on the bench. "I didn't mean to grab you by your . . . your, ahh . . ." Her behind was pressed into his groin, and for one unguarded moment, lust rolled through him like a ball of fire. He lowered his face to the side of her head. *Holy shit,* he thought, wondering if the side of her neck would taste as good as it looked. John closed his eyes and indulged a fantasy. He inhaled the scent of her hair.

"I think the five minutes are up now."

Sanity returned and he moved his hands to her waist and put several inches between them. He tried to ignore the desire twisting his gut. He told himself that getting sexually involved with Georgeanne was *not* a good idea. Too bad his body wasn't listening.

Since he'd seen her on the beach yesterday in that little halter top and shorts, he'd had to remind himself several times to ignore her long legs and deep cleavage. Even though he'd never thought he would have to, he'd had to remind himself of who she was and what she'd done. But after last night, it didn't seem to matter any longer.

Last night he'd seen behind the beautiful face and the centerfold body. He'd seen the pain she'd tried to hide with her laughter and smiles. She'd told him of table settings and silver patterns and dyslexia and of growing up thinking she was retarded and feeling lost. She'd said it all as if it didn't matter. But it did. To her and to him.

Last night he'd looked past the gorgeous eyes and the big breasts, and he'd seen a woman who deserved his respect. She was the mother of his child. She was also the star of his wild fantasies and erotic dreams.

"I'll help you back to the bench," he said, and moved them toward the stone wall. He told himself to think of her as his best friend's little sister, but thinking of her as his best friend's little sister didn't work. He decided to think of her as *his* sister, but a few hours later, after hitting gift shops and arcades, he gave up thinking of her as anyone's sister. It just didn't work.

Instead, he concentrated on his daughter. Lexie and her constant chatter provided the distraction he needed. She was like a little bucket of cold water, and all of her questions gave him the respite he needed from his thoughts of Georgeanne draped across his bed.

When he looked into Lexie's eyes, he saw her excitement and innocence, and he was amazed that he'd helped create such a perfect little person. When he picked her up and put her on his shoulders, or held her hand, his heart thumped hard in his chest. And when she laughed, he knew that everything was worth it. Having her with him was well worth the hell of wanting her mother.

During the ride back to his house, he kept himself distracted with the sound of Lexie's little voice raised in fervent song. He patiently listened to the same silly jokes she'd told him two weeks ago, and when they got back home, she repaid him by jumping in the bathtub. He'd listened to her singing, laughed at the jokes, and his little distraction deserted him for a tub full of water and a Skipper doll.

John grabbed a copy of *The Hockey News* and sat down at the dining room table. His eyes scanned Mike Brophy's column, but he didn't give it his full attention. Georgeanne stood at the kitchen counter chopping vegetables. Her hair was down and her feet were bare. He turned to a three-page article featuring Mario Lemieux. He liked Mario. He respected him, but at the moment he couldn't concentrate on anything other than the chop-chop-chop of Georgeanne's knife.

Finally he gave up and raised his gaze from the picture of Lemieux getting drilled into the nickel seats. "What are you doing?" he asked her.

She glanced over her shoulder at him, laid down the knife, then turned. "I thought I'd make us a nice salad to go with our lobster tails."

He closed the magazine and stood. "I don't want a *nice* salad."

"Oh, then what do you want?"

He looked from her green eyes to her mouth. *Something real dirty,* he thought. She'd put some pink glossy stuff on her lips and outlined them in a darker shade. He dropped his gaze to her throat, her breasts, and then down to her feet. John had never considered feet sexy. He'd never really thought of them much, but the thin gold ring she wore around her third toe did things to his insides. She reminded him of a harem girl.

"John?"

He walked toward her and looked back up into her face. A harem girl with tilty green eyes and a voluptuous mouth asking him what he wanted. After the day in his houseboat, he knew better than to kiss her.

"What do you want?"

To hell with it, he thought as he stopped directly in front of her. Just one kiss. He could stop. He'd stopped before, and with Lexie a room away in the tub playing with her Barbies, things couldn't go too far. Georgeanne wasn't his buddy's sister, or his sister, or Sister Mary Theresa either.

John slid his knuckles along her jaw. "I'll show you what I want," he said, and watched her eyes widen as he slowly lowered his head. His mouth brushed against hers, giving her time to pull away. "I want this."

Her lips parted on a deep, shuddering breath and her eyes fluttered closed. She was soft and sweet and her lipstick tasted like cherries. He wanted her. He wanted to burn. Plowing his fingers into the side of her hair, he tilted her head and dove into a soul-deep kiss. The kiss was reckless and wild. He fed off her mouth, off her desire and his. He felt her hands on him, on his shoulder, his neck, and the back of his head, holding him to her as she lightly sucked his tongue deeper into her mouth. His craving for her churned deep in the pit of his stomach. He ached for more and reached for the bow holding her blouse closed. He yanked and pulled the material wide across her chest, then he drew back, away from her moist, hot mouth. Her beautiful eyes were going all sleepy with passion and her lips were wet and puffy from their kiss. He slid his gaze down her throat to her breasts. Her blouse lay open, the white lacing crisscrossing her deep cleavage. He knew he was dangerously close to the point of no return. Close, but not quite there yet. He had a little more maneuvering room before he was over the edge.

He cupped her big breasts in his palms and lowered his face to her cleavage. Her skin was warm and smelled powdery, and he felt her swift intake of breath as he kissed the scalloped border of her satin bra. He sucked air into his lungs and closed his eyes, thinking of all the things he wanted to do to her. Hot, sweaty things. Things he remembered doing to her before. He slid the tip of his tongue across her soft flesh and promised himself that he'd stop when he came up for air.

"John, we have to stop now," she gasped, but she didn't move away, nor did she move her hands from the sides of his head.

He knew she was right; even if it weren't for their child in the next room, continuing any further was asinine. And while in his lifetime John had occasionally been an ass, he'd never been a stupid ass. Not for the past several years anyway.

He kissed the slope of her right breast, then with his body aching to continue, urging him to push her to the floor and give her nine inches of good wood, he drew back. When he gazed into her face, he came very close to giving in to his physical hunger. She looked a little stunned, but mostly she looked like a woman who wanted to spend the rest of the evening naked.

"Cryin' all night," she whispered, and reached for the edges of her blouse, pulling them together.

With that honey-sweet accent spilling from her mouth, she reminded him of the girl he'd picked up seven years ago. He was reminded of how she'd looked wrapped up in his sheets. "I guess you like me more than a bad hair day," he said.

She looked down and tied the bow. "I have to check on Lexie," she said, and practically ran from the kitchen.

He watched her go. His skin felt tight, and he was hard enough to pound nails. Sexual frustration clawed at his gut and he figured he had three choices. He could hunt her down and wrestle her out of her clothes, he could take care of it himself, or he could work out his frustration in the weight room. He chose the third and healthiest option.

It took him thirty minutes on the treadmill before he'd cleared his head of her, the taste of her skin and the feel of her breasts in his palms. He did another thirty minutes on the stationary bike, then stopped to work on his strength training.

At the age of thirty-five, John figured he only had a couple more years before he retired from hockey. He wanted to make those remaining years his best, and he had to work harder than ever.

By hockey standards, he was old. He was a veteran, which meant he had to play better than he had at twenty-five or face speculation that he was *too* old and too slow for the game. Sportswriters and front-office management wondered about all veterans. They wondered about Gretzky, Messier, and Hull. And they wondered about Kowalsky, too. If he had a bad night, if his hits were too soft, if his shots too wide, sportswriters would openly question if he was worth his big contract. They hadn't wondered when he'd been in his twenties, but they did now.

Perhaps some of the things they said about him were true. Maybe he was a few seconds slower, but he more than made up for it in pure physical strength. He'd understood years ago that if he wanted to survive, he would have to adapt and adjust. He still played a fairly physical game, but he played smarter now, using his other skills as well.

He'd survived last season with only minor injuries. Now, with only a few weeks before training camp, he was in the best physical condition of his life. He was healthy and fit and ready to shake out the rink rust.

He was ready for the Stanley Cup.

John worked on his legs until his muscles burned, then he did two hundred fifty stomach crunches and jumped in the shower. He changed into a pair of jeans and a white T-shirt before returning upstairs.

When he walked out onto the deck, he found Georgeanne and Lexie sitting together on the same chaise, watching the tide. Neither John nor Georgeanne spoke as he lit the grill, both obviously willing to let Lexie fill the strained silence. During dinner, Georgeanne hardly looked in his direction, and afterward, she jumped up to do the dishes. Since she seemed so eager to get away from him, he let her.

"Do you gots any games, John?" Lexie asked, holding her chin in her hands. Her hair had been braided down the back, and she wore a little purple nightgown. "Like Candy Land or somethin'?"

"No."

"Cards?"

"I might."

"Do you want to play slapjack?"

Slapjack sounded like a good diversion. "Sure." He stood and went in search of a deck of cards, but he couldn't find any. "I guess I don't have any cards," he told a disappointed Lexie.

"Oh. Do you want to play Barbies then?"

He'd rather sever his left nut.

"Lexie," Georgeanne said from the doorway of the kitchen where she stood drying her hands with a towel. "I don't think John wants to play Barbies."

"Please," Lexie begged him. "I'll let you pick out the best clothes."

He looked into her little face with her big blue eyes and pink cheeks and he heard himself say, "Okay, but I get to be Ken."

Lexie jumped off her chair and ran from the room. "Don't got no Ken 'cause his legs broke off," she said over her shoulder.

He glanced at Georgeanne, who stood there with a pitying look in her eyes while shaking her head. At least she wasn't avoiding him anymore.

"Are you going to play?" he asked, figuring that with Georgeanne playing, too, he could quit after a short while.

She laughed silently and walked toward the couch. "No way. You get first pick of all the good clothes."

"You can have first pick," he promised.

"Sorry, big boy." She picked up a magazine and sat down. "You're on your own."

Lexie came back into the room loaded down with toys, and John had a bad feeling he was stuck for a while.

"You can be Jewel Hair Barbie," Lexie said as she tossed him a naked doll, then she opened her arms and pastel plastic furnishings fell to the floor.

He moved to sit cross-legged on the floor, then he picked up the doll and quickly looked her over. As a kid, he would have given just about anything to touch a naked Barbie, but he'd never been lucky enough to get within ogling distance. Now that he was afforded a good look at her, he discovered she had a scrawny ass and her knees made weird crunching sounds.

Resigned to his fate, he sat on the floor and searched through a pile of clothes. He chose a leopard-print leotard with matching leggings. "Do I get a matching handbag?" he asked Lexie, who was busy setting up the beauty parlor.

"No, but you gots some boots." She dug through her stuff, then handed them to him.

He looked them over. "Just what every well-dressed woman needs, a pair of hooker boots."

"What's hooker boots?"

"Never mind," Georgeanne said from her position behind the magazine.

Playing with dolls was a new experience for John. He didn't have a sister or any close female relations his age. As a kid, he'd played with action figures, but mostly he'd just played hockey. He pulled the leotard up over Barbie's hard plastic breasts, then reached for the leggings. As he dressed the doll he realized several thing. First, getting a pair of leggings up rubber legs was a real bitch, and second, if Barbie were real, she wouldn't be the type of woman he'd want to help dress or undress. She was skinny and hard and her feet were pointed. He realized something else, too. "Ahh, Georgeanne?"

"Hmm?"

He turned to look at her. "You're not going to tell anyone about this, are you?"

She lowered the magazine a fraction and her big green eyes peered at him over the top. "What?"

"This," he said, and pointed to the beauty parlor. "Something like this could seriously jeopardize my reputation as a badass. Oh, sorry," he corrected himself before either of the two females had a chance. "Something like this could make my life hell."

Her devious laughter filled the space between them and he couldn't help but laugh, too. He imagined that he looked real stupid sitting there trying to shove boots on a Barbie doll. Then abruptly Georgeanne's laughter died and she tossed the magazine on the end table. "I'm taking a shower," she said as she stood.

"Do you want your perm now?" Lexie asked.

John watched the sway of Georgeanne's hips as she walked from the room. "Do I have to get a perm?" he asked, turning his attention to his daughter.

"Yep."

John hopped his hooker-booted Barbie over to the pink salon chair. He didn't know much about beauty parlors, but he'd had a girlfriend or two who had spent their time and his money in them. "Could you do my nails while I'm here?" he asked, then ordered a bikini wax and an apricot facial.

Lexie laughed and told him he was funny, and suddenly playing Barbies wasn't so bad.

* * *

Lexie lasted until ten o'clock. Exhausted, she insisted that John carry her to bed. By subjecting himself to the Barbie Beauty Parlor, he had scored serious points with his daughter.

At any other time, Georgeanne might have felt hurt by Lexie's defection, but tonight she had other issues on her mind. Other troubles. Big troubles. After that kiss in the kitchen, John had not only moved past bad hair day, but he'd shot past eyebrow tweezing, too. Then if that hadn't been enough, he'd sat down on the floor and played dolls with a six-year-old girl. At first he'd looked funny. A big, muscular man with big hands worrying about a matching handbag and plastic boots. A macho hockey player worrying about his reputation with the guys. Then suddenly he hadn't looked funny at all. He'd looked like he belonged on the floor, shoving leggings on a Barbie. He'd looked like a father, and she was the mother, and suddenly they looked like a real family. Only they weren't. And as they'd looked at each other and laughed, she'd felt a little ache in her heart.

And there was nothing funny about that. Nothing at all, she thought as she walked out onto the deck. She could barely see the ocean waves, but she could hear them. The temperature had dropped and she was glad she'd changed into a blue waffle-knit sweater and a denim skirt. Her toes were a little cold, and she wished she'd remembered her shoes. She wrapped her arms around her and looked up at the night sky. She'd never been good at astronomy, but she loved to look at the stars.

She heard the door behind her open and close, then she felt a blanket drape across her shoulders. "Thank you," she uttered, and wrapped the hand-woven blanket more securely.

"You're welcome. I think Lexie was out before she

hit the sheets," John said as he came to stand beside her at the rail.

"She usually is. I've always considered it a blessing. I love Lexie, but I love it when she's asleep." She shook her head. "That sounds bad."

He chuckled softly. "No, it doesn't. I can see how she can wear a person out. I have a new respect for parents."

She glanced up at his profile as he stared out at the ocean. Light from the house illuminated oblong patches of the wooden deck and threw shadows across his face. He wore a navy blue Gore-Tex jacket, and the salty breeze played with the contrasting green stand-up collar.

"What were you like as a child?" she asked, curious. Lexie and she were not as much alike as everyone believed.

"Fairly hyper. I think I must have subtracted ten or so years from my grandfather's life."

She turned toward him. "Last night you mentioned Ernie and your mother. What about your father?"

John shrugged. "I don't remember him. He died in a car accident when I was five. My mother worked two jobs, so mostly I was raised by my grandmother and grandfather. My grandma Dorothy died when I was about twenty-three."

"Then I guess we have something in common. Both of us were brought up by grandmothers."

He looked across his shoulder at her; the light from the house illuminated his profile. "What about your mother?"

Years ago she'd lied about her past, built it up, made it seem pretty. He obviously didn't remember. Now she was comfortable with who she was and didn't feel she needed to lie. "My mother didn't want me."

"Not want you?" His brows lowered. "Why?"

She shrugged and turned to look out at the black

night and the even blacker silhouette of Haystack Rock. "She wasn't married and I guess..." She paused, then said, "The truth is, I don't really know. I found out only last year from my aunt that she tried to have an abortion, but my grandmother stopped her. When I was born, my grandmother took me home from the hospital. I don't think my mother even looked at me before she left town."

"Are you serious?" He sounded incredulous.

"Of course." Georgeanne hugged herself tighter. "I was always so sure she'd come back, and I used to try to be such a good little girl so she would want me. But she never came back. She never even called." She shrugged again and rubbed her arms. "My grandmother tried to make up for it, though. Clarissa June loved me and took as good a care of me as she could. That meant getting me properly prepared to become someone's wife. She wanted to see me married before she died, and toward the end of her life, she became very diligent about finding me a husband. It got so bad that I wouldn't even go to the Piggly Wiggly with her." Georgeanne smiled at the memory. "She used to try to set me up with everyone from the checkers to the produce manager. But she secretly had her heart set on the butcher, Cletus J. Krebs. Clarissa had been raised on a pig farm and was naturally partial to a good cut of pork. When she found out he was married, she was understandably crushed." She expected a laugh out of him but didn't even get a chuckle.

"What about your father?"

"I don't know who he is."

"No one ever told you?"

"No one besides my mother ever knew, and she wouldn't say. When I was a little girl, sometimes I thought..." She stopped and shook her head, embarrassed. "Never mind," she said, and buried her nose in the blanket.

"What did you think?" he asked.

She looked up at him and responded to the gentle tone in his voice. "It's silly, but I always thought that if he'd known, he would have loved me because I always tried to be so good."

"That's not silly. I'm sure if he'd known about you, he would have loved you very much."

"I don't think so." In her experience, the men she wanted most to love her couldn't. John was an excellent example of that. She turned her head and gazed out at the ocean. "He wouldn't have cared, but it's very nice of you to say so."

"No, it's not. I'm sure it's the truth."

She was just as sure it wasn't, but it didn't matter. She'd given up on fantasies years ago.

The breeze ruffled their hair and silence stretched between them as they looked out at black and silver waves. Then John spoke, barely above the wind. "You break my heart, you know." He shoved his hands into the pockets of his jacket and turned to face her. "We need to talk about what happened in the kitchen earlier."

Georgeanne was stunned by his admission, and she didn't particularly want to talk about their kiss. She didn't know why he'd kissed her, or why she'd responded as if he'd sucked out her will to say no. Her feet were cold now, and she thought it was a good time to retreat and get her thoughts together.

"I'm obviously very attracted to you."

She decided she could stay a bit longer and hear him out.

"I know I've told you that I was immune to you, and that I find you completely resistible. Well, I lied about that. You're beautiful and soft and if things between us were different, I'd give up a lung to make love to you. But they're not, so if you catch me looking at you like I'm about to pounce, I want you to know that I won't. I'm thirty-five and I can control myself. I don't want you to worry that I'll try anything again."

No one had ever offered to give up a body organ to be with her.

"I want to assure you that I won't kiss you or touch you or try to jump your bones. I think we can both agree that sex between us would be a mistake."

Even though she agreed, she felt a little disappointed that he could control himself. "You're right, of course."

"It would ruin what progress we've made toward a workable relationship."

"True."

He turned and looked at her. "If we ignore it, it will go away." His gaze traveled to her hair, then across her face.

"Do you think so?"

A frown settled between his brows and he slowly shook his head. "No, I'm totally full of shit," he said as he pulled his hands from his pockets and cupped her cheeks in his warm palms. His thumb brushed her chilled skin and he lowered his forehead to rest against hers. "I'm a fairly selfish guy and I want you," he said, his voice lowered. "I want to kiss you and touch you and"—he paused and she saw the smile in his eyes—"jump your gorgeous bones. Even though I'm thirty-five, I find it impossible to control myself with you. Wanting you has taken over, and I think about making love to you all the time. Did you know that?"

He surrounded her, took all of her air, and sucked out her depleted resistance. Unable to speak, she shook her head.

"I had a real smutty dream about you last night. It was wild. I did things to you that we won't even talk about, because if I told you, it would get me in trouble."

*He dreamed about me?* She tried to think of something

clever and provocative but couldn't. Her remaining capacity for rational thought deserted her about the time he mentioned jumping her gorgeous bones. She'd always thought her bones were clumsy and unattractive.

"So I'm counting on you to be sensible. I'm counting on you to tell me no." He brushed his mouth against hers and said, "Tell me no and I'll leave you alone."

He was too close, and too handsome, and she wanted him too much to be sensible. She wanted to crawl inside his skin, and she didn't even consider saying no. Her hands released the blanket and it fell from her shoulders to pool at her feet. She grasped the open lapels of his jacket and held on. The tip of her tongue lightly touched the seam of his lips and he opened his mouth to her. The kiss they'd shared earlier had started out slow but had reached the flash point within seconds. This kiss lingered on their lips. Their mouths opened and their tongues lightly touched. They had all night and neither was in a hurry.

Years ago, she'd known how to please a man. The skills she'd perfected to an art form lay buried somewhere deep within her. She didn't know if she still knew how to tease, how to drive a man crazy. She moved her hands to the waistband of his pants and slowly slid her palms beneath his jacket and up his warm abdomen to his chest. Beneath her touch, his hard muscles tightened, and his mouth pressed deeper into hers, creating a soft suction. Her tongue teased him, and she felt the heavy beating of his heart. He moved one of his hands to her hips and pulled her closer against him.

Against her lower stomach, she felt him swell. He was long and hard. Passion and feminine satisfaction mingled and shot threw her, settling in the apex of her thighs. She lightly brushed against him and her passion twisted into a hot coil. His grasp on her hip tightened, then he pulled away from her lips.

"You were good seven years ago," he said as the night breeze stirred the short hair on the side of his head. "I have a feeling you've gotten better."

Georgeanne could have told him that it wasn't because of practice. In fact, she was so out of practice that she didn't have a proper sultry response. Without the distraction of his sensual mouth, and the sound of his shameless words filling her head, she felt the crisp wind slicing through her sweater and she shivered.

"Let's go," he said, and reached for her hand. He pulled her against his side, and together they walked into the house, shutting the door behind them. John kissed her softly on the lips, then he shrugged out of his jacket. "Are you still cold?" he asked as he threw the jacket on the couch.

The hairs on Georgeanne's arms tingled, but not from the cold. "I'm okay," she said as she rubbed her arms through her sweater.

"How about a fire anyway?"

She didn't want to wait that long to feel his lips against hers, but she didn't want to appear love-starved either. "If it's not too much trouble."

He gave her a lazy grin. "Oh, I think I can manage," he said, walked over to the blue and white tile mantel, and flipped a switch. Orange flame shot from the gas jets and lapped at the fake logs.

Georgeanne's smile matched his. "I think that's cheating."

"Only if I'd been a Boy Scout, and I wasn't."

"I should have guessed." She turned to look out the wall of windows but couldn't see past her own reflection. She felt a moment of panic as she hurriedly tried to remember if she wore satin underwear or if she'd changed into ordinary white cotton.

"What?" he asked as he came to stand behind her. "That I wasn't a Boy Scout?" He reached for her and pulled her back against his chest. "Or that I have a fake fire?"

Georgeanne looked at his wavy reflection. She stared into his gorgeous face, and she no longer cared if her panties were Hanes or Victoria's Secret. She arched her back a little and pressed her bottom into his groin. "Is your fire fake, John?"

He sucked in his breath and his chuckle was a little strained when he said, "If you're a good girl, I'll show it to you later." He kissed the crown of her head, then grasped the bottom of her sweater. "But for now, you show me." He pulled the sweater over her head and tossed it aside. Her first instinct was to raise her hands to shield her breasts from his view. Instead, she kept them at her sides and stood before him in her denim skirt and her blue stretch satin bra. His fingers skimmed across her stomach, then he cupped both heavy breasts in his strong hands.

"You're beautiful," he said as his thumbs brushed across the satin covering her nipples. "So beautiful I can hardly breathe."

Georgeanne knew the feeling. She felt as if the breath were pulled from her lungs as she watched his hands lift her breasts. She was unable to look away as he unhooked her bra and slowly pushed the straps from her shoulders. The blue satin slid down the slopes of her breasts, shimmered across her nipples, then fell down her arms to the floor. Suddenly embarrassed, Georgeanne tried to turn to face him, to press herself into his chest and shield herself from his hot gaze. But he moved his hands to her waist and held her where she was.

"Someone might see us," she said.

"No one is out there." He lightly brushed the tips of his fingers across the tips of her breasts.

Her breathing became shallow. "There might be."

"We're not beach level. We're up too high." She

watched as he softly pinched her puckered nipples between his thumbs and forefingers, and suddenly she didn't care anymore. A busload of Shriners could have paraded across the deck, and she wouldn't have cared. She arched her back and raised her arms. Her hands cupped the back of his head and she brought his lips down to hers. She thrust her tongue into his mouth and gave him a hot, greedy kiss. He groaned deep within his chest as he played with her breasts. He lifted and squeezed, then moved his hands to the button at her waist. Her skirt and blue satiny underwear were pushed down her hips and thighs and fell to her feet. She stepped out of them and kicked them aside, then she was naked, her bare bottom pressed against the zipper of his jeans. He was completely dressed while she was completely naked, and the feel of worn denim against her skin was extremely erotic. He tilted his hips and pressed his erection into her behind as his mouth trailed hot little kisses down the side of her throat. He lightly bit her shoulder, then sucked her skin into his mouth.

Georgeanne turned her gaze to the window, and through the blurred glass she watched his big hands slip across her body. He caressed her breasts, her stomach, and her hips. He placed one of his feet between hers and pushed them farther apart. Then he slid his hand to her parted thighs, and he fondled her gently. She was slick where his fingers stroked, and a sharp ache radiated from his touch. Her insides melted, pooling deep and low in her pelvis. His hands, his mouth, his hot gaze. She looked into the reflection of her own face and did not recognize the woman staring back at her. The woman in the window looked drugged. She heard herself moan, and she feared that if she didn't stop him, she'd reach her peak alone. She didn't want that. She wanted him with her.

She let herself savor the pleasure of his hands for a

few more wonderful seconds, then she turned and wrapped her arms around his neck. She kissed him hungrily as she slid her bare knee up the outside of his thigh. His fingers traced a sensual path down her spine, then he grabbed her behind and lifted her onto her toes, grinding his pelvis into hers. She moved her mouth to the side of his throat and tasted his skin. He groaned and she slid back down his body to stand in front of him. Her hands drifted down his stomach to the end of his T-shirt, and she pulled the stretchy cotton from the waistband of his pants.

John raised one arm over his head, reached behind his back, and grabbed a fistful of his shirt. He pulled it over his head and tossed it aside. Georgeanne lowered her gaze from his passion-filled blue eyes to the short, dark curls covering his big, muscular chest. The tips of her breasts touched him a few inches below his flat brown nipples. A trail of fine hair ran down his chest, between her plump cleavage, to his waistband.

"Look at you," he said barely above a whisper. His voice had gone all husky with lust. "You're like the best present I've ever had, like every Christmas all wrapped up in one amazing package."

Georgeanne pulled at his button fly until it lay open. "Have you been a good boy?" she asked as she slipped her hands inside his jeans.

He sucked in a quick breath. "God, yes."

She snagged the elastic waistband of his briefs and pulled them out and away from his flat belly. "In that case," she cooed, and ran one finger up his long, thick shaft, "how do you want to play? Naughty or nice?"

His breath whooshed from his lungs as he stepped on the heels of his cross-trainers and kicked them away. "I don't know how to play nice, and I've spent too many years in the sin bin to change now."

"Naughty then?" She pushed down his jeans and briefs, then ran her hands up his bare thighs. His muscles turned hard beneath her touch, and she delighted in her effect on him.

"Oh, yeah." His voice was strained as he stepped out of his clothes. He retrieved his wallet out of his pants and tossed it on a table at the end of the couch. Then he stood completely naked in front of her, a tall, solid athlete, perfectly toned from years of training. There was nothing soft about him; his physical profession showed on his powerful body.

She inched close to him, and the voluptuous head of his hot penis touched her navel. Her hands slid up his abdomen, and when she looked up into his hooded gaze, she realized that she hadn't forgotten how to please a man. She hadn't forgotten how to please *this* man. Seven years ago he'd shown her how to drive him crazy, and she hadn't forgotten. She leaned forward and touched the tip of her tongue to his flat nipple. Beneath her lips it puckered and turned as hard as leather. His hands moved to the back of her head, and he knotted his fingers in her hair.

"You're killing me. I'm dying."

Georgeanne rose onto the balls of her feet, letting the tips of her breasts graze his chest. "Then may God have mercy on your soul," she whispered as she sucked his earlobe and rubbed against his warm body. She delivered little nibbling bites to his neck and shoulder, then trailed a string of kisses down the column of fine hair trailing to his stomach and lower abdomen. She knelt in front of him and kissed and caressed and fondled until he was breathing hard.

"Time out," he gasped, and reached for her. He wrapped his hands around her arms and pulled her to her feet.

"No time out," she said as she planted her palms on his chest and pushed. He took a step backward and she followed. "This isn't a hockey game." She continued pushing until his heels hit the couch. "And I'm not one of the boys." He sat and she stepped between his thighs.

"Georgie, honey, no one would ever mistake you for a boy." One hand caressed her bottom and he pulled her closer. He sucked a nipple into his hot mouth and moved his other hand to stoke the fire with his fingers. As she watched him kiss her breast, raw emotion pumped through her veins. This was John, the man who could make her feel beautiful and desired. The man who'd ripped out her heart, then given it back nine months later. She closed her eyes and held him close. She held him while he touched her with his hands and mouth, and she told herself this was enough. When she felt herself close to the edge, she stepped back.

Without a word, he reached for his wallet on the end table and pulled out a foil-wrapped condom. He opened the package with his teeth, but before he could sheath himself, Georgeanne took the condom from him. "Never send a man to do a woman's job," she said, and stretched the thin latex down the length of him. She felt him pulse in her hand, ready and straining for release. Then she straddled his lap and looked into his blue eyes. Slowly she lowered herself onto his erection.

He was big and hard and after several attempts, he filled her completely. She sat still for a moment with him deep inside of her, feeling herself stretch to accommodate him. He felt hot, and she felt satisfied yet restless all at the same time. The muscles in his neck were ridged and she dug her fingers into his steely shoulders. His eyes were glazed and his jaw taut. She kissed his lips, then began to move. Whether from arousal or inexperience, her movements were awkward. Her knees sank into the couch, and as he thrust, she rose.

"Relax," he said, his hands cupping her behind. "Take your time."

Georgeanne crushed her mouth against his and groaned her frustration. She couldn't relax and was too far gone to take her time.

John tore his mouth from hers, then wrapped an arm around her back and bottom and turned with her so that she lay on the couch looking up at him. He was still buried deep inside her. He had one knee on the couch while his opposite foot was planted on the floor. "Never send a woman to do a man's job," he said, and withdrew. A distressed moan escaped her throat until he thrust deep inside her again. She clung to him as he drove into her over and over, pushing her toward the precipice. She uttered incoherent words of encouragement, words that would probably embarrass her later, but for now she couldn't control them, nor did she care.

"That's right, honey," he whispered as he plunged deep. "Tell me what you want."

And she did, in exact detail. His chest heaved and he placed his hands on the sides of her face. He told her she was beautiful, and he told her how good she felt to him. With each stroke, he burned her alive, and when she climaxed, she cried his name. Her body milked him hard, and just when she felt her peak subside, it started again.

John's eyes drifted shut, and his breath hissed between his teeth. He answered her cries with his groans of satisfaction. He drove into her one last time, and when he came, his muscles turned to stone and he swore like a hockey player.

# Fourteen

John sat on the edge of his bed and shoved his feet into silver and blue cross-trainers. The room looked like a war zone. Sheets were knotted in the middle of the mattress, and the down comforter and pillows were thrown on the floor. Dirty plates with half-eaten ham sandwiches were stacked on his dresser, and the oil painting he'd purchased from a local artist lay propped against the wall, the frame broken.

He finished tying his shoe, then stood. The room smelled like her, like him—like sex. He stepped over a pile of damp towels and grabbed his Walkman from his dresser. He hooked the headphones around his neck and the tape player to the waistband of his shorts.

Wild. That was the only word he could think of to describe the night before. Wild sex with a beautiful wild woman. Life didn't get much better.

Except there was a problem. Georgeanne wasn't just any beautiful wild woman. She wasn't someone he'd been dating. She wasn't a girlfriend. And she certainly wasn't one of those women who just wanted to get off with a hockey player. She was the mother of his child. Things were bound to get complicated.

He walked out into the hall. His feet stopped in front of the guest bedroom, and he paused at the half-open door and looked inside. Georgeanne's eyes were closed against the dawn seeping through the curtains, and her breathing was slow and easy. She'd changed into a white nightgown that buttoned clear up to the base of her throat, like something out of *Little House on the Prairie.* But about four hours ago, she'd been bare-ass naked in his Jacuzzi in the master bathroom doing her best imitation of a rodeo queen. With a little practice, she'd gotten real good at it, too. He especially liked the way she rocked her pelvis against him while she whispered his name with that sexy southern voice of hers.

Movement behind Georgeanne caught his attention and he lifted his gaze to Lexie. He watched her turn on her side and take most of the sheet with her. He stepped back and headed up the stairs.

Last night she'd once again shown him a slice of her past, shed a brief light on a confused and hurt little girl, lit her up for him to see, and added another dimension to the way he saw her as an adult. He didn't think she'd meant to change anything, certainly not his opinion of her. But she had just the same.

John walked into the kitchen and opened the refrigerator. He reached for a high-protein, high-carbohydrate yogurt shake. Closing the door with his foot, he popped the top to the quick-energy drink and pressed the rewind button on his answering machine. He turned up the volume, leaned one hip into the counter, and raised his breakfast to his lips. The first message was from Ernie, and while he listened to his grandfather's usual gripe about having to leave a message, he thought of Georgeanne. He thought of her voice as she'd talked so casually about her mother. She'd joked about her grandmother trying to marry her off to a butcher at Piggly Wiggly, and she thought it was silly to expect her father's love. She'd seemed embarrassed, as if she were expecting too much.

The answering machine beeped and the voice of his agent, Doug Hennessey, filled the kitchen, informing John of the meeting he'd set up with Bauer. He needed to sit down with the people who custom-made his skates and figure out why his boots had started to bother him last season. John had always worn Bauers. He always would. He wasn't as superstitious as some guys he knew, but he was superstitious enough to fix the problem rather than change the manufacturer.

He chugged the rest of his yogurt drink, crunched the can in a tight grip, and tossed it into a garbage can. The answering machine clicked off, and John walked out of the kitchen. Mist clung to his deck and the beach below. Sparse morning rays penetrated the mist and shot shards of light though the living room windows.

Last night he'd watched her in those windows. He'd watched her clothes slip from her beautiful body, and he'd watched passion soften her mouth and drug her eyes. He'd watched his hands slide over her smooth skin, and his palms cup her soft breasts. He'd watched her rub her bare bottom up and down his fly, and he'd almost exploded right there in his B.V.D.s.

Quietly John moved from the house onto the deck. He jogged as lightly as possible down the steps to the beach. He didn't want to wake Georgeanne. After the night before, he figured she probably needed her sleep.

He needed to think. He needed to think about what had happened, and he needed to think about what to do now. He couldn't avoid Georgeanne, nor did he want to. He liked her. He respected her for everything she'd accomplished in her life, especially now that he understood her a little better. And now he had a better understanding of why she hadn't told him about Lexie seven years ago. He couldn't say he was exactly pleased that she hadn't told him, but he wasn't pissed off about it anymore.

But not being pissed off and being in love were worlds apart. He *liked* her. He hoped she didn't want more because he was beginning to think he wasn't capable of more. He'd been married twice and he'd never loved either woman.

People confused sex with love. John never did. The two were completely separate. He loved his grandfather. He loved his mother. The love he felt for his first child, Toby, and now Lexie, seeped to the marrow of his bones. But he'd never been *in* love with a woman, not the kind of love that made a man crazy. He hoped Georgeanne could keep sex and love separate. He thought she could, but if she couldn't, then dealing with her was bound to get real difficult.

He should have kept his hands to himself last night, but where Georgeanne was concerned, he obviously had a hard time with what he *should* do. Wanting her had twisted him into knots, and sex had been pretty much inevitable anyway. He could tell himself to keep his hands to himself now, but he knew from experience that he probably wouldn't. He didn't have a very good track record with Georgeanne. She had a great body, and sex with her was better than it had been in a good long time.

John's feet hit the wet sand, and he raised his left foot behind him. He grabbed his ankle and stretched his quadriceps.

Their relationship was already tenuous without adding further complications. She was the mother of his child, and he should try to keep his thoughts pure. He wouldn't think about kissing her soft mouth as he slid deep inside her. He'd control himself. He was a disciplined athlete. He could do it.

And if he failed . . .

John lowered his foot and stretched his other leg. He wouldn't fail. He wouldn't even think about it. He wouldn't think about dropping by her house a couple of times a week and sweet-talking her out of her clothes either.

Georgeanne covered a huge yawn as she poured milk over a bowl of Froot Loops. She pushed her hair behind one ear, walked across the kitchen, and set the cereal on the table.

"Where's John?" Lexie asked as she picked up her spoon.

"I don't know." Georgeanne sat down in a chair across from her daughter and pulled the ends of her robe together. She put her elbows on the table and held her chin in her hands. She was dog-tired and her thigh muscles hurt. She hadn't ached so much since that aerobics class she'd joined for three days last year.

"He's probably runnin' again." Lexie scooped up a spoonful of Froot Loops and shoved it into her mouth. She'd worn her hair in a braid to bed the night before, and now it looked fuzzy and stuck out around her head like a real thin Afro. A green O fell on her Princess Jasmine pajamas, and she tossed it back in her bowl.

"Probably," Georgeanne answered, wondering why he needed to exercise after last night. They'd made love in several different locations, with the grand finale in the Jacuzzi. She'd soaped him up all over and kissed the places she rinsed. He'd paid her back by sucking drops of water from her skin. Overall, she'd say they both got a real thorough workout. She closed her eyes and thought of his strong arms and sculpted chest. She pictured herself pressed against his smooth back and muscular behind, her hands caressing his hard abdomen, and she felt her stomach go fuzzy.

"Maybe he'll be back pretty soon," Lexie said, crunching on her cereal.

Georgeanne opened her eyes. Her vision of John in the buff evaporated, replaced by her daughter eating with her mouth stuffed full of colorful O's. "Please chew with your mouth closed," she reminded Lexie automatically. As she looked into her daughter's face, she felt shameless. Having such risqué thoughts in front of an innocent child was indecent, and somewhere in the world she was positive that it was considered a breach of etiquette to visualize a naked man before morning coffee.

Georgeanne walked back into the kitchen and reached into a cupboard to pull out a bag of Starbucks and a paper coffee filter. John had made her feel alive in a way she hadn't felt in a very long time. He looked at her with hunger burning in his deep blue eyes and made her feel desired. He skimmed his fingers across her skin as if she were made of delicate silk and made her feel beautiful. Sex with John had been wonderful. Within his arms she'd turned into a woman who was confident of her own sexuality. For the first time since puberty, she felt comfortable with her body, and she felt sure of herself as a lover for the first time in her life.

But no matter how wonderful, sex with John had been a mistake. She'd known it as she'd stood in the doorway of the guest bedroom and he'd kissed her good night. She'd felt it in the empty pull of her heart. John didn't love her, and she was surprised by how much that hurt.

She'd known from the beginning that he didn't love her. He'd never said it or intimated in any way that he felt anything for her except lust. She didn't blame him. Her pain was her fault and something she'd have to deal with on her own.

Georgeanne filled the water reservoir on the coffeemaker and pushed the on button. She leaned one hip against the counter and folded her arms beneath her breasts. She'd thought she could love him with her body but not her heart. Now all her illusions were gone, burned away in the light of morning. She'd always loved John. She could admit it to herself, but she didn't know what to do about it. How could she see him on a regular basis and pretend she felt nothing more than mild friendship? She didn't know how. She just knew she had to do it.

The telephone rang, startling Georgeanne. The answering machine beeped twice and clicked on. "Yeah, John," a male voice said from the machine, "this is Kirk Schwartz. Sorry it took so long to get back to you. I've been out of the state on vacation for the past two weeks. Anyway, as per your request, I've got a copy of your daughter's birth certificate in front of me. Her mother has listed the father as unknown."

Everything inside of Georgeanne froze. She cut her gaze to the audiotape and watched it slowly turn. "If the mother is still willing to cooperate, then it won't take much to get that changed. As far as visitation and custody, we'll talk about your legal rights when you get back into town. The last time we spoke, I believe we decided that the best course of action at the present time is to keep the mother happy until we determine what to do legally. Uhh . . . I think the fact that you didn't know about your daughter until recently, and that you make a substantial income and want to provide for her, puts you in a very good position here. You'll probably be awarded the same custody as if there had been a divorce between you and the mother. We'll discuss it at length when you get back into town. Talk to you then. 'Bye." The tape shut off and Georgeanne blinked. She turned to Lexie and watched her suck a Froot Loop off the back of her spoon hand.

The trembling began in Georgeanne's chest and

work its way outward. She raised a shaky hand and pressed her fingers to her lips. John had hired a lawyer. He'd said that he wouldn't, but he'd obviously lied to her. He wanted Lexie, and Georgeanne had blithely given him what he wanted. She'd tried to put aside her misgivings and had allowed John the freedom to spend time with his daughter. She'd tried to disregard her own fears because she'd wanted to do what was right for her child.

"Hurry up and finish your cereal," she said as she turned from the kitchen. She had to get away, get away from his house and from him.

Within ten minutes Georgeanne had changed her clothes, brushed her teeth and hair, and had thrown everything into the suitcases. *Keep the mother happy . . .* Georgeanne felt sick when she thought about how happy he'd made her last night. Sleeping with her had gone above the call of duty.

After another five minutes she had the car loaded. "Come on, Lexie," she called out as she walked back into the house. She wanted to be gone by the time John returned. She didn't want a confrontation. She didn't trust herself. She'd been nice. She'd tried to be fair, but no more. Her anger fueled her like a gas line to a blowtorch. She let it burn uncontrolled through her veins. It was better to feel the rage than the humiliation and soul-numbing hurt.

Lexie walked out of the kitchen, still wearing her purple pajamas. "Are we going somewhere?"

"Home."

"Why?"

"Because it's time to go."

"Is John coming, too?"

"No."

"I don't want to go yet."

Georgeanne opened the front door. "That's too dang bad."

Lexie frowned and stomped out of the house. "It's not Saturday yet," she pouted as they headed down the sidewalk. "You said we were staying till Saturday."

"There's been a change of plans. We're going home early." She belted her into the passenger seat, then laid a shirt, shorts, and hairbrush in her lap. "Once we're on the highway, you can change your clothes," she explained as she got behind the wheel. She stared the car and put it in reverse.

"I forgot my Skipper in the bathtub."

Georgeanne stepped on the brakes and looked over at a sullen Lexie. She knew if she didn't go back in and get the Skipper, Lexie would worry and fret and talk about it all the way back to Seattle. "Which one?"

"The one Mae gave me for my birthday."

"Which bathtub?"

"The one by the kitchen."

Georgeanne shoved the car back into park and got out. "The engine is on, so don't touch anything."

Lexie's shrug was noncommittal.

For the first time since childhood, Georgeanne ran. She ran back into the house and into the bathroom. The Skipper doll sat in the soap dish stuck to the tiled wall, and she grabbed it by the legs. She turned around and almost collided with John. He stood in the doorway with his hands planted on the wooden frame.

"What's going on, Georgeanne?"

Her heart twisted in her chest. She hated him. She hated herself. For the second time in her life, she'd let him use her. For the second time, he'd caused her such pain she could barely breathe. "Get out of my way, John."

"Where's Lexie?"

"In the car. We're not staying."

His eyes narrowed. "Why?"

"Because of you." She placed her hands on his chest and shoved.

He moved, but she didn't get very far before he grabbed her arm and stopped her from opening the front door. "Do you act this way with the other guys you sleep with, or did I just luck out?"

Georgeanne whirled around and lashed out at him with her only weapon. She whacked him on the shoulder with the wet Skipper doll. The doll's head popped off and flew into the living room. Her rage boiled beneath the surface, and she felt as if her head were about to pop off just like poor Skipper.

John looked from the headless doll in her hand to her face. His brows were raised. "What's your problem?"

Inbred southern grace, Miss Virdie's charm lessons, and years of her grandmother's polite and proper influence turned to ashes within the inferno of her anger. "Get your slimy hand off of me, you immoral son of a bitch!"

His grip tightened and his eyes bored into hers. "Last night you didn't think I was slimy. I may be a son of a bitch, but not for what we did together. Last night you were hot, I was hard, and we took care of it. It may not have been the wisest choice either of us has ever made, but it happened. Now, deal with it like an adult, for Christ's sake."

Georgeanne yanked her arm from his grasp and stepped back. She wished she were big and strong and could hit him really hard. She wished she were quick with cutting words and could slice his heart. But she was neither physically strong or quick under pressure. "You made sure I was real happy last night, didn't you?"

He blinked. " 'Happy' is as good a word as any, I guess. Although I'd use 'sated,' but if you want to use 'happy,' that's fine by me. You were happy. I was happy. We were both pretty goddamn happy."

She pointed the headless Skipper at him. "You sneaky bastard. You used me."

"Yeah, when was that? When your tongue was down my throat or when your hand was down my pants? The way I see it, there was some pretty mutual using going on."

Georgeanne glared at him through her red haze. They weren't talking about the same thing, yet it was all tied together. "You lied to me."

"About what?"

Instead of giving him the opportunity to lie again, Georgeanne marched into the kitchen and rewound his answering machine. Then she hit the play button and watched John's face as his attorney's voice filled the silent room. His features gave nothing away.

"You're making too big a deal out of this," he said as soon as the tape clicked off. "It's not what you think."

"Is that your lawyer?"

"Yes."

"Then any further contact between us will take place through attorneys." She was deadly calm when she said, "Stay away from Lexie."

"Not a chance." He towered over her. A big, powerful man used to getting his way by the sheer force of his will.

Georgeanne wasn't intimidated. "You have no place in our lives."

"I'm Lexie's father, not some made-up asshole named Tony. You've lied to her about me all of her life. Now it's time she knew the truth. Whatever problems we have between us doesn't change the fact that Lexie is my little girl."

"She doesn't need you."

"Like hell."

"I won't let you near her."

"You can't stop me."

She knew that he was probably right. But she also knew that she would do anything and everything to make sure she didn't lose her daughter. "Stay away," she warned one last time, then turned to leave. Her steps faltered.

Lexie stood in the doorway to the kitchen. She was still dressed in her pajamas and her hair still stuck up around her head. Her gaze was locked on John as if she'd never seen him before. Georgeanne didn't know how long Lexie had been there, but she feared what she might have heard. She grabbed Lexie's hand and dragged her from the house.

"Don't do this, Georgeanne," John called after her. "We can work this out." But she didn't turn back. She'd given him far too much already. She'd given him her heart, her soul, and her trust. She wouldn't give him the most important thing in her life. She could live without her heart, but she couldn't live without Lexie.

Mae picked up the newspaper on Georgeanne's porch, then walked into the house. Lexie sat on the couch with a raspberry-and-cream-cheese muffin in her hand while the television blared the theme song to *The Brady Bunch*. Raspberry-and-cream-cheese muffins were Lexie's favorite and an obvious attempt to soothe the ouchie with sugar. But after what Georgeanne had told her when she'd phoned the night before, Mae wasn't sure a gooey muffin would make everything all better.

"Where's your mom?" Mae asked as she tossed the newspaper on a chair.

"Outside," Lexie answered without taking her eyes from the screen.

Mae decided to leave Lexie alone for now and stepped into the kitchen to make herself a cup of espresso. Then she headed out back and found Georgeanne standing beside the brick porch pruning her Albertine roses and tossing the dead flowers into a wheelbarrow. For the last three years, Mae had watched Georgeanne diligently coax the tangerine roses up the pergola framing her back door. A profusion of pink foxglove and lavender delphinium crowded flower beds at Georgeanne's feet and crammed the garden along the fence. Morning dew clung to the delicate petals and wet the bottom half of Georgeanne's robe. Beneath the orange silk, she wore a wrinkled T-shirt and a pair of white cotton panties. Her hair hung from a ratted ponytail and the mauve fingernail polish on her right hand was badly chipped as if Georgeanne had picked at it. The situation with Lexie was worse than Mae had thought.

"Did you sleep at all last night?" Mae asked from her position on the last step.

Georgeanne shook her head and reached for another wilted rose. "Lexie won't talk to me. She wouldn't talk to me yesterday on the drive home, and she won't talk to me today. She didn't drift off to sleep until around two A.M." She tossed another rose into the wheelbarrow. "What's she doing in there?"

"Watching *The Brady Bunch*," Mae answered as she moved across the brick patio. She set her coffee on a wrought-iron table and sat in a matching chair. "When you called last night, you didn't tell me she was so upset that she couldn't sleep. That's not like her at all."

Georgeanne dropped her hands and looked over her shoulder. "I told you she wasn't talking. That's not at all like her either." She walked toward Mae and set her pruning shears on the table. "I don't know what to do. I've tried to talk to her, but she just ignores me. At first I thought that she might be angry because she was having so much fun at the beach and I made her leave. Now I know that was just wishful thinking on my part. She must have heard John and me arguing." Georgeanne sank down on the chair beside Mae, a ratty lump of misery. "She knows I lied to her about her father."

"What are you going to do now?"

"I have to make an appointment to talk to a lawyer." She yawned and propped her chin on her fists. "I don't know who yet, or where I'm going to get the money for the legal fees."

"Maybe John won't really go through with custody. Maybe if you talk to him, he—"

"I don't want to talk to him," Georgeanne interrupted, suddenly alive. She sat up straight in her chair and her eyes narrowed. "He's a liar and a sneak, and he has no principles at all. He played on my weakness. I should have had sex years ago. I should have listened to you. You were right. I just kind of exploded and became a nymphomaniac. I guess sex isn't the sort of thing you should put off until you explode."

Mae felt her jaw drop. "Get out!"

"Oh, I'm out. I'm way out."

"With the hockey player?"

Georgeanne nodded.

"Again?"

"You'd think I'd have learned the first time."

Mae didn't know what to say. Georgeanne was one of the most sexually repressed women she knew. "How'd that happen?"

"I don't know. We were getting along and it just did."

Mae didn't consider herself promiscuous. She just didn't always say no when she should. By contrast, Georgeanne *always* said no.

"He tricked me. He was nice and so good with Lexie and I forgot. Well, I didn't really forget what a jerk he could be, I just sort of let myself forgive."

Mae didn't believe in forgiving and forgetting. She

liked the Old Testament wrath-of-God stuff and believed in an eye for an eye. But she could see how a good-looking guy like John could make a woman overlook a few things—like being dumped at an airport after a one-night stand—if the woman was attracted to two-hundred pounds of solid muscle, which, of course, Mae was not.

"He didn't have to go that far. I was giving him everything he asked for. Each time he wanted to see Lexie, I arranged it." Anger mixed with the tears in Georgeanne's eyes. "He didn't have to sleep with me. I'm not a charity case."

Even on her worst hair day, with dark circles and chipped nails, Mae really didn't believe any man would consider Georgeanne a charity case. "Do you really believe he made love to you because he felt sorry for you?"

Georgeanne shrugged. "I don't think it was a real hardship for him, but I know he wanted to keep me happy until he and his lawyer could get together and decide what to do about getting custody of Lexie." She covered her cheeks with her palms. "It's so humiliating."

"What can I do to help?" Mae leaned forward and laid her hand on Georgeanne's shoulder. She would take on the world for the people she loved. There were times in her life when she'd felt as if she had. Not so much anymore, but when Ray had been alive, she'd fought both their battles, especially in high school when big, athletic guys had thought it funny to beat him with wet towels. Ray had hated PE, but Mae had hated the jocks who ruled gym class. "What do you want me to do? Do you want me to talk to Lexie?"

Georgeanne shook her head. "I think Lexie needs time to sort everything out in her mind."

"Do you want me to talk to John? I could tell him how you feel and maybe—"

"No." She wiped her cheeks with the backs of her hands. "I don't want him to know how badly he's hurt me again."

"I could hire someone to break his knees."

Georgeanne paused before she said, "No. We don't have enough money to hire a professional hit man, and it's so hard to find good help without ready cash. Look what happened to Tonya Harding. Thanks for the offer, though."

"Ahh . . . what are friends for?"

"I've been through this heartache once before with John. Of course, Lexie wasn't an issue then, but I'll get through it again. I don't know how yet, but I will." Georgeanne pulled her robe securely around her and frowned. "And then there's Charles. What am I going to tell him?"

Mae reached for her espresso. "Absolutely nothing," she answered, then took a sip.

"You think I should lie?"

"No. Just don't tell him."

"What do I say if he asks?"

She set her coffee back on the table. "That depends on how much you like him."

"I really like Charles. I know it doesn't appear that way, but I do."

"Then lie."

Georgeanne shoulders sagged and she sighed. "I feel so guilty. I can't believe I jumped in bed with John. I didn't even think about Charles. Maybe I'm one of those women you read about in *Cosmo* who screw up relationships because deep down I don't think I'm worthy. Maybe I'm destined to love men who can't love me back."

"Maybe you should stop reading *Cosmo*."

Georgeanne shook her head. "I've made such a mess of things. What am I going to do?"

"You'll get through it. You're one of the strongest

women I know." Mae patted Georgeanne's shoulder. She had a lot of faith in Georgeanne's strength and determination. She knew that her friend didn't always see herself as a woman with grit, but then Georgeanne didn't always view herself in an accurate or objective light. "Hey, did I tell you that Hugh, the goalie, called me while you were in Oregon?"

"John's friend? Why?"

"He wanted to go out on a date."

Georgeanne stared at Mae for several incredulous moments. "I thought you made your feelings clear the day you ran into him outside the hospital."

"I did, but he asked again."

"Really? That beats all with a stick."

"Yeah, tell me about it."

"Well, I hope you let him down gently."

"I did."

"What did you say?"

"Hell, no."

Normally Georgeanne and Mae would have debated Mae's rude rejection. Instead Georgeanne shrugged and said, "Well, I guess you won't have to worry that he'll call a second time."

"He did call a second time, but I think he just wanted to annoy me. He called to ask me if I was still wrestling pit bulls."

"What did you say?"

"Nothing. I hung up on him, and he's only called once since then."

"Well, I'm sure it's best just to stay away from all hockey players. Best for the both of us."

"That's not a problem for me." Mae thought of telling Georgeanne about her latest boyfriend, but she decided against it. He was married, and Georgeanne tended to moralize about stuff like that. But Mae felt no qualms about sleeping with another woman's husband as long as he didn't have children. She didn't want marriage. She didn't want to look at the guy's face over dinner every night. She didn't want to do his laundry or birth his babies. She just wanted sex, and married men were perfect. She got to call all the shots and controlled when, where, and how often.

She never told Georgeanne how often she dated married men. Even though Georgeanne apparently had a carnal weakness when it came to John Kowalsky, she could be such a prude sometimes.

# Fifteen

After several hours of grueling drills, coaches and players jammed the ice for a two-puck scrimmage. By day three of training camp, the Chinooks were ready for a little fun. Two of the team's goalies crouched inside the creases at opposite ends of the rink, alert, waiting for someone to fire a rubber biscuit at their heads.

Raw gutter talk and the steady *slur-slur-slur* of skates filled John's ears as he zigzagged down ice. The sleeves of his practice jersey fluttered as he swerved through human traffic. He kept his head up, and the puck sailing close to the blade of his stick. He could feel a rookie third-line defenseman breathing down his neck, and in order to avoid getting knocked into the cheap seats, he shot a high-wrister past Hugh Miner on the short side.

"Eat that, farm boy," he said as he put his weight on the edges of his skates and stopped abruptly in front of the goal. A fine spray of ice powered Hugh's pads.

"Blow me, old man," Hugh grumbled, and reached behind him for the puck. He tossed it toward the other end of the rink, then crouched again and banged his stick on the red posts and cross bar, gaining his bearing without taking his eyes from the scrum.

John laughed and skated back into the free-for-all. When the practice was over, he felt bruised from battle, but happy to be back in the war. Later in the locker room, he handed his skates to a trainer to be sharpened for the next day and took a shower.

"Hey, Kowalsky," an assistant coach called from the doorway to the locker rooms. "Mr. Duffy wants to see you when you're dressed. He's with Coach Nystrom."

"Thanks, Kenny." John tied his shoes, then pulled a green T-shirt with a Chinooks logo over his head and tucked it inside his blue nylon sweatpants. His teammates wandered around the room in various stages of undress, talking hockey, contracts, and the new rules the NHL had instated for the coming season.

It wasn't unusual for Virgil Duffy to ask John to meet him, especially when the team's general manager was out of state scouting for new talent. John was the captain of the Chinooks. He was a veteran player, and no one knew hockey better than the men who had played it for thirty years. Virgil respected John's opinion, and John had come to respect the owner's business acumen, even if at times they didn't agree. At the moment they were debating a second-line enforcer. Good enforcers didn't come cheap, and Virgil didn't always want to pay millions for a limited player.

As John made his way to the front offices, he wondered how Virgil would react when he learned of Lexie's existence. He didn't figure the older gentleman would be real pleased, but he didn't fear being traded anymore. Although he wouldn't completely rule out the possibility. Virgil tended to be a hot reactor. The longer it took for Virgil to hear of what had transpired seven years ago, the better. John wasn't purposely keeping Lexie a secret, but he figured there was no need to rub Virgil's nose in it either.

He thought of Lexie and frowned. Since that morning in Cannon Beach a month and a half ago, Georgeanne had kept Lexie from him. She'd hired a lipstick-wearing pit bull for a lawyer who'd insisted on a paternity test. They'd stalled the test for weeks, then on the day the court-ordered test was to be performed, she'd done an about-face and had signed a document legally acknowledging paternity. With a stroke of Georgeanne's pen, John was legally declared Lexie's father.

A home examiner had been appointed to interview John and inspect his houseboat. The same examiner had talked to Georgeanne and Lexie and had recommended several short introduction visitations between father and child before John would be allowed to keep Lexie for longer periods of time. At the end of the introduction period, John would receive the same custody awarded fathers in a divorce situation, only he didn't even have to appear before a judge. Once Georgeanne had legally acknowledged John as Lexie's father, everything began to move rapidly.

John's frown hardened. But for now, Georgeanne still had him by the short and curlies. He wasn't getting any pleasure out of the experience, but Georgeanne obviously liked her grip. Well, she'd better enjoy it while it lasted, because in the end, what Georgeanne wanted wasn't going to matter very much. She didn't want him to pay child support or his share of Lexie's day care and medical insurance. Through his lawyer, he'd offered generous support, plus full day care and insurance. He wanted to support his child and was willing to pay for whatever she needed, but Georgeanne had refused everything. According to her attorney, she didn't want anything from him. In the end it wasn't going to matter. The lawyers were in the final stages of dotting the i's and crossing the t's. Georgeanne would have to take what he offered.

He hadn't seen or talked to Georgeanne since that morning at the beach house when she'd freaked out over nothing. She'd blown everything way out of proportion, calling him a sneaky liar when he hadn't really lied to her. Okay, maybe that first night when she'd come to his houseboat he might have lied by omission. So they'd agreed not to hire attorneys, but he'd already hired Kirk Schwartz two hours before she'd showed up on his doorstep. He'd already had a basic idea of his rights even before he'd talked to her that night. Maybe he should have told her, but he'd figured she'd just get pissed off and try to keep Lexie from him. And he'd been right. But even now, he wouldn't change what he'd done. He'd needed to know. He had to know his legal options in case Georgeanne moved or married or refused to let him see Lexie. He'd wanted to know who was listed as Lexie's father on her birth certificate. He'd wanted information. His future with Lexie was too important not to know his legal rights.

The image of Lexie standing in the kitchen at his house in Cannon Beach was still vivid in his mind. He remembered the confusion on her face, and the bewildered look in her eye when she'd glanced over her shoulder at him as Georgeanne had dragged her down the sidewalk. He hadn't wanted her to hear about him that way. He'd wanted to spend more time with her first. He'd wanted her to find as much joy in the news as he had.

He didn't know what she thought now, but he would shortly. In two days he would see her for his first short visit.

John entered the coaches' office and shut the door behind him. Virgil Duffy sat on a Naugahyde couch, wearing a linen suit from Fifth Avenue and a tan from the Caribbean.

"Look at that," Virgil said, pointing to a portable television screen. "That kid's made of cement."

Sitting behind his desk, Larry Nystrom didn't look as enthused as the owner. "But he can't hit the lake from the dock."

"He can be taught how to shoot the puck. You can't teach heart." Virgil looked at John and pointed toward the screen. "What do you think?"

John sat on the other end of the couch from Virgil and glanced at the television just in time to see a rookie Florida Panther nail Philly Flyer Eric Lindros to the boards. The six-four Lindros took his time getting to his feet before slowly skating to the bench. "I can tell you from personal experience that he hits high, like a linebacker. And he hits hard, but I'm not sure he has seed. How much?"

"Five hundred thousand."

John shrugged. "He's probably worth five, but we need a guy like Grimson or Domi."

Virgil shook his head. "Too much."

"Who else are you looking at?"

Virgil hit the fast-forward button and together the three men reviewed other prospects. The team trainer brought in a stack of paper and sat across from Nystrom. While the video played, the two men went over each sheet.

"Your body fat is less than twelve percent, Kowalsky," the coach commented without looking up.

John wasn't surprised. He couldn't afford to let weight slow him down anymore, and he'd worked hard to keep it off. "What about Corbet?" he inquired of his teammate. The Chinooks right winger had reported to training camp looking as if he'd spent his summer rooting around an all-you-can-eat barbecue pit.

"Good God!" Nystrom swore. "He's twenty percent fat!"

"Who is?" Virgil asked, and hit the stop button. The tape ejected and a local station flashed a Pampers commercial on the screen.

"That damn Corbet," the trainer answered.

"I'm going to have to light a fire under his lard ass," the coach threatened. "I'll have to suspend him or send him to Jenny Craig."

"Get him a trainer," John suggested.

"Get him on one of Caroline's diets," Virgil suggested. "When she goes on one of her diets, she gets real cranky." Caroline was Virgil's wife of four years, and only a decade younger than her husband. As far as John could tell, she was a nice woman, and they seemed happy together. "Give him a cup of white rice and two ounces of dry chicken before each game, then sit back and watch him kick ass."

The Pampers commercial ended and a voice John hadn't heard in almost two months spoke to him from the television. "You made it back just in time," Georgeanne said from the twelve-inch screen. "I'm about to add a shot of sin, and y'all don't want to miss this."

"What the hell . . ." John muttered, and sat forward.

Georgeanne picked up a bottle of Grand Marnier and poured about a shot into a bowl. "Now, if you have children, y'all will want to set aside a bit of the mousse before you add the liqueur, or liquid sin as my grandmother used to refer to all alcoholic beverages." Her tilty green eyes looked into the camera and she smiled. "If you must abstain from alcohol for religious reasons, are under the age of twenty-one, or if you prefer your sin served straight up, you can choose to forgo the Grand Marnier altogether and add a little grated orange peel instead."

He stared at her, like a dumb mesmerized rodent, remembering the night he'd served her a big dose of straight-up sin. Then the next morning, she'd whacked him with a stupid little doll and had accused him of using her. She was a lunatic. A vindictive crazy woman.

She wore a white blouse with a big embroidered collar and a dark blue apron that tied around her neck. Her hair was pulled back from her face, and little pearls dotted her earlobes. Someone had made an effort to subdue her overblown sexuality, but it didn't matter. It was all there. It was there in her seductive eyes and full red mouth. Surely he wasn't the only one who could see it. She looked ridiculous, like a *Bay Watch* babe playing at a cooking show. He watched her spoon mousse into little porcelain pots and keep up a steady stream of chatter at the same time. When she finished, she raised her hand, parted her lips, and sucked chocolate from her knuckles. He scoffed because he knew, *he just knew*, she was doing that shit for ratings. She was a mother, for God's sake. Mothers of a young daughters shouldn't behave like sex kittens on television.

The television suddenly went black, and John became aware of Virgil for the first time since Georgeanne's face had flashed on the screen. The owner looked stunned and a little white beneath his tan. But other than shock, his face gave nothing away. Not anger, nor rage. Not love, nor a sense of betrayal, for the woman who'd left him at the altar. Virgil stood, tossed the remote on the couch, and without a word, walked out the door.

John watched him go, then turned his attention to the other men. They were still in a discussion about body fat. They hadn't seen Georgeanne, but even if they had, John wasn't sure they would realize who she was. Who she was to him. Who she was to Virgil.

* * *

Georgeanne felt as if she were falling. She'd taped six shows, and the feelings got only slightly better each time. She told herself to relax and have fun. She wasn't on live television, and if she messed up, she could stop and start over. But still, her nerves churned in her stomach as she looked into the camera and confessed, "I don't know if y'all know this, but I'm from Dallas—the land of big hats and big hair. I've studied cuisine from all over the world, but I earned my spurs cooking Tex-Mex. When most people think of Tex-Mex, they think tacos. Well, I'm going to show you something a little different."

For over an hour, Georgeanne chopped mangoes, chilies, and tomatoes. When she was finished, she pulled an already-prepared, simple yet elegant dinner with a Texas theme out of the oven. "Next week," she said, standing beside a vase of black-eyed Susans, "We're going to take a break from the kitchen, and I'm going to show you how to personalize your picture frames. It's real easy to do and a lot of fun. See y'all then."

The light on top of the camera blinked off, and Georgeanne let out a deep breath. Today's taping hadn't gone too badly. She'd only dropped the pork loin once and read the words wrong three times. Not like the first show. The first show had taken seven hours to tape. It had already aired a few days ago, and she was so positive that her chocolate mousse had bombed with the viewers that she hadn't the nerve to watch it herself. Charles had seen the show, of course, and had insisted that she wasn't boring and didn't look fat and stupid. She didn't trust him not to humor her.

Lexie stepped over several cables taped to the floor and walked toward Georgeanne. "I gotta go to the bathroom," she announced.

Georgeanne reached behind her back and untied her apron. She was wired with a portable microphone.

"Give me a few minutes and I'll take you."

"I can go by myself."

"I'll take her," a young production assistant offered.

Georgeanne smiled her gratitude.

Lexie frowned and took the assistant's hand. "I'm not five anymore," she grumbled.

Georgeanne watched her daughter go and pulled the apron over her head. One of the conditions to her doing the show was that she be allowed to bring Lexie to the tapings. Charles had agreed and had given Lexie the title of "creative consultant." Lexie helped with ideas, and she came to the studio and helped Georgeanne prepare the finished dishes beforehand.

"You were great today," Charles greeted her as he emerged from the back of the studio. He waited until her microphone was taken away before he put his arm around her shoulders. "Viewer response from the first show looks real good."

Georgeanne gave a sigh of relief and looked up at him. She didn't want him to keep her show because of their personal relationship. "Are you sure you're not just saying that to be nice to me?"

He placed his mouth at her temple. "I'm sure." She felt his smile when he said, "If your numbers stink, I promise I'll fire you."

"Thank you."

"You're welcome." He kissed the side of her head, then pulled back. "Why don't you and Lexie have dinner with me and Amber?"

Georgeanne grabbed her purse from behind the kitchen counter that served as part of the studio set. "Can't. John is picking up Lexie tonight for their first visit."

Charles's brows drew together over his gray eyes. "Do you want me to be there with you?"

Georgeanne shook her head. "I'll be okay," she said, but she didn't think she would. She was afraid that after Lexie left, she'd fall apart, and she wanted to be alone if she did. Charles had been a very good friend, but he couldn't help her now, not this time.

Three days after her return from Cannon Beach, she'd told Charles about the trip. She'd told him everything except the part about the sex. He hadn't been happy to hear she'd spent time with John, but he hadn't asked a lot of questions either. Instead, he'd given her the name of his ex-wife's attorney and reoffered the half-hour television show. She'd needed the money and had accepted with the conditions that the shows be taped instead of live and that Lexie be welcome to accompany her.

A week later, she'd signed a contract.

"What does Lexie think about spending time with her father?"

Georgeanne hooked her leather bag over her shoulder. "I don't really know. I know she's a little confused about her last name now that it's Kowalsky. She has a hard time spelling it, but other than that, she doesn't say much."

"She doesn't talk about him?"

For several weeks after Lexie had learned that John was her father, she'd been cold and distant toward Georgeanne. Georgeanne had tried to explain why she'd lied, and Lexie had listened quietly. Then she'd directed all of her anger at her mother, hurting them both before letting it go. Their lives would never be the same. But for the most part, she was the same little girl now that she'd been before she'd learned of John. Although there were also times when she was unusually quiet. Georgeanne didn't have to ask her what she was thinking, she just knew. "I've told her John was coming to pick her up for a visit tonight. She didn't say much about it, just asked when he'd bring her back home."

Lexie returned from the bathroom and the three of

them walked from the studio toward the front entrance of the building. "Guess what, Charles."

"What?"

"I'm in the first grade. My teacher's name is Mrs. Berger. Like hamburger without the ham. I like her 'cause she's nice and 'cause she gots a gerbil in our classroom. He's brown and white and has little tiny ears. Everyone named him Stimpy. I wanted to name him Pongo, but I didn't get to." She kept up a steady stream of chatter all the way through the building and out into the parking lot. But in the car on the drive home, she was very quiet. Georgeanne tried to talk to her, but she was clearly distracted.

From a block away, Georgeanne noticed John's Range Rover parked in front of her house. She saw him sitting on her front porch, his feet apart and his forearms resting on his thighs. She pulled her car into the driveway and glanced over at the passenger seat. Lexie stared straight ahead at the garage door and sucked her top lip between her teeth. Her little hands tightly gripped the clipboard Charles had given her so she could write down her ideas for future shows. On the paper she'd drawn several misshaped cats and dogs and had written the words "pet sho."

"Are you nervous?" she asked her daughter, feeling her own butterflies take flight.

Lexie shrugged.

"If you don't want to go, I don't think he'll make you," Georgeanne said, hoping she spoke the truth.

Lexie was silent for a while before she asked, "Do you think he likes me?"

Georgeanne's throat constricted. Lexie, who was always so sure of herself, always so sure that everyone just automatically loved her, wasn't so sure of her daddy. "Of course he likes you. He liked you the very first time he saw you."

"Oh," was all she said.

Together they got out of the car and moved up the sidewalk. From behind her big black sunglasses, Georgeanne watched him stand. He looked casual and at ease in a pair of beige twill pants, white T-shirt, and plaid dress shirt left unbuttoned and untucked. His dark hair had been cut shorter than the last time she'd seen him; the front fell in spikes over his forehead. His gaze was riveted on his daughter.

"Hey there, Lexie."

She looked down at her clipboard, suddenly engrossed. "Hi."

"What have you been up to since the last time I saw you?"

"Nothin'."

"How's first grade?"

She wouldn't look at him. "Okay."

"Do you like your teacher?"

"Uh-huh."

"What's her name?"

"Mrs. Berger."

The tension was almost tangible. Lexie was friendlier to the mailman than she was to her own father, and they both knew it. John lifted his gaze to Georgeanne, his blue eyes accusing. Georgeanne bristled. She might not like him, but she hadn't said one word against him—well, not within Lexie's hearing anyway. Just because she wasn't willing to lie down and let him walk all over her anymore didn't mean she would try to influence Lexie in any way. She was surprised by Lexie's uncharacteristic bout of shyness, but she knew the reason. The cause for her reserve stood in front of her like a big, muscular giant, and she didn't know how to behave around him now.

"Why don't you tell John about your gerbil," she suggested, introducing the subject of Lexie's most recent fixation.

"We gots a gerbil."

"Where?"

"School."

John couldn't believe this was the same little girl he'd first met in June. He looked down at her and wondered where the chatterbox had gone.

"Would you like to come inside?" Georgeanne asked.

He would have preferred to shake her and demand to know what she'd done to his daughter. "No. We need to get going."

"Where?"

He looked into those big sunglasses of hers and thought about telling her it was none of her damn business. "I want to show Lexie where I live." He reached for the clipboard and slid it from Lexie's grasp. "I'll have her back at nine," he said, and handed the clipboard to Georgeanne.

"'Bye, Mommy. I love you."

Georgeanne looked down and pasted on one of those fake smiles of hers. "Give me some sugar, precious darlin'."

Lexie stood on her tiptoes and kissed her mother good-bye. As John watched, he knew that he wanted what Georgeanne had. He wanted his child's love and affection. He wanted her to wrap her arms around his neck and kiss him and tell him she loved him. He wanted to hear her call him daddy.

He was sure that once he got Lexie to his house and she relaxed, once she was away from Georgeanne's influence, she would turn back into the little girl he'd come to know.

But it didn't happen. The little girl he picked up at seven was the same girl he took back home at nine. Talking to her was like skating across soft ice—slow and as aggravating as hell. She hadn't had much to say about his houseboat, and she hadn't immediately wanted to know where all the bathrooms were located, which surprised him because in Cannon Beach, bathroom locations had seemed like serious business to her.

He'd showed her the spare bedroom he'd cleared for her, and he'd told her that he'd take her shopping and she could furnish it any way she liked. He'd thought she'd like the idea, but she'd just nodded and asked to go out on the deck below. She'd showed a spark of interest in his boat, so they'd jumped in the Sundancer and slowly cruised the lake. He'd watched her check out the cabin and open the compact refrigerator in the galley console. He'd put her on his lap so she could steer. Her eyes had widened and the corners of her mouth had finally tilted up into a smile, but she hadn't said much.

By the time he pulled in front of her house two hours after leaving it, his mood matched the storm clouds quickly gathering overhead. He didn't know the little girl he'd just spent the evening with, but she wasn't Lexie. His Lexie laughed and giggled and talked water upstream.

The Range Rover had barely rolled to a stop before Georgeanne was out of her house and walking toward them. She wore a loose-fitting lace dress that swayed about her ankles when she moved, and her hair was piled up on top of her head.

A little girl standing in a yard across the street called Lexie's name and frantically waved a Barbie with long blond hair.

"Who's that?" John asked as he helped Lexie unbuckle her seat belt.

"Amy," she answered, opened the door, and jumped out of the four-wheel-drive vehicle. "Mom, can I go play with Amy? She gots a new Mermaid Barbie, and I can show it to you 'cause that's the one I want, too."

Georgeanne looked up at John as he walked around

the front of the Range Rover. Their eyes met briefly before she dropped her gaze to her daughter. "It's going to rain."

"Please," she begged, bouncing up and down as if she had springs in her heels. "Just for a few minutes?"

"For fifteen minutes." Georgeanne reached for Lexie's shoulder before she had a chance to run off. "What do you say to John?"

Lexie stilled and stared at his middle. "Thank you, John," she said at practically a whisper. "I had a nice time."

No kisses. No I love you, Daddies. He hadn't expected love and affection so soon, but as he looked down at the part in Lexie's hair, he knew he would have to wait longer than he'd anticipated. "Maybe next time we'll go to the Key Arena, and I'll show you where I work." When his offer didn't get an enthusiastic response, he added, "Or we can go to the mall." John hated the mall, but he wasn't a patient man.

The corners of Lexie's mouth tilted upward. "Okay," she said, then walked to the curb. She looked both ways, then dashed across the street. "Hey, Amy," she hollered, "guess what I did. I went on a big boat, and we drove by Gas Works Park, and I saw a fish jump out of the water and John ran over it. John has a bed and a fridge in his boat, and I got to drive for a real long, long time too."

John watched the two little girls walk toward the front door to Amy's house, then he turned toward Georgeanne. "What have you done to her?"

She looked up at him and her brows drew together over her green eyes. "I haven't done anything to her."

"Bullshit. That is not the same Lexie I met in June. What have you said to her?"

She stared at him for several lengthy moments before she suggested, "Let's go inside."

He didn't want to go inside. He didn't want to have

tea and discuss things rationally. He didn't feel like cooperating with her. He was furious and he wanted to yell. "This is fine."

"John, I won't have this conversation with you on my front lawn."

He returned her stare, then motioned for her to lead the way. Following her around the side of her house, he purposely kept his gaze pinned to the back of her head. He didn't want to notice the way she moved. In the past, he'd always appreciated the way her hips made the hems of her dresses sway. Now he wasn't in the mood to appreciate anything about her.

He followed her into a backyard bursting with pastel color, a feminine kaleidoscope so typical of Georgeanne. Flowers bobbed in the prestorm breeze while a sprinkler watered the grass near a blue and white striped swing set. The little plastic shopping cart he recognized from the first time he'd met Lexie sat next to a wheelbarrow; both were stuffed with dead flowers and weeds. As he glanced around the yard, he was struck by the contrast in their houses. Georgeanne's home had a yard and a swing set, a flower garden, and a lawn that needed to be mowed. She lived on a street where a kid could ride a bike and where there was a smooth sidewalk for Lexie to skate. The moorage alone for John's houseboat cost almost as much as Georgeanne's entire mortgage. He had a great view and a great house, but it wasn't really a home. Not like this. It didn't have a garden or a yard or a smooth sidewalk.

*A family lives here,* he thought as he watched Georgeanne reach for a water spigot behind tall lavender flowers. *His family. No. Not his family. His daughter.*

"First of all," Georgeanne began as she straightened, "don't ever accuse me of doing or saying anything to hurt Lexie. I don't like you, but I've never said one bad word against you in front of my daughter."

"I don't believe you."

Georgeanne shrugged and strove for a calm she didn't feel. Her stomach felt as if she'd eaten something rotten while John stood in front of her looking good enough to gobble up with a spoon. She'd thought she could manage being so near to him, but now she wasn't sure. "I don't care what you believe."

"Why doesn't she talk to me like she did before?"

She could tell him her opinion, but why? Why help him take her daughter from her? "Give her time."

John shook his head. "The first time I met her she talked a blue streak. Now that she knows I'm her father, she hardly says a word. It doesn't make any sense."

It made perfect sense to Georgeanne. The one and only time she'd met her mother, she'd been terrified of rejection and hadn't known what to say to Billy Jean. Georgeanne had been twenty at the time, and she could only imagine how a child felt. Lexie didn't know what to say to John now, and she was afraid to be herself.

John rested his weight on one foot and cocked his head to the side. "You must have filled her with lies about me. I knew you were ticked off, but I didn't think you'd go this far."

Georgeanne wrapped her arms across her stomach and held the pain inside. His low opinion hurt even though it shouldn't. "Don't talk to me about lies. None of this would be happening now if you hadn't lied about hiring a lawyer. *You* are a liar and a lecherous jock. But that isn't enough to make me say bad thing about you to Lexie."

John rocked back on his heels and looked down at her through narrowed eyes. "Ahh . . . now we get to it. You're pissed about getting naked on my couch."

Georgeanne hoped her cheeks weren't turning red, but she could feel her face flush like some high school girl. "Are you insinuating that because of what happened between the two of us, I would try to poison my daughter against you?"

"Hell, I'm not insinuating anything. I'm saying it straight out. You're mad because I didn't send flowers or some other bullshit. I don't know, maybe you woke up the next morning and wanted a quickie in the shower, but I wasn't around to give you what you needed."

Georgeanne could no longer hold the pain inside, and lashed out. "Or maybe I was disgusted that I'd let you touch me at all."

He gave her a knowing smile. "You weren't disgusted. You were hot. You couldn't get enough."

"Get over yourself," Georgeanne scoffed. "You weren't that memorable."

"Bullshit. How many times did we go at it?" he asked, then held up one finger and counted. "On the couch." He paused to hold up another finger. "On the futon in the loft with the stars shining on your bare breasts." Three fingers. "In the Jacuzzi with all that hot water pounding our butts and sloshing on the floor. I had to pull up the carpet the next day so the floor wouldn't rot." He smiled and held up a fourth finger. "Against the wall, on the floor, and in my bed, which I'm counting as one since I only got off once, that time. You may have come more than once, though."

"I did not!"

"Sorry. I guess I have it confused with the first time on the couch."

"You've been spending too much time in the locker room," she said between clenched teeth. "A real man doesn't have to talk about his sex life."

He took a step closer. "Baby doll, by they way you

acted in my bed, I'd say I'm the only *real* man you know."

Everything she said just seemed to bounce off his hard chest while at the same time, his words bruised her heart. She wasn't going to win with him, so she did her best to look bored. "If you say so, John."

He moved until only a few inches separated them and a cocky smile curved his lips. "If you ask real nice, I just might let you polish my stick." He lowered his face closer to hers and asked in a silky voice, "Wanna ride the Zamboni?"

Georgeanne stood her ground and stared up at him. This time she wasn't going to lose her temper and call him foul names, as she had in Oregon. She raised her chin a notch and said in a voice laced with southern censure, "You're embarrassing yourself."

His gaze narrowed. "Maybe if you were a little nicer when you had your clothes on, you'd be married by now."

Just as always, John took up all the space. He took all her air, but she managed to fill her lungs with a breath suffused with the smell of his skin and aftershave. "You're giving me advice? You married a stripper."

His head snapped up and he took a step backward. She could tell by the look on his face that her words had finally scored a hit. "True," he said. "I've always behaved like a real dumb ass over a great pair of tits." He flipped over his wrist and looked at his watch. "I haven't had this much fun since I busted my ankle in Detroit, but I've got to go. I'll be back Saturday to pick up Lexie. Have her ready at three." He barely spared her another glance as he turned to leave.

Georgeanne placed a hand at her throat and watched him walk out the back gate. She'd won. She'd finally won with John. She didn't know how she'd done it, but she'd definitely put a dent in his enormous ego.

Her chest felt tight and she moved to the back porch and sat on the bottom step.

If she'd won, than why didn't she feel better?

# Sixteen

"This bites the big one," Mae muttered as she raised her Kahluá and cream to her lips and took a sip. One shiny black pump hung precariously from her toes as she jiggled her right foot. Over the top of her glass she watched a low-riding Chevy slowly roll past, bumping out bass and spewing toxic fumes. She waved her hand in front of her face and wondered if she hadn't made a mistake in choosing to sit out front. From her small bistro-style table, she had a clear view of anyone walking toward the funky old jazz bar. The melodious flow of saxophone poured through the open doors and out into the dusky sunset of downtown. Around her, couples talked of what concerned most people in Seattle: rain, coffee, and Microsoft.

She set her drink back on the table and glanced at her watch. "He isn't coming," she told herself, and shoved her foot back inside her shoe. It was Friday night. She didn't have to work for a change, and she'd put on lipstick and mascara for nothing. She'd even put on a dress. A nice little black slip dress with nothing on under it. She was freezing and her latest lover, Ted, was a no-show.

He'd probably gotten detained by his wife, she thought, and reached for her purse. She usually didn't carry a purse, but she didn't have anyplace to put her money tonight, not even her underwear. She pulled out a twenty and set it on the table. She wasn't going to wait any longer for him. She wasn't that desperate.

"Now, what's a girl like you doing all by yourself?"

Mae looked up and opened her mouth to tell the guy to buzz off. Instead she frowned and said, "Just when I thought this night couldn't get any worse."

Hugh Miner laughed and turned to the men with him. "You guys go ahead," he said as he pulled out a chair opposite Mae. "I'll join you in a minute."

Mae watched the men walk inside and she grabbed her purse. "I was just leaving."

"You can stay for one drink, can't you?"

"No."

"Why not?"

*Because I'm freezing,* she thought. "Why would I want to?"

"Because I'm buying."

Free booze had never been an incentive for Mae, but just then, a red-haired waitress walked up to the table and proceeded to make a fool out of herself. She cooed, rubbed up against Hugh's shoulder, and did everything but fall down and give him oral pleasure. She was pretty with big blue eyes and a nice body, which she asked Hugh to autograph, but to his credit, he declined.

"But I'll tell you what, Mandy," he said to the waitress. "If you bring me a Beck's and . . ." He paused and turned his attention to Mae. "What are you drinking?" he asked her.

She couldn't leave. Not now. Not when Mandy was sending jealous daggers her way. Other women weren't usually jealous of Mae Heron. "Kahluá and cream."

"If you bring me a Beck's and a Kahluá and cream, I'd be real grateful," he finished.

"How grateful?" She looked around, then leaned down and whispered into this ear.

Hugh laughed silently. "Mandy," he said, "I'm not real interested, being that what you're asking is against the law in some states. But listen, I came here tonight with Dmitri Ulanov. Now, he's a foreigner and doesn't know he could get arrested for what you're suggesting. You might get him to take you up on it."

As she laughed and walked away, Hugh leaned back and glued his gaze to Mandy's behind.

"I thought you weren't interested," Mae reminded him.

"Nothing wrong with looking," he said, and turned his attention to Mae. "But she's not as pretty as you."

Mae was so positive he said that to every woman he met that she wasn't the least bit flattered. "What did she want to do?"

Hugh shook his head and his hazel eyes shined. "Now, that would be telling."

"And you don't ever tell?"

"Nope." He shrugged out of his leather bomber jacket and handed it across the table to her. His shoulders appeared wide beneath his cream-colored dress shirt.

"Are my goose bumps noticeable from across the table?" she asked, and gratefully accepted the jacket. It was huge and warm draped over her shoulders. It smelled of musky male.

He smiled at her. "Your bumps are very noticeable, yes."

Mae didn't have to ask which bumps, and she'd been around the block too many times to get uptight and embarrassed.

"Are you ever going to answer my question?" he asked her.

"What question?"

"What is a girl like you doing all by yourself?"

"Like me?"

"Yeah," he laughed through a smile. "Sweet. Charming. I imagine that a lot of men are attracted to that warm personality of yours."

She didn't think he was funny, "Do you really want to know why I'm here?"

"I asked."

She could lie or make something up. Instead she decided to shock him with the truth. She wrapped her fists in his jacket and leaned across the table. "I'm meeting my married lover, and we're going to have wild sex all night at the Marriott."

"No shit?"

She'd shocked him, all right. Now she expected moral outrage from a man she suspected was fairly bankrupt in the morality department.

"All night?"

Disappointed by his reaction, she sat back. "Well, we were going to have wild sex, but he hasn't shown up. I guess he couldn't get away."

The waitress approached and set down their drinks. As she put Hugh's beer in front of him, she whispered something close to his ear. He shook his head and dug in his back pocket for his wallet, then handed her two fives.

The waitress had hardly walked away before Mae asked, "What did she want this time?"

Hugh raised his beer to his lips and took a long pull before he set it back down. "To know if John was going to show up tonight."

"Is he?"

"No, but even if he were here, she isn't his type."

Mae took a sip of her drink. "What's his type?"

Hugh smiled. "Your friend."

When he smiled and his eyes lit up that way, Mae could see how some women might find him very handsome. "Georgeanne?"

"Yep." He twirled the neck of the green bottle between his thumb and fingers. "He likes women who are built like her. He always has. If he didn't, he wouldn't be in the mess he's in. She's torn him up pretty bad."

Mae nearly choked on her drink. She licked the coffee-flavored liqueur from her top lip and sputtered, "Torn him up? Georgeanne is a wonderful person and he has made her life hell."

"I don't know about that. I only hear John's side, and he doesn't really discuss his personal business with anyone. But I do know that when he found out about Lexie, he kind of freaked out. He got real tense and edgy for a while. She was all he talked about. He canceled a trip to Cancún which he'd planned for months, and he pulled out of the World Cup, too. Instead he invited Lexie and Georgeanne to his house in Oregon."

"Only because he wanted to trick Georgeanne into trusting him while he screwed her over—in more ways than one."

He shrugged. "I don't really know what happened in Oregon, but it sounds like you do."

"I know that he hurt—"

"Mae?" a male voice interrupted. She turned to her left and looked up at Ted, who stood next to the table. "I'm sorry I'm late, but I had a little trouble getting away."

Ted was short and skinny, and Mae noticed for the first time that he wore his pants a little too high on his waist. He looked like a real wimp next to the piece of beefcake across the table. "Hi, Ted," Mae greeted, and pointed toward Hugh. "This is Hugh Miner."

Ted smiled and held out his hand for the well-known goalie.

Hugh didn't smile, and he didn't shake Ted's hand. Instead he stood and stared down at the smaller man. "I'm only going to say this once to you," he said in a calm voice. "Get the hell out of here or I'll beat the shit out of you."

Ted's smile and hand fell at the same time. "What?"

"If you ever come near Mae again, I'll beat you to a bloody stump."

"Hugh!" Mae gasped.

"Then when your wife comes to the hospital to identify your body," he continued, "I'll tell her why I had to kick your ass."

"Ted!" Mae flew to her feet and shoved her way between the two men. "He's lying. He won't hurt you."

Ted looked from Hugh to Mae, then without a word, turned on his heel and practically ran down the street. Mae swung around and threw Hugh's jacket on the table. Balling up her fist, she punched him in the chest. "You big butt-head!" People sitting at other tables outside the bar turned to look at her, but she didn't care.

"Ouch." He raised his hand and rubbed the front of his shirt. "For such a little thing, you hit pretty hard."

"What in the hell is your problem? That was my date," Mae seethed.

"Yeah, and you should thank me. What a weasel."

She knew he was a little bit of a weasel, but he was a nice-looking weasel. It had taken her three months to find him, and she hadn't tried him out yet. She grabbed her purse off the table and looked down the street. Maybe if she hurried, she could catch up with him. She turned to leave and felt strong fingers wrap around her arm.

"Let him go."

"No." Mae tried to jerk her arm free but couldn't. "Damn it," she cursed as she caught one last glimpse of Ted's retreating back. "He probably won't ever call me again."

"Probably not."

She frowned into Hugh's smiling face. "Why did you do that?"

He shrugged. "I didn't like him."

"What?" Mae laughed without humor. "Who cares whether you liked him or not? I don't need your approval."

"He isn't the man for you."

"How do you know?"

He smiled at her. "Because I think I'm the man for you."

This time her laughter was laced with amusement. "You've got to be kidding."

"I'm serious."

She didn't believe him. "You're exactly the type of guy I *never* date."

"What type is that?"

She looked pointedly at his hand still gripping her arm. "Macho, muscle-head, egomaniac. Men who think they can push around people who are smaller and weaker than them."

He let go of her arm and retrieved his jacket from the table. "I'm not an egomaniac, and I don't push people around."

"Really? What about Ted?"

"Ted doesn't count." He wrapped the jacket around her shoulders again. "I could tell he had that small-man syndrome. He probably beats his wife."

Mae frowned at his outrageous assumption. "What about me?"

"What about you?"

"You're pushing me around."

"Honey, you're about as weak as a wrecking ball."

He turned the collar of his jacket up around her jaw and put his hands on her shoulders. "And I think you like me more than you're willing to admit."

Mae looked down and closed her eyes. This was not happening. "You don't even know me."

"I know you're beautiful and I think about you a lot. I'm very attracted to you, Mae."

Her eyes popped open. "Me?" Men like Hugh weren't attracted to women like her. He was a well-known athlete. She was a flat-chested, skinny girl who'd never had a date until after she'd graduated from high school. "This isn't funny."

"I don't think so either. I liked you the first time I saw you standing in the park. Why do you think I've been calling you?"

"I just thought you liked to harass women."

He laughed. "No. Just you. You're special."

She allowed herself a moment to believe him. A moment to feel flattered by the attentions of a big jock she had no intention of dating. The moment didn't last long before she remembered how he'd teased her the first time they'd met. "You're a real jerk," she said.

"I hope you give me a chance to change your mind."

She grabbed his wrist. "This isn't funny anymore."

"I never thought it was funny. I usually like girls who like me back. I've never fallen for someone who hated me."

He looked so serious she almost believed him. "I don't hate you," she confessed.

"Well, that's a start, I guess." He moved his hands to the sides of her neck and tilted her chin back with his thumbs. "Are you still cold?"

"A little." The warmth of his palms on her throat spread a quivering heat to her stomach. She was shocked and somewhat dismayed by her reaction.

"Do you want to take our drinks and go inside?"

Her shock settled into confusion. "I want to go home."

Disappointment tugged one corner of his mouth downward, and he moved his hands to her upper arms. "I'll walk you to your car."

"I took a taxi."

"Then I'll take you home."

"Okay, but I won't invite you to come inside," she said. There were some women who might consider her promiscuous, but she did have her standards. Hugh Miner was handsome and successful, and he was behaving like a perfect gentleman. He just wasn't her type.

"That's up to you."

"I mean it. You can't come in."

"I believe you. If it makes you feel better, I promise I won't even get off the bike."

"Bike?"

"Yeah, I rode my Harley. You'll love it." He put one arm around her shoulders and they moved toward the entrance to the bar. "First I need to find Dmitri and Stuart and tell them I'm leaving."

"I can't ride on your motorcycle with you."

They stopped by the entrance and allowed a group of people to exit. "Sure you can. I won't let you get hurt."

"I'm not worried about that." She looked up into his face, illuminated by an orange Miller light shining above the door. "I'm not wearing any underwear."

He froze for a few seconds, then smiled. "Well, there you go. We have something in common. Neither am I."

John followed Caroline Foster-Duffy through the entry hall of Virgil's Bainbridge estate. Her blond hair was streaked with gray and fine lines had settled in the corners of her eyes. She was one of those women fortunate enough to mature with wisdom and grace. She had the wisdom not to fight her age with brassy hair dye or cosmetic surgery, and the grace to look beautiful despite her sixty-five years.

"He's been expecting you," she said as they passed the formal dining room. She paused at a set of double mahogany doors and looked up at John with concern shining in her pale blue eyes. "I'm going to have to ask you to keep your visit short. I know Virgil called you to meet with him tonight, but he's been working harder than usual the past couple of days. He's tired, but he won't rest. I know something is wrong, but he won't share it with me. Do you know what has happened to upset him? Is it business?"

"I don't know," John answered. He was into the second year of his three-year contract and didn't have to worry about negotiations for another year, so he doubted Virgil had called him to discuss his contract. And besides, he didn't handle negotiations personally, he paid a sports management corporation to take care of his professional interests. "I assumed he wanted to talk about his draft choices," he said, although he did think Virgil's request to talk to him in person was peculiar, especially at nine on a Friday night.

A frown wrinkled Caroline's brow before she turned and opened the door behind her. "John's here," she announced as she walked into Virgil's office. John followed her into a room filled with cherry wood and leather, sculptures of Japanese fishermen and Currier & Ives lithographs. The different textures blended and created an impression of wealth and taste. "But I'm only going to let him stay for half an hour," she continued. "Then I'm going to make him leave so that you can get your rest."

Virgil looked up from several papers scattered across the executive desk in front of him. "Shut the door on your way out," was his response to his wife.

Her lips flattened into a thin line, but she said nothing and backed out of the room.

"Why don't you have a seat?" Virgil motioned to a chair on the opposite side of his desk.

John looked into the older man's face, and he knew why he'd been summoned. Bitterness and fatigue pulled at the little pouches beneath Virgil's eyes. He looked every bit of his seventy-five years. John sat in a leather wing chair and waited.

"The other day you seemed genuinely surprised to see Georgeanne Howard on television."

"I was."

"You didn't know she had her own program here in Seattle?"

"No."

"How can that be, John? The two of you are quite close."

"Obviously we're not that close," John answered, wondering exactly how much Virgil knew.

Virgil picked up a sheet of paper and handed it across the desk. "This says you are a liar."

John took the document, and his gaze quickly scanned the copy of Lexie's birth certificate. He was listed as Lexie's father, which normally would have pleased him, but he didn't appreciate anyone digging into his personal life. He tossed the paper back onto the desk and met Virgil's stare. "Where did you get that?"

Virgil waved off John's question with his hand. "Is it true?"

"Yes, it is. Where did you get it?"

Virgil shrugged. "I've had someone doing a little checking on Georgeanne, and imagine my surprise when I saw your name." He held up several court documents along with John's legal acknowledgment of paternity. Virgil didn't hand them over, but he didn't need to. John had his own copies at home. "Apparently you fathered a child with Georgeanne."

"You know I did, so why not cut the bullshit and get to the point."

Virgil set the papers back down. "That's one thing I've always liked about you, John. You don't pussyfoot around anything." His gaze never wavered as he asked, "Did you have sex with my fiancée before or after she left me standing in my own backyard looking like a ridiculous old fool?"

Even though John didn't like anyone digging into his past, or appreciate the personal question, he did think it was fair. He respected Virgil enough to believe he deserved an answer. "I met Georgeanne for the first time after she left the wedding. I'd never seen her before she came running out of your house and asked me for a ride. She wasn't wearing a wedding dress, and I didn't know who she was."

Virgil sat back in his chair. "But at some point you did know."

"Yes."

"When you found out who she was, you slept with her anyway."

John frowned. "Obviously." The way he saw things, he'd done Virgil a big favor by taking Georgeanne away from that wedding. She could get downright mean, and John didn't think the older man could take being told he wasn't memorable in bed. Not like John. Virgil was better off without her. She could make a man hot and half-hard, then tell him that he was embarrassing himself. Then with that voice of hers dripping honey and daggers, remind of his second marriage to a stripper. She was vicious, no doubt about it.

"How long were you lovers?"

"Not long." He knew Virgil, and the old man hadn't called him across the sound just to hear some juicy details. "Get to the point."

"You've played some damn good hockey for me, and I've never cared where you put your dick. But when you fucked Georgeanne, you fucked me over."

John stood and seriously considered jumping across the desk and pounding the crap out of Virgil. If Virgil hadn't been so much older, he might have. Georgeanne was the most seductive and hottest woman he'd ever been with, but she wasn't just a fuck. She was more than that to him, and she didn't deserve to be talked about as if she were trash. With an effort, he held on to his anger. "You still haven't gotten to the point."

"You can have your career with the Chinooks, or you can have Georgeanne. You can't have both."

John liked being threatened less than he liked people digging into his personal business. "Are you threatening me with a trade?"

Virgil was deadly serious when he said, "Only if you force me to."

John considered telling Virgil to shove it up his wrinkled old ass. Five months ago he might have. Even though John loved playing for the Chinooks and couldn't see himself stepping into the captaincy for another organization, he didn't respond well to threats. But he had too much to lose now. He'd just discovered that he had a child, and he'd just been granted joint custody. "We have a daughter together, so maybe you should tell me what you mean by 'have.' "

"See your kid all you want," Virgil began. "But don't touch her mother. Don't date her. Don't marry her, or you and I are going to have trouble."

If Virgil had made the threat a year, or even a few months, ago, John probably would have walked out and forced a trade. But how could he be a father to Lexie if he had to move to Detroit or New York or even Los Angeles? How could he watch Lexie grow if he wasn't living in the same state? "Hell, Virgil," he said as he watched the older man stand, "I don't know who dislikes the other more, Georgeanne or me. If you'd asked me last week, you could have saved yourself some trouble, and saved me the trouble of driving over here. I want Georgeanne like I want a berry ringer, and she wants me even less."

Virgil's fatigue-rimmed eyes called John a liar. "Just remember what I said."

"I'm not likely to forget." John looked at the older man one last time, then turned and left the room. He walked from the house with Virgil's ultimatum echoing in his ears. *You can have your career with the Chinooks, or you can have Georgeanne. You can't have both.*

He waited for the ferry for fifteen minutes, and by the time he reached his houseboat, the absurdity of Virgil's threat forced a strained chuckle from him. He supposed the older man thought he'd found the perfect revenge. And it might have been a good one, too, but John and Georgeanne couldn't stand to be in the same room together. Forcing them together would have been a more fitting punishment.

Buzzers and bells, squealing tires, and breaking glass filled John's ears as he watched Lexie crash into trees, run up on sidewalks, and flatten pedestrians.

"I'm gettin' pretty good," she yelled above the chaotic atmosphere of the arcade.

He stared at the screen in front of Lexie and felt a dull ache start at his temples. "Watch out for the old lady," he warned her too late. Lexie mowed down the senior citizen and sent her aluminum walker flying.

John didn't particularly like video games or arcades. He didn't like shopping malls, preferring to order what he needed by mail, and he didn't really care for animated films either.

The video game ended, and John turned his wrist and looked at his watch. "It's about time to go."

"Did I win, John?" Lexie asked as she pointed to her score on the big screen. She wore the silver filigree ring he'd bought her from a jewelry vendor at Pike Place Market on her middle finger, and on the seat next to her sat the little hand-blown glass cat he'd purchased at another stall. The back of his Range Rover was loaded with toys, and he was just killing time before he and Lexie headed up the street to the movie theater so she could see *The Hunchback of Notre Dame.*

He was trying to buy his daughter's love. He was unrepentant. He didn't care. He would buy her anything, spend his time in dozens of loud arcades, or sit through hours of Disney if he could hear his child call him "Daddy" just once. "You almost won," he lied, and reached for her hand. "Get your cat," he said, then the two of them wove their way out of the arcade. He'd do just about anything to have the old Lexie back.

When he'd picked her up at home earlier that afternoon, she'd met him at the door without a trace of eye shadow or rouge. It was Saturday, and even though he preferred to see her sans hooker makeup, he was so desperate to see the girl he'd met in June that he'd suggested she wear a little light lip gloss. She'd declined with a shake of her head.

He might have tried to talked to Georgeanne again about Lexie's unusual behavior, but she hadn't been home when he'd picked her up. According to the teenage sitter who wore a ring through her right nostril, Georgeanne was working but was due home before he returned with Lexie.

Maybe he'd talk to Georgeanne later, he thought as he and Lexie headed toward the movie theater. Maybe they could both behave like reasonable adults and resolve what was best for their daughter. Yeah, maybe. But there was just something about Georgeanne that tweaked his nerves and made him want to provoke her.

"Look!" Lexie came to an abrupt stop and stared into a shopfront window. Behind the glass, several striped kittens rolled in a furry ball and chased each other up a carpeted scratching post. About six baby cats were kept in a large wire pen, and as she watched in awed wonder, John was treated to a glimpse of the little girl who'd stolen his heart in Marymoor Park.

"Do you want to go inside and take a quick look?" he asked her.

She glanced up at him as if he'd just suggested a felony. "My mommy says that I . . ." She paused and a slow smile lifted her lips. "Okay. I'll go inside with you."

John opened the door to Patty's Pets and let his daughter into the store. The shop was empty except for a saleswoman who stood behind the counter writing something in a notebook.

Lexie handed him the glass cat he'd bought for her, then she walked to the pen and reached over the top. She stuck her hand inside and wiggled her fingers. Immediately, a yellow tabby pounced and wrapped its furry little body around her wrist. She giggled and lifted the kitten to her chest.

John shoved the glass figurine into the breast pocket of his blue and green polo shirt then knelt down beside Lexie. He scratched the kitten between the ears, and his knuckles brushed his daughter's chin. He didn't know which felt softer.

Lexie looked at him, so excited she could hardly hold it all in. "I like her, John."

He touched the little cat's ear and brushed the back of his hand across Lexie's jaw. "You can call me Daddy," he said, holding his breath.

Her big blue eyes blinked once, twice, then she buried a smile in the top of the kitten's head. A dimple dented her pale cheek, but she didn't say a word.

"All of those kittens have had their shots," the saleswoman announced from behind John.

John looked down at the toe of his running shoe, disappointment tugging at his heart. "We're just looking today," he said as he stood.

"I could let you have that little tabby for fifty dollars. Now, that's a real steal."

John figured that with Lexie's obsession for animals, if Georgeanne wanted her to have one, she would. "Her mother would probably kill me if I took her home with a kitten."

"How about a puppy? I just got in a little dalmatian."

"A dalmatian?" Lexie's ears perked. "You gots a dalmatian?"

"Right over there." The saleswoman pointed to a wall of glass kennels.

Lexie gently put the kitten back into the pen and moved toward the kennels. The glass cubicles were empty except for the dalmatian, a fat little husky asleep on its back, and a big rat curled up in a food bowl.

"What's that?" Lexie asked as she pointed to the almost hairless rat with the enormous ears.

"That's a Chihuahua. He's a very sweet little dog."

John didn't think it should be allowed to be called a dog. It shook all over, looked pathetic, and gave dogs in general a bad name.

"Is it cold?" Lexie wondered, and pressed her forehead to the glass.

"I don't think so. I try to keep him very warm."

"He must be scared." She placed her hand on the kennel and said, "He misses his mommy."

"Oh no," John said as the memory of wading out into the Pacific to rescue a little fish for her swam across his brain. There was no way he was going to pretend to save that stupid shivering dog. "No, he doesn't miss his mommy. He likes living here alone. I bet he likes sleeping in his food dish. I bet he's having a really good dream right now, and he's shaking because he's dreaming he's in a strong wind."

"Chihuahuas are a nervous breed," the saleswoman informed him.

"Nervous?" John pointed to the dog. "He's asleep."

The woman smiled. "He just needs a little warmth and lovin'." Then she turned and walked through a set of swinging doors. A few seconds later the back of the glass kennel opened and a pair of hands reached for the dog curled up in the dish.

"We need to get going if we want to make the movie in time," John said too late. The woman returned and shoved the dog into Lexie's waiting arms.

"What's his name?" Lexie asked as she looked down into the beady black eyes staring back at her.

"He doesn't have a name," the woman answered. "His owner gets to name him."

The dog's little pink tongue darted out and licked Lexie's chin. "He likes me," she laughed.

John looked at his watch, anxious to have Lexie and the dog part company. "The movie is going to start. We have to go now."

"I've already seen it three times," she said without taking her eyes from the dog. "You're such a precious darlin'," she drawled, sounding amazingly like her mother. "Give me some sugar."

"No." John shook his head, suddenly feeling like a pilot trying to land an airplane on one engine. "Don't exchange sugar."

"He's stopped shaking." Lexie rubbed her cheek against the dog's face and he licked her ear.

"You'll have to give him back now."

"But he loves me, and I love him. Can't I keep him?"

"Oh, no. Your mother would kill me."

"She won't mind."

John heard the catch in Lexie's voice and knelt down beside her. He felt his other engine die with the ground rushing up at him. He had to think up something fast before he crashed. "Yes, she will, but I'll tell you what. I'll buy you a turtle and you can keep him at my house, and every time you come over, you can play with him."

With the dog curled up happily in her arms, Lexie leaned into John's chest. "I don't want a turtle. I want little Pongo."

"Little Pongo? You can't name him, Lexie. He's not yours."

Tears welled up in Lexie's eyes and her chin trembled. "But I love him, and he loves me."

"Wouldn't you rather have a real dog? We can look at real dogs next weekend."

She shook her head. "He is a real dog. He's just really little. He doesn't have a mommy, and if I leave him here, he'll miss me really bad." Her tears spilled over her bottom lashes and she sobbed, "Please, Daddy, let me keep Pongo."

John's heart collided with his ribs and surged up into his throat. He looked into his daughter's pitifully sad face, and he crashed. He burned. No chance of a reprieve. He was a sucker. She'd called him "Daddy." He reached for his wallet and surrendered his Visa to the happy saleslady.

"Okay," he said, and put his arms around Lexie and pulled her closer. "But your mom is going to kill us."

"Really? I can keep Pongo?"

"I guess so."

Her tears increased and she buried her face in his neck. "You're the best daddy in the whole world," she wailed, and he felt moisture against his skin. "I'll be a good girl forever and ever." Her shoulders shook and the dog shook and John was afraid that he would start shaking, too. "I love you, Daddy," she whispered.

If he didn't do something quick, he'd start bawling like Lexie. He'd start bawling like a girl right there in front of the saleswoman. "I love you, too," he said, then cleared his throat. "We better buy some food."

"And you'll probably need a crate," the saleslady informed him as she took off with his credit card. "And since he has very little hair, a sweater, too."

By the time John loaded Lexie and Pongo and the dog's accoutrements into the Range Rover, he was almost a thousand dollars lighter. On the way across town toward Bellevue, Lexie chattered up a blue streak and sang lullabies to her dog. But the closer they got to her street, the quieter she became. When John pulled to a stop beside the curb, silence filled the car.

John helped Lexie out of the vehicle, and neither spoke as they headed up the sidewalk. They stopped beneath the porch light, both staring at the closed door, postponing the moment when they would have to face Georgeanne with the shivering rat in Lexie's arms.

"She's going to be real mad," Lexie informed him barely above a whisper.

John felt her small hand grasp his. "Yep. Shit's gonna hit the fan."

Lexie didn't correct his language. She just nodded and said, "Yep."

*You can have your career with the Chinooks, or you can have Georgeanne. You can't have both.* He almost laughed. Even if he were to suddenly fall madly in love with Georgeanne, he figured that after tonight, his career was as secure as Fort Knox.

The door opened and John's prediction about the fan came to fruition. Georgeanne looked from John to Lexie, then to the shaking dog in Lexie's arms. "What is that?"

Lexie kept quiet and let John do the talking. "Uh, we went into a pet store and—"

"Oh no!" Georgeanne wailed. "You took her to a pet store? She's not allowed in pet stores. The last time she cried so hard she threw up."

"Well, look on the bright side, she didn't get sick this time."

"Bright side?" She pointed to Lexie's arms and shrieked, "Is that a dawg?"

"That's what the saleslady said, but I'm still not convinced."

"Take it back."

"No, Mommy. Pongo's mine."

"Pongo? You named it already?" She looked at John and her eyes narrowed. "Fine. Pongo can live with John."

"I don't have a yard."

"You have a deck. That's good enough."

"He can't live with Daddy 'cause I'd only get to see him on the weekends, then I wouldn't get to train him not to potty on the carpet."

"Train whom? Pongo or your *daddy*."

"That's not funny, Georgie."

"I know. Take it back, John."

"I wish I could. But the sign by the cash register said all sales are final. I can't take Pongo back." He looked at Georgeanne standing there looking as beautiful as always and mad as hell. But for the first time since Cannon Beach, he didn't want to fight with her. He didn't want to provoke her any more than he had already. "I'm sorry about this, but Lexie started crying and I couldn't say no. She named him and cried on my neck and I handed the saleslady my credit card."

"Alexandra Mae, get in the house."

"Uh-oh," Lexie said, then tucked her dog, ducked her head, and ran past her mother.

John moved to follow, but Georgeanne blocked his

way. "I have told that child for five years now that she can't have a pet until she is ten. You take her out for a few hours and she comes home with a hairless dawg."

He raised his right hand. "I know, and I'm sorry. I promise I'll buy all his food, and Lexie and I will take him to all of his puppy obedience classes."

"I can pay for his darn food!" Georgeanne raised her palms and pressed her fingers to her brows. She felt as if her head were about to explode. "I'm so angry I can't see straight."

"Would it help if I told you that I bought a puppy book for you to read?"

"No, John," she sighed, and dropped her hands. "It wouldn't help."

"I have a little kennel, too." He took ahold of her wrist and pulled her after him. "I bought a bunch of stuff for him."

Georgeanne tried to ignore the leap in her pulse as he towed her along. "What kind of stuff?"

He opened the back passenger door to the Range Rover and handed her a dog crate about the size of a deep dresser drawer.

"He's supposed to stay in that at night so he doesn't crap on the floor," he told her, then reached inside the vehicle again. "Here's a book on training, another on Chihuahuas, and one more"—he paused to read the title—"*How to Raise a Dog You Can Live With.* I have food, biscuits for his teeth, chew toys, a collar and leash, and a little sweater."

"Sweater? Did you buy everything in the store?"

"Close." He turned and ducked his head into the car.

Over the top of the kennel, Georgeanne glanced at John's rear pockets pointed in her direction. His jeans were faded a light blue in places, and a woven leather belt was threaded though the loops.

"I know it's here somewhere," he said, and she quickly switched her gaze to the back of the four-wheel-drive vehicle. It was filled with huge toy-store bags and a big box labeled *Ultimate Hockey*.

"What's all that?" she asked, motioning toward the back with her head.

John looked over his shoulder at her. "Just some things Lexie picked out. I don't have anything for her to do when she comes over to my house, so we bought a few things. I can't believe how much Barbies cost. I had no idea they were sixty dollars apiece." He straightened and handed her a tube. "That's Pongo's toothpaste."

Georgeanne was appalled. "You paid sixty dollars for a Barbie?"

He shrugged. "Well, when you figure that one came with a poodle, the other with a zebra-print jacket and matching beret, I don't think I got soaked too badly."

He'd been suckered. Within days of ripping open the box, Lexie would have those dolls naked and looking like she'd picked them up at a garage sale. Georgeanne rarely bought Lexie expensive toys. Her daughter didn't treat them any better than she did her things that were less costly, but mostly, there were a lot of months when Georgeanne couldn't afford to drop one hundred twenty dollars on two dolls.

She had a tendency to go a little crazy and spend a lot at Christmas and on birthdays, but she had to budget and set money aside for those occasions. John didn't. Last month, as their lawyers had hammered out a custody agreement, she'd learned that he made six million a year playing hockey, plus half that much through investments and endorsements. She could never compete with that.

She looked into his smiling face and wondered what he was up to. If she wasn't careful, he would take everything and leave her with nothing but that hairless dog.

# Seventeen

"Did you want your latte skinny or mocha?" Georgeanne asked Mae as she packed the metal filter with espresso.

"Skinny," Mae answered without taking her attention from Pongo, who lay curled up crunching on a doggie biscuit. "Damn, that's pathetic. My cat is bigger than your dog. Bootsie could kick his butt."

"Lexie," Georgeanne called out, "Mae is saying bad things about Pongo again."

Lexie walked into the kitchen, shoving her arms through the sleeves of her raincoat. "Don't say bad things about my dog." She scowled and grabbed her backpack from the table. "He's sensitive." She dropped down on her knees and pushed her face next to the dog's. "I have to go to school now, I'll see you later." The puppy stopped eating his biscuit long enough to lick Lexie's mouth.

"Hey now, I've told you about that," Georgeanne scolded as she took a carton of skim milk from the refrigerator. "He has bad habits."

Lexie shrugged and stood. "I don't care. I love him."

"Well, I care. Now, you better get over to Amy's or you'll miss your ride."

Lexie puckered her lips for a kiss good-bye.

Georgeanne shook her head and walked Lexie to the front door. "I don't kiss girls who kiss dawgs who lick themselves." From the entrance she watched Lexie cross the street, then she turned back to the kitchen. "She's absolutely nuts about that puppy," she told Mae as she headed toward the espresso machine. "She's had him five days, and he's taken over our lives. You should see the little denim vest she's made for him."

"I have something to tell you," Mae blurted quickly.

Georgeanne looked over her shoulder at her friend. She'd suspected something was up with Mae. She usually didn't come by so early for coffee, and she'd been acting a little distant for the past few days. "What is it?"

"I love Hugh."

Georgeanne smiled and filled the espresso machine with two cups of water. "I love you, too."

"No." Mae shook her head. "You don't understand. I love *Hugh*, the goalie."

"What?" Her hands stilled and her brows lowered. "John's friend?"

"Yes."

Georgeanne set down the glass carafe but forgot to turn on the machine. "I thought you hated him."

"I did, but I don't now."

"What happened?"

Mae looked as perplexed as Georgeanne felt. "I don't know! He took me home from a club last Friday night, and he never left."

"He's been living with you for the past six days?" Georgeanne walked over to the kitchen table. She had to sit down.

"Well, for the past six nights mostly."

"Is this a joke?"

"No, but I understand how you might think so. I don't know how it happened. One minute I was telling him that he couldn't come into my house, and then before I really realized what had happened, we were both naked and fighting over who got to be on top. He won and I fell in love with him."

Georgeanne was numb with shock. "Are you sure?"

"Yes. He was on top."

"I didn't mean that!" If there was one thing that Georgeanne wished she could change about her relationship with Mae, it was Mae's tendency to share details Georgeanne didn't care to know. "Are you sure you're in love with him?"

Mae nodded, and for the first time in their seven-year friendship, Georgeanne watched tears well up in her brown eyes. Mae was always so strong, it broke Georgeanne's heart to see her cry. "Oh, honey," she sighed, and moved to kneel by Mae's chair. "I'm so sorry." She wrapped her arms around her friend and tried to comfort her. "Men are such jerks."

"I know," Mae sobbed. "Everything was wonderful, and then he had to do this."

"What did he do?"

Mae pulled back and look into Georgeanne's face. "He asked me to marry him."

Georgeanne sat back on her heels, speechless.

"I told him it was too soon, but he wouldn't listen. He said that he loved me, and he knows that I love him." She grabbed the end of Georgeanne's linen tablecloth and wiped beneath her eyes. "I told him that I didn't think we should get married right now, but he just wouldn't listen."

"Of course you can't marry him now." Georgeanne held on to the table and pulled herself to her feet. "Last week you didn't even *like* him. How can he possibly expect you to make such an important decision in such a short period of time? Six days isn't long enough for you to know if you want to spend the rest of your life with him."

"I knew after the third night."

Georgeanne found her chair. She felt dizzy and had to sit down again. "Are you confusing me on purpose? Do you want to marry him?"

"Oh yeah."

"But you told him no?"

"I told him yes! I tried to tell him no, but I couldn't," she said, and burst into renewed tears. "It may sound foolish and impulsive, but I really do love him, and I don't want to throw away this chance to be happy."

"You don't sound very happy."

"I am! I've never felt this way. Hugh makes me feel good, even though I never knew I could feel any better. He makes me laugh, and he thinks I'm funny. He makes me happy, but . . ." She paused and wiped her eyes again. "I want you to be happy, too."

"Me?"

"The past few months you've been miserable, especially after what happened in Oregon. I feel horrible because you're unhappy and I've never been happier."

"I'm happy," she assured Mae, and wondered if it was true. With everything happening in her life, she hadn't stopped to think about how she felt. If she thought about it now, the only word that came to mind was *shock.* But now wasn't the time to pull out her feelings and look at them. "Hey," she said with a smile, stretched out her arms in front of her, and patted the table. "Let's concentrate on your happiness right now. It sounds like we have a wedding to plan."

Mae put her hands in Georgeanne's. "I know this whole thing sounds impetuous, but I really do love Hugh," she said, her face lighting up when she spoke his name.

Georgeanne gazed into her friend's eyes and let the

romance and excitement of it all override her doubts—for the moment. "Have you picked a date?"

"October tenth."

"That's in three weeks!"

"I know, but the hockey season starts on the fifth in Detroit, and Hugh can't miss the first game of the season. Then he's in New York and St. Louis before he's back here on the ninth playing against Colorado, and he never misses a chance to best Patrick Roy. I checked our schedule and we're real slow the first three weeks in October. So Hugh and I are getting married on the tenth, honeymooning on Maui for a week, then I'll come back here to help cater the Bennet party, and Hugh is off to Toronto for a game against the Maple Leafs."

"Three weeks," Georgeanne whimpered. "How can I plan a wonderful wedding in three weeks?"

"You're not going to. I want you to be in the wedding, not in the kitchen. I've decided to hire Anne Maclean to cater the whole thing. She operates out of a large banquet hall in Redmond, and she's still hungry enough to take the job on such sort notice. I only want two things from you. I would appreciate it if you'd help me pick out a wedding dress. You know I'm clueless about that sort of thing. I'd probably pick out something hideous and never know it."

Georgeanne smiled. "I'd love to help you."

"And I want you to do something else, too." Her grip on Georgeanne's hands tightened. "I want you to be my maid of honor. Hugh is going to ask John to be his best man, so you'd have to stand next to him at some point."

Tears clogged Georgeanne's throat. "Don't worry about the problems between John and me. I'd love to stand up with you."

"There's one more problem, and it's a biggie."

"What could be worse than planning a wedding in three weeks and standing next to John?"

"Virgil Duffy."

Everything inside of Georgeanne stilled.

"I told Hugh that we couldn't invite him, but Hugh doesn't see how to avoid it. He thinks if we invite his team members, and the trainers and coaches and management, we can't overlook the owner. I suggested that we just invite close friends, but his teammates are his close friends. So how can we invite some and not others?" Mae covered her face with her hands. "I don't know what to do."

"Of course you invite Virgil," Georgeanne managed, feeling her past coming back to haunt her. First John, and now Virgil.

Mae shook her head and dropped her hands. "How can I do that to you?"

"I'm a big girl. Virgil Duffy doesn't scare me," she said, and wondered if it was true. Sitting in her kitchen, she wasn't scared, but she wasn't so sure how she would feel when she saw him at the wedding. "You invite him, and whomever you want. Don't worry about me."

"I told Hugh that maybe we should fly to Vegas and get married by one of those Elvis impersonators. That would solve the problem."

There was no way Georgeanne would allow her friend to run off to Vegas because of her past mistakes. "Don't you even think about it," she warned with her nose in the air. "You know how I feel about tacky people, and getting married by Elvis is white-trash tacky. I'd have to buy you an equally tacky wedding present. Something from Ronco, like that glass cutter so you could make your own stemware from Pepsi bottles. And I'm sorry, but I don't think I could love you any longer."

Mae laughed. "Okay, no Elvis."

"Good. You're going to have a beautiful wedding," she predicted, then went in search of her day planner.

Together she and Mae got down to business. They called the caterer Mae wanted to use, then jumped in Georgeanne's car and drove up to Redmond.

Over the next week, they talked to a florist and looked at a dozen wedding dresses. Between Heron's, her work on the television program, Lexie, and the rapidly approaching wedding, Georgeanne had no time for herself. The only hours she had to sit and relax were the Monday and Wednesday nights when John picked up Lexie and Pongo and took them to puppy-training classes. But even then she couldn't relax. Not when John walked into her house, tall and handsome and smelling like a late summer breeze. She would see him and her stupid heart would flutter, and when he turned to leave, her chest would ache. She'd fallen in love with him again. Only this time it felt more wretched than the last. She'd thought she was finished loving people who couldn't love her back, but apparently not. Even though he broke her heart, she would probably always love John. He'd taken her love and her child, leaving her empty. Mae was getting married and moving ahead with her life. Georgeanne felt left behind. Her life was filled with things she enjoyed, yet the people she loved were moving in directions she couldn't follow.

In a few short days, Lexie would spend her first weekend with John and meet Ernie Maxwell and John's mother, Glenda. Her daughter belonged to a family that Georgeanne couldn't give her. A family she wasn't a part of, nor would ever belong to. John could give Lexie everything she would ever want and need, and Georgeanne was left out and pushed aside.

Ten days before the wedding, Georgeanne sat in her office at Heron's alone, thinking about Lexie and John and Mae, and feeling lonely. When Charles called and suggested she meet him for lunch at McCormick and Schmick's, she jumped at the chance to get away for a few hours. It was Friday afternoon, she had a big job to cater that evening, and she needed a friendly face and pleasant conversation.

Over clams and soft-shell crabs, she told Charles all about Mae and the wedding. "It's a week from this coming Thursday," she said as she wiped her hands on a linen napkin. "With such short notice, they were lucky to get a small nondenominational church in Kirkland and a banquet hall in Redmond for the reception afterward. Lexie is the flower girl and I'm the maid of honor." Georgeanne picked up her fork and shook her head. "I still haven't found a dress to wear. Thank goodness this will all be over soon, and I won't have to go through it again until Lexie gets married."

"Don't you plan to get married someday?"

Georgeanne shrugged and looked away. When she thought of getting married, she always pictured John as he'd looked in that formal tuxedo the day of the *GQ* photo shoot. "I haven't really thought about it much."

"Well, why don't you think about it?"

Georgeanne looked back at Charles and smiled. "Are you proposing?"

"I would if I thought you'd accept."

Her smile slowly fell.

"Don't worry," he said, and tossed a clamshell onto a pile on his plate. "I won't embarrass you right now by asking, and I won't subject myself to your rejection. I know you're not ready."

She stared at him, this wonderful man who meant a lot to her, but whom she didn't love as a wife should love a husband. Her head wanted to love him, but her heart loved someone else.

"Don't reject the idea out of hand. Just think about it," he said, and she did. She thought about how marriage to Charles would solve some of her problems.

He could provide a comfortable life for her and Lexie, and together they would be a family. She didn't love him as she should, but given more time, maybe she could. Maybe her head could convince her heart.

John tossed his T-shirt on the heap of socks and running shoes on the bathroom floor. Dressed only in a pair of jogging shorts, he covered his lower face with shave cream. As he reached for his razor, he looked up into the mirror in front of him and smiled. "You can come in and talk to me if you want to," he told Lexie, who stood behind him, peeking into the bathroom.

"What are you doing?"

"Shaving." He placed the razor beneath his left sideburn and scraped it down.

"My mom shaves her legs and her pits," she mentioned as she moved to stand next to him. She wore her pink and white striped nightgown, and her hair was messy from sleep. Last night was the first time she'd stayed with him alone, and after he'd killed the spider in her bedroom for her, everything had gone real smooth. After he'd smashed the insect with a book, she'd looked at him as if he walked on water.

"I get to shave when I'm in the seventh grade," she continued. "I'll probably be really hairy by then." She peered up at him through the mirror. "Do you think Pongo will ever get hairy?"

John rinsed his blade and shook his head. "Nope. He'll never get much hair." When he'd picked up Lexie the night before, that poor little dog had been wearing a new red sweater with jewels glued all over it and a matching stocking cap. When he'd entered the house, the dog looked at him and ran into another room to hide. Georgeanne had speculated that he might be afraid of John's height, but John figured that poor Pongo hadn't wanted another male to see him looking like such a sissy.

"How did you get that big ouchie in your eyebrow?"

"This little thing?" He pointed to his old scar. "When I was about nineteen, a guy shot a puck at my head and I didn't duck in time."

"Did it hurt?"

It had hurt like a son of a bitch. "Nah." John raised his chin toward the ceiling and shaved beneath his jaw. Out of the corner of his eye, he watched Lexie watch him. "Maybe you should get dressed now. Your grandma and great-grandpa Ernie will be here in about a half hour."

"Will you do my hair?" She held up one hand and showed him a hairbrush.

"I don't know how to do little girls' hair."

"You could put it in a ponytail. That's real easy. Or maybe a side pony. Just make sure it's high, 'cause I don't like low ponies."

"I'll try," he said, rinsed shave cream and stubble from the razor, then went to work on his other cheek. "But if you look like a wild child, don't blame me."

Lexie laughed and laid her head against his side. Her fine hair brushed his skin. "If my mommy marries Charles, will my name still be Kowalsky like yours?"

The razor came to an abrupt halt at the corner of John's mouth. His gaze slid down the mirror to Lexie's upturned face. Slowly he lowered the blade away from his face and held it under the hot water. "Is your mother planning on marrying Charles?"

Lexie shrugged. "Maybe. She's thinking about it."

John hadn't really given serious thought to Georgeanne marrying. The thought of it now, of another man touching her, tied his stomach up in a twist knot. He quickly finished shaving and turned the faucet off. "Did she tell you that?"

"Yep, but since you're my daddy, I told her to think about marrying you."

He reached for a towel and dabbed at the white cream beneath his left ear. "What did she say?"

"She laughed and said it wouldn't happen, but you could still ask her, couldn't you?"

*Marry Georgeanne?* He couldn't marry Georgeanne. Even though they'd gotten along fairly well after the Pongo incident, he wasn't convinced she would ever like him.

He could honestly say that he liked her. Maybe too much. Every time he went to pick up Lexie, he envisioned her without clothes, but lust wasn't enough to support a lifetime commitment. He respected her, too, but respect wasn't enough either. He loved Lexie and wanted to give her everything she needed to be happy, but he'd learned years ago not to marry a woman because of a child.

"Couldn't you just ask? Then we could have a baby."

She gazed up with the same pleading look she'd used to get her puppy, but this time he wasn't about to give in. If, and when, he ever married again, it would be because living without the woman was hell. "I don't think your mommy likes me," he said, and tossed the towel on the counter next to the sink. "How are we going to do that ponytail?"

Lexie handed him the brush. "You comb out the tangles first."

John got down on one knee and carefully ran the bristles through the back of Lexie's hair. "Am I hurting you?"

She shook her head. "My mommy likes you."

"Did she tell you she does?"

"She thinks you're handsome and nice, too."

John chuckled. "I know she didn't tell you that."

Lexie shrugged. "If you kiss her, she'll think you're handsome. Then you can have a baby."

Although the idea of kissing Georgeanne had always been one hell of a temptation for him, he doubted one kiss would work like magic and solve their problems. He didn't even want to think about making a baby.

He turned Lexie to the side and lightly brushed a tangle beneath her left ear. "It looks like you have food stuck in your hair," he said, careful not to pull too hard.

"Probably pizza," Lexie told him unconcerned, then they sat in silence while John combed the fine strands, fearing he was doing more harm than good. Lexie remained quiet, and John was relieved that the subject of Georgeanne and kissing and babies was over.

"If you kiss her, she'll like you more than Charles," Lexie whispered.

John pushed aside the drapes and gazed out at the Detroit night. From his room at the Omni Hotel, he could see the river looking like a long oil slick. He felt restless and edgy, but that was nothing new. It usually took him several hours to come back down after a game, especially after a match with the Red Wings. Last year the team from Motown had barely edged the Chinooks out of the play-offs with a one-goal backhanded fake by Sergei Fedorov. This year the Chinooks started the long season with a 4–2 victory over their rivals. The win had been a nice way to start the season.

Most of the team was in the bar downstairs, celebrating. Not John. He was restless and edgy and too stoked to sleep, but he didn't want to be around people. He didn't want to eat bar peanuts, talk shop, or fend off rink bunnies.

Something was wrong. Except for the blindside hit

he'd given Fetisov, John had played textbook hockey. He was playing his game the way he liked to play it, with speed, strength, skill, and hard body checking. He was doing what he loved to do. What he'd always loved to do.

Something was wrong. He wasn't satisfied. *You can have your career with the Chinooks, or you can have Georgeanne. You can't have both.*

John dropped the drape back into place and glanced at his watch. It was midnight in Detroit, nine in Seattle. He walked to the table next to the bed, picked up the telephone receiver, and dialed.

"Hello," she answered after the third ring, stirring something deep within him.

*If you kiss her, she'll think you're handsome. Then you can have a baby.* John closed his eyes. "Hi, Georgie."

"John?"

"Yep."

"Where are . . . What are you . . . ? Cryin' all night, I'm watching you right now on the television."

He opened his eyes and looked across the room at the closed curtains. "It's a delayed telecast on the West Coast."

"Oh. Did you win?"

"Yes."

"Lexie will be glad to hear it. She's in the living room watching you."

"What does she think?"

"Well, I believe she really liked it until that big red guy knocked you down. Then she got upset."

The "big red guy" happened to be an enforcer for Detroit. "Is she okay now?"

"Yes. When she saw you skate around again, she was okay. I think she really likes watching you. It must be genetic."

John glanced down at the notepad by the telephone.

"What about you?" he asked, and wondered why her answer felt so important to him.

"Well, I don't normally like to watch sports. Don't tell anyone, because as you know, I am from Texas," she drawled, "but I like to watch hockey more than football."

Her voice made him think of dark passion, reflections in windows, and hot sex. *If you kiss her, she'll like you more than Charles.* The thought of her kissing her boyfriend made him feel as if he'd taken a boomer to the chest. "I've got tickets for you and Lexie to the game on Friday. I really want you both to come."

"Friday? The night after the wedding?"

"Is that a problem? Do you have to work?"

She paused for a few long moments before she answered, "No, we can be there."

He smiled into the phone. "The language gets a little salty sometimes."

"I think we're used to it by now," she said, and he could hear the laughter in her voice. "Lexie is right here. I'll let you talk to her now."

"Wait, there's one more thing."

"What?"

*Wait until I get home before you decide to marry your boyfriend. He's a wimp and a weenie and you deserve someone better.* He sat down heavily on the side of the bed. He didn't have any right to demand anything. "Never mind. I'm really tired."

"Is there something else you needed?"

He closed his eyes and took a deep breath. "No, put Lexie on."

# Eighteen

Lexie strolled down the aisle as if she were born to play the part of a flower girl. Curls bounced at her shoulders and rose petals fluttered from her gloved hand to the carpet of the small nondenominational church. Georgeanne stood on the left side of the minister and resisted the urge to pull at the hemline of the pink satin and crepe tank dress resting two inches above her knees. Her gaze was fixed on her daughter as Lexie sashayed down the aisle dressed in white lace and beaming as if she were the reason the small group had assembled in the tiny church. Georgeanne couldn't help beaming a little herself. She was extremely proud of her little drama queen.

When Lexie reached her mother's side, she turned and smiled at the man standing across the aisle in a navy blue Hugo Boss. She raised three fingers off the handle of her basket and wiggled them. One side of John's mouth lifted, and he waved two fingers back at her.

The wedding march began and all eyes turned to the doorway. A wreath of white roses and baby's breath circled Mae's short blond hair, and the long white organza sheath Georgeanne had helped her choose looked beautiful on her. The dress was simple and emphasized Mae instead of losing her in yards of satin and tulle. The slit up the front gave her short stature a nice vertical line.

Mae walked down the aisle unescorted with her head held high. She hadn't invited her family, instead filling the bride's pew with her friends from work. Georgeanne had tried to persuade her to include her estranged parents, but Mae was stubborn. Her parents hadn't come to Ray's funeral, she didn't want them at her wedding. She didn't want them to ruin the happiest day of her life.

While all eyes were on the bride, Georgeanne took the opportunity to study the groom. In his black tuxedo, Hugh was very handsome, but she wasn't interested in his looks or the cut of his coat. She watched for his reaction to Mae, and what she saw alleviated some of her worries over the unexpected romance and hurried wedding. He lit up so much that Georgeanne half expected him to hold out his arms so Mae could run into them. His whole face smiled, and his eyes shined liked he'd just won the lottery. He looked like a man desperately in love. It was no wonder Mae had fallen so fast.

As Mae walked passed, she smiled at Georgeanne, then moved to stand beside Hugh.

"Dearly beloved . . ."

Georgeanne dropped her gaze to the toes of her beige leather T-straps. *Desperately in love,* she thought. The night before, she'd told Charles that she couldn't marry him. She couldn't marry a man she didn't love desperately. Her gaze moved across the aisle to John's black tassel loafers. Several times in her life, she'd seen him look at her with lust heavy in his blue eyes. In fact, the last time he'd come to pick up Lexie, she'd seen that "I want to jump your bones" look. But lust wasn't the same as love. Lust didn't even last past the next morning, especially with John. Her gaze traveled up his long legs, over his double-breasted jacket, and up his burgundy and navy tie. Her scrutiny moved to his face and to the blue eyes staring back at her.

He smiled. Just a pleasant little smile that sent off warning bells in her head. She turned her attention to the ceremony. John wanted something.

The women seated in the front pews began to softly weep, and Georgeanne glanced in their direction. Even if she hadn't met them briefly before the wedding, Georgeanne would have guessed they belonged to Hugh. The whole family resembled each other, from his mother and three sisters to his eight nieces and nephews.

They cried throughout the short ceremony, and when it was over, they cried as they followed the recessional. Georgeanne and Lexie walked beside John back up the aisle and through the double doors. Several times the sleeve of his navy blazer almost touched her arm.

In the vestibule Hugh's mother pushed her son out of the way to get to his bride. "You're just a doll," his mother declared as she hugged Mae and passed her around to the sisters.

Georgeanne, John, and Lexie moved out of the way as the small group of Mae's friends and Hugh's family gathered around the couple to congratulate them.

"Here." Lexie handed the basket of rose petals to Georgeanne and sighed. "I'm tired."

"I think we can go ahead and leave for the reception," John said as he moved to stand behind Georgeanne. "Why don't you and Lexie ride with me?"

Georgeanne turned and gazed up at him. He looked extremely fine in his wedding suit, except for the drooping red rose pinned to his lapel. He'd stuck the pin through the stem rather than the body of the flower. "We can't leave until Wendell takes his pictures."

"Who?"

"Wendell. He's the photographer Mae hired, and we can't leave until he takes the wedding pictures."

John's smile turned to a grimace. "Are you sure?"

Georgeanne nodded and pointed to his chest. "Your rose is about to fall off."

He glanced down and shrugged. "I'm no good at this. Can you fix it?"

Against her better judgment, Georgeanne slipped her fingers beneath the lapel of his navy suit. With his head bent over hers, she pulled out the long straight pin. She was so close, she could feel his breath at her right temple. The smell of his cologne filled her head, and if she turned her face, their mouths would touch. She pushed the pin though the wool and into the dark red rose.

"Don't hurt yourself."

"I won't. I do this all the time." She ran her hand down his lapel, smoothing out invisible wrinkles, savoring the texture of expensive wool beneath her fingertips.

"You pin flowers on men all the time?"

She shook her head and her temple brushed his smooth jaw. "I pin them on myself and Mae. For our business."

He put a hand on her bare arm. "Are you sure you don't want to ride with me to the reception? Virgil's going to be there, and I thought you might not want to go alone."

With the chaos surrounding the wedding, Georgeanne had managed to avoid thinking about her ex-fiancé. The thought of him now formed a lump in her stomach. "Did you tell him about Lexie?"

"He knows."

"How did he take it?" She slid her fingers over one

more invisible wrinkle, then dropped her hand.

John shrugged his big shoulders. "Okay. It's been seven years, so he's over it."

Georgeanne was relieved. "Then I'll drive myself to the reception, but thank you for the offer."

"You're welcome." His slid his warm palm up to her shoulder, then back down to her wrist. The hair on her arm tingled. "Are you sure about those pictures?"

"What?"

"I hate waiting around to get my picture taken."

He was doing it again. Taking up all the space and sucking out her ability to think. Touching him was both sweet pleasure and sheer torture. "I would have thought you'd be used to it by now."

"I don't mind the pictures, it's the waiting. I'm not a patient man. When I want something, I like to get it on."

Georgeanne had a feeling he wasn't talking about pictures anymore. A few minutes later, as the photographer positioned them on the steps in front of the pulpit, she was forced to endure the whole pleasure/torture experience again. Wendell positioned them with the women standing in front of the men, while Lexie stood close to Mae.

"I want to see happy little smiles," the photographer requested, his soft voice suggesting that perhaps he'd gotten in touch with his feminine side. As he looked through the camera on his tripod, he motioned them closer together with his hands. "Come on, I want to see happy little smiles on your happy little faces."

"Is he related to that artist on PBS?" John asked Hugh out of the side of his mouth.

"The oil-painting dude with the Afro?"

"Yeah. He used to paint happy little clouds and shit."

"Daddy!" Lexie whispered loudly. "Don't swear."

"Sorry."

"Can you all say 'wedding night?' " Wendell asked.

"Wedding night!" Lexie yelled.

"That's real good, little flower girl. How about everyone else?"

Georgeanne looked at Mae and they started to laugh.

"Come on get hap-hap-happy."

"Damn, where did you get this guy?" Hugh wanted to know.

"I've known him for years. He was a good friend of Ray's."

"Ahh, that explains it then."

John put his hand on Georgeanne's waist, and her laughter stopped abruptly. He slid his palm to her stomach and drew her back against the solid wall of his chest. His voice was a low rumble next to her ear when he said, "Say 'cheese.' "

Georgeanne's breath caught in her throat. "Cheese," she uttered weakly, and the photographer snapped the picture.

"Now the groom's family," Wendell announced as he advanced his film.

The muscles in John's arm tensed. His fingers curled into a possessive fist, and the hem of her dress rode up her thighs. Then he dropped his hand and took a step backward, putting a few inches between them. Georgeanne glanced at him, and again he gave her that pleasant little smile.

"Hey, Hugh," he said, then turned his attention to his friend as if he hadn't just held Georgeanne tight against his chest. "Did you check out Chelios's when we were in Chicago?"

Georgeanne told herself not to read anything into the embrace. She knew better than to look for motives or attribute feelings that just didn't exist. She knew better than to fall for his possessive embraces or pleasant smiles. It was best just to forget about it. They meant nothing, led nowhere. She knew better than to expect anything from him.

An hour later, as she stood in the banquet hall next to the buffet table laden with food and flowers, she was still trying to forget. She tried to forget to look for him every few moments, and tried not to notice him standing with a group of men who were obviously hockey players, and laughing with some leggy blonde. She tried to forget, but couldn't. Any more than she could forget that Virgil was somewhere in the hall.

Georgeanne placed a chocolate-dipped strawberry on a plate she was preparing for Lexie. She added a chicken wing and two pieces of broccoli.

"I want some cake and some of those, too." Lexie pointed to a crystal bowl filled with wedding mints.

"You had your cake right after Mae and Hugh cut it." Georgeanne put a few mints on the plate along with a carrot stick and handed the plate to Lexie. Her gaze quickly scanned the crowd.

Then her stomach did a little flip-flop. For the first time in seven years, she saw Virgil Duffy in person. "Go stand by Aunt Mae," she said, turning her daughter by the shoulder. "I'll come meet you there in a minute." She gave Lexie a little push and watched her walk toward the bride and groom. Georgeanne couldn't spend the rest of the evening wondering if Virgil would confront her and imagining what he might say. She had to get the encounter over with before she lost her nerve. She took a deep breath and, with long, deliberate strides, moved to face her past. She wove her way through the crowd of guests until she stood in front of him.

"Hello, Virgil," she said and watched his eyes harden.

"Georgeanne, you have the nerve to face me. I'd wondered if you would." His tone suggested he wasn't "over it" as John had claimed earlier at the church.

"It's been seven years, and I've moved on with my life."

"Easy for you. Not so easy for me."

Physically he hadn't changed very much. Perhaps his hair had thinned a bit, and his eyes were a little puffy from age. "I think both of us should forget the past."

"Now, why would I do that?"

She looked at him a moment, beyond the lines on his face, to the bitter man beneath. "I'm sorry for what happened, and for the pain I caused you. I tried to tell you the night before the wedding that I was having second thoughts, but you wouldn't listen. I'm not blaming you, just explaining how I felt. I was young and immature and I'm sorry. I hope you can accept my apology."

"When hell freezes over."

She was surprised to discover that his anger didn't really bother her. It didn't matter that he wouldn't accept her apology. She'd confronted her past and felt free of the guilt she'd carried for years. She wasn't young and immature anymore. And she wasn't afraid either. "I'm sorry to hear you say that, but whether or not you accept my apology won't keep me up at night. My life is filled with people who love me and I'm happy. Your anger and hostility can't hurt me."

"You're still as naive as you were seven years ago," he said as a woman approached Virgil and placed her hand on his shoulder. Georgeanne immediately recognized Caroline Foster-Duffy from her many pictures in local papers. "John will never marry you. He'll never choose you over his team," he added, then he turned and walked away with his wife.

Georgeanne stared after him, puzzled by his parting comment. She wondered if he'd threatened John, and if he had, why John hadn't told her about it. She shook her head, not knowing what to think. Never in her wildest dreams had she ever thought John would marry her or choose her over anything.

Okay, she conceded as she headed toward Lexie, who was surrounded by the bride and groom and a few tough-looking male wedding guests. Maybe in her wildest dreams she *had* envisioned John proposing more than a wild night of sex, but that wasn't reality. Even though she loved him, and he sometimes looked at her with a kind of hungry desire in his eyes, it didn't mean he loved her in return. It didn't mean he would choose her for anything more than a roll in the hay. It didn't mean he wouldn't abandon her in the morning, leaving her empty and alone.

Georgeanne moved past the stage where a band was setting up and her thoughts returned to Virgil. She'd faced him and freed herself from the burden of her past, and she felt pretty good. "How's it going?" she asked as she came to stand by Mae.

"Great." Mae glanced up at her and smiled, looking gorgeous and happy. "At first I was a little nervous about being in the same room with thirty hockey players. But now that I've met most of them, they're really pretty nice, almost human even. Too bad Ray isn't here. He'd be in heaven around all these thick muscles and tight butts."

Georgeanne chuckled and plucked a strawberry off Lexie's plate. She glanced across the room at John and caught him staring at her above the crowd. She bit into the fruit and looked away.

"Hey." Lexie scowled. "Eat the green stuff next time."

"Have you met Hugh's friends?" Mae poked her new husband with her elbow.

"Not yet," she answered, and popped the rest of the strawberry into her mouth.

Hugh introduced her and Lexie to two men in expensive wool suits and silk ties. The first gentleman, named Mark Butcher, sported a spectacular black eye. "You might recall Dmitri," Hugh said after he'd made the introduction. "He was at John's houseboat a few months ago when you came over."

Georgeanne looked at the man with light brown hair and blue eyes. She didn't remember him at all. "I thought you looked familiar," she lied.

"I remember you," Dmitri said, his accent obvious. "You wore red."

"Did I?" Georgeanne was flattered that he would recall the color of her dress. "I'm surprised you remember."

Dmitri smiled and little creases appeared in the corners of his eyes. "I remember. I wear no gold chainz now."

Georgeanne glanced at Mae, who shrugged and looked up at a grinning Hugh. "That's right. I had to explain to Dmitri that American women don't like to see jewelry on men."

"Oh, I don't know," Mae disagreed. "I know of several men who look fierce in pearl chokers and matching earrings."

Hugh pulled Mae against his side and kissed the top of her head. "I'm not talking about drag queens, honey."

"Is this your little girl?" Mark asked Georgeanne.

"Yes, she is."

"What happened to your eye?" Lexie handed Georgeanne her plate, then pointed her last strawberry at Mark.

"The Avalanche caught him in the corner and gave him a pounding," John answered from behind Georgeanne. He picked Lexie up with one arm and lifted her until they were eye level. "Don't feel bad, he probably deserved it."

Georgeanne glanced at John. She wanted to ask him about Virgil's parting comment to her, but she would have to wait until they were alone.

"Maybe he shouldn't have goosed Ricci with his stick," Hugh added.

Mark shrugged. "Ricci broke my wrist last year," he said, and the conversation turned to which man had suffered the most injuries. At first Georgeanne was appalled by the list of broken bones, torn muscles, and number of stitches. But the longer she listened, the more she found it morbidly fascinating. She began to wonder how many men in the room had their own teeth. Not many by the sounds of things.

Lexie placed her hands on the sides of John's head, turning his face toward her. "Did you get hurt last night, Daddy?"

"Me? No way."

"Daddy?" Dmitri looked at Lexie. "Iz yours?"

"Yes." John turned his gaze to his teammates. "This little worrywart is my daughter, Lexie Kowalsky."

Georgeanne waited for him to say that he hadn't known about Lexie until recently, but he didn't. He didn't offer any explanation for his daughter's sudden appearance in his life. He just held her in his arms as if she'd always been there.

Dmitri glanced at Georgeanne, then looked back at John. He raised a questioning brow.

"Yes," John said, leaving Georgeanne to wonder about the silent byplay between the two men.

"How old are you, Lexie?" Mark asked.

"Six. I had my birthday, and now I'm in first grade. I gots a dog now, too, 'cause my daddy gave him to me. His name is Pongo, but he's not very big. He doesn't got a lot of hair either, and his ears get cold. So I made him a hat."

"It's purple," Mae told John. "It looks like a dunce cap."

"How do you get the hat on your dog?"

"She pins him down between her knees," Georgeanne answered.

John glanced at his daughter. "You sit on Pongo?"

"Yeah, Daddy, he likes it."

John doubted Pongo liked anything about wearing a stupid hat. He opened his mouth to suggest that maybe she shouldn't sit on her little dog, but the band struck up a few chords, and he turned his attention to the stage. "Good evening," the lead singer said into his microphone. "For the first song of the night, Hugh and Mae have asked that everyone join them on the dance floor."

"Daddy," Lexie said barely above the music. "May I have a piece of cake?"

"Is it okay with your mom?"

"Yes."

He turned to Georgeanne and lowered his mouth to her ear. "We're heading to the banquet table. Do you want to come with us?"

She shook her head, and John looked deep into her green eyes. "Don't go anywhere." Before she had a chance to reply, he and Lexie headed across the room.

"I want a big piece," Lexie informed him. "With lots of frosting."

"You'll get a tummy ache."

"No I won't."

He set her on her feet beside the table and waited long, frustrating minutes for her to choose just the right piece of cake with purple roses only. He found her a fork and a place to sit at a round table beside one of Hugh's nieces. When he turned to look for Georgeanne, he spotted her out on the dance floor with Dmitri. Normally he liked the young Russian, but not tonight. Not when Georgeanne wore a short little dress, and not when Dmitri looked at her as if she were a serving of beluga caviar.

John wove his way through the crowded dance floor and placed a hand on his teammate's shoulder. He didn't have to say anything. Dmitri looked at him, shrugged, and walked away.

"I don't think this is a very good idea," Georgeanne said as he gathered her into his arms.

"Why not?" He pulled closer, fitting her soft curves against his chest and moving their bodies to the mellow music. *You can have your career with the Chinooks, or you can have Georgeanne. You can't have both.* He thought about Virgil's warning, and he thought about the warm woman in his arms. He'd already made his decision. He'd made it days ago in Detroit.

"Because Dmitri asked me to dance, for one thing."

"He's a commie bastard. Stay away from him."

Georgeanne leaned back far enough to look up into his face. "I thought he was your friend."

"He was."

A frown creased her forehead. "What happened?"

"We both want the same thing, only he isn't going to get it."

"What do you want?"

There were a lot of things he wanted. "I saw you talking to Virgil. What did he say?"

"Not a lot. I told him I was sorry for what happened seven years ago, but he wouldn't accept my apology." She appeared puzzled for a moment, then shook her head and looked away. "You said he'd moved on, but he's still very bitter."

John slid his palm to the side of her throat and lifted her chin with his thumb. "Don't worry about him." He stared into her face, then raised his eyes to the old man staring back at him. His gaze found Dmitri and a half dozen other men who'd taken shifty-eyed glances at Georgeanne's bustline. Then he lowered his face and his lips took possession of hers. He possessed her with his mouth and tongue and his hand moving from her back to her behind. The kiss was deliberate, long, hard. She clung to him, and when he finally lifted his mouth, she was breathless.

"Cryin' all night," she whispered.

"Now, tell me about Charles." Her gaze was a little glassy and a bit dazed. The passion in her eyes made him think of tangled bedsheets and soft flesh.

"You want to know about Charles?"

"Lexie told me you're thinking of marrying him."

"I told him no."

Relief washed over him. He wrapped his arms tight around her and smiled into her hair. "You look beautiful tonight," he said into her ear. Then he pulled back and looked at her face, at her luscious mouth, and said, "Why don't we find someplace where I can take advantage of you? How big is the counter in the women's bathroom?"

He recognized the spark of interest in her eyes before she turned her head and tried to hide her smile. "Are you high on drugs, John Kowalsky?"

"Not tonight," he laughed. "I listened to Nancy Reagan and just said no. How about you?"

"Of course not," she scoffed.

The music ended and a faster song began. "Where's Lexie?" she asked above the noise.

John looked over at the table where he'd left her and pointed her out. Her cheek rested in her palm and her lids were lowered to half-mast. "She looks like she's about to pass out."

"I better take her home."

John slid his hands from her back up to her shoulders. "I'll carry her out to your car."

Georgeanne thought about his offer for a moment, then decided to let him. "That would be great. I'll get my purse and I'll meet you out there." His grasp on her arms tightened a fraction, then he released her. She watched him walk toward Lexie, then turned to find Mae.

There was definitely something different in his touch tonight. Something in the way he held her and kissed her. Something hot and possessive as if he were reluctant to let her go. She cautioned herself not to read too much into it, but a warm little glow had settled about her heart.

She quickly retrieved her purse and bid Mae and Hugh good-bye. When she walked outside, night had fallen, and the parking lot was illuminated by streetlights. She spotted John leaning his behind against her car. He'd wrapped Lexie in his wool jacket and held her against his chest. His white shirt stood out in the dark parking lot.

"It doesn't work that way," she heard him tell Lexie. "You can't name yourself. Someone else has to start calling you something, and the name just sticks. Do you think Ed Jovanovski chose to call himself "'Special Ed'?"

"But I want to be 'The Cat.' "

"You can't be 'The Cat.' " He looked up at Georgeanne and pushed away from the car. "Felix Potvin is 'The Cat.' "

"Can I be a dog?" Lexie asked, resting her head on his shoulder.

"I don't think you really want people to call you Lexie 'The Dog' Kowalsky, do you?"

Lexie giggled into the side of his neck. "No, but I want to have a name like you do."

"If you want to be a cat, how about a cheetah? Lexie 'The Cheetah' Kowalsky."

"Okay," she said through a yawn. "Daddy, do you know why animals don't play cards in the jungle?"

Georgeanne rolled her eyes and fit her key into the lock.

"Because there are too many cheetahs," he answered. "You told me that joke about fifty times already."

"Oh, I forgot."

"I didn't think you ever forgot anything." John chuckled and placed Lexie in the passenger seat. The car's dome light glistened in his dark hair, and illuminated his blue and red paisley suspenders. "I'll see you at the hockey game tomorrow night."

Lexie reached for her seat belt and buckled it. "Give me some sugar, Daddy." She pursed her lips and waited.

Georgeanne smiled and walked to the driver's side of the car. The way John cared for Lexie touched a tender spot in her heart. He was a great father, and no matter what happened between Georgeanne and John, she would always love him for loving Lexie.

"Hey, Georgie?" His voice called to her like a warm touch on the chilled night air.

She looked across the roof of the car and into John's face, partially hidden in nighttime shadows.

"Where are you going?" he asked.

"Well, home, of course."

He chuckled deep within his chest. "Don't you want to give Daddy some sugar?"

Temptation taunted her weak will and self-control. Heck, who was she kidding? Where John was concerned, she had *no* self-control at all. Especially after that kiss he'd given her. She yanked open the driver's-side door before she had a chance to even consider his alluring proposition. "Not tonight, stud boy."

"Did you just call me stud boy?"

She placed one foot on the doorframe. "It's an improvement over what I called you last month," she said, and slipped inside the car. She started the engine, and with John's laughter filling the night, she drove out of the parking lot.

On the way home, she thought about the difference

in him. Her heart wanted to believe it all meant something wonderful, like maybe he'd gotten hit in the head with a hockey puck, and he'd suddenly come to his senses and realized that he couldn't live without her. But her experiences with John told her different. She knew better than to project her feelings onto him and look for hidden motives. Trying to decipher his every word and touch was nutty. Whenever she let her guard down with him, she always got hurt.

After she put Lexie to bed, Georgeanne hung John's suit jacket on the back of a kitchen chair and kicked off her shoes. A light rain pattered her windows as she brewed water for a cup of herbal tea. She moved to the chair and smoothed her fingers across the shoulder seam of John's jacket, recalling exactly how he'd looked standing across the aisle at the church, his blue eyes staring into hers. She remembered the scent of his cologne and the sound of his voice. *Why don't we find someplace where I can take advantage of you,* he'd said, and she'd been tempted.

Pongo let loose with a string of yapping seconds before the doorbell rang. Georgeanne dropped her hand to her side and scooped up the dog on her way to the entrance. She wasn't really surprised to find John on her front steps, raindrops glistening in his dark hair.

"I forgot to give you the tickets to tomorrow night's game," he said, and held out an envelope.

Georgeanne took the tickets, and against her better judgment, she invited him inside. "I'm making tea. Would you like some?"

"Hot?"

"Yep?"

"Do you have any iced tea?"

"Of course, I'm from Texas." She walked back into the kitchen and deposited Pongo on the floor. The dog ran over to John and licked his shoe.

"Pongo is getting to be a pretty good watchdog," she told him as she reached into the refrigerator and pulled out a pitcher of tea.

"Yeah. I can see that. What would he do if someone broke in, lick the man's toe?"

Georgeanne laughed and shut the door. "Probably, but he'd bark like mad first. Having Pongo around is better than installing a house alarm. It's kind of weird, but I feel safer when he's in the house." She placed the envelope on the counter and filled a glass.

"Next time I'll buy you a real dog." John took a few steps toward her and reached for the tea. "No ice. Thanks."

"There better not be a next time."

"There's always a next time, Georgie," he said, and raised the glass to his lips, his eyes watching her as he took a long drink.

"Are you sure you don't want some ice?"

He shook his head and lowered the tea. He sucked moisture from his lips as his gaze slid over her breasts to her thighs, then traveled back up to her face. "That dress has been driving me crazy all day long. It reminds me of that little pink wedding dress you had on the first time I saw you."

She looked down. "This is nothing like that dress."

"It's short and it's pink."

"That dress was a lot shorter, strapless, and so tight I couldn't breathe."

"I remember." He smiled and leaned one hip against the counter. "All the way to Copalis, you kept pulling at the top and yanking at the bottom. It was seductive as hell, like an erotic tug-of-war. I kept watching to see which half would win."

Georgeanne rested one shoulder against the refrigerator, and folded her arms. "I'm surprised you remember all of that. As I recall, you didn't like me very much."

"And as I recall, I liked you more than was wise."

"Only when I was naked. The rest of the time, you were fairly rude."

He frowned at the tea in his hand, then looked back at her. "I don't remember it quite that way, but if I was rude to you, it wasn't personal. My life was a pile of shit back then. I was drinking way too much and doing all I could to ruin my career and myself." He paused and took a deep breath. "Do you remember when I told you that I was married before?"

"Of course." How could she possibly forget about DeeDee and Linda?

"Well, what I didn't tell you was that Linda killed herself. I found her dead in our bathtub. She'd sliced her wrists with a razor blade, and for a lot of years, I blamed myself."

Shocked speechless, Georgeanne stared at him. She didn't know what to say or do. Her first impulse was to wrap her arms around his waist and tell him she was sorry, but she held back.

He took another drink, then wiped his mouth with the back of his hand. "The truth of it is, I didn't love her. I was a lousy husband, and I only married her because she was pregnant. When the baby died, there wasn't anything holding us together anymore. I wanted out of the marriage. She didn't."

An ache tightened her chest. She knew John, and she knew he must have been devastated. She wondered why he was telling her about it now. Why would he trust her with something so painful? "You had a baby?"

"Yeah. He was born premature and died a month later. Toby would be eight now."

"I'm sorry," was the only thing she could think to say. She couldn't even imagine losing Lexie.

He set the glass on the counter beside Georgeanne,

then he took her hand in his. "Sometimes I wonder what he'd be like if he'd lived."

She looked into his face and once again felt that warm little glow about her heart. He cared for her. Maybe trust and caring could turn to something more.

"I wanted to tell you about Linda and Toby for two reasons. I wanted you to know about them, and I want you to know that even though I've been married twice, I'm not going to make the same mistakes. I won't marry again because a child is involved, or because of lust. It will be because I'm crazy in love."

His words doused Georgeanne's warm little glow like a bucket of ice water, and she pulled her hand from his. They had a child together, and it was no secret John was attracted to her physically. He'd never promised her anything but a good time, but she'd done it again. She'd let herself hope for things she couldn't have, and knowing it hurt so much the backs of her eyes stung. "Thank you for sharing, John, but I just can't appreciate your honesty right now," she said as she moved toward the front door. "I think you better leave."

"What?" He sounded incredulous as he followed close behind her. "I thought I was getting somewhere."

"I know you did. But you can't come over here whenever you feel like sex and just expect me to tear off my clothes and oblige you." She failed to control her trembling chin as she pulled the front door open. She wanted him gone before she fell apart completely.

"Is that what you think? That you're just a lay?"

Georgeanne tried not to flinch. "Yes."

"What the hell is happening here?" He yanked the door out of her grasp and slammed it shut. "I spill my guts and you jump up and down on my insides! I'm honest with you, and you think I'm trying to get in your pants."

"Honest? You're only honest when you want something. You lie to me all the time."

"When have I lied to you?"

"Your lawyer, for one," she reminded him.

"That wasn't really a lie, it was an omission."

"It was a lie, and you lied to me again today."

"When?"

"At the church. You told me Virgil had moved on, that he was over what happened seven years ago. But you know he isn't."

He leaned back on his heels and frowned at her. "What did he say?"

"That you wouldn't choose me over your team. What did he mean?" she asked, and waited for him to enlighten her.

"The truth?"

"Of course."

"Okay, he threatened to trade me to another hockey team if I get involved with you, but it doesn't matter. Forget about Virgil. He's just mad because I got a piece of what he wanted."

Georgeanne leaned against the wall. "Me?"

"You."

"That's all I am to you?" She looked at him.

He blew out his breath and ran his fingers though the sides of his hair. "If you think I only came over here to get my rocks off, you're wrong."

She let her gaze travel to the bulge in his wool trousers, then back up to his face. "Am I?"

Anger stained his cheeks and he clenched his jaw. "Don't take what I feel for you and turn it into something dirty. I want you, Georgeanne. All you have to do is walk in a room, and I want you. I want to kiss you, and touch you, and make love to you. My physical response is natural, and I won't apologize for it."

"And in the morning you'll be gone, and I'll be alone again."

"That's horseshit."

"It's happened twice."

"Last time, you ran out on me."

She shook her head. "It doesn't matter who ran out which time. It will end the same. You won't mean to hurt me, but you will."

"I don't want to hurt you. I want to make you feel good, and if you were honest with me, like you wish me to be with you, you'd admit that you want me, too."

"No."

His eyes narrowed. "I hate that word."

"Sorry, but there's too much between us to have it any other way."

"Are you still trying to punish me for what happened seven years ago, or is it just an excuse?" He planted his hands on the wall next to her head. "What are you afraid of?"

"Not you."

He cupped her chin in his palm. "Liar. You're afraid Daddy isn't going to love you."

Her breath caught in her lungs. "That was cruel."

"Maybe, but it's the truth." His thumb slipped across her closed lips. He wrapped his free hand around her wrist. "You're afraid to reach out and take what you want, but I'm not. I know what I want." He slid her palm across his hard chest and down the buttons of his shirt. "Are you still trying to be a good girl so Daddy will notice you? Well, guess what, baby doll," he whispered as he moved her hand to the front of his pants and pressed his thick erection into her palm. "I noticed."

"Stop it," she said, and lost control of her tears. She hated him. She loved him. She wanted him to stay as badly as she wanted him to go. He'd been crude and cruel, but he'd been right. She was terrified he'd touch her, and afraid he wouldn't. She was afraid to take what she wanted, scared he'd make her miserable and unhappy. She was already miserable and unhappy. There was no way she could win. He was like a drug, an addiction, and she was hooked. "Don't do this to me."

John wiped a tear from her cheek and let go of her hand. "I want you, and I'm not afraid to play dirty."

She had to cut herself off from John, quit cold turkey. Check herself into rehab. No more hot kisses or touches or hungry glances. She had to get tough. "You just want a piece of . . . of . . ."

John shook his head and smiled. "I don't want just a piece. I want it all."

# Nineteen

John looked into Georgeanne's eyes and chuckled silently. She was trying to be tough but couldn't even bring herself to say the word "ass." It was just one of the thing that fascinated him about her. "I want your heart, your mind, and your body." He lowered his head and brushed his lips against hers. "I want all of you—forever," he whispered, and wrapped his arm around her waist. Her palms flattened against his chest as if she meant to push him away, but then she opened her soft mouth, and he felt a triumph so sweet it nearly sent him to his knees. He craved her body and soul, and he lifted her onto her toes and fed his hunger. Within seconds the kiss became a carnal feeding frenzy of mouths and tongues and hot, hot pleasure. John unzipped the back of her dress, then reached for the shoulders. He pulled down the dress, and the thin straps of her slip and bra, stripping her to her waist. Her arms were pinned to her sides, and he drew back to view her plump, naked breasts spilled toward him like his personal vision of heaven. He wrapped one arm around her waist and he lowered his face and placed a soft kiss on the very tip of her left breast. His tongue licked the puckered flesh and she moaned. She arched toward him, and he sucked her nipple into his mouth. Georgeanne struggled to free her arms, but he held her tight.

"John," she moaned. "I want to touch you."

He loosened his grasp and moved to suckle her right breast. He was ready. He'd been ready for months. The ache in his groin urged him to shove her against the wall, pull her dress up to her waist, and bury himself deep inside her hot, wet body. Now.

She freed her arms from the tangle of straps and pulled his shirttails from his pants. John straightened and looked into her drowsy eyes. Before he could give in to his urge and take her right there by her front door, he grabbed her hand and pulled her toward the rear of the house. "Where's your bedroom?" he asked as he moved down the hall. "I know there's one here somewhere."

"Last door on the left."

John entered the room and stopped dead in his tracks. The bed had a floral quilt and a lace canopy. A half dozen or so frilly pillows were tossed against the headboard. Flowers were printed on the wallpaper and on the fabric of the chairs. A big floral wreath hung above one dresser, and two vases of flowers sat about the room. He'd just stepped into girly central.

Georgeanne walked past him, holding her dress to her breasts. "What's wrong?"

He looked at her, standing there surrounded by flowers, attempting to shield herself with her hands, and failing miserably. "Nothing, except you're still dressed."

"So are you."

He smiled and stepped out of his shoes. "Not for long." Within seconds he'd stripped down to nothing, and when he returned his gaze to Georgeanne, he nearly exploded. She stood just beyond his reach, in nothing but a pair of skimpy panties and two stockings secured at her thighs with pink garters. His gaze moved from the enticing expanse of thigh just above the garters to her full hips. Her breasts were beautiful and round, her shoulders smooth, her face gorgeous. He reached for her and pulled her against him. She was hot and soft and everything he'd ever wanted in a woman. He meant to go slow. He wanted to make love to her, to prolong their pleasure. But he couldn't. He felt like a kid running toward his favorite playground, unable to stop; the only thing holding him back was his own indecision over where to play first. He wanted her mouth, shoulder, and breasts. He wanted to kiss her belly, thighs, between her legs.

He pushed her onto the bed, then rolled with her on top. He kissed her mouth and slid his hands down her back to her behind. He wrapped his fist in her panties and yanked them down her legs. His erection pressed into her smooth stomach and he ground it against her. The tension in his groin pulled tighter, tighter, until he thought he might explode.

He wanted to wait. He wanted to make sure she was ready. He wanted to be a tender lover. He rolled her onto her back and forced her panties from her legs. He sat back on his heels and looked at her, naked except for a pair of nylons and two garters. She raised her arms to him, and he knew he couldn't wait. He covered her with his body, hips cradled between her smooth thighs, and he placed his palms on both sides of her face. "I love you, Georgeanne," he whispered as he looked into her green eyes. "Tell me you love me."

She moaned and slid her hands down his sides to his buttocks. "I love you, John. I've always loved you."

He plunged deep inside her and realized immediately he'd forgotten a condom. For the first time in years, he felt enveloped in hot fluid flesh. Desperately he fought for control while the need for her clawed at his gut. He pulled back, thrust again, and they both shattered in a reeling climax.

It was three in the morning before John slipped from her bed and began to dress. Georgeanne secured the sheet around her breasts and sat up to watch him button his pants. He was leaving. She knew he didn't have a choice. Neither of them wanted Lexie to know he'd spent the night. Still, her heart ached at his leaving. He'd told her he loved her. He'd told her many times. It was still a little hard to believe. Hard for her to trust the joy she felt deep inside.

He reached for his shirt and shoved his arms into the sleeves. Tears stung the backs of her eyes and she blinked them back. She wanted to ask him if she would see him again the next evening, but she didn't want to appear grasping and greedy.

"You probably won't want to go to the arena early," he said, referring to the hockey tickets he'd given her earlier. "Lexie will have a hard enough time sitting through the game, without getting there for the early stuff." He sat on the edge of the bed and put on his socks and shoes. "Dress warm." When he was finished, he stood and reached for her. He pulled her onto her knees and kissed her. "I love you, Georgeanne."

She didn't think she would ever tire of hearing him say those words to her. "I love you, too."

"I'll see you after the game," he said, and dropped one last kiss on her lips. Then he was gone, leaving her alone with Virgil's warning plaguing her brain and threatening to destroy her happiness.

John loved her. She loved him. Did he love her enough to give up his hockey team? How could she live with herself if he did?

* * *

Blue and green floodlights circled the ice like a swirling cauldron while a half-dozen scantily clad cheerleaders danced to ear-popping rock music pumped from the sound system at the Key Arena. Georgeanne could feel the heavy bass thud in her chest and wondered how Ernie was doing. She looked over the top of Lexie—who had her hands over her ears—to John's grandfather. He didn't seem at all bothered by the loud noise.

Ernie Maxwell looked almost the same as he had seven years ago, with his thin white crew cut and gravelly Burgess Meredith voice. The only real difference was that now his blue eyes looked out from behind a pair of black-rimmed glasses, and he had a hearing aid in his left ear.

When Georgeanne and Lexie had first found their seats, she'd been surprised to see him waiting for them. She hadn't known what to expect from John's grandfather, but he'd quickly put her at ease.

"Hello, Georgeanne. You look even more beautiful than I remember," he'd said as he'd helped her and Lexie out of their jackets.

"And you, Mr. Maxwell, are twice as handsome as I remember," she'd declared through one of her most charming smiles.

He'd laughed. "I always did like a southern gal."

Suddenly the music stopped and the arena lights were extinguished, except for the two enormous Chinooks logos illuminated at each end of the ice.

"Ladies and gentleman, the Seattle Chinooks," a male voice boomed from the speakers on the huge video scoreboard. The fans went crazy, and amidst the screams and cheers, the home team skated onto the ice. Their white jerseys appeared stark in the darkness. From her position several rows above the blue line, her gaze scanned the back of each jersey until she found the name KOWALSKY printed in blue above the number eleven. Her heart fluttered with pride and love. That big man with the white helmet stuck low on his forehead belonged to her. It was so new and she was having a hard time believing he loved her. She hadn't talked to him since he'd kissed her good-bye, and since then, she'd experienced horrible moments when she'd feared she'd dreamed the night before.

Even from a distance she could see that he wore pads on his shoulders and beneath the ribbed socks that covered his legs and disappeared beneath his shorts. He held a hockey stick in the big padded gloves on his hands. He looked as impenetrable as the name he'd been given, as solid as a wall.

The Chinooks sailed from goalpost to goalpost, then finally stopped in a straight line in the middle. The lights came up, and the Phoenix Coyotes were announced. But when they skated out onto the ice, they were greeted by an arena filled with booing Chinooks fans. Georgeanne felt so bad for the other team, if she hadn't feared for her safety, she might have cheered.

Five players from each team stayed out on the ice and took their positions. John slid into the center face-off circle, put his stick on the ice, and waited.

"Kick some ass, boys," Ernie yelled as soon as the puck was dropped and the battle began.

"Grandpa Ernie!" Lexie gasped. "You said a bad word."

Ernie either didn't hear or chose to ignore Lexie's admonition.

"Are you cold?" Georgeanne asked Lexie over the noise of the crowd. They'd dressed for winter in white cotton turtlenecks, jeans, and wool-lined ankle boots.

Lexie kept her eyes glued to the ice and shook her head. She pointed to John, speeding down the ice toward them, his fierce gaze directed at an opposing team player who had the puck. He body-checked him so hard against the boards, the Plexiglas shook and rattled, and Georgeanne just knew they were going to break through the barrier and take out the crowd. She heard the heavy whoosh of air leaving both men's lungs, and she was sure after such a pounding, the other man would have to be carried away. But he didn't even fall down. The two men elbowed and hacked, and finally the puck sailed toward the Coyotes' goal.

She watched John skate from one end to the other, grind someone into the ice, and steal the puck. The collisions were often brutal, like car collisions, and she thought of the night before and hoped he didn't damage anything vital.

The crowd was wild, peppering the air with salty curses. Ernie preferred to direct the majority of his grievance toward the referees. "Open your damn eyes and pay attention to the game," he hollered. Georgeanne had never heard so much swearing in such a condensed period of time, nor had she ever seen so much spitting in her life. Besides cursing and spitting, each team delivered pounding hits, skated fast, and hammered the goaltenders. By the end of the first period, neither had scored.

In the second period, John was given a penalty for tripping and ordered to the penalty box.

"You sons of bitches!" Ernie yelled at the officials. "Roenick fell over his own damn feet."

"Grandpa Ernie!"

Georgeanne wasn't about to argue with Ernie, but she'd seen John hook the blade of his stick in the other man's skates and pull his feet out from underneath him. He'd made the whole maneuver look effortless, then he'd placed a gloved hand on his chest and looked so innocent, Georgeanne began to wonder if perhaps she'd imagined the other man sliding spread-eagle across the ice.

In the third period, Dmitri finally made a goal for the Chinooks, but ten minutes later, the Coyotes tied the score. Tension buzzed the air in the Key Arena, filling the fans and keeping them on the edges of their seats. Lexie jumped to her feet, too excited to sit. "Go, Daddy," she hollered, as John fought for the puck, then barreled down ice. With his head down, he flew across the center line, then out of nowhere, a member of the Coyotes slammed into him. If Georgeanne hadn't seen it herself, she wouldn't have believed a man John's size could cartwheel through the air. He landed on his back and lay there until the whistle was blown. Several trainers and the coach from the Chinooks bench ran out onto the ice. Lexie started to cry, and Georgeanne held her breath, a sick feeling settling in the pit of her stomach.

"Your daddy is okay. Look," Ernie said, pointing to the ice, "he's getting up."

"But he's hurt," Lexie sobbed, watching John slowly skate, not toward the bench, but toward the tunnel the team exited through between periods.

"He'll be fine." Ernie put his arm around Lexie's waist and pulled her to his side. "He's 'The Wall.' "

"Mommy," Lexie wailed as tears streamed down her face, "go give Daddy a Band-Aid."

Georgeanne didn't think a Band-Aid was going to help. She wanted to cry, too, and kept her gaze glued to the tunnel, but John didn't return. A few minutes later, the buzzer sounded and the game was over.

"Georgeanne Howard?"

"Yes?" She glanced up at a man standing behind her chair and rose to her feet.

"I'm Howie Jones, a trainer for the Chinooks. John Kowalsky asked me to come and find you."

"How badly is he hurt?"

"I don't really know. He wants me to take you to him."

"My Lord!" She couldn't imagine why he would ask to see her, unless maybe he'd been seriously injured.

"You better go," Ernie said as he stood.

"What about Lexie?"

"I'll take her home to John's, and I'll stay with her until you get there."

"Are you sure?" she asked, thoughts spinning so fast in her head she couldn't seem to grasp a single one.

"Of course. Now, go."

"I'll call and let you know what I find out." She bent to kiss Lexie's wet cheeks and grabbed her jacket.

"Oh, I don't think you'll have time to call."

Georgeanne followed Howie between the portable stands and through the passage where she'd seen John disappear minutes before. They walked on thick, spongy rubber mats and passed men in security uniforms. She took a right and moved through a big room with a draped partition. Worry knotted her stomach. Something terrible must have happened to John.

"We're almost there," Howie told her as they headed down a hallway cluttered with men in suits or dressed in Chinooks team colors. They hurried past a closed door marked "Dressing Room" and took another right through a set of double doors.

And there John sat, chatting with a television reporter in front of a big blue Chinooks banner. Hair damp and skin shining, he looked like a man who'd played hard, but he didn't look hurt. He'd removed his jersey and shoulder pads and wore a blue T-shirt that was wet and stuck to his big chest. He still had on his hockey shorts, ribbed socks, and big protective pads on his legs, but his skates were gone. Even without all his gear, he looked huge.

"Tkachuk put a good hit on you in the last five minutes of the game. How are you feeling?" the reporter asked, then shoved a microphone in John's face.

"I'm feeling pretty good. I'm going to have a bruise, but that's hockey."

"Any plans to retaliate in the future?"

"Not at all, Jim. I had my head down, and around a guy like Tkachuk, you have to be on your game at all times." He wiped his face with a short towel, then glanced about the room. He spotted Georgeanne standing in the doorway and smiled.

"The game was tied tonight. Are you satisfied with that?"

John turned his attention back to the man interviewing him. "Of course, we're never satisfied with anything less than a win. We obviously need to take better advantage of power plays. And we also need to get some momentum going in our offense."

"At thirty-five, you're still ranked among the top players. How do you do it?"

He grinned and chuckled softly. "Oh, probably years of clean living."

The reporter and cameraman laughed also. "What does the future hold for John Kowalsky?"

He looked in Georgeanne's direction and pointed. "That depends on that woman right over there."

Everything within Georgeanne froze, and she slowly turned to look behind her. The hall was filled with men.

"Georgeanne, honey, I'm talking to you."

She spun back around and pointed to herself.

"Remember last night when I told you that I would only get married when I'm crazy in love?"

She nodded.

"Well, you know I'm crazy in love with you." He stood in his stockinged feet and held his hand out toward her. In a daze she walked toward him and put her hand in his. "I warned you that I wouldn't play fair." He grasped her shoulders and forced her to sit in the chair he'd just vacated. Then he glanced at the cameraman. "Are we still on?"

"Yep."

Georgeanne looked up and her vision started to blur. She reached for him, and he grabbed her hand.

"Don't touch me, honey. I'm a little sweaty." Then he went down on one knee and looked her in the eye. "When we met seven years ago, I hurt you, and I'm sorry for that. But I'm a different man now, and part of the reason I'm different is because of you. You came back into my life and made it better. When you walk into a room, I feel warm like you've brought the sun with you." He paused and squeezed her hand. A bead of sweat slid down his temple and his voice shook a little when he spoke. "I'm not a poet or a romantic, and I don't know the words to accurately express what I feel for you. I only know that you are the breath in my lungs, the beat of my heart, the ache in my soul, and without you, I am empty." He pressed his hot mouth into her open palm and closed his eyes. When he looked at her again, his gaze was very blue and very intense. He reached inside the waistband of his hockey shorts and pulled out an emerald-cut blue diamond of at least four carats. "Marry me, Georgie."

"Oh my Lord!" She could hardly see and wiped her eyes with her free fingers. "I can't believe this is happening." She sucked air into her lungs and looked from the ring back into John's face. "Is this real?"

"Of course," he answered, slightly offended. "Did you think I'd get you one of those fake diamonds?"

"I'm not talking about the ring." She shook her head and wiped at the tears slipping down her cheeks. "Do you really want to marry me?"

"Yes. I want us to grow old together and have five more children. I'll make you happy, Georgeanne. I promise."

She gazed at his handsome face and her heart

pounded. He wasn't taking any chances. He had a television camera, a big diamond, and a crushing grip on her hand. Last night she'd wondered if he'd choose her. She'd wondered what she'd do if he did. Now she knew the answer to both questions. "Yes, I'll marry you," she said, laughing and crying at the same time.

"Jesus," he sighed, relief flooding his features. "You had me worried."

Out in the stands, thunderous applause rolled through the arena, chased by a maelstrom of several thousand cheering fans. The walls of the arena shook with their enthusiastic response.

John looked over his shoulder to the cameraman. "Are we patched into the Jumbotron?"

The man gave a thumbs-up sign, and John turned his attention back to Georgeanne. He took her left hand and kissed her knuckles. "I love you," he said, and slid the ring on her finger.

Georgeanne wrapped her arms around his neck and flattened herself against him. "I love you, John," she sobbed into his ear.

He stood with her clinging to his neck and glanced at the men in the room. "That's it," he told them, and the camera was shut off. Georgeanne clung to him as they were congratulated, and she didn't let go even after the last man filed out of the room.

"I'm getting you all sweaty," John said, smiling down at her.

"I don't care. I love you, and I love your sweat, too." She rose onto her toes and pressed against him.

He gathered her close. "Good, because you're responsible for a lot of it. There were a few seconds there when I thought you might say no."

"When did you plan all of this?"

"I bought the ring in St. Louis four days ago, and I talked to the television guys this morning."

"Were you so sure I'd say yes?"

He shrugged. "I told you I wasn't going to play fair."

She leaned back and kissed him. She'd waited a long time for this moment, and she poured her heart into it. Their mouths met, open and wet. She slanted her head to one side and licked the tip of his tongue. Her hands slid along his shoulders, up his neck, and into his damp hair.

Lust tugged at John's groin, and he pulled away from Georgeanne's sweet kiss. "Stop," he groaned, and bending his knees, he shoved a hand inside his shorts and adjusted himself. His hard plastic cup pinched his testicles like a nutcracker, and he sucked in his breath to keep from swearing in front of Georgeanne. "My jock is getting real snug."

"Take it off."

"It's about four layers down, and there's something I have to do before I start peeling to my skin." He straightened and read disappointment in her tilty green eyes.

"What could be more important than peeling down to your skin?"

"Nothing." She wanted him, and the fact that she did filled him with macho, chest-pounding pleasure. He loved her in a way he'd never loved anyone else. He loved her as a friend, as a woman he respected, and as a lover he wanted every minute of every day. And she loved him. He didn't know why she loved him. He was an ornery hockey player who swore too much, but he wasn't about to question his good fortune.

Now he wanted nothing more than to take her home and strip her naked, but he had one last piece of unfinished business first. He took her hand and pulled her with him out of the room and down the hallway. "I just need to clear something up before I can leave."

Her steps slowed. "Virgil?"

"Yep." Worry puckered the skin between her brows, and he stopped and put his hands on her shoulders. "Are you afraid of him?"

She shook her head. "He's going to make you choose, isn't he? He's going to tell you to choose me or your team."

A trainer walked past him on the way to the dressing room, and John moved closer to Georgeanne to allow the man by.

"Congratulations, Wall," he said.

John nodded. "Thanks."

Georgeanne tangled her fingers in the front of his T-shirt. "I don't want you to choose."

He returned his attention to Georgeanne and kissed the worry from her brow. "There was never a choice. I never would have chosen a hockey team over you."

"Then Virgil will fire you, won't he?"

He chuckled and shook his head. "Virgil can't fire me, honey. He can trade me to a team below five hundred if he wants to, or worse, I could find myself wearing a duck on my sweater. But only if I don't beat him to it."

"Huh?"

He squeezed her hand. "Come on. The sooner we get this over with, the sooner we can go home." Last week he'd given his agent the green light to contact Pat Quinn, the general manager of the Vancouver Canucks. Vancouver was a two-hour drive from Seattle and needed a first-line center. John needed to control his future.

With Georgeanne by his side, he walked into Virgil's office. "I thought I'd find you here," he said.

Virgil looked up from the fax on his desk. "You've been busy. I see your agent has contacted Quinn. Have you seen the offer?"

"Yep." John closed the door behind him and

wrapped his arm around Georgeanne's waist. "Three players and two draft picks."

"You're thirty-five. I'm surprised he offered so much."

John didn't think he was surprised at all. It was the usual trade for a team's captain or any franchise players. "I'm the best," he stated.

"I wished you'd talked to me first."

"Why? The last time we talked, you told me to choose Georgeanne or my team. But you know what? I didn't even have to think about it."

Virgil looked at Georgeanne and then returned his gaze to John. "That was quite a show you just put on a few minutes ago."

John pulled Georgeanne tight against his side. "I don't do anything half-assed."

"No, you don't. But you've risked a lot, not to mention the possibility of getting a rejection broadcast on ESPN."

"I knew she'd say yes."

Georgeanne looked at him and raised one brow. "A little cocky, aren't you?"

John leaned down and whispered in her ear, "Honey, 'little' and 'cocky' are two words a man just never wants to hear strung together in the same sentence." He watched her blush, and chuckled. But there had been those horrible seconds when he hadn't felt so "cocky." The sick moments when she hadn't answered his proposal, and he'd had a hazy thought of tossing her over his shoulder and running out of the room, kidnapping her until she said what he wanted to hear.

"What do you want, Wall?"

John turned his attention to Virgil. "Pardon?"

"I asked what you wanted."

He kept a straight face, but he was smiling inside.

Checkmate. The old bastard had been bluffing. "For what?"

"I made a very rash and extremely poor business decision when I threatened to trade you. What do you want to stay?"

John rocked back on his heels and appeared to give the question some thought, but he'd already anticipated Virgil's backpedaling. "A second-line enforcer might persuade me to overlook the fact that you threatened to trade me. And I'm not talking about a fourth-line rookie you can pick up for spare change. I want an experienced hockey man. Someone who isn't afraid to play the corners and hang out in front of the net. Big. Low center of gravity. Hits like a freight train. You're going to have to cough up good money for a guy like that."

Virgil's eyes narrowed. "Work on a list and give it to me it the morning."

"Sorry, I'll be busy tonight." Georgeanne stuck her elbow in his ribs, and he looked into her face. "What? You'll be busy, too."

"Fine," Virgil said. "Give it to me next week. Now, if you'll excuse me, I have other matters to take care of."

"There's one more thing."

"A million-dollar enforcer isn't enough?"

"No." John shook his head. "Apologize to my fiancée."

"I don't think that's necessary," Georgeanne sputtered. "Really, John. Mr. Duffy gave you what you wanted. I think the gracious—"

"Let me take care of this," John interrupted.

Virgil's eyes narrowed. "Exactly why would I apologize to Miss Howard?"

"Because you hurt her feelings. She told you she was sorry for running out on your wedding, but you threw her apology back in her face. Georgie is very sensitive." He gave her a little squeeze. "Aren't you, baby doll?"

Virgil stood and glanced from John to Georgeanne. He cleared his throat several times and his face turned red. "I accept your apology, Miss Howard. Now will you please accept mine?"

John thought Virgil could do a little better and opened his mouth to tell him to try again, but Georgeanne stopped him.

"Of course," she said, and placed her palm on John's back. She looked up at him and slid her hand down his spine. "Let's leave Mr. Duffy to his work," she suggested, a gleam of love and maybe a bit of laughter in her eyes.

He dropped a quick kiss on her lips and walked from the room. He held her against his side as they slowly walked down the hall toward the locker rooms, and he thought of the dream he'd had after he'd returned home early that morning. Instead of the erotic dream he usually had of Georgeanne, he'd dreamed of waking up in a huge, flowery bed surrounded by giggly little girls jumping all around. Sissy girls with sissy dogs, all looking at him as if he were a superhero for killing spiders and saving tiny fish.

He wanted the dream. He wanted Georgeanne. He wanted a life surrounded by dark-haired little chatter hounds, Barbie dolls, and hairless dogs. He wanted lacy beds, flowered wallpaper, and a woman with a sexy southern voice whispering in his ear.

He smiled and slid his hand up Georgeanne's arm to her shoulder. Even if they never had any more children, he had everything he wanted.

He had it all.

# Epilogue

Georgeanne stood on the steps of the Princeville Hotel on the island of Kauai. The tropical sun warmed her bare shoulders and the top of her head. It had taken her several days to completely master her sarong, but she now wore the fuchsia flowered material tied behind her neck and covering her swimsuit. She'd stuck a big orchid behind one ear and laced a pair of pink Hercules sandals up her ankles. She felt very feminine and thought of Lexie. Lexie would have loved Kauai. She would have loved the beautiful beaches and cool blue water. Lexie would have to settle for a T-shirt. Georgeanne and John needed time to themselves and had left their daughter with Ernie and John's mother.

A rented Jeep Cherokee rolled to a stop next to the curb. The driver's-side door swung open, and her heart swelled beneath her breast. She loved to watch John move. He was filled with supreme confidence and walked with the fluid assurance of a man at ease with himself. Only a man comfortable in his own skin would have chosen to wear that particular blue shirt with huge red flowers and big green leaves. He was so self-assured, he sometimes overwhelmed her a little. If she'd let John have his way, they would have been married the day after he'd proposed. She'd been able to hold him off for a month so she could plan a nice wedding at a little chapel in Bellevue.

They'd been married a week now, and she loved him more each day. Sometimes her feelings were too big, and she couldn't hold them all in. She'd catch herself staring into space and smiling, or laughing for no reason at all, unable to contain her happiness. She'd given John her trust and her heart. In return, he made her feel secure and loved with an intensity that sometimes took her breath away.

Her gaze followed him as he walked around the four-wheel-drive. He opened the passenger door, then he turned and smiled up at her. Georgeanne remembered the first time she'd ever seen him, standing next to a red Corvette, broad-shouldered and gorgeous, looking like her savior.

"Aloha, mister," she called to him as she descended the stairs.

A frown wrinkled his brows. "Are you naked beneath that thing?"

She stopped in front of him and shrugged one shoulder. "Depends. Are you a hockey player?"

"Yep." A smile smoothed away his frown. "Do you like hockey?"

"No." Georgeanne shook her head and lowered her voice, affecting the rich southern drawl she knew drove him wild. "But I could probably make an exception in your case, sugar."

He reached for her and slid his hands up her bare arms. "You want my body, don't you?"

"I can't help myself," Georgeanne sighed, and again shook her head. "I'm a weak woman, and you're simply irresistible."